THE REALITY OF WANTING HIM

LEXI AMBER

BEC BENSON

CONTENTS

DEDICATION

Is it weird to say we wrote this for each other? It was honestly so fun, and I hope that it can bring everyone who reads it some of the joy that we felt writing it.

CONTENT WARNING

- *Unintentional pronoun misgendering*
- *Death of a parent to cancer (off page)*
- *Cheating on a MC (off page)*
- *Homophobic parent and on page comments*
- *Calling a homophobic shitty mother a bitch*
- *Mild dominant and submissive roles during sex*
- *Breathplay*
- *Use of "straight boy" as a nickname (consensual, addressed on-page).*

PROLOGUE

Blake

"Fuck, is that clock fast?" I ask—maybe Sophie? I'm pretty sure that's her name at least—as I see the time lit up on her nightstand.

"Uh, no, it should be right," she mutters groggily.

I know we didn't get much sleep, but I'm really hoping that it isn't actually almost noon, otherwise I'm running super late *again.*

I met her at the club where my best friend Chad was celebrating his birthday. We invited a group of girls to join our bottle service, and after we'd spent the night dancing and chatting, she asked me back to her place. We had some fun, and I must've fallen asleep after the second round of shared orgasms. I wish I could stay for a third, but apparently, I'm already really late for brunch with my parents.

Oh well, it's not like they'll expect me to actually be on time. It's a Sunday morning; knowing my mother, she probably told me an earlier time than our reservation is really for, because she assumes I'll be late anyway. Her lack of confidence in me really doesn't motivate me to be better like she must think it does. If your own parents expect you to be a fuck up, it's hard not to just embrace it. I roll over and place a quick kiss on—is it Sadie's?—head. It's a good thing I'm not being quizzed on her name. I really do feel bad about not remembering it, but I've always been more of a vibes person; details like names are hard for me. "I've gotta run. Thanks for the fun night," I say over my shoulder as I search for my discarded clothes.

Having to go home first would make me even later, so I let out a sigh of relief when I locate everything. I'm sure last night's outfit will be fine for whatever fancy place my mother's chosen for this brunch.

"You don't want to exchange numbers?" Sally asks, sounding a little defeated that I'm about to just run out the door.

"Oh, sorry. I don't really do repeats. Didn't we talk about that last night?" I check, worried that I somehow gave her the wrong impression. I'm usually pretty good about setting clear expectations, so I hope I didn't give her the wrong idea about what last night meant.

"Yeah, you did. I just thought… never mind, you're right. This was fun. No need to turn it into something it wasn't." She flashes me what appears to be a genuine smile, and I relax. I hate leading people on. I really do try to be clear with the women I hookup with that I'm not a relationship kind of guy, but the older I get, the more they seem to expect from me in even the most casual situations. I smile and say my goodbyes as I order a rideshare and walk out of her apartment.

Twenty minutes later, I'm strolling into the upscale restaurant my parents always favor when they're staying at their brownstone in the city. I aim a huge grin at the hostess as I walk right past her, ignoring the side-eyed glances of the people waiting, probably judging my wrinkled outfit. I don't let that bother me, though.

Those judgy assholes wouldn't know a good time if it slapped them on the ass.

My father's face lifts into a small smile when he sees me, and I lean in for a hug before turning to kiss my mother's cheek. "Mother, you are looking absolutely divine this morning. Did you do something different with your hair?"

The amount of botox in her face makes it difficult to read her expression, but I don't think she's amused. "It's no longer morning. You're almost an hour late, and you're clearly wearing last night's clothes. Are you ever going to grow up?" she scoffs.

"Growing up doesn't sound very fun," I say conversationally as I sit down, ignoring her harsh, judgmental tone. Just because she's miserable doesn't mean I have to be. "So, what are we all ordering?"

"Have you ever managed to have a serious conversation in your life?" my mother continues. I know she gets tired of my carefree attitude, but she seems particularly upset today. Growing up, I used to try to cheer her up, but I eventually learned that any smile I earned from her was for the sake of appearances rather than anything I was responsible for.

"Do you need another martini? What's got you so tense today?" I tease.

"You," she answers immediately. "You are nearly thirty years old. Your brother was a junior partner at his firm and married with two kids by the time he was your age. Your sister was married and finishing up her residency. You've never had a real job, and you don't even have a girlfriend. You're throwing away the amazing life your father and I have tried to give you."

"I'm not throwing away anything," I insist. "I do have an amazing life that I'm very happy with."

"Ever since you gave up on your NFL plans, you've been acting like an overgrown child, spending our money with no real purpose or direction," she counters flatly. *Does she not do the same thing?* I know that my dad has worked hard for his money, but my mom has never hesitated to spend it, and I've never known anything different. Not like they ever taught me how to budget. Hell, I wouldn't even know where to start.

"Oh, come on," I say lightly, trying to keep this conversation light and not focus too much on how sad it is that there's probably some truth to what she's saying, even if she's saying it as harshly as possible. "You guys have way more money than you could ever know what to do with. And I didn't 'give up on the NFL,' they gave up on me. Isn't me being happy and enjoying my life enough?" I ask, looking to my father for support. I'm his youngest son; he can never say no to me. Except, he isn't even looking at me. He's glancing uncomfortably out the window, fidgeting with his cufflinks.

"No, it isn't enough. If you don't want a job, you could at least work for my charity as a bare minimum," my mother suggests.

"Yeah, okay. I can help with that," I agree, perking up at the suggestion. Other than spending more time with her, that honestly doesn't sound bad at all.

"Ugh, that's not the point!" she exclaims, voice laced with frustration. "You need to do more than that. Maybe if you cared about someone other than yourself, you'd understand our concerns and finally have some real direction in your life. You need to settle down."

"Settle down? What does that even mean?" I ask, confused how we're still having this conversation.

"Get married."

I blink a few times, not sure I heard her right, but when I look back at my father, he's looking at me with such hope in his eyes that I can't think of anything to say against the idea. All I can do is try to swallow the sudden lump that's formed in my throat at her suggestion.

"Your father and I have been discussing it, and we've come to a decision," my mother remarks, looking all too pleased with herself. "The best thing we can do for you at this point is give you an ultimatum. You need to get married by the time you're thirty, or we're cutting you off—completely. No more spending money, no help with rent or groceries. Nothing. You'll be entirely on your own."

Forget learning how to budget; she wants me to be homeless?

I take a moment for her words to really sink in. I can't believe she's giving me an ultimatum because I haven't lived up to her idea of success by thirty. I've never given much thought to marriage before, but I guess if it's a wedding or getting completely cut off from the only lifestyle that I've ever known, then it doesn't even really feel like a choice to me.

I'm going to find a wife.

"So as long as I get married in the next two years, you won't cut me off?" I confirm, needing to make sure before I invest time into trying for more than my usual one-night stands.

"We just want you to have a full life, son," my father finally chimes in. "Find someone to share it with. I know I found my true purpose after I met your mother and had you kids. I want you to find that, too," he says softly, patting my hand. I give him a small smile because I know he's always wanted what's best for me, even if he wasn't around much to show it, and that means he truly believes this is a good idea.

Fuck, maybe he's right. Just because I haven't considered settling down before doesn't mean I hate the idea of sharing my life with another person. Regular sex and always having someone to hang out with sounds like a good time. I can change my bachelor ways if it means keeping my expensive way of life. I can't imagine what I would even do if I needed to get a real job. I have a business degree, but I was so focused on football back then that I barely remember anything I learned in college. Not to mention, I have zero work experience.

Maybe Sandra from last night would want to go on a date?

Fuck, I didn't actually get her number, and I honestly can't even remember her name, just that it started with an S… I think. Shit, what is wrong with me? Why can't I remember something as important as people's names? Plus, it would be super embarrassing to show up at her house again after I gave her the whole "I don't do repeats" speech multiple times.

Okay, it'll be fine. No need to panic. The next time I'm interested in hooking up with a girl, I'll try actually dating her instead. It's not like I'm incapable of dating; I've just never had any motivation to try. Even with my clear expectations, it wasn't like Samantha was the first woman who asked to see me again after we hooked up.

If I just put in some effort and actually try, it should be easy. I get along with everyone, and I bet I'll find a girl who's also looking to settle down and be engaged in the next six months. I probably won't even need the two years they're giving me. It can't be *that* hard to find a girlfriend.

Right?

1

———

BLAKE

Sixteen Months Later

"So, how was the date last night?" Chad asks as he looks over the menu at the new taco place we're trying.

"Awful. She looked nothing like her profile pictures, and all she wanted to talk about was celebrity gossip. Every time I tried to ask about her life, she would give super short answers, and she couldn't stay off her phone," I say with a sigh, trying not to remember the latest in my long list of failed dating attempts.

"What are you going to do? You only have eight months left to get married," he points out, like I'm not hyperaware of that fact.

"Chad, will you marry me?" I suggest desperately, only half joking at this point.

"You know your parents would never go for that," he says with a laugh, clearly not understanding just how much I'm starting to wish he'd agree. "What about going on a dating show? All the contestants on those claim to want to be married at the end of it."

A dating show? How do people even get on those? "Like one of those reality shows all the streaming services keep promoting everywhere?" Those seem so vapid, but I guess I'd be applying for the same reason more or less. So maybe it isn't the worst idea. "Are there any happening soon enough for me to pull it off?"

"Yeah, I saw an ad yesterday for one that's doing an open casting call for singles who live in or around NYC. I think it's brand new, and you're, like, the perfect contestant: you're not ugly and you don't have a job. I'm sure they'd pick you," he insists, sounding excited about the idea.

My first instinct is to laugh it off, but I really am desperate. I haven't been able to keep a girlfriend for more than a month since my parents gave me their stupid ultimatum, and I'm running out of options. I had no idea that being in a real relationship required so much hard work. I've tried to be better, but I'm so used to being on my own, and women don't like it when you lose track of time or forget that you said you'd come to something they care about. I've been alone for so long that I've never needed to worry about the details of being in a relationship, and I wish that I was better at it.

Growing up, I didn't exactly have the best examples of healthy, supportive relationships. I think my dad tried his best when he was around, but he was always traveling for work, and my mom would've rather handed me off to nannies than spend time with me herself. My siblings are older and had each other; they never wanted to spend any time with the baby of the family.

Honestly, I think the only real affection I ever got came from our Samoyed puppy, Lady. She followed me around like a little fluffy white shadow and would always snuggle up to me. I don't know what I would've done without her warm, sunny presence in my otherwise cold home.

I tried to make sure she had the best dog life possible. Losing her in my senior year of high school was definitely one of the hardest things I've ever gone through. She was twelve and had lived a full life, and I knew she was uncomfortable in the end, but it still gutted me. I think about her often, even ten years later.

Sometimes I wonder if growing up that way left me broken when it comes to dating. I really feel like I've given it my all with the girls I've attempted to date, but no matter how hard I try, or how much I want it to work, I keep fucking it up. I found out pretty quickly that the women I was picking up in bars and clubs weren't looking for real relationships, even if they did want to hookup again. So I moved to the apps, but I keep striking out there as well.

Maybe a reality show is a good option for me.

"Do you still have the link?" I check, getting more excited about the idea. I have nothing to lose at this point, and I do really like the idea of meeting someone who's already hoping to get married quickly.

"Yeah, I sent it to my cousin, so I should still have it," he says, and a moment later, my phone lights up with his text.

"Thanks." I follow the link and am brought to a website for *Love Without Labels*—a new reality show designed to test people's preconceived notions with completely blind and gender-less dating. The casting call is for anyone above the age of eighteen who is looking for their forever person, regardless of their gender identity.

The website gives a brief overview of the premise, stating that contestants can't disclose names, ages, or gender, explaining that there will be voice altering technology so you can't decipher voices. Everyone will have their own apartment at first, and if you find a match, you can ask them to move in with you to continue dating. The show wants to see if people can make a deeper connection without looks or labels.

That sounds like a cool idea. I don't have any specific type physically, so I'm not worried about not knowing exactly what they look like. I'm sure I'll be happy with whatever girl I end up vibing with.

The website continues to explain that if you do find someone to pair with, you'll meet the person you've been talking to and decide if you want to take things further. Ultimately, each couple will have the chance to tie the knot, and if they do, there's a small amount of prize money on the table to sweeten the deal.

I guess they want to make it seem like a success, even if it's all just a ploy. But hey, that's all my parents want too—me to get hitched. They never specified it had to be *real*.

They're planning to start filming in about a month, and it looks like the deadline to submit an application is tomorrow. "This could totally work," I agree, getting more excited about the idea as I continue to think about it.

Chad must have also followed the link because he flashes me the website from his own phone. "What if you end up talking to a really ugly girl? Or what if it's a dude?" he says, sounding concerned.

"Come on, they always cast hot people for these things," I point out. "Plus, I feel like it'll be kind of obvious if I'm talking to a man or a woman, right?"

"Yeah, I guess it might, depending on what you talk about," he concedes. "So, are you actually going to go for it?"

"I like the idea." I shrug. "I'm running out of time, and everyone who signs up for the show is at least open to the idea of getting married in the next few months. Plus, I'm so sick of my mom trying to set me up with her friends' daughters. They only seem to care about our appearances, so a little depth might be nice. I'm worried about leaving Lucky alone for that long, though," I admit.

Lucky is the Samoyed puppy I got in Lady's honor when I was cut from the NFL and had no idea what to do with myself. I hadn't gotten another pet before then because I assumed that I'd be traveling across the country every week with my team. When that didn't go according to plan, being able to have another pet was truly the only silver lining, and probably the only thing to keep me from spiraling off the deep end into the New York City party and drug scene that some of the guys I knew from college fell into.

I've never gone longer than a night or two away from her, and when that has happened, I've been kind of a mess trusting her with other people. I pay someone to take her out, feed her, and keep her company if I do go out for the night, but I know that no one else will give her the proper snuggles that I do, and I miss her comforting presence at my side whenever I do have to be gone for more than a few hours.

"You know that she can move in with me while you're gone. I still have the binder you made me with all of her care instructions. I promise to snuggle her as much as I possibly can," he assures me, and I can't help but smile. Chad is probably the only person I'd trust with Lucky for that long. I know he loves her almost as much as I do. The thought of being away from her for weeks makes me not want to apply, but I don't want her to be homeless either, so it's time to find a wife.

"Okay, if you're sure?" I check, and he nods enthusiastically.

We spend the rest of dinner mapping out everything I should include in my application.

When I get home, I start filling it out, trying to make sure I include everything important. I write down the basics: styled blond hair, hazel eyes, a decent tan most of the year. I even throw in that I'm six foot three because if I'm putting in this much effort, they might as well know I'm tall.

Once it's all written out, I spend way too long triple-checking everything, making sure I don't leave anything out that might cost me my shot. I attach a bunch of pictures too—some where I'm in swim trunks showing off the body I work hard for, and others where I'm dressed up for charity events. I'm hoping to show them that I can clean up well but also know how to have a good time.

Seems like important reality show contestant skills, right?

The last thing I need to do before submitting the application is record a short video about why I want to be on the show. I'm pretty sure "my parents threatened to cut me off and I'm terrified of losing their money because I have no idea how to budget, pay taxes, or be a functioning adult" isn't the best selling point.

So I go with a half-truth instead.

I sit in front of my laptop and press record. "Hey, I'm Blake, and I'm hoping that you'll consider me to be a contestant on *Love Without Labels*. I'm twenty-nine years old, from New York City, aka the greatest city in the world, and I'm looking to settle down." I flash the camera what I hope is a dazzling smile that hides how nervous I really am. "I've always assumed I'd be married by now, but the dating world isn't what I thought it would be. The bars and apps haven't panned out the way I'd hoped they would.

"But I have a really great feeling about this. I love the idea of building a connection with someone before you jump into the more physically focused dating routine. I'm a fun, easygoing, open-minded guy, and I think I'd be a great fit for the show. Can't wait to chat with you all soon, and who knows? Maybe wedding bells are in my near future. Fingers crossed," I tease with a wink at the camera.

I watch it back once to make sure I don't look too stiff, but it's fine. I look good, and I don't think I seem awkward.

What more could they want for a reality dating show?

LIAM

I can't believe I'm doing this.

If my mom could see me now, she'd be beside herself. I was always the shy, reserved one in the group and never felt the need to be the center of attention, so to actively apply to go on a dating show for the whole world to see seems insane even to me.

I don't even post on social media, which I guess needs to change as part of the show's rules. They say the viewers love learning more about the contestant's lives and want to know what happens after the show actually airs. The concept seems a little silly to me, but then again, I'm the one who signed up for *Love Without Labels*—filmed the application video, answered way too many personal questions, and even did multiple interviews with producers. I knew my entire life was going to be put on blast for keyboard warriors to criticize and judge, but I try not to think about that and focus on what I'm really here for: finding my person.

I know as soon as I get there, I'll need to film my introduction video that they'll use in show promos and the first episode. That has me more nervous than I was during the entire application process, probably because I never really thought I'd get picked. Even though, deep down, I wanted it. I also didn't want to let myself get too hopeful or invested either. As a small-town farm boy, I don't exactly scream *reality-show material.*

But now that it's actually happening, I feel completely unprepared. Despite it consuming my every waking thought, I still have no idea what to say. They told me to prepare some basic things: a one-liner about what I'm looking for in my forever person, a hidden talent of mine, and why I think I would make a great husband. Based on the other reality shows that I've been studying in an attempt to prepare myself, I know most people go for something bold or funny, maybe trying to win the favor of the audience or producers, but I want to take this seriously. I *really* want to be married by the end of filming.

This feels like my last chance at finding a relationship, and I know that may sound a little dramatic for a twenty-eight-year-old to say. But I've tried everything else. Maybe I'm just destined to be single and marriage isn't for me.

My last "serious" relationship was in college, and it turned out to be *not that serious* to my boyfriend since he was cheating on his girlfriend from high school the entire time with me. I found out when I tried to surprise him with dinner while he claimed to be studying and found them in bed together. I was completely blindsided, heartbroken, and fucking pissed off for a long time. I've struggled with really trusting people since then, but eventually I decided to try dating again.

I've tried all the apps. Despite my best efforts at wit, charm, and genuine conversation, nine times out of ten, they just completely fizzled out. We'll go on a first date, both say how great a time we had, and text each other about meeting up again. Sometimes, it works out for two to three dates, and then it's just… over. Every time.

The very rare times that it progressed beyond the initial first few weeks, it turned into a situationship where, as soon as the words, "So, what are we?" were muttered, everything came to a screeching halt. Even when they claim to be looking for a relationship in their profile, it's like our generation is terrified of commitment.

How is it that we're all glued to our devices but have no clue how to communicate?

Don't get me wrong, I'm not a prude. I've enjoyed my fair share of hookups in the past, but lately, they've been leaving me feeling empty. I'm chasing connection, and all I'm left with is the reminder that I'm still alone. It's gotten to the point where I don't even want to hook up anymore.

I absolutely want more, but finding someone to have that with has felt impossible. I feel like *Love Without Labels* is the perfect next step for me because everyone there is actively looking to get married. At least, I hope they are. I don't know how seriously people take these shows, but since this is season one, I feel like the applicants are more focused on the concept and less concerned with becoming famous.

I want someone to settle down with, someone who will stand by my side as I take over my family's farm and help me turn it into *our* future. Right now, it's just my dad and me running it. We've been doing it together my entire life, and he's ready to retire and move on from such demanding work. He's done so much for me over the years, and I want to give him an easy retirement where he knows I'm happy and that his life's work is in good hands.

We have a small farm that's a little over twenty acres. He has his own house on the land, where I grew up, and when I graduated college, we built a house for me on the opposite side of the property, giving us each some privacy. We have three acres dedicated to produce, which we sell locally, and we also raise chickens for fresh eggs.

Our farm's been successful enough to keep us both afloat and our bills paid, but neither one of us is rich with this lifestyle. My dad did his best, especially when I went away to college, but it's been nearly impossible to expand the way we've always dreamed of. I have endless ideas—I just don't have the finances to make the improvements we'd like to.

I've always wanted to find a partner to settle down with who cares about the farm as much as I do, who could see its potential and share my dream. But with it being my dad's last year working, I know the time to find someone is now. I have no idea how I could ever have the time to date someone new while also taking over all of the farm's responsibilities.

Besides the fact that this show feels like my last shot, I love the concept. The anonymity of not even knowing the person's gender is so unique, and honestly, exciting to me. Growing up, I was fairly confident that I was bisexual, but it wasn't something I could explore in my small hometown in upstate New York with its microscopic dating pool and everyone knowing everyone else's business.

When I left for college two hours away, it felt like a fresh start. At one of my first parties, a cute guy came up to me, and for the first time, I didn't hesitate to flirt back. I wanted to know if my curiosity was just that or if there was more to it. We didn't do much—just exchanged handjobs in the bathroom—but it was enough for me to know, without a doubt, that I'm bisexual.

When I came home for Christmas break that year, I came out to my dad. I was nervous, but he was everything I hoped he'd be —completely supportive. I still remember his words. "As long as you're happy, with someone who treats you well, and you're living your life authentically, I'm the happiest and proudest dad in the world." It hit me so hard, I couldn't help tearing up.

Which is why I shouldn't hesitate to tell him that I found out I was cast for the show today. My feelings are all over the place. I'm thrilled at the chance to find someone who truly gets me, someone who could maybe even love the farm as much as I do. But there's also the practical side of things. My biggest worry is leaving my dad to handle everything on his own while I'm away. Thankfully, it's winter so there isn't much to do, which is why I didn't hesitate to apply, but we still have chickens that need us every day.

I walk the field over to his house and see him sitting on his front porch with a mug in his hand. I know he'll be completely supportive of me going on the show and tell me not to worry, but I will. It's just who I am.

"Hey, Dad. Got a minute?" I ask, sitting down next to him.

"For you, always," he replies with a smile.

I take a deep breath. I know it'll be okay, but I still fear I'm letting him down or putting too much pressure on him. "You know that dating show I applied for?"

"Yeah. The anonymous one where you don't know who you're falling for?" He chuckles.

"That's the one, and well… I got accepted," I force out, holding my breath for his reaction.

"Really? That's great news, Liam! I'm so happy for you," he responds, sounding genuinely excited for me, just like I knew he would.

"Thanks." I smile shyly, wishing I didn't have to tell him the next part. "There's just one thing: I'll have to be away from the farm for a while to film. I'm not sure how long I'll be gone, I guess it depends on if I continue the process with someone after the blind dating portion or not. I've got a couple pieces of furniture almost ready; I'll make sure I sell those before I go so you can have the cash."

"I appreciate you considering me, but this is a big opportunity for you, and I'd never stand in the way of that," Dad insists. He's always so supportive. I don't know what I did to deserve a father like him. "I know you want this, and I want you to have it without stressing about me and the farm. It's winter. There's not much to do right now anyway. And I'm sure I can hire some extra help while you're gone if I find myself needing it, but there's not much to do this time of year."

"I know, but hiring help adds up quickly," I respond, completely ignoring the part about him not wanting me to worry. I can't help it. "We've always made it work, but I hate the idea of putting more on you."

He reaches over and puts a hand on my shoulder. "Listen to me, Liam. You've spent your whole life working hard for this farm and this family. If this show is what you want to do, then it's worth it. If you want to find a partner, I want you to prioritize that. Don't worry about me; I'll be fine. We'll manage. We always do."

Hearing his reassurance slightly eases the worry in my chest. "Thanks, Dad. I promise I'll make it count. I really do want to find my person."

"I know you will," he says, smiling back at me. "And who knows, maybe you'll bring back someone who can wrangle the chickens and keep up with you out in the fields. Maybe even work on that list of expansion ideas."

I find myself letting out a laugh. "Here's hoping."

3

BLAKE

I feel like a spy with all of this cloak-and-dagger shit—getting us all to the same apartment building at separate times to avoid seeing any of the other contestants. Not that I would know if anyone I saw in the airport was a contestant, but I guess if someone else was being escorted by a production assistant with a clipboard and a nametag lanyard with the show's logo on it, it would be pretty obvious.

The show booked all our plane tickets to stagger arrivals, and as soon as I cleared security, a staff member was waiting—probably to make sure I didn't wander off and screw up their schedule. They led me straight to a blacked-out SUV that took us to the underground garage of what looked like a midsize apartment building.

The producers explained that it's cheaper to film in Georgia, so even though all the contestants are from New York this season, they've set up in Atlanta for the initial filming. Plus, if the show does well and they end up shooting more seasons, they can keep casting contestants from different cities and bring them here.

I should probably be more nervous about meeting the other

contestants and all the cameras that'll be on me, but despite the pressure, I can't help but be excited about this whole experience. At some point over the last year and a half, I've actually started to like the idea of getting married. Having a partner I connect with and enjoy everyday things with sounds pretty great. Like, if I was attracted to Chad, he'd be my perfect partner.

I also really love the show's whole premise of finding a connection before worrying about appearances. It feels like exactly what I need after all the women my mom's tried to set me up with. Most of them only seemed to care about looks and status, so getting a break from that sounds nice.

By the time we get to the building, there's a whole crew waiting for our arrival. They add makeup to my face, carry off my luggage, and confiscate my phone—something I'd already consented to in the mountain of legal paperwork I signed to be on the show.

Someone steps forward from the swarm of assistants and camera crew, a person in dark jeans and a headset, holding a clipboard. "Hi, I'm Remi, one of the producers. It's nice to meet you in person," they say quickly, continuing before I even respond. "Filming will start right away. All of the hallways, as well as every room in your apartment, is fitted with full video and audio recording from almost every angle. The only blind spots are in your shower and the toilet area. Everywhere else, assume you are being filmed. Most of the footage will obviously not make it onto the show, but our editors will see it all. Don't do anything to piss them off, or they have the power to edit you to look like a complete asshole for all of the world to see," they warn.

I think it's meant as a joke, but I take it seriously, just in case.

"Even though we want everyone to remain in their assigned apartments at all times, you aren't locked in or anything," Remi continues. "We have staff watching the feeds at all times, and there will be a chat with staff as well as emergency help options within the show's communication app that we ask you to use in the case of a nonemergency. If the fire alarm goes off, exit the building using the emergency stairs like you normally would, but please don't start any fires, otherwise the whole premise of the show would be completely fucked." None of this is new info; it was all in the legal paperwork, but it's a nice reminder. I'm excited to see where I'll be living while I'm here.

Even though I was anxious to be chosen, I wasn't exactly surprised when I got the call that I'd be on the show. I know that one internet search of my name brings up a bunch of articles with "NFL draft pick" next to it. These producers don't care that I never made it past training camp; it's an easy hook for the show, and I'm sure they'll use it to their advantage, even if I wish they wouldn't.

I don't exactly love being reminded that everything I'd spent my life working toward was within my reach, and I fumbled it just before the endzone. But I have new goals now that include walking away from this show as a married man. I'll get to keep access to my money and hopefully find someone I connect with —feels like a win-win to me.

Remi leads me to a room full of different backdrops where a photographer and videographer are waiting to shoot promo for the show. I'm introduced to the host, Andy, who leads me through a short interview, asking me to introduce myself, say some interesting facts, joke around, and pose a whole bunch of times. I can't tell if he's naturally the most peppy person I've ever met or if it's an act for the cameras, but he never falters. By the end of it, I can't remember anything I've said so I hope it works and doesn't make me look like an idiot.

Next, Remi escorts me to an elevator where they scan their ID card before hitting a floor number. There will be no sneaking around in this place, that's for damn sure. We get out of the elevator and are in a small entryway with a door to what must be my apartment. The door is painted to look like the LGBTQIA+ flag.

Remi uses a key to unlock the door, and I walk into my new home. The bold decor choices don't end at the door. The small two-bedroom apartment is decked out in rainbow everything. I don't think there are any two pieces of furniture that are the same shade or color, and I kind of love the commitment this must have taken to put together. It might be a little bright at first glance, but it definitely works. Why go for boring neutral tones when you can say "fuck it" and do *all* of the color instead? It's cheery and happy, so there are no complaints from me. It also drives home the fact that I *am* on a queer dating show.

When I filled out the application, I wasn't really thinking about the fact that this show is more geared toward queer contestants. Genderless is in the tagline, but still, I didn't mind. I just figured there'd be fewer people for me to match with. No big deal. It's not like I have a problem with the idea of dating a man; I've just never looked at a guy and thought, "I wonder what it would be like to kiss him?" the way I definitely have with women.

The casting crew seemed a little hesitant when I told them I've always identified as straight, even though I'm an ally. After I assured them I wasn't worried about who I formed connections with—because I'd probably be drawn to a girl, and be able to tell if I was talking to one—they just exchanged a few meaningful looks among themselves and moved on to their next question. By the end of my interview, they had promised me a spot on the show, and I'm so excited to finally be here.

On the bright yellow kitchen table, I see what must be my new iPhone. I open it up and see there are a few apps preloaded onto the device. One looks like a messaging app for the show that's got a heart over a chat bubble. There's also an app with two overlapping hearts for its icon, and when I open it up, there are instructions on the screen:

WELCOME TO YOUR VIBE BOARD. PLEASE TAKE THE TIME TO ADD SOME INFORMATION ABOUT YOU FOR YOUR FELLOW CONTESTANTS TO SEE DURING YOUR BLIND DATES. THIS CAN INCLUDE IMAGES OF ANYTHING YOU WOULD LIKE TO USE TO DESCRIBE YOUR "VIBE" THAT WILL BE SHOWN ON YOUR FEED. ALL BOARDS WILL BE APPROVED BY THE PRODUCERS PRIOR TO THE FIRST BLIND DATES TO AVOID ANY IDENTIFYING INFORMATION BEING GIVEN.

Sweet. I move over to the deep sectional set up in front of a massive flatscreen TV. The producers explained earlier that the content from our phones will be mirrored onto the TV screen, and we're expected to verbally react as much as possible—talking through our thoughts, reading things aloud, and making it clear what we're thinking—so they can follow along with what's happening.

There's a mirror option, and I'm able to easily get the vibe board set up on the television. "Sorry for not reading the directions out loud. Hopefully someone better at following instructions than me remembered," I apologize with a small smile and a shrug at the hidden cameras. This is definitely going to take some getting used to, but I also kind of love the idea of people caring enough to want to watch me lounging around my apartment.

Starved for affection and approval? Who, me?

"Okay, let's pick some vibes," I say, clicking into the search bar. I start pulling up some generic stock images—football, dogs, working out, NYC—narrating as I go and explaining why I'm choosing each one.

"Should I put something about going out to bars and clubs with my friends on weekends?" I wonder aloud. "I don't want them to think I'm some party boy. That's just... what we've always done." I pause, considering. "But if I'm in a relationship, I hopefully won't be doing that as much. So maybe I'll leave it out."

I scroll through the app's suggested favorites and add a few: tacos for food, Prague for my favorite vacation spot, and fall as my favorite season.

By the time I'm happy with my vibe board, I feel like I'm already half asleep. I raid my fridge, throwing together an easy sandwich before I head to bed with a huge smile on my face.

Tomorrow is the day I meet my future spouse, and I can't wait.

I'm so excited for today. I love talking to new people, and the element of surprise—not knowing what they look like or even their name—makes everything more exciting. Our blind dates are set up in the second small bedroom, and I was told we'll stay here for most of the day. It's a simple but cozy room with a loveseat in front of a TV screen, and a desk off to the side with a small lamp and a water bottle. The room is dimly lit but comfortable, with just enough space to feel intimate without being claustrophobic. It has a good date ambiance if you forget that you're talking through screens.

Before the dates start, the TV screen lights up with a video of Andy, the show's host, welcoming us all to the process. The production assistant mentioned Andy will be our guide throughout the experience, but somehow my memory didn't do him justice because I'm still blown away by the sheer energy this guy brings.

"Welcome to *Love Without Labels*!" he booms, his smile so bright I half expect the screen to glare. You can tell he's made for this sort of over-the-top gig, and I love his positive energy. "You're about to embark on the most exciting and unique journey of your lives. This isn't just any dating show—this is about making true, lasting connections that go deeper than physical attraction, gender, or age. Are you ready to open your hearts and minds?" I'm sure it was rhetorical, but I nod along because I know this place is littered with cameras.

"Here's how this works," he begins. "You'll stay in your date rooms for the duration of the morning. You will get ten minutes with each of the other contestant for a speed date. Your voices will be modified to stay anonymous, and remember, *no names or gender-revealing pieces of information.* Use only initials and write down notes to help you eventually narrow down your connections."

The dramatic background music swells as Andy leans closer to the camera, his tone growing more serious. "Now, a few things to remember for this once-in-a-lifetime opportunity: be open, be vulnerable, and don't hold back. The only way to find a true connection is to be yourself. The producers will be there to support you every step of the way, and I'll be checking in regularly. So... who's ready to fall in love!?"

The screen cuts to Andy throwing his arms wide open, grinning like he's just announced the lottery numbers. "Good luck everyone, and remember—love is love! Now, let's get started!"

The video ends with a swirl of rainbow glitter and the show's logo flashing across the screen. I stare at it for a moment and notice a smile on my face I don't remember forming. The production assistant had said Andy's job was to keep us hyped, and well... mission accomplished.

The first few dates are kind of a blur, but I've just finished up a call with someone that I think I'd like to talk to again. I have a journal that I can take notes in, and I put a checkmark next to KD—their initials. Their vibe board had a lot of makeup on it, which I guess I used to think would automatically mean girl. But here, with how the show's set up, I remind myself that isn't necessarily the case. It's just someone sharing what they're into. Same way I put football on mine without thinking twice.

Maybe that's the point. Stuff doesn't have to be for one gender or the other. It's just... you.

The vibe board for my next blind date loads for LM, and I smile—I've been on enough dates this past year to recognize farmhouse design inspo when I see it. Maybe they're an interior designer?

There's also a few pics of fruit and veggies so they're probably into healthy eating, which I can get behind. I might not play football anymore, but I've never stopped hitting the gym and taking care of my body.

The rest of the board is full-on fall vibes: changing leaves, pumpkin patches, cozy everything. Looks like we picked the same favorite season.

"Hello, I'm LM," the mystery contestant introduces themself. The voice changer has everyone sounding like a robot.

"Hey, L. I'm BB," I say.

Let's see if I'm talking to the person of my dreams.

4

LIAM

Producer: "What scares you most about dating?"

Liam: "Being treated like my partner's second choice."

I glance at BB's vibe board in front of me, and at first, it looks promising. *Fall?* Great, who doesn't love a crisp autumn day? It's my favorite season, too. *Dogs?* Cute. *Tacos?* Yes, obviously. But then… *football*. My stomach twists.

Growing up, I was never a fan of sports. I played soccer and basketball because I felt like I was supposed to—all my friends did. But I quickly realized it wasn't for me. I tried for a couple of years until I finally had the courage to sit my dad down and tell him I didn't want to play. I gave it a shot, but I've always preferred to spend my time with my dad on the farm. He was, of course, incredibly understanding and happy to let me quit if I didn't enjoy playing anymore.

Now, as an adult, the idea of spending my weekends glued to a TV watching grown men chase a ball? *Absolutely not*. It's just so… pointless. I'd still prefer to spend my time outside on the farm, digging in the garden, washing produce, and hanging out with the chickens in the quiet.

And beyond just a general dislike, football carries some baggage for me.

This is my tenth date out of seventeen. We only get ten minutes per date today, which is just enough time to decide if there's a spark. I've already got a short list of people I'd like to talk to again, and the last date with JR was probably my easiest and most natural connection so far.

I promised myself I'd keep an open mind throughout this entire experience since it feels like my last real shot at intentionally trying to find love. So, unless someone is waving red flags all over the place, I'll say yes to a second date—just like Andy requested.

"Hi, L, tell me about the farm vibes, is that a design thing?" BB leads with.

"Well, I live on a farm, so it's pretty much my whole life. We have produce and chickens; I love it."

"That's so cool, I love animals, but I don't have any experience with ones who live on a farm."

I pause to see if they'll say anything else, but it's quiet so I guess it's my turn for a question.

"Tell me about yourself, B. Why fall?" I ask, mirroring their question by picking something from their vibe board.

"It's always been my favorite season," BB replies. "I grew up in the city, but every fall, I'd tag along with my best friend's family, and we'd all drive out to a farm to pick pumpkins. It's one of my favorite memories. And, of course, it's football season." Their short laugh sounds distorted by the voice changer, but it's obviously there.

I fight the urge to roll my eyes because I set myself up for this by asking about fall, but I manage to hold back because *cameras.*

"I know it might sound silly, but football's always been more than a game to me," B continues. "Most of my best memories with my dad and friends are because of football. Sundays I'm with my friends, watching football, strategizing fantasy leagues, and just being around people who feel like family. I love how it brings people together."

It sounds like they chuckle again, but my mind is spinning over the fact this sounds all too familiar. The last time I dated someone who was into sports, specifically football, I got my heart broken. I didn't even know I was "the other guy" until over a year in. When I confronted my ex about cheating on me, he claimed he'd been "figuring himself out" while never breaking up with his long-distance girlfriend. He'd said I helped him understand himself better and that I should be flattered he chose me to experiment with.

What a fucking asshole.

Right now, all I can think about with all this football talk is how I spent my weekends back then pretending to care about the game, because I thought that was what you did when you loved someone. I wanted to be what he needed, but when he finally got caught, he had no problem going back to his high-school sweetheart like I never existed.

Fuck that. That clearly wasn't love. It took me a long time to even want to trust someone again, and as much as I know being attracted to men is nothing to be ashamed of or hide, the fear of another jock using me as some sort of experiment is one I can't quite shake.

Truthfully, I don't know if I could spend weekends on the couch watching a game I don't care about again, even if it was with someone else.

"Uh, that's a lot of football," I say, forcing a polite laugh, which probably sounds robotic coming through the other side. "So, you're a diehard fan then?"

"Uh, yeah, I guess so," B answers. "Football's always been important to me. I love the energy, the strategy, watching guys put everything on the line for a win. The games are so fun in person too. Have you ever been tailgating? I actually have season tickets for a few of the different sports teams in the city. Going to the games is, like, my favorite thing to do."

"I can't say that I have," I respond feeling defeated and almost grateful they can't hear my voice. Every word they're saying is bringing back an all-too-familiar feeling like déjà vu.

It's not fair, I know. B is not my ex, I'm positive of that because they have different initials, and last I saw, my ex was married to his then-girlfriend. B hasn't done anything wrong, but sitting here, listening to them talk so passionately and enthusiastically about football brings back that buried ache of not being good enough, even though my therapist told me that situation had nothing to do with me. I've worked hard to get past that relationship, to stop seeing myself as someone who could be used like that.

The last thing I want is to end up with someone who makes me feel like I don't fit into their life because we have vastly different passions. I want to be chosen on purpose, not as an experiment or a phase.

So yeah, B's probably a great person, but not *my* person.

5

———

BLAKE

Producer: What's the first thing you look for in a partner?

Blake: To be honest, in the past I've been more focused on what my partner looks like than anything else… but that obviously wasn't working out for me, which is why I'm here. I really like the idea of actually being friends with the person I'm dating. I don't know if I've ever had that, and it sounds amazing.

The final speed date wraps up, and Andy's bubbly familiar face pops up on the screen. "You did it! The first round is officially over! Can you believe it? Some of you might have already talked to your future spouse." He pauses dramatically. "Any guesses on who it might be?" I'm not sure how responsive we're supposed to be, once again, so I shrug with a small smile for the camera.

"Here's what happens next," Andy continues. "After you take a break to eat and decompress, spend some time reviewing your notes and thinking about who you'd like to talk to again—and who you're ready to say goodbye to forever. You can request up to ten people to match with for the next round. Make sure to rank your top three for a better chance of connecting with them again."

He leans toward the camera. "If both of you request each other, you'll be able to directly message them in our app so you can plan your next date, which could be as soon as tonight. While you absolutely can message whenever you want, we strongly encourage you to plan daily dates if you want to stay matched. If you need prompts, we have some in the rooms and you can find additional ones on your app.

"Now, here's the twist. If only one of you requests the other, unfortunately, that's the end of the road for that connection." Andy makes an exaggerated pout, only to immediately perk up and hold up one finger. "*Unless* that person is in your top three! If someone ranks you in their top three but you didn't initially request to talk to them again, you'll be given the chance to accept another date with them. That's your opportunity to reconsider and give someone a second chance if you think you might have overlooked a potential connection."

Interesting. Although, I'd hope that everyone I want to match with will also feel a strong connection to me. I felt like those dates went really well, and I connected with most of the people I talked to, so now I'm even more excited to see where this goes.

Andy adds, "Of course, no one should feel pressured to say yes to a date with someone they're not interested in. This process is all about genuine connections, not forcing something that isn't there. But, sometimes, second chances lead to surprising outcomes."

He claps his hands together and smiles. "Once everyone's results are submitted on the app, you'll get a message from the producers with your matches. Also, if someone picked you in their top three and you didn't rank them at all, but you do give them that second chance, they'll never know. Your secret is safe with us," he says with a dramatic wink at the camera.

Yeah, and with anyone who watches the show.

How embarrassing would that be if I picked someone in my top three who didn't pick me at all?

Andy finishes up his video by saying, "Best of luck, everyone! Remember, love is love. Follow your heart, ignore labels, and let's see where it leads you!"

The video cuts off, and I finally make my way back out into the main living space of my apartment to make a late lunch and pick my top ten. Unfortunately, we're responsible for making our own food. The show asked us what groceries we wanted stocked, but it's up to us to actually cook them. Not exactly ideal for someone like me who's used to buying most of my meals.

To be fair, they warned us about this, so I've been practicing. Or attempting. It's not like I'm a gourmet chef now or anything, but I can at least put together something edible without burning the place down. Remi's warning comes to mind, and I can't imagine being the reason for the show being "ruined," as they put it, if I set off the fire alarm. Chad would have a field day with that.

Hopefully having to make my food will end up being a good way to pass the time, though. It's a little comforting, in a way, to focus on something simple when everything else feels so big and uncertain. There's no denying being in this setup is isolating. I miss Lucky's constant presence at my side, and all of the walks and dog parks that usually fill my day. I wish I could check in with Chad to see how she's doing. I can't even leave this apartment for the next week and I don't have my phone, so I'm just stuck in silence with my own thoughts. At least I'm not on dates with people who sound like robots right now.

Wait... what if I was talking to robots, and this whole thing was some high-tech version of Punk'd that Chad set up? Like that Jury Duty show where everyone was an actor except the one guy—except now I'm the lone human on an AI dating show.

Nah, Chad knows how important it is for me to get married.

He wouldn't waste my time like that unless he plans to financially fund the rest of my life, and as much fun as that sounds, I don't think my parents had him in mind as my future spouse. Still… a show like that would be hilarious in a different context.

I'm so used to going out and being surrounded by my friends that this experience is throwing me off balance. For once, it's just me. No distractions, no group plans, and no loud city noise to drown everything out.

I take a deep breath and glance around the apartment, staring into the fridge as I try to figure out what to eat. Maybe that's part of the point of all this—to slow down, sit with myself, and actually figure out what I want, instead of rushing from one thing to the next. It's uncomfortable, sure, but there's something about it that feels… necessary.

I wonder what I'll discover about myself by the end of this.

The show provided us with a news app that's updated with daily current events so that we're not completely cut off from the world, and the TV does have some on-demand show and movie options we're free to watch. But there are none of the typical social media apps that I'm used to scrolling through to mindlessly fill my time. It's strange not having that automatic distraction.

I definitely plan to work out while I'm here too, but there are only so many hours in a day one can actually work out.

One thing I'm looking forward to is when we get access to message the other contestants. After talking to everyone today, I feel like I've barely scratched the surface. I'm curious to see who's genuinely interested in talking again and seeing if we can build a connection. I'm not sure yet who will make my top ten, but I'm definitely filling all the slots to maximize my chances of finding a match. There's no way I'm leaving here single, I feel way too good about this experience, and I really want to get married.

My mind is so focused on deciding who my top three should

be that I can't bring myself to focus on cooking, and I opt for a microwave meal. I'll try to actually cook next time.

I go through my notes as I eat and put stars next to the initials I remember having the most fun with—and who I think are the most likely to be women. This whole thing would be a lot easier if I was also attracted to men, and being here all by myself has certainly given me the time to think about that option for the first time. On paper, hanging out with a guy that I'm friends with all the time sounds great, but whenever I try to picture being with a man physically, it's like my brain gets stuck on the logistics and gives up on the idea. It's too bad too, because outside of the physical stuff, it does seem like a great setup.

I know it's a possibility I could match here with a man and not know until we meet. I guess if I do, I'll have to do a lot more than consider a hypothetical, but I'll deal with it if it comes to that. There's no use stressing about something that probably won't happen. I just don't want to waste other contestants' time. They deserve someone who might actually fall for them since we're all here looking for something real, and I don't want to lead the other guys on when I can't give them what they're looking for. When I was applying for the show, I didn't really think about taking away someone else's chance to find their person, and now I feel a little guilty they cast me at all.

"Okay, time to narrow down my top three," I say aloud. "Starting with RR. Their vibe board was full of fashion stuff, and they seemed really sweet. After our brief conversation, I think they might be from the city as well. They also kind of reminded me of the girls I've dated, except that by being on this show, they've shown they're actually ready for commitment, which makes them a much better choice than my exes."

I skim my notes again. "MW was another standout. Their vibe board had a lot of cooking and baking stuff, which sounds amazing right about now as I eat my microwaved meal. They seemed a little less outgoing than RR, but I think I can be confident enough for the both of us if we progress our relationship," I explain as I rank them.

"LM is also definitely in my top three. They seemed so supportive when I talked about football, even when they admitted to not liking sports. I loved that they didn't interrupt me or try to talk over me. And the farm thing sounds so quaint. How much fun would it be to have actual pigs and cows in your backyard? *So cool.* I know my friends would all love to visit a real-life farm, and Lucky could have little chicken friends and run all around the open space."

With my top three settled, I pull up the vibe boards on the TV and fill the spots with anyone else who I think might be a woman. There are only eighteen people on this show, which I know means that statistically, I'll be adding a couple of men—but hopefully I don't string any along for too long. I'm less confident about the ones I add at the end, but hopefully with more time talking, I'll know who I should keep focusing my efforts on.

When I have my final top ten, I submit my list to the producers in the show's app, then work out as a distraction until my matches are confirmed. An hour later, I've run out of patience and am anxious to know what's taking so long. I know they said they'd give us time to choose, *but it's not that hard, people.*

When my phone lights up with a message almost another hour later, I practically jump out of my seat, except it's just from the producers asking if I want to give SJ another chance.

Ugh.

I look at their vibe board again and try to remember the conversation. SJ and I talked about my sister being a doctor when SJ mentioned they were finishing up school for dentistry. I remember being kind of bored during that one, and honestly, a dentist would probably get annoyed with me. My mother's always making comments about how it's a good thing I'm attractive because I'm "not the brightest," as she so lovingly put it. I don't want to be with someone who's constantly making me feel like I'm not smart enough, so I decline SJ's invitation.

And I just tell myself that my top three must've matched with me instead.

LIAM

Producer: Describe your ideal partner in three words.

Liam: Loyal, honest, kind.

"I'm honestly not sure what to do here," I say aloud to my empty apartment. "I just got the notification that I'm in BB's top three." *For some unknown reason.* The producers reminded us in the notification to say as much of our reactions out loud as possible, so viewers know what we're thinking. "I don't know how B possibly felt a connection when all they did was talk about football."

I really want to decline. I mean, how did they pick up on any chemistry between us when they dominated the whole conversation while I spiraled over how much they reminded me of my college relationship?

But I've told myself repeatedly that I wouldn't say no to anyone who wanted to keep talking unless they were a walking red flag. While B stirred up some not-so-great emotions, I know it isn't their fault. They're not my ex.

"I came into this process promising to keep an open mind,

and no matter how much my head is telling me they aren't the one, I keep reminding myself first impressions aren't everything," I say, not feeling the urge to dive deep into my past relationship trauma on TV. I've learned that lesson hundreds of times, and I feel like it's a much better narrative to go into for the cameras.

I stare up at the message that's projected on my screen as I pace back and forth in front of the TV. "Personally, it can take me a bit longer to warm up to someone new. I've always been a little awkward around people I don't know," I admit. It's like I can't quite figure out how to navigate the small talk without overthinking every word that comes out of my mouth. Add cameras, producers, and the whole anonymity angle, and it's like my social skills have decided to pack up and take a vacation. I'm sure the others here are likely feeling the same way. "I know that once I get past my initial awkwardness and start warming up to people, I usually like them more the longer I'm around them. So maybe that'll be the case with B," I explain.

Maybe B has more to offer than just a passion for football. Surely they have other hobbies. I try to remind myself that people aren't one-dimensional. B's love for football could have just been the loudest part of their personality in that moment because it's something they're comfortable with. Maybe I was more distracted thinking about my ex than I realized.

I take a deep breath. "No one is going to dive straight into the more intimate parts of themselves during a ten-minute speed date. I'm going to bet that football was drowning out the quieter pieces of B that actually matter," I continue my debate for the cameras.

"If I'm being honest, my own interests—gardening, my chickens, my farm—might sound boring to someone else if they don't get the bigger picture either. Maybe I didn't give B enough credit, and I was too focused on how different we seemed with my disinterest in sports to see them for who they are."

Or maybe I'm overthinking all of this because I don't want to be the guy who shuts someone down on a dating show without really giving them a chance, and I don't want to hurt their feelings. That's just as likely. But does the why of it all really matter?

I glance at the app notification again, debating. B's name sits there, bold and bright, next to ten others I actually do want to see again. I had my list pulled up when his notification came through, giving me the chance to decide what I want to do here. It won't kick another person off my top ten, but I just can't decide if it's worth it. I have to admit, today was exhausting, and we're not done yet. We can request dates with people during the afternoon and night too, so I need to perk up and make a decision.

I still haven't made up my mind, and all I can think is maybe I'm being too harsh. Maybe there's more to B than football. People can surprise you, and not always in a bad way.

Somehow, our three-hour break to decompress, look over our notes, pick our top ten, and make lunch is nearly over. Before I overthink it anymore, I decide. "I'll give B another chance. Maybe they'll surprise me," I say with a shrug to the cameras.

Or maybe, I'll just give the show really good ratings for how badly round two will go.

Either way, I'll know I kept my promise to stay open to any and all possibilities.

I JUST GOT my matches back, and I'm feeling pretty good about it. I matched with six of the ten people I ranked in my top ten.

Plus BB.

I don't really mind that four people didn't match with me. The important thing is, I matched with my top three and that's where I want to focus. Even if it doesn't work out with them, I still have four other matches I'm excited to get to know.

Seven feels much more manageable to date than seventeen.

I'm still conflicted over how to feel about BB. I've tried to really think about it more, but I'm not sure how they felt any kind of connection. But maybe that's part of the process—learning to slow down and accept that people can be different than you assume at first glance.

I scroll through the profiles of the people I matched with, mentally ticking off the ones I'm genuinely excited to chat with again. There's AP, who was surprisingly funny and quick-witted. JR, who had this calming energy that made the whole conversation feel easy. And RL, who talked about their love of photography in a way that made me feel like I was appreciating the world through their lens. Maybe that's what B was trying to do with football. It just didn't land the same way RL's passion did.

With each profile I look at, I feel a little more hopeful about this whole process. Maybe this experiment isn't so crazy after all. Maybe I really did already meet my future spouse.

I glance at the messaging app and wonder if I should make the first move messaging anyone or see who reaches out to me. There are so many factors to consider, and I want to remain as true to myself as possible so I can find my person. I don't want to put on a show for the cameras and end up with someone who likes a fake version of myself. I put my phone down and take a deep breath, mentally preparing to dive back in. Seven matches. Seven chances to make a connection—or rule one out.

As much as I'm hesitant about it, I know I'll end up talking to B again. It's part of the experiment, right? To challenge myself and stay open, even when I'm nervous they're not the one. If nothing else, I'll know I gave it a fair shot, and I won't leave here with any regrets.

And who knows? Maybe this time I'll figure out what they saw in me that made them want to match in the first place.

7

BLAKE

Producer: Describe your ideal partner.

Blake: Um, I'm not sure… I've never had a specific type before. That's why I wasn't worried about coming on this show—hair color, height, curves, doesn't matter. I've never had a preference.

"*F*ive fucking matches? That's it?" I question out loud, because seriously, *what the fuck.* I should have ten. "Why wouldn't people want to keep talking to me? I'm a cool guy," I insist, talking to the cameras. I'm sure they'll use this footage, and I don't want to come across like a completely conceited asshole, so I try to spin my reaction with some humor. I turn to where there's obviously a camera built into the wall above the television and look straight at it. "You guys like me, right?" I ask with a pleading smile, shrugging my shoulders.

Fuck. I seriously need to focus though. I'm counting on walking away from this show as a married man. I can't get kicked off because no one likes me on day fucking one. *Deep breaths, remember what your coaches always told you.* You can't win if your head isn't in the game.

I just need to concentrate on building connections with everyone who's left. The person I'm going to marry is on this list, and it doesn't matter how many other people didn't want to keep talking to me—because they did, and that's who I'm meant for.

I force a more relaxed smile on my face as I compare the initials that are on my screen with my notes. "My top three all matched, so that's awesome," I say as I confirm them. "I definitely want to continue exploring my connection with everyone on this list. There's no use waiting around for them to make the first move. I'll send them all a message, so they know I'm interested," I narrate as I open the message app.

Not to brag, but I feel like I'm really nailing this reality TV contestant thing.

I send the same message to everyone:

BB

> Hey! I'm so glad that we both recognized the potential in this connection. I would love to set up another date if you're interested or to keep chatting here if you would prefer that first.

We have the option to send an invite link where they can see our availability to schedule a date. It's super convenient so that you don't need to ever tell someone you're booked with another date when they want to meet. These producers really thought of everything.

I send all five of them an invite with my message so that they can schedule something that works for them. RR responds to my message almost immediately.

RR

> Hey B! I'm so glad that you felt our connection too! I scheduled another date. See you soon xoxo

Now that's the kind of response I'm hoping for from everyone! I'm glad that I wasn't completely off-base assuming people would want to talk to me. MW, JH, and TS also respond fairly quickly confirming dates for tonight or early tomorrow.

After about thirty minutes, I realize that not everyone has replied. "LM hasn't responded," I say out loud as I check my calendar to see if they scheduled something without sending a message. But nope. I pull up my message to make sure it sent and see that it was read almost immediately after I sent it. *That's weird.* "If we matched, I'm assuming they want to keep talking," I say. *Why would they ignore me?* "Maybe they got caught up in a conversation with someone else and plan to respond later," I think aloud.

I don't like waiting around, though, picturing them bonding with someone else. I also have a date scheduled in about fifteen minutes so I don't delay. "I'll send another message and pull their attention back to me," I tell the camera.

BB

Already change your mind about me?

I can see them read the message and am on the edge of my seat, waiting for a reply. They sure are taking their time. Fuck, did they actually change their mind? I was going for teasing, but maybe they think that was pushy.

BB

Sorry, I meant that in a flirty teasing way, but now I'm worried you think I was trying to pressure you into something you don't want to do.

My leg is bouncing up and down as I see the indicator that they're typing. Did I already fuck this up? How am I so bad at dating?

LM

> I read it as teasing, don't worry. Sorry I hadn't responded. Today has been a lot and I'm trying to mentally prepare myself for more of it before I schedule anything else.

That's cool. "I'm glad I didn't mess this up already," I say after reading their text aloud. "And I'm glad that they're being so honest right off the bat and not pushing themself to do something that they aren't up for."

BB

> Well I definitely don't want you to overextend yourself. It has been a crazy-busy day. Thank you for being so honest with me. If the dates are too much right now, I'd love to keep chatting here when you're free. But if you need the night off, I totally get that too. I have to go for a bit, but I hope that the rest of your evening goes well and we can talk soon.

I go straight to my scheduled date instead of sitting around anxiously waiting to see if LM responds. I hope they do, because their message definitely sparked my interest. It felt like the most genuine moment of this experience so far, and I want more of that.

Going into this second round, I need to figure out what went wrong in the first place to only have five matches, and change my ways quickly. None of the dates in the first round were the same, of course, but looking back I realize I did a lot of the talking. I tend to do that when I'm excited, and don't always recognize when it's my turn to shut up, so I want to make a conscious effort to be an active listener as much as I can during this next round. Letting the other person talk should also help me figure out who I vibe with the most, so it's a win-win.

I try to focus on the dates for the next few hours. These are a bit longer than the first round—thirty minutes—and the show provides flash cards full of label-free icebreaker questions for us to use if needed. I answer the questions that my dates ask me, but I try to not monopolize as much of the time, and to really listen to what they're saying.

My date with RR definitely seems like the easiest of the three I have tonight. They have no trouble filling the silence, but also didn't interrupt me when it's my turn to talk. I wouldn't say that we necessarily have a ton of interests in common, but based on some of their stories and the places they mention, it's fairly obvious that they're also from a well-off family. We're also both from the city which gives us a lot to talk about, and the time is over quickly.

The whole time I'm in these dates, though, I can't stop the nagging questions in the back of my mind from drawing my attention. *Did LM respond? Will they want to talk to me again?*

When the dates are over and I finally get to hang out in the living room, I don't even pretend to play it cool. I get comfortable on the couch and immediately pull up the messaging app to check for a response.

LM

I scheduled a date for tomorrow. Thanks for being so understanding.

"Fuck yes!" I say pumping my fist and doing a little happy dance. "Oh shit, are we allowed to swear? I definitely should have asked that sooner," I say as I throw an apologetic look to the camera above the TV. *I like pretending that's where the audience is to entertain myself.* I think I'm already going a little stir-crazy without dog cuddles or interactions with other people face-to-face. "Sorry, I'm just excited that LM scheduled a date," I explain with a shrug.

BB

Can't wait!

I don't want to be too pushy with anyone, so I hold off on sending any more messages after I respond to LM. I spend some time preparing an actual dinner, and then when I'm still too hyped up from the day to go to bed, I do another bodyweight workout. I saw an option to schedule gym time on the calendar so that no one else is there at the same time, and I definitely plan to take advantage of that option, but for now this will do. When I've finally worked off some energy, I take a shower and get ready for bed.

The entire time, I'm tempted to send another message to LM. Maybe ask them how the rest of their night went, or reassure them that they aren't alone in feeling a bit overwhelmed by this whole process. But I hold off. They already seemed a little more hesitant than my other matches and I don't want to scare them off yet.

I'm really glad they scheduled a date though.

8

———

LIAM

Producer: What's a red flag you couldn't ignore when you first start dating someone?

Liam: Dishonesty.

BB

Good morning, looking forward to our date!

I think about the cameras and remind myself to speak my thoughts out loud, "B definitely seems excited to connect again, and their eagerness is starting to rub off on me—just a little. I've never been one for overbearing or clingy partners. So much of my work on the farm is independent, and I can't have someone expecting a response from me 24/7. I need space, and I'm still not sure if B's energy is something that complements mine or if it's going to exhaust me, but I guess we'll find out."

I went on two more dates last night before I hit my social limit. I could've crammed more in, but I knew I'd get overwhelmed and wouldn't give anyone a fair shot. I also know that I only have so much time before the dating part of the experience is up and I need to pick a match or go home alone—obviously not the goal. Today, I'll get through the rest, which still feels like a lot, but I'm hoping for some actual clarity on who I want to keep talking to. It's only two and a half hours total this morning that I need to talk to people. Then I'll have freedom to spend time just talking to who I want.

I talked to JR again last night, and I think we're going to be really good friends. I picked them because our first ten-minute conversation felt so easy, and the second conversation was the same. I don't feel a connection in a romantic way, but in the kind of way where you meet someone and immediately think, *Oh yeah, this person's going to be part of my life.* There was no pressure or awkwardness, and I felt like I could actually breathe for the first time during one of these dates.

We spent half our time talking about the show itself. Then we somehow got onto the topic of bad dates, which led to JR telling me about the time a date took them to a cemetery for a "romantic" nighttime stroll and then tried to perform a spoken-word poem about soulmates next to someone's gravestone. I was actually crying from laughing.

By the time the timer buzzed, I didn't feel like I was cutting off a date—I felt like I was just hanging up on a really fun conversation with a friend. I decided then and there that they're staying in my rotation, not for romance, but because this show would be unbearable without at least one person I can fully be myself around and go to for comfort.

Speaking of dates today, I need to message B back.

LM

Me too!

Simple, but it's a response. And I added an exclamation point so that's got to count for something.

I finish getting ready and make my way to the second bedroom to start my dates. There was a producer who stopped by yesterday to set some things up, and they left flash cards full of icebreaker questions. I didn't use them with JR since the conversation flowed so naturally, but I think on my first date with AP, they might have used them a time or two. I wonder if I'll need them with B, or if they'll just talk about football again for the entire thirty minutes. I take a deep breath as I hear the distorted sound of the door closing coming from the speaker.

"Hello, L?" the robotic voice asks.

"Hi, B. I'm here," I reply.

"I'm so excited to talk with you again. I'm glad we matched. I realized last time I talked so much, and I'd love to hear more about you this time."

Interesting. They seem to be making an effort to balance the conversation, so that's a good sign. Maybe they really were just nervous and talking about something that was easy for them. I can't say I blame them. Speed dating so many people in one sitting was completely draining.

"That's nice of you to say," I reply, leaning back into the loveseat. "What do you want to know?"

"Anything, really," B says, their enthusiasm bubbling through the voice distortion. "I realized after our first conversation that I barely know anything about you, but I left wanting to know more. So, tell me, what's something you're passionate about?"

"My farm, mostly," I say. "It's my whole life. I grew up helping my dad run it, and now I'm working on taking over full-time. It's hard work, but I love it. It's really important to me to find someone who understands and appreciates that."

B makes what I assume is a thoughtful hum. "That's really cool. Farm life sounds so interesting—like, you actually get to live off the land and be self-sufficient. That's gotta feel rewarding."

I nod even though they can't see me, but I know the cameras can. "It is. But it's also exhausting in the best way; there's always something that needs to be done. A lot of people romanticize the idea of farm life, but it's not all front porch swings and sunsets over an open field."

It sounds like B chuckles. "I love a good sunset, but I get that it's real work. I spend a lot of my time helping my mom with charity work. I think that's why I love sports so much, it's my escape and my way of feeling like I'm part of something bigger."

They help their mom with charity work? Maybe they don't work since they didn't mention anything about a job… I won't bring that up yet, though. I've wondered how everyone else was able to drop everything and come on the show. It could be a touchy subject, maybe they had to quit or were fired if they couldn't get the time off. The last thing I want is to make them feel uncomfortable.

"That makes sense. I think everyone needs something like that—an outlet," I admit.

"Exactly! It's less about the game and more about the experience. The connection, the energy, the people. That's why I love it."

It's the first time I think I understand BB's perspective. I still don't *relate* to it, but at least now I'm able to move past it just reminding me of my ex. I think we both have outlets, just in different ways.

Admittedly, I probably should have an outlet that *isn't* the farm because that's where I spend most of my time, and it's not exactly a hobby. It's my job and my entire life. I guess I have woodworking, but that's more to make extra cash during the winter when the farm is quiet even if I do like it. So I don't know if I could call that a hobby.

I just haven't found *my thing* yet. I don't choose to go to the gym because I do enough physical activity on the farm, and that type of "working out" feels much better than spending my time trapped inside. I also don't like sports—*obviously*—so I've never been interested in joining any adult leagues.

Maybe I'll focus on finding a new hobby when I'm back, or maybe I'll pick one up from my future partner I'm hoping to find on this show. The idea of doing something together sounds nice.

B pulls me out of my thoughts and surprises me when they say, "But enough about sports. We could do a lightning round with the cards they left in our rooms—might be fun. What do you think?" I like that they're considering my wants and actually asking me, instead of assuming.

I pick up the pile of cards in my room and flip through them quickly. Nothing looks too bad, so I say, "Yeah, let's do that."

We take turns pulling cards, asking each other questions like, "What's your love language?" and "What's your biggest green flag in a partner?" The conversation starts feeling more like a fun game than an interrogation, which makes it easier.

Some of the questions dig a little deeper. "What's a hard no for you in relationships?" and "Are you more of a go-with-the-flow dater or do you like to have a plan?" Others are more life-focused, leading us into easy back-and-forths. "What's something you've always wanted to do but haven't yet?" and "If you could only eat one food for the rest of your life, what would it be?"

Before I know it, we've gone through half the deck—not that it was a big deck—and the conversation actually feels effortless. *Fun, even.*

I learn that B's love language is physical touch, while mine is acts of service. And based on my earlier thoughts, I'd say my second love language is likely quality time, just like his.

"Oh, so you're the kind of person who's always offering to do little things for your partner?" B asks. "Like planning a date, or cooking, or bringing your partner coffee, things like that?"

"I'd like to be," I admit. "For me, it's about showing I care by making life a little easier for the person I'm with. If I'm into you, I'm probably making sure the coffee is set the night before or planning meals and cooking so we don't end up stuck in the constant 'what's for dinner' debate."

"That's sweet," B says. "I've got to admit, I'm not sure I'd be the best at that. I'm trying to do better, but I've been a little forgetful in the past, which I'm working on. I think it'll be easier when I find the right person, though. For me, I just want to be close to them. Like, casual touches, cuddling, sitting next to each other on the couch, all of that. I'm usually snuggling with my dog whenever I'm at home, and I think I'm going through withdrawals already." They laugh again.

Physical touch isn't something I *dislike* by any means, but it's never been the first thing I look for in a relationship. It's interesting how people show love in such different ways.

We talk about their dog, Lucky, for a while, and I learn that B's biggest green flag—other than getting along with Lucky—is someone who can communicate well, and that's something we easily agree on. For me, it's not just about talking—it's about being open, honest, and willing to have the tough conversations. Emotional openness is just as important, and I know exactly where I got that from.

"My dad never believed in bottling things up. Growing up, he made sure I knew it was okay to express how I felt, whether I was frustrated, overwhelmed, or just needed to talk something out. He wasn't one of those emotionally distant 'toughen up' types. If something was wrong, he'd sit with me, work through it, and remind me that ignoring your feelings doesn't make them go away," I tell B.

That's probably why I have no patience for people who shut down, or refuse to communicate, or simply lack depth. I don't need constant emotional deep dives, but I do need honesty. A relationship should feel like a partnership, not a puzzle you're trying to solve with half the pieces missing.

That also might be why I've had such a hard time dating in the real world because it always seems like everyone wants you to be a mind reader. Here, you actually have to talk about what you want, and I've really appreciated that part so far.

Another thing we agree on immediately is that a hard no in any relationship is lying. It's one of the quickest ways for me to lose trust in someone, and B feels the same way.

Along with their admission that they've been forgetful in past relationships, B admits that they struggle with keeping up with time and that they're sometimes late for things as a result. *I appreciate the honesty.* It's refreshing to hear someone own up to a personal flaw instead of pretending they've got it all together. I'd rather know up front than be frustrated later when plans don't happen on time.

Where I love to plan, B says they like to be spontaneous, which I can see. They seem like the type of person who loves to chase experiences without worrying about logistics. Not sure how that would translate to farm life, but they didn't hate the idea of hard work when I mentioned it, so maybe that's a good sign.

"So, if I said, 'hey, pack a bag, we're leaving in an hour for a surprise trip,' that'd stress you out?" B asks.

All I can do is laugh and confirm that I'd be *very* stressed. "It's not that I need a down-to-the-minute itinerary, I can go with the flow, but the farm makes it hard to just drop everything and walk away. Coming on this show was already a huge step for me, and leaving my dad to handle things without me wasn't easy, even though he swore it was fine. I'm grateful I didn't leave him hanging completely, but I still stress about it," I admit.

There's a high schooler who lives down the street who is always looking for extra cash. He's been our go-to for years, ever since he first knocked on our door at fourteen asking if we needed an extra set of hands. Most of the properties around ours are no longer functioning farms like they were fifty years ago. When he first started, he had no experience, but he was eager to learn, and I've spent quite a bit of time showing him how everything works. He wasn't lying about wanting to put in the work, and now he probably knows just as much as I do. Anytime we need someone to fill in, he's the first person we call. It makes being away slightly less stressful, even though there isn't much going on right now since it's winter, but knowing my dad isn't handling everything alone makes me feel better.

The conversation keeps shifting between different topics without the awkward pauses or one-sided conversation from our first date. It's easier this time, and before I know it, the thirty-minute timer buzzes.

How fast it felt catches me off guard. I can't believe how much more I enjoyed this date with them. I'd definitely been too quick to write them off and I'm glad I followed my gut and gave them a second chance.

After this final structured round, the rules change again. There are no more timers or "forced" conversations with our picks. We'll be able to talk to whoever we want, for as long as we want. In a few days, there will be another formal 'ranking' that will result in us having a smaller list of contestants to continue talking to. They want to try to encourage us to focus on finding our one match, but until then, how we spend our time is up to us.

And to my complete surprise, I think I'm actually looking forward to planning another date with B.

9

BLAKE

Producers: What's something your future spouse might see as a red flag?

Blake: I can't cook, like at all. Let's hope they fall in love with my personality and don't mind takeout.

*W*as that seriously the timer already? Damn. That went by quickly. Before our date started, I was a little worried that LM would be more reluctant to talk after they admitted to being overwhelmed by the process last night. Lucky for me, they must have had some renewed energy today because that was probably the best date I've had so far.

There's something about them that seems so much more *real* than the other contestants. While everyone has been nice, I'm still having to refer to my notes to remember the details about what we've talked about for most of them. Not LM though. We've covered some important topics already, and I remember them all.

Hopefully I didn't turn them off too much by being so honest about my struggles in past relationships—being late and forgetful aren't exactly selling points. Some people find that kind of thing charming, but others? Not so much.

Maybe my mother was onto something, and I can blame all the hits I've taken to the head when they eventually find out I used to play football.

Football has been such a huge part of my life beyond just watching it, but I know I can't say that yet, not on the show. The fact that I was drafted would give away my gender and that would defeat the purpose of this whole experiment. I definitely don't want to risk getting kicked off for breaking the rules. Still, it feels weird to hold back something that was my entire life for so long—like I'm being honest about everything *except* the one thing that probably shaped me the most.

L said honesty is really important to them, and it is to me too, that's why I wanted to be as real as I could tonight. The last thing I want is for them to feel like I'm hiding things. I know the truth about football will come out eventually, but for now, I just hope that what I did share was enough to show I'm serious about this —about talking with them, and about what this is becoming.

And if they decide my flaws are deal breakers... well, I guess I'd rather they know now than be blindsided later.

I love the idea of a partner cooking for me or doing small acts of service like that to show they care, but I didn't want to give them the wrong impression about what I bring to a relationship. There's a chance that I just haven't been with the right person yet, and that's why it's been hard for me to remember the "little things," but I've also never been particularly good at that stuff for friends either. I don't want to be a disappointment if it's what they're expecting.

Although, LM didn't seem like they wanted their partner to show love the same way they were describing. If anything, I got the sense that they'd rather be the one doing the acts of service. And when I talked about liking the idea of spending a lot of time with my future partner, and how I like to show affection in more physical ways, they didn't seem put off by it either.

This was my final date of this round, which means the next couple of days are less structured. We can schedule as much time as we want for these more formal date calls when we come into this room, but now we're also able to message or call directly from our phones through the app, which still changes our voice.

Before we go back to our apartments, I want to figure out LM's preferred method of communication. "Hey, before we go, I'd love to keep talking with you if you're open to it," I say.

"Yeah, I think I'd like that too," LM responds, and I let out a breath I didn't realize I was holding.

"I know yesterday was a lot, and I want to respect your boundaries as much as possible, so how should I contact you? Would you prefer to schedule more dates in here, or would you rather message in the app? We can even message first and see if the other person is free for a call from our phones now too," I suggest, kind of rambling as I tell them things they already know. Why am I so nervous right now? They already said they want to keep talking.

"I do like to have a plan, so maybe we can set up another formal date, but I'm also open to the idea of talking more in the apartments," they suggest.

"I like the sounds of that! Best of both worlds," I agree. "I'll send you another formal date request for tomorrow, but hopefully we can talk before then too?"

"Okay. I'll talk to you soon, B. Bye."

"Talk to you soon, L," I say, and I hear their door click as they must leave their date room.

BB

So what's the best part about living on a farm? I keep picturing cute cartoon versions of farm animals running around with Lucky lol.

LM

LOL. We only have chickens on our farm for eggs as of right now. They're basically my pets though. I think they're as cute as whatever cartoon you're probably picturing and are definitely one of the best parts. I would love to build them a new coop though, the one we've got right now is pretty old.

BB

Ohh like a mansion for the chickens? I love that, you could decorate it to look like a mini house or something, give them the space they deserve. You said for right now, do you want more animals?

LM

There are a lot of things I would love to do for the farm and getting more animals is one of them. But the investment required for that sort of thing is a lot more than I think most people would assume. And I wouldn't want animals for slaughter, I don't think I could ever be that kind of farmer. But I'd love to have some more animals for milk, and just for selfish reasons because I really enjoy their company.

BB

Doesn't sound selfish to me, I bet they would love your company too. You should totally do it with the money you'll get from the show.

LM

Maybe. What about you? What would you want to do with the money?

BB

> I'll just be happy to leave the show married.
> My new spouse can decide what they want to
> do with it.

I CATCH myself before I say wife instead of spouse. Before being on the show, I wasn't used to being so careful with words that imply gender, but I think I've adjusted quickly. It's not like it's actually difficult.

LM and I have been casually sending messages back and forth since the end of our date this morning. I sent another date invite right away and they scheduled one for early tomorrow. I'm glad that we have another one planned because I had such a blast this morning, but I'm also super relieved that we won't need to wait until then to keep talking.

I've been reading the texting conversation aloud as we have it, but I should probably add even more for the camera. "I'm not sure if I should talk too much about money yet. What I told LM is true, I don't care about the prize money. I feel weird not telling someone that I'm building a potential relationship with that I come from a wealthy family, but I also don't want someone to pursue me because of that," I explain.

I also reassure myself that not telling them makes sense when my own financial situation is so dependent on my success on the show anyway, and it's not like I could explain the ultimatum my parents gave me. Anyone who agreed to marry me after knowing about it, or because of it, would most likely be after the money for themselves. The last year and a half of trying to find a spouse has led to it being about so much more than the money for me. I'm hoping to find someone I actually want to spend my life with.

I go back to thinking aloud. "I can always bring that up in a later round when I'm focused on less people." I've sent some messages to my other matches today too, and I have a few more dates scheduled either tonight or tomorrow. I look to the camera again so that the audience can know where my head is at in regards to the other contestants. "My chat with LM is definitely holding most of my attention. The more I talk to them and the more I learn about them, the more excited I am about this entire process," I admit.

Maybe it's naive, but after talking to some of the other contestants, I've started to get my hopes up about this actually working. I know my best shot at finding the right person is to be genuine with all of them. Not the shallow, surface-level way I've handled relationships in the past. Starting with L, I focus back on our messaging app and read the next one aloud.

LM

> Not sure if that's meant to be a romantic statement or if you really care so little about money...

"I definitely don't want to lie to them, we talked a lot about honesty in our date today," I tell the camera as I think over how to respond.

BB

> I guess it's a little of both. I grew up with money so I've only had to start thinking about it more recently. But I also really like the idea of having a partner to share big decisions like that with.

LM

> That does sound nice, having someone to weigh-in on important choices, be there for the tough times, or celebrate victories with. That's pretty much why I signed up for the show. I've always wanted a partner for those moments, but spending so much time on the farm made it harder to find that person.

BB

> Being in a big city of people didn't work out for my dating life any better. Maybe we were both meant to end up here, and that's why things haven't worked out for us yet.

LM

> That's a nice thought. I've got to go for a bit but maybe we can find a time to call tonight?

BB

> Definitely, just let me know when you're free!

I end up chatting with RR for a bit over text while I wait for my next formal date. If LM is busy, RR is probably the one who's got my attention next. Our conversation flows easily, and I definitely have a great time talking with them, but it feels like my previous relationships where we don't actually talk about anything important.

I have a date with MW, then another with RR before dinner. They're both *fine*. With RR, I try to dig a little deeper than our texts by asking about their passions, and they talk about fashion, different fabrics and when the best time to wear them is. I find myself doodling a chicken in my notes instead of focusing on what they're saying. I'm not ready to write them off—it's only day two—but my gut keeps pulling me back toward LM. And I've learned to trust that feeling.

When I'm back in the kitchen, I decide to shoot my shot and see if LM is free to talk while I cook.

BB

> Any chance you want to try out the call function on this app to talk while I'm making dinner?

LM

> Sure, I was just about to make something too.

I tap the call button in the app and LM answers on the second ring.

"Hello?" they ask in that robotic distorted tone I've started to get used to. The only option for the calls is speakerphone so that the audience can hear too.

"Hey, L. So, what are you making?"

"I think I'll make a casserole so that I can have the leftovers another time when I don't feel like cooking."

"Wait, that's so smart! I need to start doing that. I'm having some chicken and a salad because I'm still worried I'll be the one burning my meal and causing the fire they warned us not to start," I admit.

"Wow, I think I might be morally obligated to teach you to cook then, for everyone's safety," L teases. Even with the voice changing the show uses, I think I've adjusted to the way LM speaks enough to know when they're joking around.

"That would be amazing actually. Maybe we can do more calls like this where you walk me through it?" I suggest hopefully.

"I'd be happy to," L responds, and I realize I'm beaming.

We chat throughout the rest of our meals. I tell them a bit about my life in the city, my friends, and a little more about my mom's charity for cancer research. When I mention what the charity raises money for, L gets quiet. I don't want to push them to open up about anything potentially sensitive if they're not ready, so I pivot. I ask for the names of their chickens and tell them that I've been trying to draw them today. It gets the laugh I was hoping for, and the tension lifts. Then they launch into stories about growing up in a small town, and just like that, the conversation flows again.

It sounds nice. I'm sure there are some things I would miss

about the city, but if I'm being honest with myself, there's nothing keeping me there—and I'm sure Lucky would love the open space and time outside. I love hanging out with my friends, but they're starting to settle down too. It's not like I hope we're still watching football and drinking four nights a week together in a few years. And my mom's charity events don't really *need* me. I've enjoyed the time I've spent working there over the last year, but the foundation has plenty of volunteers. I'm not offering anything special.

L is definitely tied to the farm, though. And the more I think about it, the more I hope I get to see it for myself once we're out of these apartments.

Which makes me realize something else. I really hope they pick me.

I have the phone on speaker on the pillow next to me as I lay down, and I wonder if L is doing the same thing.

"Is it embarrassing if I admit that I'm laying in bed, but I'm not ready to stop talking to you?" I ask.

"I hope it's not embarrassing because I'm doing the same thing."

I can't seem to relax the permanent smile that's been on my face the whole time we've been talking. "Cool, then I won't say goodnight yet. Tell me something about yourself that your future spouse should know," I ask, feeling bold as I get comfortable in my bed.

They don't respond right away, and I wonder if they fell asleep.

LIAM

Producer: How does your family feel about you being on this show?

Liam: It's just my dad and I now, and he's my biggest supporter. He's excited that I have this opportunity.

*E*ven though my mom passed away almost twenty years ago, it's still hard to talk about. I miss her, and I wish I'd had more time with her. But at the same time, I know how lucky I am to have such an incredible dad who helps keep her memory alive.

I take a deep breath, knowing this is something I need to bring up with B—especially since they're now in my top picks. *What a plot twist.*

When B mentioned helping their mom with her cancer volunteer work, it caught me off guard. For a moment, I completely shut down. I think they noticed, too, but they didn't push, and I really appreciated that.

Still, if I'm serious about seeing where this could go, I can't avoid the conversation forever. It's part of who I am and part of why I value the relationships I have as much as I do.

My dad loved my mom so much, and I remember how they prioritized each other even when I was little. Looking back, knowing what I know now, I've come to realize that what they had was special and *real*. The kind of love I'm hoping to have one day.

My dad hasn't dated again. He says that once you find the love of your life, you don't need another one. I used to think that sounded romantic, but now that I'm older, I see the weight of it, too. He *chooses* to be alone because what they had was enough for him.

I don't know if I believe in one great love. I'd like to think there's more than one chance at something real for everyone. But I do know I want what they had, I want the real deal. It might sound strange coming from someone who signed up for a reality dating show, but I'm not willing to settle just because time is passing or because people expect me to get married. If I'm going to be with someone, really be with them, I want it to be the kind of love that feels like home.

Maybe that's why this whole thing feels so terrifying. Because what if I get it wrong? I'd like to think that I can ignore the pressure of the show, forget about the cameras and what happens next to focus on getting to know the people I'm talking to. But what if I convince myself I've found something real, only to walk away and realize I was chasing a version of love that doesn't exist?

Or worse, what if I do find something real and it slips through my fingers anyway?

Thinking about all the what-ifs is terrifying. But, I know that if I want my best shot at finding my person, I need to be honest and put myself out there, starting now with opening up to B.

"My mom died when I was ten," I say on a shaky exhale. "It

was really hard—still is, of course—but my dad has always made sure I knew how much I'm loved. My mom had cancer and fought as hard as she could for two years. She was one of the kindest and most compassionate people I've ever met, along with my dad, and I desperately wish I'd had more time with her. I treasure every memory and am so thankful that I was old enough to at least have that."

I pause, and it feels heavy. This is the first moment where I've really wished I could see my date's face, not because I actually care what they look like, but because I'm completely unsure as to how they'll respond. I can't tell if that was too much, too soon. We've only really spoken to each other for a couple of days, and I just told them something that usually takes me a lot longer to open up about, *if I talk about it at all*. It's such a hard topic for me to bring up without getting too emotional, and I hate the pity in people's eyes when I do tell them, so I usually avoid it if I can.

B still hasn't responded, so I add, "Sorry, I feel like I just trauma-dumped. Not sure if it was too quick to share something so personal."

B quickly responds to that. "No. I'm really glad you told me. Thank you for trusting me with that."

I exhale, feeling a smidge of relief. I shift onto my side, getting even closer to my phone.

"It's just when you talked about your mom's cancer work, it threw me for a second. I think I shut down without meaning to." I exhale slowly. "I don't talk about her a lot. Not because I don't want to, but because it's still hard to find the right words."

"I can't even imagine losing a parent so young. But it's clear how much she meant to you."

"She was the best," I agree. "And I don't want it to be this thing I avoid bringing up. I just… sometimes I worry that talking about it makes people uncomfortable."

"It doesn't make me uncomfortable," B says without hesitation. "And for what it's worth, I think it's really special that you had that kind of love in your life. Not everyone gets that."

The way that B is actually talking with me about this rather than pretending everything is fine to avoid a tough conversation is making my chest ache in a way I wasn't prepared for.

I'm so glad I didn't write them off after that initial conversation because they reminded me of my ex. I know I've probably messed up plenty of first impressions too. I mean, four of the dates I picked on this show didn't choose to keep talking to me.

People are complicated. We're all carrying things that aren't always obvious right away. Some people need time to let their guard down, while others come on too strong before settling into who they really are. I don't want to be the kind of person who judges someone entirely on a ten-minute conversation or decides their worth based on a single interaction. *And yet, I almost did just that with B.* I'm so grateful they put me in their top three so I could reconsider.

I realize I've been so in my head that I didn't even respond to their last statement, and they surprise me when they speak again.

"Do you ever think about what she'd say if she could see you now?"

Wow. I let out a slow breath, taken aback by this question, and admit, "Yeah. All the time."

I don't say more right away and B doesn't cut in. They just wait for me to respond this time, giving me space to process.

"I think she'd be proud of me," I finally say. "For the life I've built, for taking care of the farm, for the way I love people. She was so full of love. She always made people feel like they belonged. I try to be like that, even when it's hard."

"You are like that," B says without skipping a beat. "Even talking to you for such a short time, I can tell already."

I'm glad my voice is altered through this phone call because I'm getting more emotional and choked up than I intended as I pour out my innermost thoughts. Then I remember that I'm on a reality dating show for millions of people to judge. It's a testament to how comfortable I already am with B that I forgot that for a moment. I take a second to compose myself, knowing I need to shift the attention off myself.

"What about you, B? What's something you think your future spouse should know about you?"

B doesn't respond right away, dragging out the pause like they're really thinking about what to say to the same question they initially asked me.

"I mean… I don't know," B says hesitantly. "I feel like I should have some deep, meaningful answer here, but the truth is —I've had a really privileged life. And I'm aware of that." They pause, clearly unsure how to keep going. "I guess I just don't want to make something up to sound more interesting, you know? I haven't had a lot of struggle, and I know that's not everyone's experience. I'm just grateful—and maybe trying to figure out who I am beyond the comfort I've always had." They laugh a little, like they're not even sure if that's the right thing to say either.

I smirk into my phone. "So what you're saying is, you're perfect?"

"Oh, absolutely," B says without hesitation. "Flawless, really. My future spouse should know that I'm a catch."

I roll my eyes, but before I can prod them further, they add, "Okay, okay, seriously though, I guess they should know that I like to keep things light. I don't stress about much, I don't typically get super deep about things, but that doesn't mean I don't care. I just… I don't know. I try to see the good and the positive in everything because I know the bad can quickly take over."

It's not exactly a deep revelation, but somehow, it still tells me a lot about them. They like to keep things happy and easy. They don't dwell, don't overthink, and don't get weighed down the way I sometimes do. I kinda like the idea of that, honestly. But that last part sticks with me.

Because you don't say, *I know the bad can quickly take over,* unless you've experienced it yourself.

Maybe they've had to confront something hard too and now work twice as hard to keep from getting pulled back in. It seems like B's not ready to bring that up yet, and I won't push or ask for clarification. We've got time.

B was so supportive just a few minutes ago when I was talking about my mom. They didn't brush it off or try to change the subject, instead they listened. They asked the kinds of questions that make it clear they were actually paying attention. And when I admitted I still have a hard time talking about it, they didn't try to fix it. B was just *there*, and sometimes that's all you can really ask for.

Maybe it would be fun to have a partner who knows how to be serious when they need to be but can also break down my walls and pull me out of my own head sometimes. Someone whose immediate reaction to things is a little more optimistic than mine, who knows how to laugh through the frustrating moments instead of letting them weigh them down. I've spent so much of my life planning, worrying, making sure everything runs smoothly. What would it be like to have someone who pushes me to let go a little?

It's so hard to imagine a future with someone when I don't know their gender, their voice, or even any details of what they look like. I've been attracted to a range of men and women before, so I truly don't have some secret hope that I'm talking to a petite blonde woman or some tan super buff bodybuilder man. Every time I try to imagine B on the other end of this call, it feels impossible. I know they talked a lot about football initially, but it was all about watching it, enjoying the atmosphere of the game and the camaraderie of the fandom. I'm not going to assume a fan looks like one of the players. I know anyone can enjoy sports. The point of the show is to build an emotional connection, and I'd definitely say it's working.

"You ever feel like you're too much?" B asks suddenly, drawing my attention back to them and not what they might look like.

I wasn't expecting that at all after what they just said about staying positive. "What do you mean?"

"Like, too much for other people. Too loud, too talkative, too *something*."

B has always seemed so confident, but once again, *layers*. I don't want to admit that's exactly the way I felt about them after our first date, so I finally go with the truth. "I think everyone feels that way sometimes. Like they're either too much or not enough."

B lets out a long exhale. "Yeah. I don't know. I was just thinking about what you said earlier. How your dad always made sure you knew you were loved, how he let you feel everything. I think that's really rare."

Here's the conversation we were likely meant to have earlier when they brushed it off. I could tell there was something more, but they just didn't know how to say it. "You didn't have that?"

"I mean, my parents are fine, don't get me wrong," B says quickly. "I've had a great life, no complaints. I just..." He pauses for a few seconds. "They weren't the feelings type. My mom's the kind of person who shows love by making sure you have the newest, shiniest things and that you're dressed well for family photos. My dad... well, I guess he's very focused on success. Being the best at something, earning some kind of award or achievement. He isn't cold, but it's like the only time he ever really knew how to show affection was when I was accomplishing something. I think that's why I crave physical touch so much in relationships. I can't remember ever having that from anyone but our dog growing up. But like I said, it's not like I had a bad childhood or anything."

B's trying to say it doesn't bother them. It's obvious that they don't want to speak poorly of their family when there are so many cameras recording our every breath and movement, but I know what they're getting at. They just want to be loved for who they are as a person, without some type of condition tied to it.

I swallow as I pull my blanket up higher. "I think people show love in the ways they know how."

"Yeah," B agrees. "I just... sometimes I wish I felt more connected to the people around me, you know?"

I do know. Probably more than they realize.

I hear some odd noise come through on the other end of the line, and I'm trying to make out what just happened when B says, "I can't stop yawning."

I glance at the clock and realize it's nearly midnight, and I have no idea how that's possible when it feels like we just picked up the phone to cook dinner.

"You should go to sleep," I say, even though I don't really want to end the call.

"Probably. But I like talking to you."

That does something to me. It shouldn't—I mean, it's not like no one's ever said that to me before—but the way B says it makes me really want to just ditch this show and meet them face-to-face tomorrow.

"Yeah," I admit. "Me too."

There's a long stretch of silence, but it's not awkward. It's the kind of silence that means neither of us want to be the one to hang up.

"I'm gonna regret staying up this late," B finally mutters.

"You definitely will," I say, smirking. "And I'm not responsible for any of it."

He lets out a dramatic sigh. "Wow, no accountability. Noted, L. That'll bode great for us in the future."

We've only known each other for a short time, and yet... the idea of an *us* doesn't sound so impossible. I shake my head, still smiling into my pillow. "Goodnight, B."

"Night, L."

The call ends and I stare at my phone for a moment before setting it down on the nightstand, reflecting on that conversation.

Yeah. Maybe it would be fun to have a partner who's less serious than I am. I haven't felt this light in a while, even if we did talk about heavier topics.

BLAKE

Producer: Do you prefer to plan a date, or be invited on one that's already planned?

Blake: I think both? I'd like to bring my partner to do fun things with me, but I would also appreciate them inviting me to things that they want to do too.

*D*ay three is a little hectic, but I manage to fit in dates with all five of my matches. The first hour flies by with LM. Even though we talked all night, it's easy to pick up right where we left off. They tell me about a neighbor who's helping out with the farm while they're here, and I share a story about my mom's last charity gala—where she spent the whole night trying to set me up with her wealthy donors' daughter. I leave out the part about how badly one of those dates went. L doesn't need to hear how rude the woman was to our waiter, or how she said it was *so great* we were both blond no less than five times. There hasn't been any chemistry with any of the women my mom has tried to set me up from her circle. I'm disappointed when the timer goes off, but we both agree to schedule another date for day four.

The next two dates don't go nearly as well. Maybe it's because my time with LM feels so effortless that everything else feels forced and awkward by comparison. I catch myself glancing at the clock more than once, silently willing the date to end.

When I got here, I was confident I'd want to keep my options wide open, play the field, and talk to as many people as possible to increase my chances of ending this show with a wife. But after today, it's clear my strategy needs to change. It's not about quantity anymore—it's about the right connection.

And I think I already know who mine is with.

If I'm still struggling to hold a conversation with someone at this point, I don't want to force it, so I don't plan any more dates with my second and third matches.

After lunch, things pick up again. My final two dates with RR and MW feel more relaxed. The conversations aren't as deep as the ones I've had with LM, but that doesn't mean they don't have potential. I don't want to count them out just because LM and I connected over something heavier early on. If I'm not bringing anything deep to the table, I can't expect them to either. It's not less valid—just different.

That said, LM is definitely monopolizing my time outside of the dates, and I'm not complaining. They talk me through making meatloaf while we laugh and joke the entire time. We stay up late again, and I find myself smiling like an idiot when we finally say goodnight.

At one point, they ask where I'd go if money wasn't an issue. I tell them about some of the places I've traveled, and they say they've always dreamed of Hawaii. Their parents went there on their honeymoon and they remember their mom talking about how it was the most beautiful place in the world, and that they've wanted to visit it ever since.

As they're telling me that, I catch myself imagining us going together. Even though I don't know what they look like, it's easy to imagine a vague daydream of holding someone's hand as we walk along a beach, palm trees and ocean waves lapping against the sand. I've never subconsciously planned a future with anyone. That's gotta mean something, right?

Day four feels a lot like day three, just with fewer dates. Since I've narrowed things down to only LM, RR, and MW, I finally have time to check out the apartment gym, which is a nice break. I message all three of them while I work out, so totally still being productive with dating.

That evening, Andy appears on the TV screen with a new update informing us it's time to narrow down our connections to our top four. Which is irrelevant when I only really want to keep talking to the three of them that I have left anyway, so I only rank three.

Bright and early on day five, I wake up to a message from the producers reminding us that we'll have to narrow our connections down to our top two by tonight. That gives us the next two days with just our top two to figure out who we want to move forward with as our final match. On day seven, we'll determine if we want to ask someone to move in with us as the next step before an eventual proposal.

It's cool that we have the opportunity to try out living together before getting engaged. Living with someone is more serious than any relationship I've ever been in. It almost feels like a bigger step than a proposal, because hopefully, by the time you propose, you already know their answer—and that you work well together as a couple. Living together means no pretending to be a better boyfriend than I am; they'll see *all* of me.

Today's twist is "planning" our own dates. We each get to request props that the producers will deliver to the other person to use during our time together.

It might be kind of lazy, but I requested the same activity for all my dates. I want to see how each of them reacts to the same setup. Plus, I think doing a puzzle says a lot about a person.

I did pick a different puzzle for each date, though, but I made sure we'd both be working on matching ones. That way, it still feels like we're doing it together.

"A puzzle?" RR asks as soon as we're both in our rooms.

"Yeah, I thought it could be fun to work on together."

"Umm, okay. I asked them to set up fondue, do you have some?"

"Yup! The chocolate looks great. Should we do that first so the puzzle doesn't get dirty?"

"Sure."

I pick up a strawberry and dip it in some chocolate. "So why fondue?" I ask.

"I forgot to ask for chocolate on my grocery list and I was craving it. No special reason," they say, followed by what I now know to be the distorted sound of a laugh through the voice changer.

"Valid," I agree. But, I'm also kind of disappointed that there *isn't* something deeper. I still feel like I've barely scratched the surface with R.

We enjoy the fondue and move on to the puzzle. They don't seem super into it or anything, but they make some comments while we're talking that make it clear they're actually working on it. We also talk about vacations, but they seem more focused on which of their vacation posts got the most likes on social media than what they actually enjoyed during their travels. I've always appreciated social media and sharing my experiences with other people, but not at the expense of those experiences. I finish the puzzle well before our time is up and try to focus on talking.

"So, do you want kids?" they ask.

I perk up a bit. *Finally something real.* "For sure. I've always thought about what I would do differently than my parents. I'm not in a rush or anything, but eventually I do," I say. I'm not trying to be intentionally leading with my answer, but after I've said it, I wait to see if they'll ask me about my parents or what I'd do differently.

Instead they reply with, "I think I want two kids, but I also don't want them right away or anything."

Not quite as deep as I was hoping, but still great to know. Our time is up, so we say our goodbyes. I have my date with MW soon, but the producers ask me to go back to the main area of my apartment so they can set up for the next date. I drink some water, and they eventually give me the okay to come back in.

"Oh, there's a puzzle here?" MW asks when they join the call.

"Yeah, I thought it could be fun to work on together."

"But we're not even together, this will take forever by myself."

"I just thought it would be nice to be doing the same thing even if we're in different rooms," I explain.

"Okay. Well, I thought it would be fun to share some wine," they say.

I eye the bottle and glass that are set up for me wearily. I'm not usually one to turn down drinking, but it's only my second date of the day. I don't want to judge M—maybe this is their last one, and they figured a drink would help us open up a little. Nice in theory, but I'm not about to risk messing up my date with L just because I got a little buzzed with someone else.

Besides, I should probably get along with my future partner sober. I've done enough drinking in my single days, I think I might actually be ready to focus on more important things, whenever I figure out what they are. *Holy shit, do I actually want to be better for someone else? Is this what my dad meant about finding purpose in a relationship?* I shake off that disturbing thought and focus on my date.

I hear the cork pop on M's end, and debate opening mine so that they won't realize I'm not drinking, but decide against it. They don't call me out on not opening it, and I'd rather some producer enjoy the unopened bottle later than waste the entire thing.

M definitely enjoys the wine, bringing up different wine tastings they've been to and what they know about this bottle, but when I ask if they've started the puzzle, they make a noncommittal noise and I'm pretty sure they never even open it. They do a lot of talking about themself and their friends and family. I'm a little impressed that they're able to keep all the details vague enough not to give away their gender or age, even as their topics get more and more random—and they obviously enjoy more and more of the wine.

I'm relieved when it's finally over, and I wish them well, but I think our ignored date ideas make it clear that we're not on the same page.

I take another short break before my date with LM. I'm so glad this is my last date of the night so I can end on a high note after the second one was such a flop.

"A puzzle?" L asks when we're both in our rooms.

"Yeah, I thought it could be fun to work on together," I explain for the third time today.

"Awesome. I also brought something for us to do together. Great minds," they say, making me laugh as I let out a sigh of relief.

"So do you paint?" I ask, looking down at the art supplies in front of me.

"Not exactly. I really enjoy being artistic and creative, but I don't have nearly enough time to make what I'd like to. I love to make things out of wood. My dad and I built a lot of the furniture that's in my house actually. Now, I mostly make or refurbish wood furniture to sell. It helps us in the winter."

"That's so cool! I love those videos of people flipping old

furniture to make it pretty. I'm not sure how they ended up on my For You page the first time, but I'm glad they did," I tell them, picturing all the girls I've seen painting old dressers to make them look like new. I wish I knew what L looks like so I could picture them instead. Every time I try, they have a different hair color, height, or build. After all our conversations, I'm fairly certain we're similar ages, but their actual looks remain a complete mystery. It's also kind of fun not knowing for sure. I've gotten pretty good at using the gender-neutral wording for everything so I don't mess up the show, but I still can't help picturing the other contestants I'm talking to as women because that's all I've ever known, even if I don't know any specifics of their looks beyond that.

"And that's super impressive that you built your own furniture. I don't think I've ever owned a toolbox. You should totally build that mansion for your chickens."

"That's not a bad idea. For now, though, I thought watching the same instructional painting video could be fun. The producers agreed to exchange our artwork, too, if you want, so I could get yours and you'd get mine when they're done."

"Um, yes, please. I love that idea," I respond, already opening my paint.

"The producers said they'll start our videos at the same time whenever I send them a message so that they're synced up, and it won't mess up the audio in the footage of our date. Ready for me to text them?" L asks, and I agree.

It's not a super long video, but the person instructs us on how to paint the background first, eventually adding in colors that turn into mountains and trees around a lake. Or at least that's what it's meant to be. "I think mine might be a little more abstract than they intended," I warn L, making them laugh.

We wrap up the paintings and set them aside. I can't wait to see what L's looks like compared to mine.

"So, why puzzles?" they ask, and I'm glad someone finally thought to.

"My older siblings and I used to do them when we were growing up. I'm the youngest by about five years, and I always wanted to join in on whatever they were doing. Usually they acted like they were too cool for me, but our grandparents would bring over puzzles for us whenever they visited, and my siblings couldn't argue that I couldn't participate when it was a shared gift. It was my job to sort the pieces by their color, and if they were on the edge, and they would work on the actual picture, but I always loved getting to do that with them. I haven't touched a puzzle in probably fifteen years, but for some reason, it was the first thing I thought of when it was time to plan a date."

"I love that, I'm glad we get to do it together now," L responds.

I'm suddenly wishing that I had only brought the puzzles to *our* date, to share this with only L. Then again, seeing how the contestants reacted so differently to the same thing *did* help me see where I'm at with each of them. "I know that you don't have any siblings, but do you think you'll want kids someday?" I ask.

"Oh, uh… yeah. It seems like a kind of faraway dream right now, but I've always pictured having my own kids to pass the farm down to one day. What about you?"

"I don't have a farm to pass down," I tease. "But yeah, I would like to have kids. I've thought a lot about what I'd do differently than my parents, and I hope to have that opportunity one day."

"Like what?" L asks.

I can't help but smile at their reply, the way they obviously want to know the little details that make me, *me*. "Like…" What do I say that won't make my parents sound like complete assholes on television? "Like, I was always jealous of the kids whose parents coached their teams, and as much as I loved most of the activities I did, I would put less pressure on my own kids.

I think having a good time should be more important than winning or being the best," I explain.

"I think you'll make a great parent one day," L replies easily, and my throat closes up a bit. What the fuck? Am I about to cry?

"Thanks. You too, L," I manage to choke out.

We move on to lighter topics as we finish off our puzzle. As we go on, we get more and more competitive about who will finish first. It's kind of silly when either of us could claim to be done at any time, but we're both laughing and having a great time. I finish before L says they're done, but I decide to let them have the win and pretend like they beat me. I've had another great date with them, and that's what actually matters to me.

Picking my top two at the end of the night is easy. I have a brief moment of panic while I'm waiting to get back the results, and I realize how invested I've become in my relationships in such a short amount of time. Or at least, one of the relationships. Luckily, it isn't too long before LM and RR both confirm me as one of their top two as well.

This process might be fast, but I'm feeling great about where I'm at. Two more days, and hopefully I'll be meeting my future spouse in person. I truly don't care what they look like, I know that we'll be starting the next chapter of our relationship as a stronger couple than I ever was with any of my previous girlfriends, and I can't wait.

LIAM

Producer: Is there anything about this process that concerns you?

Liam: Um, I guess my biggest concern would be that I find someone I want to be with, and they don't want to move to my farm. I've tried to set the expectation with everyone I've talked to that the farm is my future, but thinking you could live somewhere is different than seeing it.

The last few days have been a lot, and I'm so grateful I decided to keep an open mind—especially considering the fact that my only interest now is in BB. *Yup, the disastrous first date, wasn't-even-in-my-top-ten, is now the* only *one I'm interested in.*

I've put all my mental energy into making sure I'm confident in who I still want to be dating. I've slowly ended my other connections one by one. All RL wanted to talk about was photography. Which is fine, I get it, that's their thing. But when every conversation circles back to camera settings, lighting techniques, and the philosophy of capturing a moment, I started checking out. I'm happy they're passionate, but I don't think I need to spend my life hearing about cameras and photography.

Then there was AP who was great, and I did like them, but as time passed, our connection started to feel like it was fading. I wouldn't be surprised if they found someone they connected with more, and I can't be mad about that. That's what this whole thing is about—finding the person who really fits—and I wasn't going to keep forcing something that wasn't what either of us really wanted.

The only other person I've really connected with is JR, but we both agreed it was completely platonic. From the beginning, talking with them has felt like an easy, no-pressure friendship. We even agreed to keep each other in our top two for emotional support. I've loved having someone I could just talk to openly while here since I couldn't talk to my dad or my friends back home.

Which leaves BB as my other top-two choice. My *only* romantic focus, and that's absolutely terrifying. What if they don't pick me? What if I'm feeling this connection so much stronger than they are? What if I meet them in person and end up feeling the same way I did about them on our first date?

I think that last thought is the most concerning, like maybe I've made up this entire layered, kind, funny person in my head, but when we actually meet, they'll just revert back to only talking about football.

The possibility of leaving here single, and having to return to dating apps as my only way to meet people—dealing with awkward first dates and meaningless small talk—*that's the scariest thought of all*. I can't ever do that again. If that's my future, I'd rather give up on dating altogether.

This experience has been so much better than I'd dare to hope for before coming. And after making this connection with B—feeling like I might have found a real partner, picturing what it would be like to have them back on the farm with me—I can't bear the thought of having to start over with someone else if it does end up falling apart.

I also don't want to convince myself to settle for someone I don't actually care about just to avoid being alone. So as much as it really is BB or bust for me, I know there's still a very real possibility I could be going home alone if the connection changes after we meet.

All of this back and forth as I try to manage my expectations of what could happen with what I'm hoping will happen, is only stressing me out more. I have a good feeling about BB, and I should focus on that. I want to keep dating them, to see where it could lead.

I text JR to help calm my nerves since I know they're in a similar situation.

LM

On a scale of "mild anxiety" to "full blown freak out" how stressed are you about tonight?

JR

LOL, full blown panic. Who knew only leaving one person as your top pick would be so nerve-wracking.

LM

We definitely should have thought of that sooner. Not that I had any other options I actually liked haha. I really don't want to leave here alone. I can't fathom the thought of dating again outside of this experience.

JR

I'm right there with you. At least we formed a solid friendship out of this, right? But from what it sounds like on your end, BB is likely to pick you too.

LM

I really, really hope so. How are things with KD?

JR

Good! I think we've built a really strong connection, it's almost like I've known them for years instead of a few days. But then again, it's my ONLY connection so I hope they feel it as strongly as I do.

LM

I get that. That's how it is with BB for me. I didn't expect it at all, but now I can't imagine leaving here without them.

JR

I feel the same way. Although, KD has been in my top since the beginning, unlike BB for you, haha. But it's terrifying not knowing for sure if you'll be picked and if they feel the same way about us that we feel about them.

LM

Here's to hoping for double dates in the future! Keep me updated on how it goes. I want to know everything.

JR

Same to you!

I put my phone down after that last message.

I meant what I said—I really do hope we both leave here engaged. And not just because I don't want to leave alone, but because I don't want to leave without BB.

I don't know exactly when the casual dates turned into something real, but I feel it now. It's different with B.

Every time I talk to them, the rest of this ridiculous experiment fades into the background. I don't think about the cameras, the producers, the pressure to find someone. It's just them. They're all I care about.

I loved our puzzle and painting date. I wasn't sure what to expect going into it, but BB kept things fun, just like they always do. Even when we're just on the phone cooking our own separate dinners, or decompressing from the day, they've continued to surprise me. I've found myself really enjoying it.

I already submitted my top two, so now I just wait, staring at the blob of colors that loosely resemble a mountain that B painted. It really is bad, but every time I look at it, I can't help but smile. The waiting is causing me so much more stress than I ever expected. I kind of want to text BB and beg them to pick me, but I won't. Obviously, it needs to be their decision.

I've been trying to envision leaving this two-bedroom apartment to move into a one-bedroom with BB, but it's so hard to do without knowing their gender or looks or voice. It's going to be interesting to see how our relationship feels once we've met each other, and to try connecting everything I know about them from my limited perspective to reality.

Finally, after what feels like days, I get the notification that BB wants to continue with me, and the relief I feel is monumental. I immediately open our texts and send one.

LM

Well, that was the longest wait of my entire life.

BB

I had to keep you on your toes ;)

LM

Mission accomplished lol. Now I can breathe again.

BB

Glad to hear you really wanted me. Like I said, I'm a catch.

LM

A humble catch, clearly. Good to know what I'm signing up for.

BB

You already signed up. No take-backs!

LM

Guess I'll just have to deal with it then.

BB

Yep. And trust me, you won't regret it!

BB

To be honest though, I've been waiting too. I think the show held back our answers to add drama, I was just about to message you when yours came through. I'm glad this isn't over.

DAY SIX FLIES by in a blur. I spend most of it talking with B, having another formal date in the other room where we just continue our conversation from our texts. I'm trying really hard not to overthink everything and panic, but I can't stop myself from anticipating *something* going wrong.

I also may or may not text JR one too many times because I'm definitely freaking out. But, in my defense, having someone to talk and vent to was the whole reason we decided to pick each other. There weren't any rules against that. Not having my phone to talk to my friends about this big decision would have left me absolutely spiraling. I *never* expected to be this invested in the show.

Luckily for JR, KD picked them in their top two as well, so we've both made it to the last day at least. I haven't heard from JR yet on if KD agreed to move in, but I know they're planning to ask today.

Now, I'm sitting in the date room again, waiting for B to come in so I can ask them if they want to continue this experi-ence and move in with me. I'm confident, but definitely still freaking out. I mean, how can I not be when my entire future depends on it? Dramatic much?

I want to believe BB feels the same way I do, but I have no idea how they're actually feeling. I know it's not just me in their top two, there's still one other person they're considering. We can view each other's calendars to send requests to schedule dates when they're free, so I know that they had other dates scheduled in this top two period. I really doubt that they also decided to have a completely platonic friend as their second option.

I hate that I don't know for certain where I stand with B. Every conversation we've had has felt real, like we're both all-in, but what if I've misread everything? What if I've let myself get caught up in something they don't feel as strongly about? What if their other connection is stronger?

Panicking doesn't even cover it.

Especially since we had the really important conversation about kids. I didn't realize how much I was holding my breath, waiting for that answer, until I heard BB say they wanted to be a parent too.

I've always envisioned the farm with a few kids running around—helping feed the chickens in the morning, spending time outside with my dad and I, learning the same lessons he taught me growing up. I want that kind of life, and I want it even more with someone who wants the same thing.

Yesterday, we talked more about what kind of parents we'd be and what values matter most to us. They joked that they'd be the fun one while I'd be the responsible one. They're probably not wrong, and yet, it doesn't bother me. Even though neither of us specified that we'd be parenting the *same* kids, it sure felt like that's what we were talking about, and I loved it.

We talked about their dog, what we like to do to unwind, and how we handle stress. BB joked that I'd probably have to remind them where they put their keys every day if we lived together.

My stomach definitely had some butterflies at the casual suggestion. I admitted that I have a bad habit of leaving dishes in the sink just a little too long. Curse of living alone and spending all my time outside of the house.

It was those conversations that made everything feel less hypothetical and more like this could actually turn into a real, lasting, life-long relationship. That's always been my intention, but it's never felt like such a real possibility.

As I'm waiting for B to enter their room, I'm so grateful they can't see the nerves that are definitely radiating off of me. "I'm so anxious right now. It all comes down to this," I say into the cameras I know are recording in the otherwise quiet room. "I'm going to ask them to take the next step and move in with me."

After a few more minutes of waiting, I hear the sound of the door closing, and B says, "L? Are you here?"

"Hey, yes!" I'm now also very grateful they can't hear my real voice because I know that would have been incredibly squeaky and high pitched.

"So, how are you doing? Are you nervous?" B asks, like they're completely calm and collected over there while I'm barely able to stay in my seat with how fast my leg is bouncing.

"Yes, definitely." I let out a little laugh because I honestly think I'll cry if I don't. The amount of pressure I'm feeling right now is unreal. I don't think I've ever felt *this* nervous before.

There's a muffled sound as they let out a deep breath. "Yeah. I mean, it's a big decision, right? We went from strangers to this in, what, a week?"

"Yeah." I swallow hard. "But it doesn't feel rushed, does it?"

B is quiet for a moment, and somehow my fear manages to multiply, even more terrified that I've misread everything. But then they speak, and their voice seems softer this time. "No, it doesn't."

I take a breath, steadying myself. They wouldn't have said

that if they were done with me. *Right?* "So… I guess there's only one thing left to do."

B exhales a short laugh. "Yeah. I guess so. L, will you move in with me?"

Wait, did I just hear that right? I was so sure I'd be the one asking. I had this whole nervous speech prepared in my head. I'd already accepted having to put myself out there first. But now, here B is, flipping the script and asking me instead.

Somehow, it makes this moment even better.

I let out a breath I didn't realize I was holding as a massive smile takes over my face. "Yes! Of course. Yeah, I will."

B lets out a relieved laugh. "So, it's official," B says, way louder than before. "We're moving in together!"

It's happening. This is really happening! This is no longer just an idea or a hypothetical next step in the show—we're actually going to be sharing a space. I'm nervous and excited. My adrenaline is through the roof, but I feel good, like I've made the right choice.

"You sure you're ready for this?" B asks.

"I don't think anyone's ever actually ready to move in with someone they've never seen before," I joke. "But with you? Yeah. I think I am."

My face hurts from how hard I'm smiling. I finally get to meet them face-to-face. A whole new wave of nervous energy flows over me, but I know that this time, it's also full of excitement. *I can't wait to meet you, B.*

13

BLAKE

Producer: So you've previously told producers that you identify as straight, what made you want to sign up for a show where you could end up dating men without knowing it?

Blake: I guess that I assumed I would know if I was talking to a man or a woman, but after actually being a part of this experience, it's clear that my initial confidence might have been a little misplaced. Things certainly aren't as cut and dry as I had pictured. But, to answer your question, I've struggled with finding my person. After seeing the ad for the show's sign ups, I really liked the idea of getting to know someone for who they are before physical appearances came into play. I'd like to think looks aren't important to me, but when you're dating in the real world, it's hard *not* to take appearance into consideration.

The television in the date room suddenly lights up and Andy appears on the screen. "Congratulations to the happy couple! You've agreed to advance your relationship to the next step in our experiment—living together!" He's jumping up and down and clapping like we've already won something.

Except, if I'm being honest, L agreeing to be exclusive and move in with me feels like the real prize, so I can't blame him for being excited. I might not be actually jumping, but the excitement is there. Even though I went into the final round with two choices, I think a part of me has always known it would be LM.

As much as RR seemed like a good option on paper—obviously from money, living in the city, liking all the fashion trends that my mother is into—we just never clicked the way I did with LM. Maybe if we'd met on an app before this show I would have wanted to date them, but now, after everything that I've experienced with LM as our connection has grown, I know RR and I would have ended up with yet another shallow relationship. We wouldn't have been happy.

But LM? This feels like it could be the real deal. This is the most mature, yet also the most fun relationship I think I've ever been in. I can't wait to meet them, and I can't wait to see what they look like, even though at this point, I truly don't care.

Andy continues talking. "It's time to grab your packed bags and a producer will escort you to your new shared home! Whoever gets there first, please wait to unpack until *after* you've met your partner in the main living space." His expression falls dramatically and he leans in to whisper to the camera. "If, for whatever reason, you decide upon meeting that you no longer want to continue with the show, please be respectful and excuse yourself from the apartment. A producer will help you from there."

Then he steps back and his whole face lights up again. "I'm sure that won't be the case for you, though! This is *Love Without Labels* and you wanted to find someone who would love you despite those pesky first impressions. And you have! I am so excited for you to continue on this journey! Now, the moment you've all been waiting for... it's time to go meet your partner!"

The screen goes black again, and I'm out of my seat, practically sprinting to grab my bags. They had us pack up this morning, knowing we'd either be moving in with our partner or heading home, and now it's finally happening.

I'm about to meet L!

And I'm so fucking excited, I can barely think straight.

Remi is escorting me to L's and my apartment, and they're on the phone coordinating so we don't get there at the same time. It sounds like I'll be getting there first. We take the elevator up a few floors and they open the door for me. It's a more traditionally styled apartment this time. There are still rainbow touches, but the whole kitchen screams boring model showroom. After living in the rainbow explosion that was my studio apartment for the last week, this is kind of a letdown.

Not important. Don't give a shit about the apartment.

L is almost here! What the fuck should I do while I wait? Should I be sitting? Standing so we can hug? Will we kiss right away or will we need to build up to that? I'm standing in the middle of the room, undecided on how I should play this, when I hear the door open. My heart jumps into my throat as I spin around, a huge grin already plastered on my face—

And then it falls.

Because it's not her.

There's a large, rugged-looking man standing in the doorway. He's got dark hair, a flannel, and bright blue eyes. *What is he doing here?*

"Sorry, I think you've got the wrong apartment," I say with a nervous laugh, hoping this guy will hurry up and leave before L gets here.

"B?" he asks, sounding kind of breathless. His brows are furrowed as he checks me out, like he isn't sure if I'm who he's looking for either.

"Oh, are you a producer or something? Should I be standing in a different spot for the big reveal?" I check, looking around and positioning myself so that I'm facing the door.

"A producer? What are you talking about?" he asks, stepping fully into the apartment.

And that's when I see the suitcase he's wheeling in behind him.

Into the apartment.

The apartment I'm going to share with L.

Because we just agreed to move in together.

To advance our relationship.

L, who I've been picturing this entire time as a woman… *why the fuck did I do that?*

This is L, who I decided I want to be exclusive with.

L, who I shared parts of my life with that I've never shared with anyone else.

L, the person I've decided I want to build something real with for the first time in my life.

I'm completely frozen in place, like I don't even have control of my body right now as I try to mentally catch up to what's happening. I knew it was a possibility. When I first got to the show, I thought about how much easier this would be if I was attracted to men. Chad had even suggested this exact scenario when we first talked about the show, and I shrugged it off, assuming that I would know if I was talking to a man.

Except I *didn't*.

I didn't know.

I chose him.

A man.

And now he's standing in front of me, looking exactly as confused as I feel.

"Wait, you're L? LM?" I finally question.

"Uh, yeah?"

I feel like I'm having an out-of-body experience, like this isn't actually happening to me right now. Everything I pictured during our dates—the way I imagined *her* laughing, the way I thought *she'd* look at me when we finally met—it's all unraveling in real time. Every late-night conversation, every inside joke, every stupid little thing we shared—it was all *him*. LM was always a man.

He's the one who's been teaching me to cook. He's the one who I've lost sleep over, staying up late because I didn't want to say goodbye. He's the one I imagined taking me to his farm, showing me his world, maybe even letting me be part of *his* dream. My head is spinning as all the details from the last week are suddenly merging with the man in front of me.

"Is something wrong?" he asks, clearly thrown off by the reaction I'm having. I take a deep breath, shaking my head before I finally seem to remember how to speak.

"You're a man," I finally point out.

"And that's a problem?" He looks somewhere between confused and mad now, so whatever vibe I'm giving off is clearly not the excited meeting he was probably hoping for.

I focus on my breathing so I can answer him. The thoughts are flying through my head way faster than I can process them. I take a moment to try to sort through the emotions. I'm surprised more than anything. I'm embarrassed that I didn't more seriously consider this as a possibility. I'm not angry, though. At the end of the day, I wouldn't have wanted to pick anyone else. L is the only one I had any true connection with, and I don't regret my decision.

That has to mean something, right? Is there a chance that we could still have a real relationship, even if I've never seriously considered one with another man? I'm sure everyone watching this will love this set up after how confidently I labeled myself as the straight contestant on a queer dating show.

"I've never dated a man before," I admit.

The words are out of my mouth before I can even really consider stopping them. I don't have anything against men dating other men, it's just something that I'd never considered for myself before this show. Even when I thought about it in the abstract early on after getting here, the hypothetical felt very different from the man I have a real connection with, who is standing here across from me.

"Is that a problem? Did you not know what show you signed up for?" he asks as he turns for the door, and I race forward, grabbing his arm to stop him.

"Wait, don't go!" Even though this isn't what I was picturing, I'm not ready for him to walk away.

"What do you expect me to do? You saw me and were obviously disappointed. Then you pointed out that you don't date men," he says, emphasizing each word like I need help understanding. "I'm a man. You look absolutely terrified right now, not like some closeted baby bi who's excited for his first gay experience. This whole interaction didn't exactly scream 'I'm so excited to be in a relationship with you,' " he huffs, glaring at where my hand is still on his arm. "I don't want to be with someone who isn't excited to be with me. So I think I should just save us both the embarrassment and go."

"Shit, L, I'm so sorry. Please don't go. I *am* excited—I was so fucking excited when you said you'd move in with me. I was a mess all morning, worried you'd choose the other person still in your top two. I know I want to move forward with you. I didn't mean to offend you. I don't even know how to explain myself right now, and I know I sound like an idiot—and an asshole—but I'm sorry."

I take a deep breath while looking right into his bright blue eyes, pleading for him to understand. I'm momentarily distracted by the stormy array of blues and greys staring back at me. "Yes, I knew when I signed up for the show that I'd be talking to other guys, but I really liked the idea of the whole connection without looks thing." *And the convenient timeline for the ultimatum, but now is so not the time to tell him about that.*

"I guess I assumed I would be drawn to the women on the show because that's who I've always dated in the past. I was surprised when I saw you because it was easier for me to picture the vague idea of a partner that was similar to the ones I've had before. I think that maybe, on some unconscious level, I was always okay with this outcome?" I say it like it's a question, although I realize the truth of it as I voice the thought. "I was thinking that I was the token straight man on the show, but maybe a truly straight person wouldn't have signed up in the first place," I admit.

He's still just staring at me so I keep going. "And now that I know it's *you*, I still want to do all of it. I want *you* to give me cooking lessons in person this time, I want to go to *your* farm and bring Lucky to meet the chickens. I haven't been this excited about anything in my life in a long time. Please don't tell me I've fucked it all up already. Can you give me another chance? Let me prove there's a reason we picked each other."

He doesn't look convinced, so I let go and step back, finally taking him in. He's a big guy, maybe an inch shorter than my six foot three with wide shoulders that fill out the open flannel he's wearing over a tight T-shirt. A backwards baseball cap completes his farm-boy getup, and the full beard that covers the bottom half of his face makes his blue eyes seem brighter. He's still a bit tan even though it's winter, and I can only imagine the contrast in the summer when he's on the farm all day. He's definitely a good-looking guy, even with how pissed off he seems to be with me right now.

But am I attracted to him? Could I kiss him? Date him?

I'm surprised that I'm not opposed to the idea. I'm actually kind of... intrigued? A part of me does want to kiss him right now, just to see what it would be like. *Which isn't a super straight thought to have.*

Other than the times I'd wished I could just marry Chad to fulfill my parents' ultimatum, I've never considered dating a man before. I've never really had a reason to before the ultimatum. I've had a lot of fun with women over the years, and I've never had any doubts about my interest in them. But what I have done hasn't worked. I came to this show determined to get married.

I wonder what my parents will say when I tell them I'm engaged to a man? They want me to be married, though, and they never specified to whom.

I just thought *when* not *if...* I'm totally doing this if he'll agree to give me another chance.

If I didn't completely fuck it up already.

Plus, it's not like I actually need to propose right now—we still have time. I can prove to him that the connection we've been building is real, even if I fucked up the in-person first impression. Even if I need to ease into the physical aspects of being with another man. The next step is just living together, which doesn't sound bad at all. I've already been spending all my free time talking to L anyway, so clearly we get along.

There's no timeline for anything physical. It's not like we need to consummate the relationship tonight. We can start with kissing and go from there. I don't know if I'm just hyping myself up for it or what, but the longer I look at him—*or, I guess, I'm checking him out*—the more I like that idea... yep, I think I'm fully on board with kissing him. He's definitely not ugly.

He's hot, but I'm sure he knows that.

And it's L. The last week with *him* has been way better than any of my previous relationships, so I do want to give this thing between us a chance. I care about him in a way that I don't think I've ever cared about someone before, even if I didn't know L was a "him" until now. I think I owe it to the both of us to embrace this opportunity.

I fully realize that being open to dating a man isn't, like, peak straight behavior. Neither is thinking about kissing him, or doing more, but I actually don't think I care about the whole "straight" label. It might be what I've always assumed, but that doesn't necessarily mean it's true.

"So, what's your name?" I eagerly ask, finally over my

shock. I'm getting more excited the more I think about what this next phase of the show will really look like—about spending real time with L. I've been eager to meet them, to be with them, and now that I can finally picture this man in all the moments I imagined us sharing, I'm just as excited to live with them.

"Liam." He rolls his eyes at me, but it looks like maybe he's trying to fight a smile too, and that only makes my smile grow more. Now that I've gotten over the initial surprise, all I'm really feeling is nervous anticipation—the kind I used to get before a big game I was desperate to win. Maybe I should be upset, disappointed, even confused. But the more I think about it, the more the butterflies in my stomach seem to multiply as I wait for him to agree to continue this experience with me. "I'm Blake. Nice to officially meet you," I say, sticking out my hand. He eyes it wearily before reluctantly shaking. "So, are we doing this?" I check.

Can he tell how desperate I am for his approval?

"You really still want to?" He looks completely unconvinced, but he hasn't left, so I'm taking that as a good sign.

"Definitely! If you give me a chance, I promise to prove to you that I'm taking this seriously, and I'm excited to be doing it with you. I'm still glad I asked you to do this with me, Liam. Just because I've never dated a man before, doesn't mean I can't start now. Maybe that's what I've been doing wrong this whole time," I joke, hoping to win him over.

14

LIAM

Producer: What's your favorite feature—the first thing you notice when you meet someone?

Liam: Probably their smile. When someone else is happy, it's hard not to be drawn to that.

I feel like I'm on a bad sitcom, like this is all some kind of joke. Why didn't I follow my gut and initially say no to B? I would have been able to avoid this entire situation, and honestly, all this embarrassment.

I actually started picturing my future with B. With Blake.

I imagined us on the farm, cooking together, going to markets, and *maybe* even watching a random football game together every once in a while. Yeah, that's how far gone I was.

Now all those dreams feel like they were ripped away the moment he looked at me when I told him who I was.

There's no way this will work between us.

Despite the seemingly sincere apology and the way he's smiling at me now, I'm just not buying that he's ready to date a man. He's definitely not going to be ready to get married to one in a few weeks. How could he be?

This is what I get for telling myself to be open-minded when B kept surprising me. Apparently I've managed to surprise him even more.

I feel like a fucking idiot.

The person who chose me over everyone else thought I was a woman the entire time we'd been talking, then announced it on national television. The one who asked me to move in with him, to continue this experience, and yet, he assumed I worked for the show before considering that I could be the one he's been dating.

This is going to be a meme. This is going to catch like wildfire when it airs. Blake's shell-shocked expression because he thought I was a woman is going to be their multi-million-dollar marketing clip. I will literally *never* live this down. It doesn't matter that he followed it up with the least convincing bi-awakening moment ever. He probably realized there are cameras everywhere—and that he looked like a completely prejudiced asshole—before backpedaling and claiming that he still wanted to see me. I guess we'll see what he really thinks when we get into our bedroom that doesn't have any cameras. The bedroom we'll be sharing.

I assume I'll get another apology, then he'll want to plan some amicable breakup where he can say we didn't end things because I'm a man, but because we just aren't as good a match as we'd hoped. That has to be his plan—because why the hell would he want to keep going if he thought he was straight ten minutes ago?

I should turn around right now and walk out the door. I should grab my bags and pretend this never happened. End this experience now before I become an even bigger laughingstock.

Even on the off chance that everything he said was true, and he genuinely wants to try to continue building a relationship with me, do I even want that? I'm almost thirty years old. I don't have time to be someone's bi-awakening sexual experiment. I learned that lesson with my ex. It's not fun. Especially not on TV.

Except, despite all these very rational thoughts, I don't move. I stay right where I'm standing.

As much as I hate to admit it, there's a tiny part of me that wants to explore this, despite the embarrassment. The part that has *actual* feelings for him. For Blake. And it has absolutely nothing to do with how attractive he is.

Blake is huge, he looks like he's an inch taller than me. His blond hair is styled in that effortless, tousled way that definitely took effort. It's long enough to run my fingers through and grip —not that I'm thinking about that. His clothes look expensive too. He's got on dark jeans and a green Henley with the sleeves pushed up, showing off his impressive forearms. Ones I'm definitely not paying any attention to. I force my gaze back to his face and meet his hazel eyes. They're filled with so much hope, pleading for me to give him some sort of confirmation that I'll give him a chance.

He claims that just because he hasn't dated a man before, it doesn't mean he's opposed to it. He even acknowledged that he knew this was a possibility when he signed up for the show, but saying he'd date a man and actually doing it are different things.

Finally, Blake opens his mouth to speak again. "Well, I had this whole plan to kiss you when I saw you... do you still want me to do that?" He chuckles again, sounding nervous, and I'm not sure if that was meant to be a serious offer or a joke to ease this tension.

I say nothing, just raise an eyebrow. Does this straight guy really think he can "date" me if he's freaking out over a kiss he made up in his head?

I cross my arms. "I'm pretty sure that plan was for a girl, not me. So we can skip that for now."

He nods once, but still seems way too determined to hold onto this experience. I'm not sure if it's because he actually wants to be here with me or if his ego just won't let him walk away, but I'll have to take him at his word for now that he wants to continue until we can get away from the cameras.

"Well, should we unpack then?" I reluctantly ask, figuring that will get us some privacy.

"Yeah! Yes, let's do that," Blake agrees easily.

We both turn around to wheel our luggage further into the apartment, and that's when I see exactly what we're dealing with tonight.

One bed.

One *queen-sized* bed.

For two guys over six feet tall.

"Guess we're getting cozy," Blake says with a laugh.

I turn to look at him, waiting for some kind of freak out or acknowledgment that this is a problem for him. But nope. 'Course not. He's just grinning at me like he can't wait to cuddle up together. Or maybe it's for the cameras. This is so fucking confusing.

15

BLAKE

Producer: In past relationships, do you jump right in with physical affection, or wait and build up to it slowly?

Blake: Most of my past relationships have started physically. Can't say many have progressed beyond that…

"I can sleep on the couch if you actually want to stay tonight," Liam offers, and I get why he's hesitant. I really should have tried to keep my reaction to him being a guy more to myself. I just assumed he'd be a woman because that's who I've dated in the past. But none of those relationships lasted more than a month… hmm. Maybe this will be better. The thought of him spending the night on the couch doesn't sit right with me, though.

If we're trying to figure out if we can be in a relationship—and not just that, but be *married*—by the end of the month, I'm going to need to get over the fact that I've never been with a man and do it quickly. We already have a connection, and what I feel for him is real. It's the strongest connection I've ever had with another person. The best way to do that is to not tiptoe around each other. I need to prove to him I'm still committed because all I've wanted as of recently is to have a real connection with someone—and he's it. I'm going to treat Liam like I would anyone else I was dating. I'm not concerned about us sleeping together.

Okay, real talk, I'm a little *concerned about the sex "sleeping together" aspect of things.* But just sleeping? Chad and I have fallen asleep in the same bed before and it was no big deal. Plus, being that close all night can only help us become more comfortable together.

"Nah, fuck that. Sleep in here, we can share the bed," I assure him. Then I shut the door to make sure we're alone. When they had us pack, the producers mentioned the new apartment won't have cameras in the bedroom to give us privacy. They asked us to spend as much time as we could hanging out in the main living spaces so that the show could still get footage of the relationships building, but they're not trying to film *that* kind of content.

"If you're sure?" Liam asks slowly, sounding wholly unconvinced.

"I'm sure! Plus, I think it will be good for us to have a camera-free space together, right?" I offer what I hope is an encouraging smile his way, but he's looking at me like I have two heads.

"So there's nothing else you want to say to me, now that there aren't cameras?" he asks, looking like he's expecting me to add something.

"I'm sorry again. My reaction really was nothing personal, you're a good-looking guy, you have to know that," I say, gesturing toward him.

He's still looking at me like I have two heads. "And you really want to sleep together?"

"Come on, it's just a bed. It'll be great. What side do you prefer?"

"I'll take this one," he says, sitting on the edge closer to the door. "I usually sleep in my underwear, would you rather I wear sweats or a T-shirt?" he asks, still sounding confused that I'm not requesting separate sleeping arrangements or building a pillow wall in the middle of the bed.

"I don't care what you wear. I usually sleep naked, but I'm assuming you don't want me to do that," I tease as I plug my phone charger in on my side of our bed. He isn't looking my way, but the tips of his ears are red, so I think he might be blushing. The thought of Liam blushing because he's picturing my naked body makes me smile. I definitely don't hate it. I kind of want to tease him some more, but I don't want to push my luck.

I wonder what he *looks like naked?*

"Yeah, probably best that you don't," he mutters. "I'm going to shower before bed, if you don't mind."

"Not at all." He grabs some of his stuff before heading into the en suite, and I unpack my suitcase, leaving him plenty of room for his things. *I'm already such a good boyfriend.* I really have to piss by the time I'm done, so I grab my toothbrush and head into the bathroom.

"What the fuck are you doing?" Liam yells when I open the door.

"Uh, I was going to pee and brush my teeth?" I say, meaning to answer confidently, but it ends up coming out like a question.

"While I'm in the shower?"

Shit, he sounds mad. How do I keep fucking this up? Maybe I'm not such a great boyfriend after all.

"Um, yeah. Is that not okay?" I ask, genuinely confused. "We're both guys, it's not anything we haven't seen before. I honestly didn't think anything of coming in," I explain. The shower even has a frosted door—not that I knew that coming in here—so it's not like I can see more than the blur of him.

"Well, I would prefer some privacy while I'm in the bathroom. Thanks," he spits out.

"Sorry." I quickly leave, and go out to see if there's another bathroom in the main living space.

I hadn't noticed it earlier, but I do find one. When I get back to our room, he still isn't done. I showered before our final date earlier, so I throw on a pair of my boxer briefs and sit on the bed to wait for him, ready to apologize yet again. I can't believe it was only today that I was so worried about LM not choosing me, and now, I'm living with *him*. At this rate, though, I won't be surprised if I wake up to find he's snuck out in the middle of the night—done with me before our first full day together.

Maybe I really am a shit boyfriend. No wonder all my relationships barely begin before they get tired of me.

As soon as he walks into the room, I launch into my apology without giving him time to speak. "I'm sorry. I didn't notice the other bathroom earlier, and I've been in so many locker rooms over the years, I honestly didn't think twice about there being a privacy issue. Please don't leave." It all comes out in one long breath. Hopefully he understands my rant and I didn't say it too quickly.

He's standing still, frozen by the door, staring at me, and it takes me a moment to realize he's checking out my naked chest. I automatically sit up straighter and flex, trying to impress him. *Huh, do I normally try to show off for men?* Probably. I work too hard to look like I do to not let everyone appreciate it.

"Locker rooms?" he finally asks, sounding unamused as he meets my gaze. He's slowly rounding the bed toward his side, which I take as a good sign that he isn't immediately leaving.

"Yeah, I couldn't tell you before because it would give away my gender, but I played football for most of my life."

"Of course you did." I swear I can hear the eye roll in his tone. "It's fine. It's been a long day, let's just get some sleep."

"Okay," I say, getting under the covers as he turns off the light. Once we're both settled, facing away from each other, I feel like there's still awkward tension. "Hey, Liam? Thanks for giving me a chance," I whisper.

FINALLY. My dick is rock-hard as the pretty brunette on their knees in front of me wraps their lips around the head and sucks. It's been so fucking long since I've gotten any action. I can't remember the last time I got off with another person and not my right hand. I can't stop my hips from jerking forward, chasing more of this feeling. They let out a deep moan in response to my obvious desperation, and I close my eyes, tipping my head back as pleasure overwhelms my senses. I thread my fingers through their hair—hair that is much shorter than I realized.

That's strange.

I open my eyes and look down into the familiar bright blue gaze of the person with their lips wrapped around my cock.

Liam.

I jolt awake from my dream to find I'm spooning Liam in our bed, my very obvious erection digging into his ass. I should probably be more embarrassed or worried about Liam's reaction, but all I can focus on is how great this is.

"L, guess what?" I whisper, moving back so that we aren't tangled together as I gently nudge him.

"Hmm?" he hums, seemingly already awake.

"I just had a sex dream about you," I tell him excitedly.

"What?" he asks, surprisingly alert as he rolls over to look at me.

"I had a sex dream about you and woke up super hard, isn't that great?" His brow is furrowed and he's still looking at me like I'm speaking a language he doesn't understand.

"It's great?" he echoes the question, obviously not following me.

"Well, as you know, I haven't been with another man before,

and to be honest, I was a little nervous about the physical aspect of that, but obviously I'm attracted to you on top of the emotional connection we've already been building."

I pause trying to find the right words. I want to tell him that once I caught up to the reality that LM is Liam—a man—it'd be easy enough for me to get on board. I've always been a go-with-the-flow person, and we do have a strong emotional connection, which has been the thing that's been missing from all my other relationships. I really don't care that he's a man, I just haven't ever considered dating one before.

"I'm not scared of figuring this out," I say. "Not if you're the one I'm in a relationship with."

"Well, I'm glad you think that's a positive thing and you're not freaking out…" he trails off as he shakes his head and runs his hands through his short hair. I wonder if it's as soft as it felt in my dream. "I'm going to go start breakfast."

He heads out of our room, shutting the door behind him. I can't stop thinking about my dream, and what it would really be like to be with Liam like that. *Fuuuck,* I can't remember the last time I was this turned on. My cock is still aching by the time I get out of bed, so I take a quick shower to rub one out. I don't know if I should feel guilty or excited about it, but I can't help but picture Liam as I do.

As I'm getting dressed, the smell of bacon overwhelms me and I practically skip out of our room to see how much Liam made. I hope I'll get to experience his cooking firsthand now that we live together.

"Fuck, that smells amazing. Is there enough for me?" I ask, stepping right up behind him and placing a hand on his hip to steady myself as I look over his shoulder at the sizzling pan.

"Shit, you scared me," he says with a jolt.

"Sorry," I say, stepping back as I open cabinets until I find plates and silverware for us. Unless he's planning to eat a ton of food by himself, it looks like he made us both breakfast. My heart feels a little lighter in my chest at the realization that he might not have given up on me yet. "Any cream or sugar for that coffee?" I ask as I set the table.

"Just cream."

I get that out too and pour us each a cup, placing them on the table with the cream since I don't know how much he likes yet.

When he brings the food over, he's eyeing the table suspiciously. "I thought you said you were bad at little things in relationships?" he accuses.

I eye the coffee and plates I grabbed. "I'm bad at small romantic gestures, not basic human decency," I offer him a small smile, still unsure where we stand.

"I just figured that the rich city boy might be used to being served and waited on," he teases back, making me fully smile.

Holy shit, is this flirting? The fluttering nervous feeling in my stomach certainly seems to think so. Obviously I liked talking to LM before we met. But now, having met Liam, spending time with him and acknowledging how nervous and excited I am around him, it's clear that his gender isn't affecting those feelings.

"Thanks for making me breakfast," I say earnestly. "This is nice—eating together. Way better than you trying to teach me how to cook over the phone with those robot voices."

He laughs, a warm sound that makes my stomach flip all over again.

LIAM

Producer: What's the best date you've ever been on?

Liam: I'm more of a slow evening at home kind of person. I'd rather just stay in, cook together, talk. Something simple where it feels like we're actually getting to know each other.

Blake really does seem completely unaffected by the idea of being with a man, and honestly, it's confusing as fuck.

It's like none of this even fazes him. Like waking up next to me, sharing a space, living with a guy he thought was a woman this whole time, is just another normal day. He passed right out last night too. No late-night tossing and turning, contemplating if he really wanted to do this. He just accepted it without barely a moment of reflection or hesitation.

Maybe that's just who he is—completely confident that everything will always work out for him. It's messing with my head.

Him coming into the bathroom while I'm showering so he can pee and brush his teeth? *Not considerate.* But then thanking me for making breakfast and getting our coffees and plates? *That definitely is.*

I'm trying to put all the pieces together from all our dates and it just doesn't add up. I don't know what to think about him.

Then there's the thing I've been trying to get out of my head since this morning, but can't seem to stop thinking about. He was hard this morning when I woke up. I was lying there trying to figure out how to escape from his hold without waking him so he wouldn't realize how he'd wrapped himself around me in his sleep. But before I could figure it out, he was awake, and he didn't even care. *At all.* I was expecting him to finally have some sort of sexual identity crisis realizing his hard dick was rubbing against me, but Blake wasn't even remotely panicked. He was even excited about it.

I don't know what to make of him. Every time I think I have him figured out, he surprises me again. It's like, no matter how hard I try, I can't get a read on him, but I can't help but think the way he's handled his apparent sexual awakening is... sweet? Endearing?

Which just makes this harder. I'm not sure how to describe him, and I hate that I'm spending this much time thinking about a potential relationship with him when this will probably be over before it really begins anyway.

"So," I start, trying to stop the loop my mind is on. "You mentioned football and locker rooms last night. Is there anything you didn't tell me when we were blind dating that you want to tell me now?"

He seems to consider it for a moment before nodding his head. "I think there are two things, really. One likely isn't a surprise, though, since you've made a comment already."

Okay, that has my curiosity piqued.

"The first thing is that I do come from money, but my parents are kind of sick of my shit, so we'll see if I still have it by the end of this." He laughs. Maybe his parents don't approve of him on this show. "The other is that I don't have a job. I've actually never had a real job. It's why I help my mom with her charity work. It was a compromise of sorts. At least, initially. I really do like it now."

He never mentioned a job when we were talking and I didn't want to ask in case it was a touchy subject, but I guess that makes sense. No one's mom does charity work seemingly full-time unless they're rich. It's not a luxury the working class has.

Blake sighs. "I know how it sounds."

"Do you?" I ask before I can stop myself.

"Yeah, I do. Trust fund baby, parents cutting me off, no real ambition, the whole stereotype. I get it."

I cross my arms. "And is it wrong?"

Blake shrugs. "Not really. But to be fair, I did have a plan. It just… didn't work out."

"Let me guess, something with football?"

Blake rubs the back of his neck, he's smiling but it doesn't reach his eyes. "Yep. I got drafted to the NFL, thought I was set, and then… well. I wasn't."

I just look at him, unsure what to say. I didn't realize you could be drafted and *not* actually play in the NFL, but that just goes to show how little I know about sports.

He shrugs then continues. "It never went anywhere. Didn't even make it through training camp. I thought it was my entire future, and then it was nothing."

I give him a nod and think about what he just said. "So, what, you played football for a while, it didn't work out, and then you just… didn't try anything else?"

He doesn't react right away, but I can see him lick his lips before he swallows and looks up at me.

He finally exhales. "Uh, yeah. It's kind of embarrassing when you put it that way. I was pretty lost for a while until I got Lucky. She keeps me busy and a lot of my friends were in similar situations—not needing to work—so I didn't think much of it until my parents called me out. The last year and a half has really given me a lot of new awareness."

At least he acknowledges it. It explains why he said he didn't care about the money from the show. It won't do anything to change his life, but it'd sure as hell change mine. There have been moments since we met where I think I could really like him. Moments when he's funny, or thoughtful, and he actually seems like a real person with depth. And then there are moments like this, where I'm just left staring at him, wondering what the hell I got myself into.

There are layers to everyone, him included.

So, instead of making him feel worse, I decide to lighten things up and switch the conversation back to the here and now.

"Well, since I cooked, do you think you can handle the dishes? Can't burn those," I tease.

Blake perks up instantly, like the emotional moment never even happened. "You're assigning me chores now? Damn, so bossy. At least take me out to dinner first."

I shake my head, pushing my plate forward. "You're about to eat my cooking every day. That's better than paying someone else to cook for us."

"Is it?" he questions, but his tone is still teasing. "Fine. Since you asked so nicely, I guess I can grace you with my dish-washing skills."

Except, I quickly learn he does not have dishwashing skills. After watching what's unfolding in the sink, I don't know if Blake has ever washed a dish in his life. He turned the water on full blast, grabbed a plate, and just sort of waved it under the water like that's enough. He hasn't even reached for the soap or the brush, and then he just sets it on the counter.

"What are you doing?" I can't take this anymore. As amusing as he is, I have to say something.

"Uh, washing the dishes?" he responds with a smile, but his tone makes it clear he's confused about why I'm asking.

"Well, if you're going to wash the dishes, you need to actually *wash* the dishes. That means getting soap on the sponge and scrubbing them clean," I explain. I know what I'm about to ask is likely condescending, but I need to know. "Blake, uh, have you ever washed dishes before?"

He scoffs. "Duh. Of course I've washed dishes before."

"Okay, whatever you say." I laugh and shake my head. "But this is painful to watch." There's no way he's ever washed a dish *properly*. I'm sure he had a housekeeper or someone come in behind him and rewash them all without him knowing. It's kind of cute, really.

"Then don't watch." He tosses me a wink before going back to *not* washing the dishes, and I can't help but laugh again.

I should be annoyed, but the way he's standing there, sleeves pushed up, abs peeking out where his too tight shirt rides up? I can't look away, and I hate myself a little for even noticing. But damn, he looks good. What am I supposed to do? Not look?

Ignoring my intuition, I come up right behind him and say, "I'm taking over. There's no use when I'll have to rewash everything anyway at this rate."

My shoulder is brushing against his, and I feel him lean in a little when I reach around him for the sponge, before he steps aside, motioning toward the sink. "Be my guest. But if you wanted to get all handsy with me, you could've just said so."

I go still for half a second, dropping the sponge into the sink as I stare at him like he's lost his mind. What the actual hell is happening right now?

This man—this *allegedly-self-proclaimed-straight-man-as-of-yesterday*—is flirting with me. *Intentionally* flirting with me, after being excited about apparently getting hard thinking about me this morning. No hesitation, no awkward backpedaling. He's just *in it* like he said.

I'm moving before I really make a conscious decision, and apparently the only thing my brain can think of in this moment is to take the now wet and soapy sponge and throw it at him. It hits him square in the chest when he doesn't move out of the way in time. His eyes are wide and his mouth is hanging open as he stares at me in shock. I'm a little surprised myself, I don't know why I even did that, but I clearly did.

"Oh, you little—" He doesn't finish, and I see why a second too late to react. He lunges for the sink hose, grinning like crazy, and squeezes the handle as he aims it at me. Cold water sprays me right in the face, and Blake absolutely loses it laughing.

"You asshole!" I cry, laughing too.

He drops the sprayer like it's on fire and starts running through the apartment, still laughing his ass off. When I catch up to him, I don't think as I grab his wrist and pull him back into me. We're chest to chest as we crash into each other, and for a moment, neither of us moves.

We're both breathless from laughing. Water is dripping down my hair and face, and my fingers are still curled around his wrist. I can feel the rapid flutter of his heartbeat in my grip as his breath ghosts across my face. His hazel gaze bounces between my eyes, and I get distracted by all of the colors I hadn't noticed in his before this moment. Are they more brown or green?

I have no idea how long we've been standing here staring at each other, chests heaving, when Blake ruins it by opening his mouth. "I don't think you know how to wash the dishes either."

Jesus. His comment pulls me out of whatever trance I was just in. I shake my head and let go of his wrist, stepping back with a shaky laugh. I don't know what else to do. I'm definitely way too turned on to think properly, so I point toward the sink. "Wash the dishes, Blake. With soap and a sponge this time."

Then, before he can say anything else, I turn on my heel and walk away.

Because what the fuck was that?

Of course, Blake has to get in the last word. He calls out, "Yes, sir!" with so much innuendo in it that I almost turn around to see if his expression is all teasing or if he might actually be into the idea of me bossing him around. But I stay strong in my resolve and continue into the safety of the bedroom.

Our bedroom. Where we share a bed. Fuck, this isn't helping.

I take out my phone, because I desperately need a distraction, and send a text to JR.

LM:

I think I'm losing my mind.

JR:

Dramatic much? What happened now?

LM:

He called me 'sir' with the filthiest fucking tone I've ever heard in my life and I swear we almost kissed.

JR:

What did you do?

LM:

I got the hell out of there before I did something stupid. I don't want to let myself fall for him if this is all one big experiment or something he's doing to save face in front of the cameras.

JR:

We really ended up in weird situations, huh? Wouldn't have called it for either of us two days ago.

LM:

You could say that again.

BLAKE

Producer: During the blind dating round, we asked you to not discuss detailed sexual preferences out of concern that it might reveal your partner's gender. Are you worried about being compatible now that you've met Liam?

Blake: You know, I probably should be. I mean, I thought I was straight when I signed up for this. But no, I'm not into anything wild. If my partner is happy, I'm happy. That's kinda the whole point, right?

As much as I was kidding about calling Liam "sir," I don't hate the idea of him ordering me around a bit. Especially when we do explore the more *physical* aspects of our relationship since I'll have no idea what I'm doing. And at this point, I'm pretty sure it is a *when* and not an *if.*

Hypothetically, when I had considered kissing him last night, I was into the idea. But when he was holding my wrist and we were standing inches apart? All I could think was how much I wanted his lips on mine. I wanted to know what it would be like. Would it be different to kiss a man than all the women I've been with? *None of them have ever been able to manhandle me like that.* I think I liked it.

Actually, I know I liked it.

But then at the last second, I chickened out and decided to make a dumb comment instead. As fun as that was—and as much as I appreciated his somewhat flustered and stern reaction —I'm determined not to lose my nerve the next time the opportunity to kiss him presents itself. *I need to stop hesitating.* Obviously I came here because I want to get married to keep my money, and if it works out that way, then I'll be relieved to not have to stress about finances, but that hasn't been my focus since I really started building a connection with Liam. Being with him is fun. Part of me feels like a teenager again when I'm around him, nervous and excited to be near my crush, wanting to be closer, to kiss him, but worried about how it'll go.

I watch TV for a bit since it seemed like Liam wanted some space, but after the second episode, I'm bored and restless. *That was probably enough alone time, right?* So I knock on the bedroom door. *See? I can respect privacy.*

"Come in."

"Hey, sorry if you wanted to be alone, I was just wondering if you'd want to come to the gym with me," I ask, flashing him my best smile.

"Like to workout?"

"That is typically what people do in a gym."

"Uh, sure. I don't think I've been to a gym since college," he says, almost to himself with how quiet he is.

"Bullshit."

"Excuse me?"

"There's no way you look like *that* without a gym," I insist, gesturing to the massive arms and chest that are filling out his T-shirt. He doesn't have a flannel on over it right now, so his muscles are on full display. *And they're sexy as hell.*

"Working on a farm isn't exactly easy," he explains. I just

give him a skeptical look in return. If he's really bigger than me from only his farm work, I'm seriously questioning what running a farm actually involves. I was wrong about all of the assumptions I'd made about LM being a girl, but surely collecting eggs from chickens wouldn't make you look like *that?*

"Okay, while we workout I'm going to need you to tell me more about what you do on this farm to be in *that* good of shape," I say, waving my arm up and down in his direction, making him laugh. I like that I can do that, especially when he drops all his concern about me never having been with a guy before and can just enjoy himself. The moments he seems to give in to how much fun we have together are my new favorite things. That's how it was during our blind dates, and I know that's how it can be again once we embrace this relationship.

I sent a message to the producers earlier to see about using the gym and they confirmed it was free for us to use whenever we want now that we've met our partners. No one else is in the gym when we arrive, but we'll meet all the other contestants tomorrow for a group event that's planned. It will be interesting to meet some of the other people I talked to—if they're still here —and see who they ended up with.

Liam confidently approaches the equipment. I watch him as he sets up the weights, so obviously he's been in a gym before, even if it really was almost ten years ago. "Wait, how old are you?" I ask when I realize we haven't covered that yet.

"Twenty-eight. You?"

"Twenty-nine. I'll be thirty a month after the show ends."

"Couldn't bear the idea of entering another decade without a partner?" he teases, not knowing how close he is to the truth.

"Something like that," I mutter. As much as I want to be completely honest with him—and I've debated telling him the truth about my parents' ultimatum a hundred times now—I just can't. Not yet, anyway. Things still feel too shaky between us right now, and I want our relationship to be solid first. I'm scared if I tell him all that, he's going to assume I'm only with him for the money. But the truth is, I really don't want to lose him. Sure, I did join this show for the money, but the more I talked to Liam throughout the dating portion, the less I cared about the ultimatum. Money isn't the only thing I want anymore.

When I met him yesterday and discovered he was, in fact, *not* a woman, the money obviously crossed my mind. But I'm secure enough to admit that I'm more than a little curious about what being with Liam physically would be like. I wanted to kiss him earlier, and I definitely enjoyed my dream about him. He's different from the soft curves I'm used to, but his hard body seems to really be doing it for me. My reaction to him wasn't meaningless.

And I honestly don't care about his gender.

I've been thinking a lot about my sexuality over the last twenty-four hours, and I think I can easily admit that I'm less straight than I had assumed going into this show, and that doesn't bother me at all. I've never given a fuck about who people choose to be with. I truly don't know why anyone cares.

I'm pretty sure that I already came out to the world last night by begging a man to date me on reality TV.

It's cool I won't have to stress about doing it later. Win-win if you ask me.

I really would like to confirm my new suspicions though. As I eye Liam working out, I'm glad I get to explore things with not only someone that I already care so much about, but that he's such a good-looking man as well. He's the kind of guy I might see at the gym and ask about his diet or workout plan because I'm jealous of how hot he is. But maybe a part of me was always attracted to those guys and I just didn't understand my feelings of admiration.

And Liam's beard? I've always been obsessed with beards. But my light blond hair always comes in patchy when I attempt to grow it out, so I've never been able to have one. Do I actually want one, though, or am I attracted to guys with beards?

I try to focus on my own workout, but my brain keeps circling back to Liam—and all the questions I suddenly have about what I thought I knew when it came to guys. Then he lifts up his shirt to wipe the sweat off his face before seeming to give up on the idea and removing the shirt entirely. *Holy shit.* How does he have actual abs if he doesn't even go to the gym? And the prominent V of his hips draws all my attention to his dick with a dusting of dark hair… has that always been so fucking hot? The urge to run my hand over his abs is so strong. "What the hell do you have to do on a farm to look like that?" I ask, trying to keep the mood light as I openly check him out while I set up one of the weight machines.

He laughs. "Well, I pretty much never stop moving. There's a lot of carrying around feed and equipment, fixing things as they wear out. We don't have the money for the newer equipment that can automate things, so I do a lot of the planting and harvesting myself."

I nod, realizing my vision of a farm has always been about a slow, easygoing life with some guy in overalls sitting on a tractor. "Huh, yeah, that does sound harder than what I was picturing. Maybe I can help when we go. I can't wait to see it."

Liam's head snaps in my direction with wide-eyed confusion again. "Go where?"

"To your farm?"

"You're coming to my farm?"

Why is he acting like he didn't know this?

I let out a short laugh. I can't tell if he's joking or not. "Obviously. We'll be there next week for the hometown visits for the show, and I assume that's where we'll live when we're married. I know how much you love it there."

His shocked expression is comical.

"I guess with everything that happened yesterday, I haven't really thought past our next few days," he admits.

That stings a little. I don't know if I should be offended by how uninvested he seems in our relationship, but I'm not wasting time on hurt feelings. I need to focus on finding a way to show him that there's a reason we picked each other. That just because I was expecting LM to be a woman, that doesn't mean I'm not happy to be doing this *with him*. I just need to convince him I can handle being with a man. *And prove it to myself.*

"Well, I'm excited," I assure him, and I mean it. I want to go. I want to meet his dad, see the farm, catch a glimpse of what his day-to-day life is like.

"Oh yeah?" he says, raising an eyebrow. "You sure you're ready for farm living? It's early mornings and hard work, there's no staff to help you with chores and no one around to cook for you, rich boy."

"But you'll be there," I say, grinning. "You can cook for me."

He barks a laugh as I bat my eyelashes at him. "And what will you be doing while I do all the farm work, chores, and cooking?"

"Playing with the animals, eye candy, moral support, comedic relief?" I suggest. Liam just shakes his head, but he can't hide his smile. *I'm totally winning him over.*

We spend the next hour comparing his tiny town to my life in the city. He tries to convince me that waking up at sunrise to work is "fun," and I try to convince him that a twenty-dollar oat milk latte from my favorite swanky coffee bar is worth it. We're laughing the whole time, and every time our eyes meet or I earn a laugh from him, that fluttering in my stomach intensifies, and my heart races a little faster.

Later, back in the apartment, we take turns showering, and I'm excited to find the producers dropped off more puzzles. I start working on one at the breakfast bar so we can talk as Liam cooks, and after lunch, he joins me working on it. I hope I'm not the only one feeling the tension between us as our arms occasionally touch, reaching for pieces. *He has to be as aware of me as I am of him, right?* We're not doing anything special or extravagant, but I'm really enjoying our time together. *I hope he is too.*

I lose track of time puzzling, and when we finish, it's already time for dinner. "Can we do an in-person cooking lesson?" I ask, coming up beside him while he starts to pull out ingredients.

"Yeah, maybe you will be able to cook something for me soon," he teases.

"Eh, I wouldn't get your hopes up." I wink, and this time I get to see when his cheeks darken. *Yup, I definitely like that.* Without really considering what I'm doing I brush my fingers over the blush and his breath hitches.

"You always blush this easily?" I murmur. "Or is it just when you're around me?"

He swallows, but doesn't move away. "I-I think it might be you."

My hand lingers a second longer than it probably should. "Good."

We've been flirting, and the tension between us has been building since we met, but I don't know how to take that next step forward. I'm too nervous, too in my head about it being my first time with a man, but I want to. I want more.

"What are you doing?" His voice is breathy and his wide eyes are locked on mine.

I let my fingers linger for just a second longer before letting them fall away, but I don't move back. "I was thinking that it's cute how your cheeks get so red from a simple wink. And I was wondering how you'd react if I kissed you."

His lips part slightly like he's about to say something, but then a slow smirk spreads across his face, completely replacing his previously shy expression. There's a newfound confidence there and a glint of something wicked in his eyes that I haven't seen yet, but it makes my pulse pick up even more. I think I like it.

"Fuck it. You want me to kiss you, straight boy?" he taunts, voice dripping with amusement.

Now I think I'm the one blushing. I give a slight nod as I hold his gaze.

As soon as I give him permission, he steps closer. His breath fans over my lips, and for a second, we just hover there. Close enough to feel it, to want it.

He closes the distance, and when his mouth finally meets mine, I'm surprised by how soft his lips are.

As confident as I was pretending to be, I feel like I'm frozen in place. I'm usually the one initiating things with my partners, but not now, and I kind of love it. He's cupping my jaw and tilting my face to deepen the kiss, and my brain feels like it's completely short-circuiting. *Why have I never kissed a man before? I'm definitely into it.*

I gasp, completely unprepared for how good his beard rubbing against my skin feels. He takes full advantage, slipping his tongue past my parted lips, licking into my mouth with a confidence that makes my knees feel unsteady. Without permission, a soft moan escapes my throat, and that finally snaps me into focus. I grab his hips and lean in more.

That must be all the encouragement he needs, because the next thing I know, he's spinning us, pressing me back against the counter, our mouths never separating.

My entire body melts into him. It's a visceral reaction. His tongue moves against mine, and I give into him willingly, loving this display of dominance. I've never been kissed like this before. Never had someone take over like they physically couldn't hold back, like they couldn't help themselves.

It's so fucking hot.

And more than that, it feels like proof that he hasn't

completely dismissed the future I'm still hoping for with him, that he *wants me.*

His hand slides into my hair, gripping tight as he tugs my head back just enough to deepen the kiss even more. It's like he needs to be closer to me, and *god, I want him to be.*

I'm positive I've never felt this wanted. And I like it. No, *I fucking love it.* This is all I want now. I don't think anything else could ever live up to the way this kiss is undoing me.

A whimper slips out this time before I can stop it, and I don't even care. I want him to know how badly I want him. I realize I'm grinding my very hard cock into his thigh where he's positioned it between my legs. I've fully crossed the line from experimental curiosity to *holy shit, I want him so badly, I can't think straight.*

Ha. Not thinking straight at all, this is very much not-straight thinking. I'm definitely into him.

His other hand slips under my shirt, fingertips tracing over my abs, and I can feel his erection digging into my hip. It only makes me more desperate for him, and I grind into him more forcefully. I don't want to stop. If only he'd move his hand a little lower—

But instead of playing into my fantasy, he pulls back.

"Okay," he says breathlessly, laughing softly as he steps away. "I think that's enough for today."

For a second, I can't even process what he's saying. My brain is too fogged up with want and desire to think of anything other than kissing him. I'm sure I heard him wrong. *Right?*

"What? No, why'd you stop?" I whine. My body is buzzing. I'm so needy for him, I can barely stand it. I'm desperate for his hands, his mouth, anything he'll give me. I'm not even picky. I just want *more.*

Liam gives me an amused look like he's enjoying watching me suffer and nearly beg. "Because you don't need to jump straight into the deep end. I get it, you're okay with me being a guy, but we can ease you into that a little before we get our cocks out."

"Liiiiam," I whine again because my still-very-hard dick is *not* loving this plan.

"Blaaaake," he taunts back, raising an eyebrow as he smirks at me.

I bite back a groan. "Fine, but I would like to state for the record that I'm more than willing to speed things up." I cross my arms and sink back against the counter with a huff.

He relaxes too before laughing at my disappointed expression. "Want to get back to cooking?" he offers, and I reluctantly nod.

Not like I have much of a choice.

As much as I kind of really want to excuse myself to go finish things myself in the shower instead, I also don't want to give up this time with him. I liked our phone-call cooking lessons, but I'm even more excited to get the live version.

I just need to stop distracting myself with how fucking hot that kiss was and enjoy this time together.

18

LIAM

Producer: Do you usually make the first move in a relationship, or wait for the other person to take the lead?

Liam: I'm not usually the first to make a move, but once we're both in it, yeah, I like to take the lead. As long as they're into it, too, and consenting, of course.

I can't believe what just happened. I didn't want to stop. *Nothing in me wanted to stop.* But I knew I had to.

Despite my best judgment, I know I'm falling for Blake, and the last thing I want is to push too far too fast or end up as another experiment. I didn't want to risk doing something Blake wasn't ready for, and I don't want to risk getting too attached, only for him to realize he isn't actually into men.

I know he'd seemed confident with all his flirting and teasing, but still, it's his first time doing *anything* with a man. There's a very real chance he could freak out later on, and I absolutely don't want him to do something he'd regret or end up resenting me for. I also refuse to be someone's experiment again,

129

someone who they string along until it's no longer convenient for them.

And then there were the cameras. Fuck. I just thought about the cameras.

It's not like I actually forgot they were there, but in the moment, when his hands were on me and I could feel how badly he wanted me, I hadn't given them a single thought.

Great. I'll just die of embarrassment when I see how completely gone I looked, watching it back. There's no way I wasn't staring at Blake like some lovesick fool. Which also means there's absolutely no way I'm letting my dad watch this. If he chooses to ignore me and watch it anyway, he'd better do it far, far away from me, because there is zero chance I'm sitting next to him while he watches that scene.

Deep breaths, that's a problem for future Liam. I urge my body to calm the hell down because my boner is definitely still noticeable.

Well, maybe the reality TV gods are on my side and they won't actually show those clips on TV if my hard cock is clearly visible. *One can only hope.*

Blake and I continue to cook, and I try to stop my mind from reeling about our future. If anything, tonight proved there's a real chance at something between us. Which is exactly why I had to slow it the fuck down before we both ended up in over our heads.

No matter how much I try to distract myself, though, I can't stop thinking about how easily he mentioned moving to the farm. He even said, "when we're married," like it was inevitable. When he first found out the "L" he'd been falling for was actually a man—and not the woman he'd imagined—any thoughts I had about a future with him came to a screeching halt. Especially when he admitted he'd never dated a man before.

I know I agreed to see where things would go, but if I'm being honest, a big part of why I stayed was because he's hot.

I'm not a saint—I wasn't about to turn down a man who looks like *that* and was practically begging to date me. But even after saying yes, I didn't actually expect him to be at this level of *all in*.

But he's still thinking about it. We didn't even need to discuss it—no debate about who would move in with who, who would give up the life they had before the show, none of that. Finding someone who wouldn't want to move to the farm was one of my biggest concerns when I came here. I certainly wasn't expecting him to be so eager to give up his lavish lifestyle in the city and move to my farm simply because he knows how important it is to me.

He's willing to leave behind his whole life to be a part of mine, to build something new with me—and I've never had anyone choose me like that before. That's what makes it so terrifying.

What happens when we're out of here and reality hits? When real life happens? When I need to work from sunrise to sunset, and he wants to spend four nights a week watching football? Does he actually see himself happy in a long-term relationship with me, or is he just saying all this for the cameras because he thinks it's what he's supposed to do?

This is really sounding more and more like the bi version of a Hallmark movie.

While I've been busy spiraling over our possible future together, we've finished putting away the dishes.

"Wanna watch something?" Blake asks as he grabs the remote from the coffee table.

"Sure." No need for him to know I've been freaking out.

Blake grins as he clicks on the streaming service they've given us access to. I sit down on one side of the only couch in the living room, and instead of Blake sitting on the opposite end, he sits right next to me. Close enough that our legs press together and I can feel the heat of him.

I try to ignore it and give him the space I just told myself we needed—so we don't ruin this before it's really even started—but I feel a little stiff, hyperaware of where we're touching.

"This okay?" he asks, hovering over a show I've never seen before and I nod. I won't be able to focus on anything anyway. "Perfect," Blake says to himself as he presses play.

He relaxes into the couch and drapes one arm over the back of it behind me. *Subtle, Blake, real subtle.* He's not exactly touching me, but he's so close I can feel him there—and it's distracting as hell. I try to focus on the show but I can't care less about what's happening on the screen. Especially not when I feel the subtle movement of his fingers touching my hair. They're lightly grazing the base of my neck and sending a slight shiver down my spine. It's such a soft touch, though, that I wonder if he's even aware he's doing it. But he has to be, right? I can't be the only one aware of this simmering tension.

His fingers slide down to my shoulder, and I give in to the pull I've been trying to resist. Every plan I made to keep my distance vanishes as I shift toward him, like I can't help it. He leans in too, and when I turn to look at him, I find him already watching me. I should probably say something to break the tension, but all I can think about is how close we are—and before I can move, he does.

His hand lifts to my chin, and I can't help leaning in. But then I take control, pressing forward to kiss him like I mean it. He melts into me instantly. *Fuck, I love that.* This big football player of a man handing me all the power gives me such a rush. I've always liked to be the one in charge in the bedroom, but I've never been with someone bigger than me, even if it's only by an inch. I've never felt like I was *actually* dominating my partner before, and I'm taken aback by the heady feeling. The fact that he's obviously enjoying this dynamic makes it that much better.

His body relaxes, fingers curling into the fabric of my shirt. The moans of pleasure from Blake assure me that he's fine letting me take the lead. So I do. I slide a hand into his soft blond hair, tugging just enough to see how he'll respond, and the softest whimper escapes his lips before he leans into me even harder. Fuck, I've wanted to do that since I first saw him. That noise went straight to my aching cock and my desperation has me gripping him tighter, kissing him deeper, needing even more.

He climbs into my lap and his arms circle around the back of my neck as I continue to fuck my tongue into his mouth—trying not to question this or him. I focus on the way he enthusiastically gives into everything I do, how he obviously loves it when I take control.

My mind wanders to the way he called me "sir" when I asked him to do something and my cock grows even harder. As much as I want to push him back to fully lay on the couch, to cover his body with mine and give into this fire between us, that nagging voice in the back of my mind warns me against it. I'm not ready to stop kissing him, though.

I don't know how long we sit there, tangled up in each other, but I do know one thing.

I am absolutely fucked.

Everything about this feels too easy and natural, like we've been doing this for way longer than a couple of days. Like I've known him far longer than just over a week.

I groan as I force myself to pull back and rest my forehead against his. His hands are still around my neck, my fingers are still tangled in his hair, and I don't think I've ever wanted to keep kissing someone this badly. I could probably come just from kissing him.

But I know we need to stop. I tell myself it's the right thing, trying to remember all my plans from earlier. "We should go to bed."

He doesn't move or drop his hands. He doesn't put even an inch of space between us. *Fuuuuck, of course he has to make this harder.*

Then, with the most satisfied smirk on his sexy face, he says, "Yeah? Should we?"

I know exactly what he's implying. I shake my head, a quiet laugh escaping as I finally lean back. "Yes, *to sleep*."

He sighs dramatically, finally letting go of me to drop his head against the back of the couch and throw his arm over his face. "Fiiiine," he whines, just like earlier, before he drops his act and smirks at me once more. "But don't think I didn't notice how long it took you to pull away. I'll figure out how to prove to you I want this. Want all of you. Including your cock, if that wasn't clear." He raises his eyebrows a few times, somehow managing to hold that fucking smirk.

I can only stare at him. He said that so casually, like he's been interested in dick his entire life. I'm so screwed. I finally snort a laugh and follow him to the bedroom. We get ready for bed, but my mind is nowhere ready for sleep and it's entirely Blake's fault.

I don't hate it though. I can't remember the last time I've had this much fun.

I ROLL OVER IN BED, feeling the warmth of Blake still wrapped around me. The guy sleeps like he doesn't have a care in the world, and it's so fitting for him. His arm is slung around my waist, his leg tangled in mine, and he's already treating me like I'm his personal body pillow. He's talked about cuddling his dog a lot, and I know he's missing her, but I kind of hope that when he's reunited with her, he still wants to cuddle me, too.

I carefully grab my phone from the nightstand, squinting at the screen before sending a text to JR.

LM:

You awake yet? B is still out like a baby despite falling asleep first again last night.

It takes less than a minute before my phone buzzes with a reply.

JR:

Not sure what's worse—finding out you're dating a straight man, or finding out you're dating the person who's hated you for the last fifteen years. Tough call.

I smirk, shaking my head as I type back.

LM:

I'll take my relationship, thanks. It actually isn't so bad.

Everyone watching this show is going to think this was so scripted. I mean, what are the chances the guy who *only* wanted to match with women ended up in a relationship with me? I know the viewers will say we were matched up together intentionally or that we're playing it up for the cameras. But the thing is, none of this feels fake, especially not with the way he kisses me.

My phone buzzes again.

JR:

We've made it through our first few days, we got this.

I let out a small huff of laughter, shaking my head as I type back.

LM:

> Yeah, we do. Excited to finally meet you later! Gonna be so weird but cool, haha. Can't believe I still don't know what you look like.

Today's a big day—we finally get to meet the other contestants who matched up with their partners face-to-face. It's the first time we'll all be in a group setting, and as much as this whole process has been weird as hell, I'm looking forward to it.

Mostly because I'll finally get to meet JR—who I now know is a man named Jace—in person. We both had eventful and unexpected reveals, and talking to him the last few days has made everything feel more grounded. I already know we're going to be good friends, and I'm grateful that I have someone who understands exactly what it's like to be falling for someone who they might not have the best chance with.

While I didn't find anyone else I truly connected with, I know Blake did. I feel good about us, but I can't be sure he won't change his mind today if he finds out his number two choice is actually a woman. He came into this show looking for a *wife*. He thought he would only match with women and he ended up with me. And even though he keeps telling me he's okay with this, that it doesn't bother him, that he wants me, tonight's actions will really prove it to me in a way words alone can't. Wanting someone in the heat of the moment is different than choosing them as your partner for the rest of your life.

It's easy for him to say all the right things when we're wrapped up in each other, but what happens when the real world sets in? When people see us together? When he's really with a man out in the open? When his friends ask him about his sexuality? When his parents meet me at his hometown visit?

What happens if I believe him now, let myself fall all the way for him, and then he changes his mind about dealing with all that?

To say I'm stressed about how today will go is an under-statement.

I TRY to calm my nerves as we walk onto the rooftop bar the show has created at our building. I don't remember a time I've ever felt this nervous. Well, besides right before walking into the shared apartment and meeting Blake for the first time, and that sure didn't go the way I'd hoped it would. But he's been giving our relationship real effort since his initial moment of surprise, so I'm trying to ignore my hesitations about being the first man he's been with.

Before we left our apartment, producers delivered nametags to our room. Mine says, "LM - Liam," and Blake's, of course, says, "BB - Blake," both in bold black ink. It's a stark reminder that after tonight, no one will be anonymous anymore, every conversation we had will be remembered as we meet the other contestants. Are people going to act like strangers? Or bring up the things we talked about?

Blake seems calm, which feels very on-brand for him. If he's nervous, he doesn't show it.

As we walk in, everyone turns to look at us expectantly, and Blake takes that as them looking for an introduction. There are only six other people here. I guess I forgot that if people didn't match up, they went home. I know JR will be here because they matched with KD, but I'm not sure who else is left.

"Hey, I'm Blake, also known as BB," he says, flashing his trademark grin that's starting to really grow on me, before slinging an arm around my shoulder. "And this is my partner, Liam, or LM as you might know him."

Excuse me while I fucking melt. I can't help it—with how nervous I am that he's going to drop me for a safer option, the way he said "partner" like it didn't faze him makes me swoon.

Maybe I do mean more to him than I've let myself believe.

We walk into the crowd and one more couple joins the bar after we arrive. JR thankfully comes up and introduces himself as soon as Blake steps away to grab us drinks.

"Hey, man! It's so good to finally meet you." He laughs, pointing to his name tag. "I'm Jace."

It's so surreal to finally put a face *and* voice to him after all our conversations. After talking for a short time, it's obvious that we get along just like I expected we would. As hard as I try, I can't give him my full attention, though. I'm really interested in what's happened between him and KD, but I'm too distracted when I realize that the attractive woman who stopped Blake on his way to the bar is RR.

RR, who is, in fact, a woman. A woman who's wearing expensive clothes with a face full of makeup, long nails, and bleach-blonde hair. RR who looks like the perfect trophy wife for the rich, hot, ex-NFL drafted man who was making out with *me* on our couch last night.

They're standing closer together than needed, her hand casually brushing his arm as she leans in. My heart is racing. This is exactly what I was worried about, except the reality of watching it happen in front of me is so much worse than the hypothetical. He isn't doing anything, they're just talking. *He picked me,* I try to remind myself.

"I'm sorry, one second," I mutter distractedly to Jace. Before I can make the conscious decision to move, I'm walking toward Blake, but I don't make it far. Suddenly, a guy who seems like RR's partner appears, who also looks to be in his late twenties or early thirties, and as he notices Blake, RR's hand falls away. *Good.*

I'm close enough to hear them, even if no one's seemed to notice me. "Wait, you're Blake Barclay? Like NFL-draft Blake Barclay?"

I freeze mid-step as I see the muscles in Blake's back tense slightly before nodding.

He immediately perks up, asking Blake question after question: "What happened? Were you injured? Did the pressure get to you? How did it feel to be so close to your dream only to have it slip through your fingertips?' "

Blake told me he was drafted, but I didn't realize it was this big of a deal. Or that he was the kind of player people recognized. I feel guilty for dismissing it the way I did. It has to be painful to have people bring up your failures and prod you with questions about why you weren't good enough.

The guy walks away after RR asks him to get them food from the buffet that's set up across the roof. I'm standing behind Blake, and RR seems to only have eyes for him, so they still haven't noticed me. I want to talk to him about it and let him know that I'm sorry I was so dismissive about football. I also want to know why he hasn't told me how big of a deal he was. I'm feeling like a pretty shit partner right now for not asking more questions when it was clearly such a big part of this life.

RR gives a sideways glance at her partner like she's waiting for him to be far enough away before she says something for only his ears. I should walk away, but I don't. Maybe I'm self-sabotaging or just desperate to hear Blake shut her down and mention me. Either way, I stay frozen in place. It's like my feet are stuck to the floor as my stomach flips and twists, anticipating what will happen next. RR starts talking, and Blake seems just as focused on her as she is on him.

Are they already so absorbed in each other that he's forgotten me already?

"You know, it isn't too late to fix our mistake. We both know we should've ended up together." RR's voice is almost sickeningly sweet, and my stomach fucking drops as I watch her touch him *again* as soon as her partner is out of sight.

My blood turns to ice, and it feels like the air is knocked out of me at her suggestion. But what makes me more sick is the fact that Blake doesn't pull away in disbelief, and it's exactly what I feared coming here tonight.

Every doubt I've tried to bury crashes back over me at once, ripping through whatever fragile hope I'd built. All the smiles he gave me. Every laugh he pulled from me. I shoved my fears aside and let myself believe he might actually be different. That this could be real. I've been so stupid for thinking I meant more to him than the thrill of something new. He was just saving face in front of the cameras. I actually let myself get carried away with someone else who was ready to drop me at the first opportunity. I can't believe I thought he was different, that we could be something real. I should've known better than to fall this fast.

I can't stay here and watch this blow up in my face. I need to pull the fuck back before it's too late.

If it isn't already.

19

BLAKE

Producers: Would you describe yourself as someone who struggles with apologies or accepting blame?

Blake: As someone who accidentally fucks up a lot, I'm definitely not afraid to apologize.

*M*y mother paid the nannies to raise me to be polite toward women. I'm trying to remember that when all I want to do is snap at Rachel—aka RR—to *let go of me*. I've tried to be nice, but she's ignoring all my not-so-subtle attempts to put space between us. Her grip on my arm might look casual, but it feels like her fake nails are digging into my forearm. I wish Liam would come over here and save me.

I had a great time talking with RR during the blind dating portion of the show. It was easy. She is exactly the kind of woman I expected to leave the show married to. But I am so relieved I followed my gut and chose Liam. I'm not having any doubts about it, but seeing Rachel in person only confirmed my suspicions that I could never be in a truly happy relationship with her. She's beautiful, she clearly puts a lot of effort into her

141

appearance—lots of makeup, curled hair, those sharp-ass painted nails. I'm sure my mother would love her and her designer clothes. None of my friends would question me marrying this woman.

But I would be so fucking bored.

Our dates would be easy because we're used to the same life-style: living off our family's money in New York City, focused more on image and fun than on anything *real*. Our conversation flowed because I've talked to a hundred girls just like her before. There's nothing about Rachel that stands out, or that makes me want to spend time learning every detail I can about her. Not like I want to get to know Liam. When Rachel talked about her life, I wasn't imagining myself as a part of it like I've always done with Liam's farm. I doubt I'll ever be bored with him.

Her partner, a guy who looks around my age, must be a big football fan because he immediately jumped into the same inter-rogation I've heard a hundred times now. *"What happened? Were you injured? Did the pressure get to you? How did it feel to be so close to your dream only to have it slip through your fingertips?"*

It actually felt fucking fantastic dude, thanks so much for bringing it up so I could relive it now.

Rachel must have wanted him out of here because she quickly asked him to go grab them food. She seems even more interested in talking to me after finding out that I was nearly an NFL player.

Then she opened her mouth and left me speechless. "You know it isn't too late to fix our mistake. We both know we should've ended up together."

It takes me a moment to answer, needing to process her suggestion. "Excuse me? What?" I finally scoff. What the hell is she talking about? I know I should say more, but I'm honestly too shocked by her comment to truly make sense of what she said, let alone form some sort of lengthy response.

"Come on, Blake, have you ever publicly dated a man before?" The look on my face must answer her question because she continues. "You were in the NFL. You might be okay with being with a man here, on a queer positive show, but do you think your football buddies are going to want to hang out with you and your *husband*? God knows I was surprised to find out Kieth only knew so much about expensive cars because he's a fucking mechanic." She scoffs like that's some horrible offense. She drops her voice to a whisper. "I can't bring him back to my family, they'll laugh at me. I only stayed so I could meet you, and I'm so glad I did. No one will blame us if we go to the producers and explain that we made a mistake in the final round and that we should have picked each other. They'll love the drama for the show, and we can both get the relationship we were looking for when we came here. We're not getting any younger."

Her explanation is ridiculous, and I give up on being polite, yanking my arm out of her grip so I can step back.

"Rachel, I don't know what's going on with you and your partner, but I'm very happy with who I chose. I *want* to be with Liam, and I don't give a shit what anyone else thinks, including my football buddies."

"You seriously want to marry a man at the end of the month?" she asks, eyebrows practically in her hair, not accepting a word I just said.

"Yes, I want to marry *Liam* at the end of the month," I emphasize. "Why are you even here? You sound really homophobic right now. I don't care that he's a man. I care about who he is as a person. I feel really fucking lucky that he chose me and that he wants to give us a real chance at a future. Rachel, we could never be happy together. Other than talking about wanting kids, I don't think we had one meaningful conversation that whole week."

I feel like I owe her an explanation with how confused she

still seems, but I'm also so fucking *over* this whole conversation. I'd much rather be talking with Liam and his friend. I wanted to meet JR after finding out he was only in Liam's top two so they could be there to support each other as friends.

But when I turn to where I think Liam is talking to JR, I can't see him anywhere. I only see who I'm assuming is JR glaring at me. Fuck. What did I do now?

"Rachel, I wish you the best, but I want to be very clear that things are done between us. I need to go find Liam," I say, not waiting for her to respond before I'm hurrying toward the man I've obviously pissed off. "Hey, did you see where Liam went?" I ask JR, or Jace, after glancing at his name tag to confirm it's him.

"He said something about not wanting to be dumped in front of the cameras. What the fuck were you and Rachel talking about?" His angry words feel like daggers piercing my chest as I try to catch up and figure out what I did wrong. "Are you really planning to dump him for the first hot girl to throw herself at you? I know you thought you were straight, but that's low."

"What the fuck are you talking about? I don't want her. I want him. Where is he?" I repeat, trying and failing to stay calm. I don't give a shit about what this guy obviously thinks he saw happen between Rachel and me. But with each passing second, the ball of dread in my gut grows. I need to make sure Liam isn't thinking the same thing.

"Probably packing up his things before you humiliate him further," JR spits out.

Fuck!

I'm practically running out the door before he even finishes his sentence. Liam has to know that I don't care about Rachel. *Right?* After yesterday's makeout session, I was ready for more. *I still am.* I know he said we should take things slow, but I thought he finally believed that I'm into him. What could he possibly have seen to think I would ditch him that easily?

I crash into our apartment door, trying to open it quickly, but it seems like the faster I try to get to Liam, the slower time feels. I swear my heart is trying to escape my chest with how fast it's beating. I'm so fucking worried that he'll already be gone that I nearly burst into tears when I find him still in our bedroom.

"Oh, thank god! You didn't leave." I'm panting as I try to gulp down enough air to keep talking.

"I needed some time away from the cameras," he mutters, not looking at me from where he's sitting on the edge of the bed, picking at his nail, staring intently at his thumb.

I move to stand in front of him, heart pounding—unsure if he wants space or closeness, but needing to be near him all the same just to reassure my racing heart that he's still here. He didn't leave.

"Liam, what the fuck happened? Why did Jace think I want to end things with you?" I ask desperately. He doesn't respond immediately, and I can't handle even a second of silence. "I don't. I really don't want that. I want nothing more than to be with you. That's all I want. You, L."

His head whips up, eyes roaming over my face like he's searching for the lie in my expression.

"Blake, I heard you and Rachel talking. Don't try to deny it. I'm not anyone's *mistake*. You came on the show expecting to leave with a wife. Congratulations, looks like everything worked out for you." He drops his head again, and I can't hold back from touching him any longer. I grab his wrist, desperate for him to keep looking at me, to believe what I'm saying.

"Liam, the only one in this room who looks like they might be ready to leave the other is you. I don't know how much you heard, but you must have left before I told Rachel how happy I am *with you*. That at the end of the month, I'm hoping to marry *you*. She might be regretting her own choices, but I'm not. I wanted to date LM, and I still do. Hell, I want to *marry* you, Liam!"

He finally meets my gaze, but he definitely doesn't look convinced.

"I told her I chose you. That I still choose you. That I'm not interested in what could've been with someone else when what I have with you is real."

"I want it to be real," Liam finally says. "I'm afraid of just how much I like you. I knew I had feelings for you when we were in the first portion of the show. But then, when I found out I wasn't what you expected, I tried to hold myself back from falling even more. It's hard, though, because you're so charming and silly. You're carefree and so the opposite of how I feel most of the time. And while I admire that, I'm still scared that I'm going to keep falling and you're going to realize my gender is a dealbreaker for you. That you'd prefer someone else, and I'll get hurt."

My stomach flutters at his admission. I know that I'm all in, but the confirmation that he actually likes me so much—even after our somewhat awkward introduction—makes me feel like I'm soaring. I can't hold back the giant smile on my face as I answer him. "It's not." I step closer. "The fact that you happen to be a man isn't a dealbreaker. You're the deal. A big fucking deal because you're the thing I didn't know I was waiting for."

His brows lift slightly, and I see the hint of a smile that he's not ready to give me yet.

"I mean it, Liam. I want to prove to you how much. Not because I have to, but because I *want* to. You said you were afraid of being someone's mistake. I've never been more sure that you're the best thing that's ever happened to me. I know it's only been three days since we officially met, but I mean that."

He exhales shakily, his shoulders easing just enough that I can breathe again.

"Fuck, Blake," he mutters, and it's not in anger.

"What?" I ask, hopeful now.

"I just—when I saw how she was acting and heard what she

said, I panicked. You chose me, you're *mine*, but I've been worried ever since you found out I was a man that you'd change your mind. I guess a part of me didn't expect you to go meet your second choice tonight and still want to come back with me, to still be saying all this. I figured I should leave before I tried to stake some sort of barbaric claim over you on national television that I wasn't even sure you wanted. I'm sorry I overreacted."

"It's okay, you don't need to apologize for your feelings. And I do want it, I want to be yours. I want you to claim me. You feeling so possessive over me is pretty hot. I just wish I could convince you of how I feel so that those doubts can stay in the past." My wide smile morphs into a more mischievous grin. "I know I don't have to prove anything. But I want to. I wanted to do more than kiss you last night. I've wanted to do more all day," I say, stepping closer.

His lips twitch at that.

"And the idea of groveling a little?" I lean in, my voice dropping. "Super fucking hot."

Liam smirks as he stands, moving his mouth right next to my ear. "Oh yeah? What's your idea of groveling, straight boy? You want to earn that forgiveness?"

I can't help but groan. "What the fuck? Even you taunting me with that nickname is hot. Hell yes, I'm into that."

His eyes widen and he laughs a little. "I don't even know where that came from, but I'm kinda into it too."

"You can call me whatever you want, as long as it means you'll let me touch your dick." I don't hesitate before dropping to my knees right at his feet. "I really want to explore more together, Liam."

I can't help my smug grin when he's obviously surprised by the move. I promised myself that I would stop hesitating. *I want him.* I want to be with Liam in every way that I can imagine.

"I'm already on my knees, L, did you want me to blow you too?" I offer.

His pupils expand, making his blue eyes appear almost black as he stares down at me. He hesitates for another moment before finally taking in a very deep breath, searching my face, maybe checking how sincere my offer is. He must finally believe me, though, as he straightens to his full height and looks down his nose at me. "You want my cock in your mouth, straight boy?"

Fuuuuck. My dick is already thickening at his commanding tone as I nod up at him. *Where did that deep voice come from and why did I like it so much?* I love blowjobs. Having my dick sucked is one of the best feelings in the entire world. Watching a woman attempt to swallow my cock, gagging and coughing when it hits the back of her throat, has always been far more appealing to me than penetrative sex.

But now, picturing myself in that position, being the one on my knees, making Liam feel good as I choke on him… *That might be even hotter.* "Yes, please," I confirm aloud when he doesn't respond to my nodding.

He stares at me for another moment, assessing, before something in my expression convinces him that I'm serious. "Take it out then," he commands, and I'm instantly grabbing at his pants to undo the zipper. I should probably be more hesitant about this since I've never touched another man's dick before, but all I can think about is how much I want to touch him. This is about so much more than proving to Liam that I want to be with him. My aching cock certainly agrees that this is a good plan.

I get his pants open, quickly pulling them and his underwear down to free his erection. He kicks his pants out of the way, and I take a moment to fully appreciate him. His cock is long and swollen, jutting out toward me like it's inviting me to touch, to taste. I have no idea what the hell I'm doing, but I reach out and wrap my fingers around the thick base, give an experimental tug, and rub my thumb over the prominent vein running up the side.

"I didn't think you'd actually be so eager, straight boy," he says, his tone somewhere between a taunt and disbelief.

"I told you I want you. And my cock digging into my zipper in response to touching your dick isn't making me feel very straight right now."

"Well, what are you waiting for? I thought you wanted to blow me. Wanted to prove to me that you're all in. Do it. Suck my cock, B. " Each word sounds more confident. Something about his large body towering over me, about him bossing me around, does something to me. My whole body feels alert, buzzing with this electric anticipatory energy that I've never experienced. I shiver as I realize how much I'm enjoying this dynamic. He's certainly taken control when we kissed, but this is even better—freeing in a way I've never experienced.

I want to give in to this feeling. Lose myself in following his demands and focus only on making him feel good.

So, I do.

I stop thinking and lean in. Using my hand that's still firmly gripping the base of his cock, I guide him to my mouth, licking up the underside before wrapping my lips around the head. The salty taste that explodes in my mouth takes me by surprise. I have no idea what I was expecting, but I definitely don't hate it. Why have I never tasted my own cum before?

He lets out a soft moan as I hum while sucking on his tip. I swirl my tongue around his cock as I explore my new toy. And his dick really does feel like my new toy as I think about all the things Liam and I can do together. If I already like this so much, what else have I been missing out on?

My cock is aching, begging to be freed from my uncomfortable pants, but even ignoring that, in favor of making Liam feel good, gives me a rush. It's intoxicating. Sure, I want to give him control, but I'm still the one ultimately making that choice. I know he wouldn't be doing any of this if I didn't want him to be.

I love that he isn't falling at my feet like that guy tonight at the bar asking about football. I love that Liam hasn't once asked about my family's money in a way that makes me think he'd be after using it for his own gain. It's obvious that Liam is passionate about the things he cares about without making a show of it. He talks about his dad with so much love, it makes me ache for a family like that of my own someday. He's steady in a way I didn't know I needed. He's safe without being boring, solid without being controlling, and he's the only person I've ever truly connected with on this deep a level. I love that Liam seems to know what I want without me having to tell him—that he can read my body language and boss me around while still completely respecting me.

I didn't realize just how much I trust Liam until this moment. More than I've ever trusted another person. It's kind of scary to acknowledge the hold he has on me already, but I know I'm not the only one feeling this way. He wouldn't have been so upset tonight thinking I would leave him for Rachel if he didn't want this thing between us just as much as I do.

With all of these thoughts racing through my mind, I'm determined to make this good for him. I leave sloppy, open-mouth kisses up and down his shaft, wanting to get his cock nice and wet before I try to take more of him into my mouth. It's no easy task with how big his dick actually is—bigger than mine at least—and I only manage to get maybe half of it into my mouth as he thrusts forward before my gag reflex kicks in and I start coughing.

He doesn't apologize or let up, though, and I love that he isn't treating me like I'm fragile, or like I can't handle this. That's not what we need right now. I know firsthand how hot it is to have my partner gagging around me. The fact that Liam is watching me do the same to him has me leaking. He cups my jaw with one hand, and I finally look away from his swollen dick, up through my lashes, to meet his gaze.

"Fuck, Blake, watching you choke on my cock has to be the hottest thing I've ever seen," he says in that gravely tone that I'm now obsessed with. "You doing okay?" he checks, cupping my jaw and swiping away the tears in my eye with his thumb.

I nod, still working him in my mouth.

"Tap my leg twice if you need me to stop, okay? Do it now to show me you understand." I do exactly what he asks without hesitation.

"That's good, B," he praises, and I sink even further into the amazing feeling of this new experience. "Now, I need to ask you a question, and I want a real answer, so you need to stop for a moment." *Yeah, that's not happening.* I try to take him deeper again when Liam suddenly slides his fingers through my hair, gripping tightly so he can yank my head back, forcing me off him.

"Hey, what the fuck?" I demand, not because I hate him pulling me like that, but because I don't want to stop.

"I thought that you were enjoying following my directions?" he taunts, so I reluctantly nod. "Good, now do you want to keep exploring on your own, B? Or do you want me to completely take control and fuck that mouth like I've been wanting to since we met?"

My eyes widen at the suggestion, but his words only make the heat pooling in my gut grow, the desire spreading to make me feel even needier, even more desperate for him. "Definitely that one," I agree.

"Good, get my cock back in your mouth and relax as much as you can," he instructs.

I hurry to do as he says, attempting to hold as still as possible. He moves his hand to grip the back of my head again, and I focus on taking deep, relaxing breaths through my nose. Far slower than I expected, he starts to shift his hips, pushing his dick deeper but only slightly. I don't know if I expected him to jump into anything super rough too quickly, but the proof that he's taking this slow to gauge what I can handle makes me melt all over again. I'm able to relax even more, and he gradually picks up his pace.

"Is this really what you want, straight boy? You want to turn down that hot woman at the bar so you can come home to me? So I can fuck your face and order you around?"

I press down on my aching cock, trying to find some relief as I moan, hoping he understands it as a yes. I do. I really want to do this with him again and we're not even done with round one yet. His grip on my hair is controlling my head, and his thrusts are picking up speed. My eyes must have drifted closed because I have to force them open to look at him. I want Liam to see how needy I am right now, how much I'm loving this.

"Are you hard?" he taunts as he fucks into my mouth. "Take out your cock so I can see just how desperate you are to have me inside of you."

Finally.

Obviously, I could have done this sooner, but it somehow felt wrong to do without his permission.

I rush to rid myself of my pants, Liam pausing to give me space to do so before guiding his cock back into my open, waiting mouth. "Look at you—how needy you are. You're leaking just from having my cock in your mouth. What else are you going to let me do to you?"

I should probably be more concerned by that question than I am. "Anything" seems like the wrong answer for someone as new to sex with another man as I am, but it's still the first thought I have.

"Make yourself come while my cock is inside you," he says, and I immediately move my hand to my dick. I'm so close already. Every word out of his mouth goes straight to my balls. "Tap twice on my leg if you want me to pull out, and once if you're okay to swallow," he warns, and I make sure to clearly tap on his leg one time. I want the full experience.

"Do it, come for me," he demands, and it's like I've been

waiting for his permission yet again. *Maybe I have been.* My release paints the floor of our bedroom as pleasure crashes over me in waves. His praise is drowned out by the high of my orgasm. His cock twitches in my mouth, and his cum shoots down my throat. I want to handle this like a pro, but even though I love the taste of him, I definitely end up choking and coughing a bit. Liam's look of awe as he cups my face after makes it pretty clear he doesn't care, though.

He drops to his knees, still cupping my face as he brings his lips to mine, not minding that I taste like him. The kiss is softer than I expect after he was just so dominant. This is sweet and unhurried. Eventually he pulls away, smiling, looking at me with such adoration that my instinct is to look away. Somehow, I'm shy, even after everything else we just did.

"Blake, what the fuck am I going to do with you?" he teases, making me laugh.

"Hopefully everything."

"So, you're okay then? That wasn't too much?" he checks, and I love that he cares, but I'm definitely good.

"That was so fucking hot," I assure him, and now he's laughing. "When can we do that again?"

2 0

LIAM

Producer: They've been in their room for awhile... think they made-up?

Second producer: We pulled audio from the rest of their apartment to make sure we had proof of life and didn't need to intervene in a physical altercation... let's just say, they definitely made-up.

I've had sex before. I've even had *good* sex before. But nothing—truly nothing—has ever felt like that. That was officially the hottest sexual experience of my life, and it was only Blake's first blowjob.

I don't know what I expected when Blake dropped to his knees for me, but it sure as hell wasn't that. He wanted it so badly too, his eyes pleading like he needed me to tell him exactly what to do. I might have acted mildly dominant before, but I didn't know I had that in me. It was the first time in my life I could truly take what I wanted without holding back, and I was only comfortable doing it because of how obvious he was about how much he was enjoying the experience.

I know our exchange was about a lot more than him convincing me that he actually wants to be with me, but I can't deny it worked. I feel like I finally channeled the hurt and frustration I was feeling—to let go of the worry and insecurities that drove me back to our apartment and away from the cameras in the first place. The stress of tonight might have led us to fall into the roles of domination and submission in a way that we wouldn't have otherwise, but I don't think it will be a one-time thing.

I want it again, but I don't just want to see Blake on his knees. I want to *put* him there and watch as he does it without hesitation. Maybe it's the part of me my ex broke all those years ago that craves the validation of seeing his eyes go hazy as he hands over control—feeling a rush knowing he's giving himself to me completely because he wants this as badly as I do.

I've never had this kind of power in a relationship before. I've always been the one who adjusts, the one who makes things easier for the other person.

But with Blake? I don't want to be careful or hold back. I want to push him. I want to hear him beg for me. I want to take him apart piece by piece and watch him melt under my touch, my voice, my control.

And the craziest part is that he wants it too.

Maybe he's so used to coasting through life, with everyone catering to his wants and needs, that he actually likes not getting to do that with me. I can tell he enjoys it when I push him, when he has to be the one to put in the effort. His eyes light up when I take the decisions out of his hands and show him exactly what I want. He seemed so eager to earn my praise, to please me, to make me happy. Has no one ever made him put effort into a relationship before? I love being the one to bring out this side of him.

It's fucking addictive.

Even though I'm vers and prefer to top, I've never been in a position where I wanted to completely take over. Even with guys I've dated in the past, things have always been balanced—give and take, back and forth, a shared dynamic where we each had moments of control.

But with Blake, I don't want to share the control because he doesn't want it.

I take a deep breath, forcing myself to come back to reality, because if I keep thinking about what just happened, I'm going to want another round with him already.

Blake is still leaning against me, his cheek nuzzled into my shoulder. When I nudge him slightly, he looks up at me with a completely sated expression. I need to get him in bed before I do something stupid.

"Was I good for you, Sir?" he asks, voice hoarse, low, teasing, full of the over-the-top innuendo he used in the kitchen when he first called me that.

Oh, fuck him.

My spent dick twitches at his taunt, despite the fact that I *just* came down his throat. Obviously, I'm really into this power dynamic we've naturally fallen into. He might think he's being funny, but I also think there's a big part of him that craves the validation and praise, and he only knows how to ask for it in a joking way.

I grit my teeth and reach down, threading my fingers through his hair, gripping just enough to tug his head back and make him look at me properly. He better never cut his hair.

"Careful," I murmur. "You keep talking like that, and you're gonna be right back on your knees before you even get a chance to recover."

His smirk widens, *the little shit.* "Don't tempt me with a good time."

I will myself to get a grip as he waggles his eyebrows at me. He's testing me, and I know better, so I shake my head and release my hold of his hair.

If he wants to push, I'll show him how far it could go. Even though I'm definitely not entertaining this idea tonight, part of me is curious to see his reaction, so I don't stop myself from saying, "If we don't stop now, I'm going to want to toss you face down on this bed and have my way with your other hole."

His breath hitches, and for a second, he actually seems surprised before a look I've never seen on his face takes over. His brows are furrowed like he's nervous, but there's also clear excitement in his eyes. "I—"

"Nope," I cut him off, even though every part of me is screaming to just give in to those instincts, to throw him around and ruin him. I won't do it. *Not yet.* "We're going to sleep."

He looks at me like I just told him his football game was canceled, dramatically huffing out a deep breath. "Fine," he relents. "But I'm holding you to that."

I shake my head as I huff out a laugh. I have a feeling my straight boy is going to become a needy bottom the first time I touch his hole. Taking a deep breath in an attempt to clear my head, I stand up first before pulling him to his feet.

"Are we done cuddling?" he asks, sounding disappointed.

"Do you need to be cuddled more, Blake?"

"Yeah, I think I do." All the teasing is gone from his voice now, and I'm surprised when he softly adds, "I really like cuddling you, L."

I squeeze his hands, unsure how to respond as I smile to myself. I guide us to the bathroom, and after we get cleaned up and brush our teeth, we get into bed. Blake hardly waits until I'm under the comforter to tangle himself around me like a damn octopus. He puts his head on my shoulder and snuggles into me as he lets out a contented sigh, and I wrap an arm around him. It's quiet for a long moment, and I think he's fallen asleep, but then barely above a whisper, I hear, "I really like you, Liam."

My chest tightens and I swallow past the lump in my throat

as I press a kiss to the top of his head. "I really like you, too, B," I say, my voice just as quiet.

And then he's out.

THE REST of the week passes by in a blur of mutual blowjobs, cuddles, cooking, and forced hangouts with the other contestants. Blake goes down on me like he's starving every single time. I return the favor whenever I can, learning exactly what earns the loudest moans or causes his fingers to tighten almost painfully in my hair. He likes it when I tease him with my tongue before taking him deeper until I can swallow around him. I love the way he groans my name when he comes, always sounding so needy and desperate for me.

We only leave the apartment when we're forced to. How could I ever want to leave when I have Blake eagerly swallowing my cock at every opportunity?

But after the drama that unfolded during the first group session, the producers insist on scheduling more, claiming they want to "capture the dynamics between the couples" now that we've all met in person. I'm not exactly thrilled, but at least it gives me an excuse to see Jace more and his partner, Kieran. We've been sending each other memes and dumb texts and we hang out during the two additional group dates we have over the next four days.

Blake and I make it a point to avoid Rachel at all costs, even though the producers seem like they really want more interaction —holding us back to arrive at the same time, trying to have Blake sit next to her at a dinner. They go so far as having our names on place cards at each seat. *Fuck that.* I sit next to her instead and she's all too happy to ignore me. Not that she tries too hard to talk to Blake after that first night when he made it clear he wasn't leaving me. She seems to get the message and stops wasting her time trying to get her claws into him, but from what Blake told me about their interaction, I'm surprised she's still here.

Things between Blake and I, though, are good. Really good.

Two nights ago, we found ourselves tangled up in bed, talking. Blake was trailing his fingers over my chest, and I felt so settled by his now familiar touch. He looked up at me and whispered, "I know when we met in person, you were worried about me freaking out about this being my first time with another man, that I would change my mind or something, so I want to remind you how serious I am about you—about us."

I'm glad there aren't cameras in our room for many reasons, but I'm particularly happy that I won't have evidence of the stupid smile I'm sure was plastered on my face as I ran my fingers through his hair. "Yeah?"

"Yeah," he confirmed without hesitation. "I know the show is kind of a wild way to meet someone, but I don't care. This doesn't feel fake. You don't feel fake." He shifted, propping himself up on his elbow so he could look me in the eyes. "I know I can be a dumbass sometimes, and I know I don't always think before I act, so if something ever bothers you, tell me. Please. I want this, Liam. You make me feel something I never have before."

It was in that moment, that I felt like we could really go all the way, and I let myself finally admit how much I want us to. "Okay."

He gave me a small smile. "Good. 'Cause I don't want to screw this up, I haven't been this excited for the future in a long time."

I didn't know what to say to that—not in a way that didn't make me sound completely gone for him—so I kissed him instead.

His words are still at the front of my mind. I've never had a relationship where these conversations came so easily. I've always felt like I was trying to bend to make someone else happy, but with Blake, we just fit. We work for each other without either one of us having to change. I push him and take control in bed, which he loves. And he helps me relax and let out a more playful side of myself the rest of the time, which I love.

The time I've spent with Blake feels like everything I've ever wanted in a relationship. He always finds his way to me at night, snuggling as close as humanly possible—and I'm surprised by how completely obsessed with his clinginess I've become. I always thought a cuddly, needy partner would be a huge turnoff because of how much independence I'm used to, but with Blake, *I want more.* I don't feel suffocated at all.

He's still insisting I teach him how to cook. He seems genuinely interested in all our conversations and learning more about the farm. He's curious about my life in a way no one ever has been before, and it's so fucking easy to just exist with him.

I really like him.

Which is why the next phase of the experiment—the hometown visits—now feels like an even bigger deal than I'd originally thought they'd be. This is where reality is going to pop the bubble we've been living in.

This is when we see who we truly are outside of this show. And, more importantly, we'll find out if Blake actually fits into my world.

If he actually *wants* to.

I'm terrified he'll take one look at the work a farm actually requires and decide he prefers his easy life in the city.

I'm not sure my heart could handle that rejection, but as much as I wish we could stay here, away from the stresses of the real world, the show must go on. So we pack our bags and head to the airport. I'm just grateful Blake's visit is first and we can put off my fears for a little longer.

BLAKE

Producer: Are you worried about bringing Liam to meet anyone since you've never dated a man before?

Blake: Not really. I don't see why anyone but me should care about the gender of the person I'm dating. And if they do? That says more about them than it does about me.

As soon as the producers confirmed that we would be on the show, we had to submit ideas for our potential hometown visits. They wanted a few options so they could choose the best filming locations and get everything set up, encouraging us to include as many friends or family members as possible to make the whole "getting married quickly" thing still feel real.

When I asked my parents to be a part of it, my mother laughed, saying, "There's no way you'll find a wife on a television show," before she left the room. My father was also dismissive about it. "I know you've been trying, son. If it works out we'll be sure to be in town for the wedding, but I've got a work trip that your mother is joining me on, and I couldn't possibly reschedule."

So, of course, neither of them is here today.

Which leaves me with my friends. Don't get me wrong, I love hanging out with them, and we always have a good time, but most of my friends are the kind of guys I go to a football game or a club with, places that involve more alcohol and entertainment than conversation. I don't think any of them are going to be truly homophobic, but I'm also a little worried that most of them will think I'm kidding when I tell them I'm planning to marry a man. The last thing I want is anyone to laugh in Liam's face because they don't believe me, especially with a whole camera crew there as part of a reality show. I'm terrified to embarrass Liam any further than I already have, even if it's by way of my friends, so I'm really glad my initial hometown plan only involves me seeing Chad.

He was the one who told me about the show in the first place, so I think he'll take me seriously when I explain everything to him. Plus, he's my best friend and the only one I actually spend quality time with one-on-one, so I know he'll just want me to be happy. I'll tell him all about Liam, and he can back me up tonight in front of the rest of our group if anyone gives us a hard time, because there's no way I'll allow anyone to be a dick to Liam. I don't care who they are or how long I've known them. None of them matter more than Liam.

We all wake up super early to fly back to New York. I'm pretty dead on my feet, and Liam teases me about not being cut out for farm work. I know he's only joking, but I'm worried that he actually thinks I won't be able to handle it. So, I chug a large coffee and make a point to not nap on the plane like I'd originally planned.

We spend the flight talking about the things we've missed the most about being away from home, *mostly Lucky,* and the time flies by. Hanging out with Liam is always so fun and easy. It's not just that we're both guys either. I've never cared this much about making any of my friends laugh, and my heart has never raced because I made any of them smile. *Liam is special.* I can't wait for this next week when I finally get to see the farm and we can really start planning a future together.

This is the final week before the show expects us to get engaged. Then we'll all be meeting back at the hotel they're hosting us at in NYC to start wedding planning. They didn't mention what would happen if you *don't* end up engaged, but I think it's pretty obvious that would mean you've broken up and your journey on the show is over.

Hopefully I won't have to worry about that. I'm positive I want to marry Liam. I don't care that we've only known each other for a short amount of time, or that there's a lot more physically for us to explore. *Judging by how much I love blowjobs, I'm sure I'll love the* more *just as much.* Obviously, I came on to the show intending to get married, and that's still my plan. It no longer feels like an ultimatum requirement though, but the beginning of a future I never knew I wanted.

Once we arrive at the airport, there's a bus waiting for us to bring us to the hotel the next phase of the show will be headquartered at. One of the producers takes most of the bus ride to explain how the next week will go for each couple since some of us are from the city and others are further away. I squeeze Liam's hand, already dreading being away from him today. He has to spend the morning doing interviews for the show while I get to meet up with Chad and tell him about Liam.

I've loved spending all my time with Liam over the last few days, and I'm worried I'm going to go through some sort of withdrawal if I can't be cuddled up with him for hours. I wish Liam could just be there with me. I'm not worried about Chad's reaction at all, and any time spent with Liam is better than being apart. I've never wanted to spend this much time with any of my previous partners.

When we have to separate so Liam can go to his interview at the hotel, I give him a deep kiss, completely unbothered by who might be around. "I miss you already," I say before pulling him into a tight hug.

"I'll miss you too. Have fun with Chad and Lucky. Can't wait to meet them later!"

We break apart, and I'm escorted to a cab to go to my apartment to meet Chad. I ordered us lunch so he can bring Lucky back home. I only got my phone back from the producers this morning, and they warned us not to give anything away off camera. So I just confirmed the time for him to come over in a text, saying I'm excited to see him and update him on everything.

Now I'm anxiously pacing in my living room. The show has a barebones crew assigned to follow me, but they asked me to try to forget they're here. *Easier said than done.* Finally, the door opens and Lucky runs in, jumping up with her front paws on my thighs, balancing on her back legs like she wants to give me a hug as her tail wags rapidly. I kneel on the floor so I can properly hug her and pet her stomach when she drops down to roll onto her back, tongue hanging out of her mouth while she pants in excitement.

"Who's a good girl?" I coo as I try to pet her all over, desperate to make up for the lost time we've had. I know Chad took great care of her, but I missed her like crazy, and I don't want her to think I left because of anything she did or because I don't care about her. "How's my little princess? I missed you so much, my sweet girl."

"She was a perfect angel the whole time you were gone," Chad says, reminding me that he's here.

"Hey, man! It's so great to see you," I say, reluctantly getting up to lean in for one of those bro hugs that start as a handshake but turn into a quick back slap.

"You too! I can't wait to hear all about the lucky lady you've convinced to date you," he teases, and I'm really regretting following the producers' instructions to not warn him. Why am I so nervous when I know Chad will be cool? I can't seem to settle the nerves dancing around in my stomach. I take a deep breath and decide to just put it all out there.

"So, I actually have a lot to tell you," I start, and Chad raises his eyebrows, already looking amused. "Remember what you said when we were first talking about the show, when you asked me what would happen if I ended up choosing a guy?"

"You didn't," he says, eyes wide shining with amusement.

I give him my best smile, scrunching up my nose a little as I shrug. "Turns out, I shouldn't have been so confident that I would know the gender of the person I was blindly dating."

"So you chose a man? I fucking called it, bro, why would you want to talk to a girl if you could hangout with a dude!" He sounds far too proud of himself as he laughs. "But wait, I thought they would only be filming this week if you were still dating someone?" His comment is casual, not sounding judgmental or negative; just curious.

"That's accurate," I confirm, nodding as I wait for the pieces to all fit together for him.

I don't think it would be possible for his smile to be any bigger. "So, you're actually dating a man? You're going to get married?"

"Yeah." I know I should say more but I can't get anything else out, the nerves seeming to take over all of my ability to function as I wait for his response.

"And you want to? You're happy about it? You really like him?" he asks seriously, all of the previous amusement gone from his expression. I appreciate that he isn't bringing up my parent's ultimatum in front of the cameras, but his concern for my feelings seems sincere, not like he's worried about money.

"Yeah, I really am happy with him," I admit, a small smile

forcing its way onto my face despite my nerves. "I've never felt like this about anyone before. I want to marry him."

"Congrats, man! I'm happy for you." He only sounds excited by the idea, and I let out a breath I didn't realize I was holding. I didn't think he would be an asshole. Still, I guess this was my first coming-out moment, and I didn't anticipate how scary it would actually be.

"Thanks." I'm beaming at him now, and we both burst out laughing. "So, want to come ring shopping with me?" I ask when we finally settle down.

"Obviously. But first, I want to hear all about him. Holy shit, have you guys, *you know?*" he asks, pumping his eyebrows. He's asking if we've fucked, but we're being filmed so I'm not sure how much to admit.

I smirk, hoping to give a vague but still honest answer. "Turns out, consensual sex is always fun, it doesn't matter what the gender of my partner is."

He holds out his fist for me to bump and we both laugh again. I'm lucky to have him as my best friend, and I'm so glad he was in town today. I'm really excited for Liam to meet him.

The food arrives and I spend the meal telling him all about the show, the process of matching with other people, ranking them, and how Liam was always in my top three. I tell him how shocked I was when we finally saw each other face-to-face because, like an idiot, I'd assumed Liam was a woman. But as soon as the initial surprise wore off, I realized it didn't matter. Not even a little, because I liked him for him. Then I tell him about Rachel, and how she tried to make a move once we met in person, but that it only made me more confident in my choice with Liam. By the end of the meal, he's caught up, and just as excited to shop for a ring as I am.

After taking Lucky on a short walk and making sure she's settled back at home, the camera crew follows us to a jewelry shop nearby. They tell us to wait outside first so they can confirm if it's okay for us to film inside before letting us in. Guess, they weren't too happy I kind of sprung this on them, but how was I supposed to know before the show started that I'd care this much about picking out a custom ring? The show had a variety of rings we could choose from to propose with, but call me old-fashioned, I want to do it right.

I want to propose to Liam with a ring that means something, that represents the commitment I want us to make to each other. I like the idea of going in and picking out the perfect ring for him, not just using some generic one that's offered to me.

"Hello, how can I help you today?" the middle-aged woman behind the counter asks us when the crew gives us the go-ahead to proceed inside.

"I want to get an engagement ring for my boyfriend," I say, and realize it's the first time I've referred to Liam that way. *My boyfriend.* The title makes me smile; I like having that claim on him.

"Do you know what style you're looking for?" she asks, turning to Chad.

"Oh, I'm not the boyfriend," he says with a laugh. "Just here for moral support."

"My mistake. Do you know what type of ring you're looking for?" she asks, smiling at me this time.

Shit, I guess I should have done some research. If I'm being honest, I've always assumed ring shopping would involve getting a huge diamond in whatever setting the girl I was dating told me to get. Do two men both wear engagement rings? Are there still diamonds involved?

The woman must read the confused panic on my face because she doesn't wait for me to answer. "Does your boyfriend wear any other jewelry? What does he do for a living?"

"Uh, no other jewelry, and he works on a farm." Now that I think about it, I don't think Liam would want anything flashy.

"You might want to consider a silicone ring for when he's

working to reduce the risk of injury, but we have some lovely stackable rings for a more formal option." She leads us over to a display case, pulling out a tray full of rings varying in color and design. My gaze is drawn toward a black one.

"I think he'll want something classic and simple," I say, forcing my attention away from the rings with stones in them. Even though I think they're really cool, *maybe for me,* I can't imagine Liam wanting to wear diamonds with all of his flannel. "Maybe these darker ones. You said stackable, does that mean a ring for the engagement and a ring for the wedding?" I feel like such an idiot that I haven't thought about this before, but she doesn't seem surprised by my lack of knowledge so maybe she's used to clueless customers.

"Yes, it's all personal preference of course, but some same sex couples choose to both wear an engagement ring, and then get a second band for the marriage," she confirms.

"Those dark ones are cool," Chad says, pointing to the row of black rings I thought Liam might like.

"Yeah, I think he'd like that better than the gold or silver options," I agree.

We spend some time comparing the different rings, seeing how they would look stacked together, and eventually I find one I really like. It's got a brushed black finish, but the angled edges are shiny, and it isn't too thick so it can be paired well with a second band. Sophisticated, nothing over the top. I hope Liam will like it.

I also get a similar silicone option he can wear while he works, but I want him to have one that's fancier and costs a bit more too. It's a symbol of my commitment to him and our relationship. I don't want to go the cheap route and have him take it the wrong way.

Chad and I head back to my place to get changed for the game we're going to with Liam tonight. I probably should have given Liam a heads up about planning something sports related, but in all of my excitement thinking about going to his farm, my own hometown visit slipped my mind. It isn't football season, but I have hockey season tickets as well, and the games are always a good time. He's going to meet us there so the show can film him meeting Chad, but I wish we could all show up together. It's only been a few hours since I saw him, but I really do miss him already.

After updating Chad on everything, our relationship is feeling even more real, and I'm really excited for Liam and Chad to hang out together. We have great seats in a box, and I can't wait… but I hope Liam doesn't hate it.

LIAM

Producer: What's surprised you most about this process so far?

Liam: How fast a connection can form when you're not distracted by everything else. I didn't expect to feel this sure about someone so quickly, but here I am, getting ready to bring them to my farm to meet my dad.

I knew these one-on-one interviews were coming, but that doesn't make me dread them any less. The producers warned us that, at different points in the process, we'd have to sit down and reflect on everything so they could splice it into the episodes for dramatic effect.

Well, they didn't say that exactly, but we all know what it's for. But now I'm sitting in the middle of the room they've turned into a studio at the hotel, mic'd up with all the cameras and big microphones pointed at me, as I sit opposite Andy and his beaming smile. Why am I so nervous? This feels far more formal than the previous ones they've done where they sat us in a chair in the hallway outside of our apartments and had random producers ask the questions.

Besides the drama with Blake and Rachel—which admittedly was me assuming the worst—I've just been completely wrapped up in Blake. Falling into this thing with him has been almost terrifyingly easy. I've never felt this way before and I don't think he has, either. And that makes me more than a little nervous for what questions are about to come out of the producers' mouths. I have no idea how to talk about any of this.

Andy smiles at me from across the small studio setup, leaning forward in his chair like he's about to dig into me. "Alright, Liam. Let's start with something simple. Can you tell us how it's been living with Blake?"

Easy enough first question, I can totally do this.

"Living with Blake has been interesting," I start. They told us to repeat back the question in our answer like we're playing Jeopardy so the future viewers will know exactly what we're talking about. I can see the camera operator nodding, encouraging me to continue. "I think people expect me to say that I was shocked by the whole *straight guy picking me thing* or comment on how Blake assumed that I was a woman, but honestly? I think I was more surprised by how much we get along."

"Just how much *do* you like him?" Andy asks, propping his chin in his hands as he dramatically blinks at me, obviously intrigued.

My mind immediately wanders to Blake last night and how he rested his head on my chest as we talked about our future together. It also flashes to him on his knees, looking up at me with want in his eyes, but I quickly cut that thought off. I can't risk getting hard on TV. *Again.* He isn't even here, but just *thinking* about my future husband is enough to make that a very real possibility.

And fuck, if that title isn't sobering. *My future husband.* It's not even some far-fetched daydream; we could be engaged in just a few days.

I take a deep breath, trying to center my thoughts and focus on the conversation. "I… I don't know," I finally answer, licking my lips to buy a few more seconds. "I mean, I do know. But I also… Blake and I are very different people, and I thought that was going to be a problem. But instead, it's working. I think it might be working really well."

Andy grins and changes direction. "Let's talk about the hometown visits coming up. Blake is heading to your farm soon. What are you most excited for?"

I can't help but smile as I picture Blake on my farm. "I can't wait for Blake to come to the farm. I want him to see my life. I want him to meet my dad. And…" I trail off, my throat tightening.

"And?"

I let out a slow breath. "I want to see if he fits there. If he'll be happy. If he can adjust the image in his mind to the day-to-day reality of what running a farm is really like."

As easy as this bubble we're living in has been, I know Blake is used to expensive dinners, and fancy bars in the city. He's used to very little responsibility, and my life is basically defined by it. There are early mornings, followed by long days of hard work struggling to keep my family's farm running. Blake says he doesn't need luxury, but I have to see that for myself. If I let myself love him and it turns out he can't handle my world?

I don't know if I'm strong enough to deal with that kind of heartbreak.

I'm a little surprised by how honest my answer is. This whole process is so wild when I think about just how much Blake and I have already shared with the public when it comes to our relationship. My first instinct is to try to hold back, to keep what little privacy we have left and not share any more details than I have to.

But I also know we had an unconventional start with the gender confusion. And then there was the drama with Rachel—even if it was minimal, I know they'll still eat it up. As much as I hate to think about it, we'll probably get a lot of screen time with all our drama aired. Although, I'm not entirely sure what's going on with the other couples, so maybe that's a little egotistical of me to think. Jace and Kieran certainly have their own drama. I want to show that there's more to us than those potentially viral moments. I want people to understand that we're a surprisingly good fit, a couple who has a real shot at making it.

Andy lets out a chuckle, pulling my attention back to him. "I think we're all excited to see how Blake fares on the farm. You two certainly had an interesting beginning. Can you tell us a bit more about your dynamic—what it is that's worked so well for you both when Blake is new to dating a man."

"Believe me, no one is more surprised than I am after that first in-person meeting that Blake and I have ended up where we are in such little time," I say with a laugh. "But our relationship is better than I could have even hoped for. He pushes me to let go, to loosen up, and enjoy every moment. I'd like to think that I've helped him find out who he is outside of the lifestyle he's accustomed to here in the city. Blake makes me feel something I haven't ever felt before, and even though this whole thing started under weird circumstances, it somehow feels more real than any other relationship I've been in."

Andy's smile softens slightly, looking less fake than I've ever seen it.

"I think I speak for everyone who's going to see your romance unfold when I say that I wish you both the best, and I can't wait to see what happens next for the two of you!"

We wrap up the interview without any other painful questions, and I think, overall, it went pretty well. Now I get to be nervous for a whole other set of reasons—time to meet Blake's best friend.

Blake didn't actually tell me what we're doing tonight, and I didn't think to ask, so I can only imagine what he's planned. I'm finally arriving in a car that the show coordinated to meet him, and I can't wait to be able to touch him again. I didn't realize just how much I'd missed him until I was done worrying about the interview. I step out, taking in the arena and all the people around, wearing matching jerseys.

I should have guessed we'd be doing a sports related activity.

Whatever, I'm sure it'll be fine for one night, plus I want Blake to be happy.

There's a producer with me who directs me to a security line, and once we're through, they scan our tickets. When I finally step into the lobby of what I'm guessing is a fancy VIP entrance by the lack of crowds, I see Blake waiting for me with that charming smile already in place as he rushes to me. I smile right back, and I can't help but reach out, gripping the back of his neck to bring his lips to mine. I kiss him hard on the mouth, needing to feel close to him after the stressful day we spent apart, not caring for a second that we have an audience or a camera pointed right at us.

Blake lets out a surprised noise but immediately melts into my hold. He places both of his hands on my hips, holding tight as he enthusiastically kisses me back, like maybe he's missed me just as much. When I finally pull back, I catch the flush that spreads across his cheeks, and it sparks a possessive desire within me that I have no right feeling while in public.

"Sorry. I missed you and I couldn't help myself," I say quietly, just for him.

I'm hoping I didn't embarrass him in front of his friend. But when I turn to face the man next to him, who I'm assuming is Chad, he's watching us with what's got to be the biggest grin I've ever seen in my life. I swear it rivals Andy's.

Blake groans and shoves Chad's shoulder. "Don't be weird."

Chad just laughs, the wicked glint in his eye giving away just how much he's enjoying this. "Who's being weird? I'm literally being so normal about you casually kissing your boyfriend right in front of me. No big deal." Then he turns to me and sticks out his hand. "Liam, right? At least, I hope you're Liam and not some random dude kissing Blake right on the mouth."

"Yeah, I'm Liam," I laugh as I shake his hand. "It's good to meet you, Chad."

"I've gotta say," Chad says, glancing between the two of us with that shit-eating grin still in place. "This was *so* not the outcome I expected when Blake signed up for this show. But I like it. I think you're going to be really good for him. It's pretty obvious with how he hasn't been able to go more than thirty seconds today without bringing you up, and how he hasn't stopped smiling when he does."

Blake rolls his eyes. "You like it because you love being right."

"Obviously." Chad grins. "And because you're, like, weirdly into him. I've never seen you like this before, man. It's kinda cute. Makes me think I should try dating a guy."

Blake just glares at his best friend, and I bite back a laugh. *I like Chad already.*

"So," I say. "What's the plan?"

Blake perks up immediately. "We have a box for tonight's Dragons' hockey game."

Even though I had guessed as much walking in here, I still want to give him a hard time. "You do remember that I don't like sports, right?"

Blake grins guiltily, he likely knew that was coming. "Yeah. But *we do*." He gestures between him and Chad. "And more importantly, I had to give the producers ideas of what to do before I was even on the show, remember? I thought whoever I brought would just be happy to spend time with me in a box. It's a whole experience."

He waggles his eyebrows like this is supposed to be cute. *And damn him, it is cute.* Infuriatingly so, because I know I'm going to find myself in a stadium full of people cheering loudly for a sport I don't care about.

But I also know that I'm going to do it because it's what Blake wants to do, and I am happy to just spend time with him.

I sigh dramatically, rolling my eyes. "Fine."

Blake lights up. "You really are the best."

Chad claps a hand on my shoulder. "Don't worry, Liam. We'll make a sports fan out of you yet."

I snort before my face breaks out into a smile. "Yeah, that's not happening."

Blake grins wider, throwing an arm around my shoulders. "You don't have to like the sport to have fun at a game. Have you ever been in a box before?"

"No, but watching sports is still watching sports, it doesn't matter how fancy the room is," I point out. Blake laughs like I'm missing out on an inside joke. And with that, I let them drag me onto an elevator toward the fancy private suites at the top of the arena.

I really do want to do things Blake likes, and I know part of marriage is compromise. But I'm silently hoping we can find *other* things to do together that we both enjoy. Blake and Chad, on the other hand, are thriving. They're hyping each other up and talking about what they think will happen in the game.

When we finally make it to the box, my gut sinks as we step inside. I knew that Blake would probably have more friends here, but I guess I was naive in hoping there would only be a couple more people joining us. Instead, the private room is packed. There are a few cameramen and people here with the show, and at least ten or so other guys standing around, all wearing matching Dragons jerseys. A hush falls over the room as they all turn to face us. Some obviously look confused, glancing around, not focusing on me at all.

Do they think I'm also working on the show? Are they waiting for some hot girl to appear behind Blake?

Won't they be surprised.

"Okay, listen up everyone," Blake says loudly to the group,

despite the room already being so quiet you could hear a pin drop. "I'm only going to say this once, and if you have a problem with it, you can get the fuck out of my box." There are a few nervous chuckles as they all focus on Blake expectantly.

"You obviously know about the show by now, I'm sure they've made you sign a bunch of shit saying you're okay being on TV. In case it wasn't clear, I signed up to go on a dating show hoping to finally settle down and get married."

No one seems surprised by that part at least, and the room remains quiet as Blake continues. "The thing that makes this show unique is you're anonymously dating, so no names, no ages, no faces, you don't even know people's genders or what they sound like until you decide to move in together. I was super lucky to find someone who's way cooler than anyone I've dated before, and I'm really happy they've been willing to put up with me so far. So, I'm going to be really pissed if any of you assholes say anything to scare him away, okay?" Blake levels the room with a serious look as they all continue to look confused.

One of the men finally speaks up, breaking the silence. "Did you say 'scare *him* away'? Are you dating a guy?" He sort of sounds like he's in shock, but I'll take that over angry or disgusted.

I didn't fully appreciate that today would mean Blake was coming out to all his friends, and I really admire how he's just going for it. I should have known he wouldn't ease anyone into this with how confident he's been, but seeing it in action is making me a combination of nervous and so damn proud of him. I really am glad to be at his side. I might not know these people, but I also didn't get the impression in our previous conversations that Blake's group had any queer friends in it, and I don't think he knows how his friends will take the news of him being with a man.

He might be risking years of friendship with these guys right now by announcing our relationship this way, but he isn't hesitating. Blake really is an amazing person. I'm glad we've gotten through all the hurdles we've faced so far. I want to walk up to him and hold his hand for comfort and support, but I'm going to let him have his moment first.

"I don't get it, are you saying you're gay now?" one of the other men asks curiously.

"Nah, I think I'm bi," Blake announces casually, turning to me to grab my hand and pull me to his side. "This is my boyfriend, Liam."

"And everyone is going to be really nice and accepting of their relationship, *right?*" Chad cuts in before Blake can say anything else. There's a chorus of "yeah," "of course," and "cools" as the group finally reacts. Some of the men seem genuinely unfazed, while a few others still look confused as they exchange glances with each other, but no one says anything against us.

It's not lost on me how big this moment is for Blake. He lived almost thirty years thinking he was straight and then he walked right into a relationship with a man without even realizing it. And instead of running or panicking or trying to deny it, he's fully embraced it. And now, he came out to his friends and labeled himself for the first time. I'm so damn proud of him, and more than that, I'm excited because this means something big for him and for us.

Conversation returns among the group and a few guys come forward to introduce themselves. When that part's done, I'm left standing with Chad and Blake again. I know I need something to distract myself with because this has been *a lot*, even if it has been in a good way. "So, where's the beer and nachos?"

Blake just grins. "See? You'll fit right in. But there's way fancier food than that in the box."

"Cool, I need something to occupy myself with for the next hour of my life."

"At least two hours," Chad corrects with a grin.

I glare at him for a moment before I drop the act and finally shrug, smirking as I let out a chuckle.

If Blake can come out to his friends so fearlessly, I can sit through a hockey game tonight and be a good sport.

The three of us make our way over to the fancy buffet that's prepared against the back wall, making plates of the gourmet sliders and sides they have prepared. A waiter comes around and takes our drink orders, then Blake guides us out onto the balcony to find seats. We're practically on the ceiling of the gigantic arena, and I quickly claim a seat so that I don't feel like I'm about to trip and fall to my death. I focus on my food while Blake and Chad talk about the season and the team.

The announcer introduces some of the players, and someone sings the national anthem before the game starts. For the first twenty minutes, I think I might actually survive this. I zone out, let my thoughts drift, and nod along whenever Blake nudges me and informs me of what's happening on the ice, but I just can't get into it. Blake is shouting, jumping up, gripping Chad's arm, losing his mind over every tiny thing that happens. I swear, I've never seen him this animated before. *Not even when I was literally sucking his dick.*

When the buzzer sounds and Blake tells me the first period is over, we all head back into the private box. He's quickly pulled into a conversation with one of his friends, and I hang back, letting him catch up. Still, I feel a little out of place. These aren't my people, at least, not yet, and I've never been great in big social settings where I don't know anyone, especially ones where I feel like I'm being quietly sized up. A few guys glance my way, and I can't help but wonder what they're thinking. I'm sure they're trying to figure out what Blake sees in me, or who fucks who, since that seems to be a thing straight people obsess over for some reason.

I try not to let it get to me, but it's hard not to feel like I stick out. So, rather than hover, I head to the bar and scroll through my phone, pretending to be absorbed in something. I'll give Blake his space—he deserves it without feeling like he needs to look out for me.

"No way Blake is actually going to marry a dude, he isn't gay. I played football with him for years, and he never checked anyone out in the locker room. He probably lost a bet or something," I overhear one of the men say on the other end of the bar and the two guys he's talking to both laugh.

Awesome, casual homophobic stereotyping. Just great.

"Don't listen to them," another guy says, drawing my focus before I can say anything to the ignorant man claiming to know more about Blake than I do. "I'm Ash. I also used to play football with Blake back in the day, and despite being very attracted to men, I can assure you I never checked anyone out in the locker rooms either. Wasn't trying to paint that target on my back," he says quietly.

Well shit. One of Blake's friends coming out to me wasn't on the list of things I thought would happen tonight.

"Nice to meet you, Ash," I say with the first genuine smile I've probably had in the last hour as I offer him my hand. "Are you out now?" I ask quietly.

"Nope, and I'm kind of freaking out about how casually I just told you that," he says with a nervous laugh. "But I don't actually know you, and Blake storming in here with a hot boyfriend announcing he's bi like it was no big deal made me very jealous. So here we are." He shrugs, giving me another hesitant smile.

I beam at him. "Welcome to the club."

"Thanks." He laughs again before asking me more about the show and if I went into it wanting to date a man. We're pretty absorbed in our conversation, so I don't care when everyone else makes their way back out onto the balcony for the next period.

"Not into hockey?" Ash asks when I don't make a move to leave the bar.

"Not into sports."

"Wow. Blake must really like you if he still wants to be with you knowing that," he teases.

"More like I must really like him to sit through tonight." I laugh knowing that even though this hasn't been my idea of a dream date, I'm still happy Blake's happy.

23

BLAKE

Producer: You're a huge sports fan. How are you handling that the person you're falling for isn't into them at all?

Blake: *Horribly.* No, I'm kidding, but if you told me that before the show, I'd say it was a dealbreaker. But now, I kind of don't care. I like watching sports, but I like Liam way more.

This game is crazy. I'm so glad we were able to make it tonight. It's only the second period and both teams have scored multiple times. We're currently winning, 3-2, but things can change quickly. The players are getting frustrated, and another bullshit penalty was just called against us for tripping, so we'll be down a guy for the next two minutes.

"That didn't look like tripping to me." I roll my eyes as I turn to Liam to see if he understands what the penalty was for, only to see he isn't actually there. Did he not come back out for the start of the second? I know he went to the bar inside, but I thought he'd joined the crowd back out here. Shit, how did I not even realize?

I rush back into the box, and heave a huge sigh of relief. He

182

looks fine. He actually looks happier than I've seen him all night, talking with Ash at the bar.

"Everything okay?" I ask as I walk up to them, still wondering why they're in here when the hockey is out there.

"Yeah, everything's fine, B," he says, sounding confused by my question.

"So why are you in here?"

"Ash and I are hanging out," he replies.

I know he isn't a sports fan, but I still feel like a complete asshole for not realizing he was in here. I should have known this wouldn't be his idea of a good time. I think part of me just hoped he'd come and see it was more fun than he'd made it out to be in his head, but I also kind of threw him to the wolves with a dozen of my friends after announcing I have a boyfriend.

I'm an idiot.

"Do you want to get out of here?" I suggest, hoping it isn't too late to fix my mistake.

His head snaps in my direction, and the confused look on his face is so cute. "Out of here?" he repeats, like he doesn't understand the words.

"Yeah, you're obviously not watching the game, and I know big crowds aren't your thing. This whole night was a stupid idea," I admit. "We could go back and have a drink at my place instead. Ash, you're welcome to come too. We haven't had a chance to catch up yet, so that would be great. I can text Chad, but I don't know who else would want to leave."

"Blake, I'm fine here, really. I promise. I don't want you to miss out on the game you've been so excited watching," Liam offers, but I've already texted Chad to see if he'd want to go with us, and I can see him standing from his seat on the balcony to come back inside.

"Can't get rid of me that easily," Chad teases before walking right out of the box to lead us out of the arena.

"I guess we're leaving," Liam says with a laugh, getting up to follow Chad. "Ash, are you joining us?"

"Yeah, I think Blake and I have a lot to catch up on." He smirks, and I raise a brow at my friend. Ash and I have never been super close, he's always been one of my more reserved friends, but he's a good guy and our families are friends, so we've known each other our whole lives. "I'll tell you more at your place," he says, looking at me this time. I follow them all out, surprisingly okay with leaving even though Liam told me he was fine with staying. I believe him, but maybe some things really are more important than sports.

"OKAY, I was trying to be chill while your rich friends were here, but seriously, Blake? I can't get over how fancy this place is. I can't believe you live here," Liam says, looking around my condo in awe.

Ash and Chad just went home after hanging out for a couple of hours. Lucky has been loving the attention from the extra people around. A two-person camera crew followed us back from the game to get some footage of us all hanging out together, and after they left, Ash told me he's bi. It was a complete surprise to me, but I understood why he kept it under wraps—his asshole family has always been obvious about their disapproval of queer people. I don't get why people care. It has no effect on their life. Plus, our friend group has never really talked about same-sex relationships, so he's been in the closet this whole time, unsure how we'd react.

I hate that he felt the need to hide a huge part of himself for so long, but it's really cool knowing Liam and I helped inspire him to feel comfortable enough to share his truth, even if it was just with us and Chad for now. I haven't given much thought to the implications of us being on this show and how our relationship unfolded, but I hope it can help others feel inspired to live their truth too. If they don't write me off for looking like an asshole for assuming Liam was a woman.

The most fulfilling part of tonight was that I finally got to see the real Ash. Once he shared his sexuality and was met with complete acceptance, he finally relaxed in a way that I've never seen—more outgoing and talkative, just happier. I've always liked having him as a friend, but I'm hoping we'll be closer now that he knows I fully support him.

"It's just a house," I shrug, finally responding to Liam's comment. I know it's nice, and I'm not trying to downplay how fortunate I am, but I also know Liam is worried about me seeing his farm soon, and I don't want him focusing on how different our homes are when we'll be sharing one soon enough.

He snorts at my response. "Your kitchen is probably the size of my whole house and you don't even cook."

"So I clearly don't need it," I tease, earning an eye roll from Liam. "Stop focusing on my place, I need you to focus on meeee," I whine, grabbing both of his hands to drag him with me as I walk backward toward my room.

"And why should I focus on you, B?" he taunts in that deep voice that instantly has my cock thickening. "Are you feeling needy?"

"Obviously. I had to go all morning without touching you, and on top of that, Ash spent the last hour checking you out, completely ignoring the fact that your *boyfriend* was sitting right next to you."

"Is that why you threw your legs over mine to sit sideways on the couch? Staking your claim?"

"Yes," I respond simply. No reason to sugarcoat how much I want it to be known that Liam is mine, even if I do want Ash to be comfortable being himself around us.

Liam's answering smile makes my breath catch. I love seeing

him look so happy, but knowing that I'm the one making him feel that way makes my heart feel too big for my chest.

"Is your shower as fancy as your kitchen?" he asks, confusing me. I definitely thought we'd be going straight to my bed.

"Uh, I guess?"

"Shower first, then I want to try something new tonight if you're up for it," he says, grinning at me.

"I'm up for it," I insist. I've loved the blowjobs, but I also want to explore everything that I possibly can with Liam. Having him boss me around is hot as hell, and I am *so* here for more of it.

"You don't even know what I want to do," he points out with a laugh.

"If you want it, I want it too."

"Fuck, B," he groans. "You are going to be the death of me." He leans in for a soft kiss, and I try to deepen it, but he's pulling away and tugging me through my room into the en suite before I can. "Shower first," he repeats softly, like maybe he's saying it more to himself than me.

He spends a lot of time washing my body, running his large calloused hands over every inch of my skin to spread the soap, and then again to clean it off. His touch is electric, my skin buzzing everywhere that his hands trace, leaving me desperate for more. My cock has been aching this entire time, the blood completely draining from the rest of my body, redirecting south, making thoughts of anything other than Liam touching me very difficult.

"Look at your hard cock straining out toward me like it knows exactly who it belongs to," Liam says. His voice is low as he completely ignores my erection. He moves around me, stepping in close to my back, grinding his own rock-hard cock between my asscheeks, and I let out a whimper at how good even that motion feels. My entire body is oversensitive, and every stroke of his fingers sends jolts of pleasure straight to my balls.

Liam has both arms wrapped around my hips now, one hand slowly inching closer and closer to my aching dick as the other grips my hip tightly. He moves his mouth to speak right into my ear in that gravely tone I love. "Are you going to let me play with your ass tonight?"

My cock jerks as I subconsciously grind my hips back into his erection. "Yes. Anything, please."

"Fuck, you're so good for me, already begging to have your hole played with. Have you ever had anything inside of you there, straight boy?" he asks, stepping back to run a finger down my crease right over the hole in question.

"No, never."

"But you'd be okay with that? You want it?" he checks again. I love how even though he's bossy and dominant when we both want him to be, he never lets me forget that I'm still the one making decisions about what I'm comfortable doing. I'm the one choosing to give him the control here, and if I no longer want that, I have no doubts he'll immediately stop whatever we're doing. I don't think I'd enjoy this dynamic with anyone but him, but I fucking *love* it.

"Yeah, I do. I'm not promising I'll like it, but I definitely want to try. I had no idea I would love having a dick in my mouth as much as I do, and I want to know what else I might enjoy."

He lets out a short laugh, squeezing my ass before smacking it firmly. The unexpected sharp sting only makes my cock ache even more. He shuts off the shower and hands me a towel. "Come on, get on the bed on your hands and knees with your ass in the air. Do you have lube?"

"Nightstand," I answer, drying off quickly before I do exactly what he asked. Crawling onto the bed, I fold my arms in front of me on a pillow and rest my head down on them so my ass is in the air as requested. The position has me feeling more exposed right now than I probably ever have in my life. *What does my hole look like on display like this?* But somehow, the potential embarrassment or shame I might be experiencing over being so vulnerable only makes this situation even hotter.

Liam grabs the lube and comes onto the bed to kneel behind me, spreading my cheeks with both hands. "Fuck, knowing I'm the first man to ever see you like this, to ever touch this virgin hole…" He lets out a slow breath and little moan while running his finger over my rim. "Blake, you're so fucking sexy. I still can't believe I get to do this with you," he admits.

"Not just the first man, the *only* man," I remind him. "I'm yours, Liam."

The sound he lets out can only be described as a growl. "Yes, you are, baby. You're *mine*."

Oh fuck, I like that name. Then before I can really process what he's doing, the most incredible feeling overwhelms me as a warm, wet pressure starts at my taint and moves up over my hole. It's unlike anything I've ever felt before, and I need more of it.

"Ohmyfuckingjesuswhatdidyoujustdo?" comes out of my mouth in one long jumble, and I immediately regret saying anything when the sensation stops. I try to shift my hips up or back, chasing my new favorite feeling, and Liam lets out a soft laugh.

"Sorry, I should have warned you before I started eating you out. My caveman side took over for a second when you said you're mine." His voice is deeper than I've probably ever heard it, and that sexy tone only makes me needier.

"Well don't fucking stop," I whine, shifting my hips again.

He chuckles before bringing his mouth back to my hole, fingers digging into my cheeks. He's licking and sucking and kissing my hole with so much enthusiasm that any thought or worry I might have had about what he's doing doesn't even have time to form. His moans, as he focuses his tongue on my open-ing, make it clear he's enjoying this.

Not as much as I am, though. There's no way. His mouth on me like this has to be the single greatest thing that has ever happened to me. Fuck penetrative sex, I'll gladly never stick my dick in another person ever again if I can have this. I want Liam's mouth on me all the time. "Oh, holy fucking Christ, why haven't we done this before? Wait, don't answer that! Don't you dare stop." Why can't I just shut up and enjoy this?

Then he uses his tongue to actually spear inside of me and my mind melts, any hope I have of forming a complete thought is gone. All I can focus on is how amazing this feels, the warm wet pressure is so naughty and forbidden, and it's lighting up nerve endings I didn't even know existed. "Ohmygodohmygod," flies from my mouth. I definitely don't have control over what I'm saying but I can't shut up.

My cock has probably never been harder in my life, and it's leaking like crazy. I'm desperate to touch it, to give myself any relief, but I also never want this to end, and I'm already worried that I'll come just from how incredible his mouth feels. *Is that even a thing?* Can you finish without anything touching your dick?

He pulls back for a moment, and a needy whimper leaves my throat, but I'm so past caring about how desperate I am for Liam.

"Can I use my fingers?" *Ugh, that voice isn't helping how close I am.*

"Yeah, absolutely, just don't stop. Please." While Liam's voice has that sexy gravely tone all deep and masculine, mine is way higher than I'd like it to ever be. I should probably be embarrassed about that, but right now, I don't care. I want this—and him—so badly.

He goes back to fucking me with his tongue, and I hear the click of the lube cap opening. Then his tongue is replaced with what must be his slicked-up finger. It's a little firmer, and the pressure is deeper than before as he slowly enters me.

"Stay nice and relaxed for me. Deep breaths, B." I focus on his instructions, and before long, I'm rocking my hips trying to get him to go deeper. "I'm going to add another one. Deep breath in and bear down on the exhale."

I do as he says, and the pressure increases, but he moves so slowly, and he's obviously been generous with the lube. There's a slight burning sensation, but I focus on how hot it is, knowing that Liam is *inside of me,* and it helps me to relax enough that the uncomfortable feeling is replaced by pleasure.

"You feel so fucking tight, Blake. I can't wait until it's my cock stretching you like this." I let out another whimper at the thought. I definitely want that. Want him to fuck me and claim me in that way. "Get up here." Liam grabs my shoulder with his free hand, guiding me to an upright kneeling position. His arm wraps around my chest so that he's gently gripping my neck to hold me up, not actually applying any pressure to affect my breathing, but in a way that makes me feel completely owned by him. *It's so fucking hot.*

I twist around for a sloppy kiss, the angle is awkward, but I need his mouth on mine. He's pushing his fingers into me slowly, and then he shifts the position, and I swear to god my soul leaves my body. He hits some magical spot that completely lights me up from the inside out, and sparks of pleasure spread throughout my entire body.

As much as I never want this to end, it's time to admit that clearly isn't an option.

I give up on trying to hold back, focusing instead on the feel of Liam's fingers fucking me as they rub over that magical spot with each thrust. The pleasure is overwhelming.

"Oh my god. Holy fucking Jesus Christ. Liam, how does that feel so good? Don't stop, right there, fuuuuuuuuck!" My rambling turns into a moan as my cock jerks, shooting thick streaks of my release all over the bed.

The orgasm is unlike any I've had before, starting in that magical place Liam's fingers are still brushing against inside of me and spreading throughout my whole body. It's so intense, and the high feels like it goes on forever. I slump back into Liam's hold as I finally calm down and think about what the fuck just happened. *I guess it is possible to come without touching your dick.* That's so crazy!

"That was so fucking hot," Liam growls in my ear. "I need your mouth."

"You can have whatever you want after that," I respond in my post-orgasm haze. "I can't believe I just came hands-free. Holy shit."

He chuckles and helps me to lay back on the bed, propped up on some pillows as he kneels over me, lining up his swollen cock right in front of my mouth. "Do you want to suck me, or should I fuck your face?" he asks, running his hands through my hair, gazing at me with affection in his eyes, but it's mixed with something darker.

I look up at him through my lashes, taking the time to appreciate how fucking hot he looks looming over me like this, muscles straining with his need to come, gaze hooded and dark. The choice is easy, giving up the control to him always is.

"Fuck my face."

He doesn't waste any time, tightening his grip in my hair to control my head as he thrusts his dick into my mouth. I try to focus on keeping my jaw relaxed and breathing through my nose as he takes what he wants from me. My gaze is still locked on his, vision watering as tears form when he hits the back of my throat, and I fucking love it. I love knowing that I'm the one putting that wrecked look on his face, that I'm the only one he wants to be with in this way.

It only takes a few more thrusts before he's shooting down

my throat, and I attempt to swallow as much as I can. He moves his hands to cup my face, wiping away a tear before leaning down for a deep kiss, licking into my mouth and no doubt tasting himself there.

"You're fucking perfect," he whispers when he finally pulls away.

"I came without even touching my dick!" I excitedly remind him, still not over that.

"Yeah, you did, straight boy. It was so hot."

"I really shouldn't like that nickname," I say, smiling. "But I do."

"You'll always be my straight boy," he taunts, making me smile. "But what about when I called you baby, was that okay?"

I bite my lip as I nod quickly. "I liked that too. Maybe even more."

He chuckles and leans in to kiss me one more time. It's soft and sweet, and I am so happy I get to spend forever doing this with him. "You got any extra sheets?" he asks.

"Yeah, I'll grab them."

"Nah, B, I got it. I'll get you cleaned up and get the bed ready for us. You can stay right here, looking thoroughly wrecked."

I tell him where to find more sheets in my closet and do just what he said, enjoying having someone to pamper me. Liam is the best boyfriend ever.

I can't wait to call him my fiancé.

24

LIAM

Producer: What's it been like seeing Blake's world for the first time?

Liam: It's been a lot, in a good way. Honestly, I think I like the city more than I thought I would, probably because I'm seeing it with him. Watching him here, in his element, makes me feel like I'm getting to see a whole new side to Blake.

I wake up to a wall of warmth pressed against my chest. I love that Blake has naturally taken the place as the little spoon in bed.

My mind immediately drifts back to last night. Based on how quickly he embraced giving blowjobs, I had a feeling he'd like my tongue in his ass. Still, I didn't expect him to lose himself in it the way he did, giving in completely and not holding anything back. Turning him into a whimpering, begging mess is my new favorite thing in the world.

Not to mention, I've never seen anyone come hands-free before. *Fuck, that was… something else.*

Blake doesn't just accept pleasure—he surrenders to it. And I *love* that. Love that he completely gives himself to me. I never expected to enjoy having control over someone like I do with him. The second I start bossing him around, he absolutely melts. I want to give him everything he desires.

I bite back a groan, shifting slightly so my morning wood isn't pressing directly into his ass. *Not that he'd care.* Hell, if he was awake, he'd probably be grinding against me and making some dirty comment that would have me flipping him over and pinning him to the bed.

Christ. I need to think about something else before I wake him up in the filthiest way possible.

I carefully slide out of bed, managing to untangle myself from him while he continues sleeping. When I stand, I take a second to look around since I have yet to see his place in the daylight. *And yep, Blake's apartment is just as ridiculous in the morning as it was last night.* Floor-to-ceiling windows over-looking the NYC skyline, sleek modern furniture that I bet costs more than my dad's entire house, and way too much space for one person.

I knew he was wealthy, but this? This is stupid rich.

I want to pretend it doesn't bother me, that it doesn't make me question what the hell he sees in me. But seriously, what the fuck is he going to think when we get to my farm?

His life here is so far removed from mine that I don't know how they're supposed to fit together and that absolutely terrifies me. Blake keeps telling me he doesn't care, and maybe he won't. Maybe he really will love it like he keeps claiming he will, but the tiny voice in my head saying he won't even want to stay for the entire hometown visit is deafening.

I head to the kitchen to start making coffee and pull out my phone to text Blake. His house is so large, I don't know how long it'd take him to find me, and I don't want him to think I left after our night together.

LIAM:

You awake yet?

BLAKE:

No.

LIAM:

Well, someone's a little grumpy this morning. I thought you'd be happier after what we did last night.

BLAKE:

If you didn't want grumpy, you shouldn't have left me alone in bed.

LIAM:

I'm making you coffee, baby.

BLAKE:

Not the point.

I smirk to myself as I pour a cup, questioning why I'm so worried about what Blake will think about my life. While he may be rich as fuck, at the end of the day, he's still just Blake—clingy, needy, kind of a brat. *Mine*.

I take a sip, leaning against the counter just as he comes stumbling into the kitchen, hair a mess, eyes still half-lidded with sleep. He spots the mug in my hand and frowns.

"Where's mine? Thought the whole reason you had to leave me all alone in bed was to make me coffee?"

There's my needy brat. I turn and hand him the cup I made for him, and he smiles at me with so much affection that I feel my heart skip a beat.

After he takes a sip, he turns to me and waggles his eyebrows. "So, about last night... I want to do that again, and again. Basically, all the time. I'm so happy I picked you. I had no idea dating a man would be the best thing I ever did."

I freeze mid-sip, my coffee forgotten, not nearly as interesting as the words that just came out of his mouth. He's looking at me with that wide, self-satisfied grin of his, and I can feel my own smile take over my face.

"You're serious?" I ask, watching for any hesitation or flicker of doubt.

His grin only grows. "Dead serious. But I want the real deal too. If your fingers and mouth were that mind blowing, I can't wait to see what your cock feels like. That was the hottest fucking thing I've ever done in my life. I don't know why I wasted so much time thinking I only liked women, when clearly, I've been missing out on this the entire time." He gestures between us before taking another sip of his coffee, still looking at me like he just won the lottery. "And by this, I don't just mean being with any guy. I mean *you*, Liam."

I'm completely awestruck. I didn't realize how badly I needed to hear those words. How big of a deal him saying it really is. This isn't just some experiment to him. He keeps proving over and over again that he's invested in this. In *me*.

I step in close, gently taking his face in my hands. "Jesus, baby… you really know how to make a guy emotional first thing in the morning," I say with a soft laugh, sure my smile is revealing how hard I've fallen. "This—you—mean so much to me, too. It's not just that you're hot or full of surprises. It's the way you make me feel like I can just be myself. I didn't expect something real here… but I found it. With you."

"Me too," he says with a nod of his head. "I mean every word, Liam. I don't care that I never expected this. I don't care what anyone else thinks. I'm so glad I have you."

I close the distance between us, pulling him in by the back of his neck, pressing my lips to his. He kisses me back instantly and sighs into my mouth. There's no way I'll ever get used to this feeling. How right being with Blake feels.

When I finally pull back, he's breathless and his cheeks are flushed. "Fuck," he murmurs, lips brushing against mine. "See? Best decision of my life."

BLAKE DECIDES to spend the day treating me like a tourist in his city, which, apparently, means overpriced brunch, unnecessary shopping, and checking out every landmark. The brunch alone costs more than a week's worth of groceries, and when the bill comes, Blake doesn't even glance at it before handing over his card. Somehow, instead of annoying me, though, it makes me laugh.

As we make our way through the city in cabs and on the subway, I think about how much fun I'm truly having with him. As a person who genuinely dislikes crowds and commotion, I never thought I'd truly enjoy being here, but Blake has this way of making everything feel exciting. He talks a mile a minute, pointing out things like a native New Yorker giving a tour as we briskly walk from building to building to get out of the cold, and even though I have a feeling that half the "facts" he told me are completely made up, it's still the best tour anyone could've given.

He lights up every time he shows me something "quin-tessential New York," and I find myself watching him more than the sights. Although, I have to admit, the views are cool too. We hit up all the classics—Times Square, Central Park, the Empire State Building, the Statue of Liberty, and some fancy coffee shop that Blake claimed was the best in the city. It's a nice break to get out of the cold. He tells me it's the same place he mentioned when we were at the gym back in Atlanta, and though the drinks really do cost twenty dollars each, I'm not blown away. *Not about to tell him that, though.* The whole time, I try my best to ignore the camera person following us around, and eventually, I can almost forget they're there, especially since there are so many other people surrounding us, filming everything on their phones.

By the time we make it to a high-rise bar with an incredible view, I can definitely understand why Blake loves this place so much. It's special in its own way. For the first time since we started this grand tour of NYC, we aren't rushing anywhere and can just enjoy the night. I don't care about the cameras or the other people around us; I'm locked in on Blake and how happy I am to be here with him before we drive to the farm tomorrow.

When we get back to the apartment later that night, I'm exhausted. Between the running around, the cameras, and Blake himself, it feels like I've lived an entire week in two days.

Blake made me fall a little in love with his world during this visit, but I have no idea if he's going to feel the same way about mine.

All I can do is hope.

25

BLAKE

Producer: You've never been on a real farm, but you seem pretty confident about wanting to live on one. What makes you so sure you'll like it?

Blake: Okay, true. I've only been to a pumpkin patch when I was a kid, but I kind of feel like it could be exactly what I need. I love animals, and I'm excited to have the space and time to dedicate to more of them. And honestly, I just want to see what Liam's life is like. He gave the city a chance for me; I'm ready to see his world.

We're almost at Liam's farm, and despite the three-hour car ride to get here, my excitement hasn't faded. He keeps making comments about how "simple," "old," and "run down" parts of their property are, and he's reminded me multiple times to "lower my expectations," so I'm trying to contain how outwardly eager I am to finally see it.

Not sure how successful I am as my leg bounces up and down in my seat.

Liam and I are in the back of the car, a producer and cameraperson up front, and they have a few cameras set up in the car itself to record our conversations and reactions. I'm pretty used to the whole camera thing by now, though, so it's easy to ignore them and focus on Liam. I wish we could have brought Lucky with us today, but the producers requested that she stay back in the city, so she's with Chad again.

"We're almost there. That's our neighbor's property," he says, pointing at a dirt driveway on the narrow country road. "It's just an older couple living there now, all their kids have moved away. They don't farm anymore, but I try to help them out if they need anything." He shifts in his seat, fiddling with a loose thread on one of his shirt's buttons as he looks around. "And the house across the road is where the highschooler lives who's been helping out my dad while I've been doing the show. He's a good kid, a senior now, and his family's property hasn't been used for farming for the last few generations, but he's a huge help."

My smile couldn't possibly be bigger. It's so cute to see Liam nervously ramble on when he's usually so sure of himself. I also love hearing about his life and getting to add a visual to some of the people and places he's told me about.

We finally pull into the driveway of what must be Liam's farm. There's a fence bordering the property that's made of mismatched wooden posts, like it's been repaired over the years with different materials. We're driving really slowly now as he points out everything.

"That's my dad's house. It was his grandparents' when they first bought the farm, and has been passed down in the family since," he explains as we pass an older white farmhouse not far from the main road. "But my dad wanted me to have my own space, so we built my house a few years ago. It's deeper on the property so you can't see it from here. And that red building used to be stables when my grandpa had horses and cows, but we just have the chickens now, so we mostly use it for storage."

Sure, everything could definitely use a fresh coat of paint, but it's all even better than I'd hoped. There's real history here, each peeling layer representing a chapter in his family's legacy. *I'd love to be a part of that.* I've never felt that way with my own family's polished-to-perfection impersonal properties. They could belong to anyone with money. None of them hold the memories that this farm clearly does.

"The smaller barn near the entrance is where we pack and have people pick up their produce for that community program I told you about—the one where people buy a subscription to our farm and come each week to get the food we grow directly from us."

I nod along, trying to pay attention as he explains everything, but I can't focus on any one thing for too long. The property is gorgeous, huge trees surround the area, but a lot of the land has obviously been cleared, I'm assuming to grow food. I can't tell what they're growing or if it's even the right season for that sort of thing, but there's a lot of dirt so I think that would probably be where the food grows.

I'm going to be such a great farmer.

"Where are the chickens?" I excitedly ask when I can't hold back any longer.

Liam chuckles. "The coop is set further back that way." He points down a fork in the road that seems to connect all the buildings on the property. There's another building within a large fenced-in field, but that fence looks like it's got metal mesh or something between the posts. *There's actual real-life chickens running around.*

"Ohmygodohmygodohmygod, it's real! Why are we driving away from them? The chickens need to meet their new daddy!"

Liam bursts out laughing. "I thought maybe you'd want to see my house? You know, the one you've mentioned wanting to move into multiple times?"

"Liam. Honey. Lover of mine. I don't think you understand.

There's actual real-life chickens. Right over there! Plus, you literally built your fucking house. That automatically means I love it. I don't need to see it to know I want to live here."

"Lover of mine?" he repeats back like I just spoke a foreign language.

"Uh, yeah, that's what you are. Would you prefer I shorten it and just call you *lover*?" I say as dramatically as I possibly can, really drawing out the L and waggling my eyebrows. "In fact, I think I will. If I'm your 'straight boy,' I think you get to be my 'lover.' "

Liam groans, but he can't suppress his smile. "Whatever, let's let 'daddy' meet his new chickens," he teases, instructing the driver to pull over.

The car isn't even turned off and I'm jogging toward the coop. I'm careful as I open the fence, not wanting any of my precious babies to escape. They immediately flock around me, and the squeal that escapes me at their attention would be embarrassing if I wasn't so completely focused on taking them in.

I immediately drop to my knees, careful to avoid any of the chickens, so that I'm closer to their level. "Hello, everyone. Wow, it is such an honor to meet you all! I'm Blake, but you can call me daddy."

They're all vying for my attention with their cute little squawks, poking me with their beaks, saying hello. It's everything I'd hoped this moment would be, and so much more. "This is amazing, there's so many of you! And you're gorgeous, I had no idea how many different colors chickens can be! Don't worry though, your other dad is going to teach me everything that I need to know to take care of you, and I'm going to build you the biggest, nicest coop that money can buy. Well, I probably won't do much of the actual construction, but your dad is great at that stuff, so I'm sure it will be amazing. We'll make such a good team."

Their coop seems pretty shabby to me. I'm confident Liam is

a great chicken dad so I know it serves its purpose, but I'd still like for them to have somewhere they can be proud to live. It'll probably help egg production, too, if the chickens feel appreciated in a fancy new home, right?

"You do know that the camera guy followed you and this little introduction will probably be all over the internet when the show airs, right?" Liam says with a bright tone, obviously amused by my display.

"Do you hear that, babies? You're going to be famous!" I'm trying to pet as many of them as I can, not wanting any of them to feel neglected. I'm already in love with them all. Liam finally joins me in the fenced-in area and picks up a chicken, showing me how to hold them. Choosing just one to hold is stressful, but I remind myself that there's no rush, I'll have the rest of my life to get to know each and every one of these precious birds. Then my heart sinks right to the grass as Liam fucking tosses the chicken he's holding into the air.

"Stop!" The scream I let out is a much higher pitch than I've heard it before. But instead of crashing to its death like I had feared, the chicken flaps its wings and glides back to the ground, and to my immense relief, is completely unharmed.

"What's wrong?" Liam obviously doesn't understand my reaction to him throwing the chicken because, *well, I guess it was a stupid reaction.*

I look down at the chicken in my large hands, hoping Liam won't judge me too much for my answer. "I thought maybe they were like penguins, and didn't know they could fly," I mutter.

He doesn't laugh like I expect, though. "Oh, baby." His tone is soothing as he reassures me, like he regrets causing my panic. "I would never hurt one of the chickens." He comes up behind me to wrap his arms around my waist, placing his chin on my shoulder.

"Thank god."

"Should I be offended that you wanted to greet the hens before me?" a deep voice I don't recognize calls out.

"Hey, Dad." Liam turns toward the man approaching us.

He's got a huge grin on his face, clearly excited to see his son. I don't think he actually cares that we didn't find him right away; he looks thrilled as he pulls Liam into a big bear hug.

"I've missed you, son," he says when they finally break apart. "And who's the lucky person that you've brought back with ya?"

I know from Liam's stories that his dad already knows he dates men. He's always described him as so supportive and welcoming, so I've been really excited to meet him. "Mr. Moore," I say, stepping forward to offer my hand after gently shifting the chicken in my grip into a one-armed hold, tucked under my arm like a football. "I'm Blake, it's an honor to meet you, sir."

"Pleasure's all mine, Blake. If you make my son happy, then you make me happy," he says with a firm shake. "Call me Dad if you'd like, or Wyatt if you prefer, but Mr. Moore has always seemed too formal for a modest farmer like myself." He chuckles, and the sound reminds me so much of Liam that I instantly warm even more to the man.

Liam lets me have some more time with the chickens while he catches up with his dad. Since we needed to travel to get here, the producers didn't insist on splitting us up like they did back in the city, but the cameras stay pretty focused on them.

Eventually, he convinces me to see the rest of the farm, and Wyatt joins us as we walk all around the property. They both tell me about the half-started projects, future ideas for different parts of the farm that they'd like to upgrade, each detail bringing the place to life even more. They have a ton of great ideas for expansion, but they always mention how expensive everything is as they describe it. *That's where I come in, even if I haven't told them yet.* This farm will be even more amazing when I can fund all their plans.

I love their idea of expanding the amount of pumpkins they plant to try to take advantage of the families who want to visit a real farm in the fall, but they explain that would require creating a larger store than the area they have set up now for their local produce subscribers, and it doesn't sound like they plan to do it anytime soon.

Liam also points out that they'd need more than just pumpkins to draw people in to choose their farm over the others in the state. I suggest a petting zoo, and Liam teases me about just wanting more pets, but I think it's a great idea. Some goats, a few cows, maybe even one of those super adorable really hairy ones. We're definitely having a petting zoo.

At night, we eat dinner with his dad at his place, and I'm having such a great time that I don't realize how late it's gotten until Wyatt yawns for the third time in one story, and Liam assures him that we'll handle the morning chores and tells him to get some rest.

I got so caught up in my excitement with the farm, that I forgot we haven't actually made it into Liam's house yet. It might be late, but I'm still full of energy, riding the high from what an amazing day it's been.

"Ready to see your future home?" Liam asks as we head across a field from his dad's place.

"Fuck yeah! Show me our house, lover," I say dramatically, earning a smirk and a head shake from Liam that makes me laugh. But then he grabs my hand, interlacing his fingers with mine, and we walk in sync toward the picturesque modern farm home hidden in the back of the property. It's definitely the most modern building on the farm, but it also fits in perfectly.

Part of me can't believe Liam built it, but I'm also starting to believe he can do anything. I really do love it already. It's so cool to think about it still being here in another hundred years, with

Liam's great grandkids telling their dates that he built it. Everything here feels so much more important than my life back in the city.

Even with my mom's charity, I never got to really interact with the people we were raising money for. Everything was about planning the events and how to earn the highest amount of money from the donors. I'd like to think I made a positive impact on someone's life in the time that I spent there, but it all felt very impersonal.

But here? Every decision Liam and Wyatt make regarding the farm and its future feels significant. The proof that those choices could impact generations to come is all around us. I was optimistic about coming here, and I had assured Liam I wanted to move to the farm with him, but now that I'm here, I want it more than ever.

LIAM

Producer: What's it like having Blake here on the farm?

Liam: It's great. I was nervous about him seeing it, but he took to it better than I could have imagined. Almost too well. It definitely feels like we could have a future here together, but a part of me is still waiting for the other shoe to drop. Like, things can't really be this easy… Can they?

I didn't think today would go this well. I've spent the last week worrying about bringing Blake here, wondering if the farm would be too much for him, if the reality of my life would be too different from his. But today proved to me, again, that I had nothing to worry about.

He didn't just tolerate the farm, he was *into it*. He asked questions, shared his ideas—some of which were actually really solid—and even had the audacity to start calling himself daddy to the chickens. Which… yeah. That was surprisingly adorable.

We'll see if it's the same story tomorrow when I actually make him help with the morning chores, but I'll probably just put him with the chickens since he seemed so eager to spend more time with them. I really do want him to enjoy his time here.

My dad seemed to love Blake too, which I wasn't worried about, *but still*. My dad has always trusted me to make the right decisions, to bring the right people into my life, but seeing the two of them together and getting along made me happier than I expected.

Today felt like the last piece clicking into place for me. I've been trying to keep some kind of guard up—*though, even I can admit I've done a shit job of it*—just in case he didn't love it here. Just in case this was the thing that made him realize he didn't actually want a life with me.

But now that I've seen him here, I can't hold back anymore.

I need to show him exactly how much I want him and how deep this goes for me. I want to strip away any last shred of hesitation or doubt he might still have until the only thing in his mind, the only thing he feels, is me.

But first, I need to show him around my house, what he confidently called our future home. *Fucking swoon*. The stupid cameras are still following us, and I don't think they'd appreciate me pinning Blake against the nearest surface the second we walk through the door.

Well… maybe they would. But I'm not about to find out.

Blake and I walk hand in hand up the porch steps. I unlock the door and push it open, letting him walk in first, then the cameras, before I follow. He's quiet as he takes it all in. My place is nothing fancy, especially compared to his condo in the city, but it's functional for everything I need.

"I can't believe you built this!" he finally says, sounding truly amazed. "I mean, *I can*, you're incredible, but wow. It's amazing, Liam."

"Well, I did most of the work with my dad. And my best friend, John, is an electrician. His brothers still live here, so he came back into town and they all helped us with it. Plus, we did hire a few contractors for other things we couldn't do ourselves, like the foundation. It's not much, but—"

"It's *yours*," he finishes for me, glancing back at me with awe in his eyes. "That's insane. You actually built a whole-ass house!"

I chuckle. "Not by myself," I remind him again, but it's cool that he's so excited about this. I've always loved my house and that it's something my dad and I did together, but having Blake be so impressed, so proud of me, is making me surprisingly emotional. "So, you could actually see yourself living here?" I ask, needing to hear it again. *Just one more time.*

He turns to me with obvious affection shining in his eyes. "Yes. I want this, Liam."

I nod, my throat suddenly tight. I knew bringing Blake here would be a big deal, but I didn't expect this type of reaction, and I guess I'm still processing it all. I hate that I couldn't just accept his answer when he said he was excited. I know my past relationship trauma has left me jaded, but it's never really come up again before now. Probably because it's the first time I've truly cared this much about anyone else I've dated, and I'm terrified that this will still blow up in my face for some reason.

This is the first time I really want a future with someone. I want to be enough for him. Given my ex, and the fact that Blake had never considered wanting to date a man only a few weeks ago, it's been hard not to doubt that he feels the same way I do, but as I look around at him in my home—*our home*—all I can picture is our future together.

"I want you," he adds, stepping closer. His hands settle on my hips before snaking around my back, the feel of him grounding me.

I reach for him, sliding my fingers into his hair as I pull him into a slow, deliberate kiss. He chases my lips when I pull back to respond. "Me too. You ready for me to show you how much?"

Before I can deepen the kiss and show him how badly I want

him, someone clearing their throat from the doorway has us both jerking back. One of the producers stands there, giving us an expectant look. "Uh, mind if we grab some footage of you showing Blake around before we wrap for the night?"

Actually, I do mind, but I know that wasn't really a question so much as a reminder of what they're here to do.

Blake sighs dramatically, and I do my best to will my growing erection to calm down. *Why the fuck do I keep getting hard on TV?* Nothing like getting cockblocked by the production crew shadowing your every move while you're in the can't-keep-my-hands-to-myself phase of a relationship. I swear if Blake looks at me a little too long with his fuck-me eyes again before they leave, I'm going to shove them through the door myself so we can get some privacy.

"Can't we do that tomorrow?" I plead, already knowing the answer is going to be a resounding no.

"Sorry, we need his first reactions. It won't work if we come back tomorrow morning after a night together."

Fuuuuck. "Fine. Let's get it over with," I sigh.

I grit my teeth and start the tour. I'm extra grateful right now that I don't have a large house so I can get this over with quickly. I walk Blake, and unfortunately the crew that are following us with their cameras, through the house pointing out specific details. But I mean, clearly a bedroom is a bedroom and a kitchen is a kitchen. The whole time, I'm trying to not be rude but my body is still on high alert, and I know the tour is the last thing either of us care about right now.

Blake is not helping. *At all.* He's being extra animated and throwing out reactions that are obviously meant to keep torturing me. "Wait, you built these cabinets with your own hands? Babe, that's so hot, I'm so turned on right now."

I shoot him a look—hopefully off camera—trying to communicate that he'll pay for that later. But all he does is grin wider and waggle his eyebrows.

When we make it to the bedroom, Blake immediately throws himself onto the bed. "I can't wait to feel these flannel sheets on my naked body." He's intentionally pushing me and it feels like the last of my self-control is breaking. Honestly, I can't be held responsible for my actions at this point. They might have to just blur some footage out if they really want to keep filming tonight because Blake's ass is *mine* the second they walk out that door.

Thankfully, though—and I'm not sure if they actually got what they need, or if it was the way Blake is looking at me while obnoxiously running his tongue over his lips—they tell us they've got enough and they'll be back in the morning. I'm not even sure what usable footage they have, but that's the last thing I care about. We walk them to the door and lock it behind us so there's no chance they can come back in.

Blake is immediately on me. His lips crash against mine and I let him take what he wants—for now. His tongue teases my lips and I open easily for him. His kiss is full of desperation, like he's making up for every second we had to play nice for the show, but I pull back as soon as I feel him start rutting against my leg and grip his jaw in my hands.

"Bedroom. Now."

He shudders against me, nodding immediately before turning to literally run toward the bedroom. *Fuck, I love his enthusiasm.* I follow, and the second we're inside, I'm back on him, taking the lead this time. He melts against me as I push him into the wall and press my body against his. I want him to know just how turned on he makes me, and the wall is much closer than the bed. The moment he feels my growing erection, his hips rock forward, and fuck, if that doesn't make me even harder.

I lean in, dragging my lips along his jaw, obsessed with the way his breath hitches. He tilts his head back to give me more access to his neck, and I make my way down. I take full advantage of his responsiveness, pressing open-mouthed kisses along the column of his throat, nipping lightly to feel him shiver beneath me.

I pull back just enough to look at him—his flushed skin, his kiss-swollen lips, his blown-out pupils. Fuck, he's so beautiful when he's turned on and desperate like this.

"I want to take my time with you tonight." My voice is low and gravely. "But if you keep looking at me like that, I'm going to lose every ounce of self-control I have."

His smirk is almost cocky, but the way he shivers under my hands tells me he's just as gone as I am. "Who said I wanted you to have self-control, babe?"

"Fuck, B." I groan because he's really testing me. "Tell me exactly what you want tonight."

Blake bites his lip and looks at me through his lashes, eyes dark with lust. He leans in and whispers in my ear, "I want you to fuck me." Then he shakes his head and adds, "And I don't want you to hold back because you're worried that it's my first time. I want you to own me. Ruin me. I want to feel you everywhere. Whatever you want L, I want it too. Make me yours."

Jesus. This man. Heat surges through me and every single part of me is screaming to give him what he wants. To take him apart piece by piece and put him back together so he never forgets he's mine.

I step back just enough to pull his shirt over his head before doing the same to mine. Then I slam my mouth to his in a sloppy, claiming kiss, and feel his fingers dig into my back. I reach behind me and grab his wrists before pinning them against the wall. "You *are* mine," I practically growl, unable to control myself with what he's offering me. "You're sure, baby? You really want me to ruin you? You want me to stretch out your virgin hole and fuck you so hard that you feel me for days?" I ask as I trail bites down his jaw and throat.

I'm trying to focus, but I'm struggling. I've thought about this, about fucking him. *A lot.*

I've loved every moment that Blake and I have spent exploring each other's body and making each other come. And as amazing as his hand and mouth are, I haven't been able to stop myself from imagining what it would be like to fuck him. I love the idea of stretching him open slowly, making him take me inch by inch, teasing him until he's shaking and desperate to come. I've imagined him on all fours, on his back, up against the wall, bent over—every way I could possibly have him begging for more.

But no matter how many times I've pictured it, nothing could prepare me for hearing him beg for it. For feeling his body tremble against mine as he whimpers, "Yes. Please."

"Get on the bed," I demand, voice rough with need.

Blake doesn't hesitate as he scrambles back onto the mattress like he's been waiting for this all night too, and maybe he has. His lips are parted and his chest is heaving, already struggling to catch his breath even though I've barely touched him.

I strip out of my pants then crawl up his body, taking my time, letting my weight press him down into the mattress. My fingers trail lower over his stomach, teasing just enough to make him squirm before I grip the button of his jeans and pop it open. I slide the zipper down slowly, watching the way his chest rises and falls with uneven breaths. I peel off his jeans and underwear in one go, admiring how he's completely spread out and *mine* beneath me.

I take a second to admire him and how fucking sexy he is. How pretty. His tan skin and defined muscles that he's obviously worked hard for, his normally perfectly styled blond hair, already disheveled. His thick cock is swollen, the tip red and leaking before we've really even begun, and the proof of how much he wants this, how much he wants *me* is such a rush. I run my hands down his thighs to his knees and back up again, delighting in how responsive he is to my touch, each tense or twitch of his muscles feeding the addictive high of knowing Blake has asked me to take control.

"You look so fucking good like this," I whisper, leaning forward to press a slow kiss to his hip bone. "Been thinking about you in my bed all damn day."

"Then stop thinking about it and touch me already," he taunts, but the waver in his voice gives away just how badly he needs me. He lets out a breathy laugh at the glare I aim his way, but it dies in his throat when I grip his cock, giving way to a desperate moan instead.

"You don't get to rush me. I feel like I've waited so long for this moment, and I'm going to take my time with you."

I lean in, licking up his shaft, tasting the precum already gathered at the tip. His hips jerk up automatically, but I press him down, keeping him right where I want him. I wrap my lips around the head, sucking just enough to make him whimper. His thighs tense beneath my hands, and I can feel the way he's fighting the urge to thrust again. I love knowing I have him like this—so desperate, so needy, so completely at my mercy.

I bob my head down, taking him to the back of my throat and the way he moans sends a jolt of lust straight to my own leaking cock. I want him to know that I'm in control. That he can trust me to give him exactly what he needs, *but only when I decide to.* I drag my tongue along the underside of his head, swirling it around the tip, watching as his cock twitches, leaking even more for me.

"Fuck, Liam," he groans, dragging his hands through my hair, gripping like he can't decide if he wants to push me back down or pull me up for a kiss. I let my teeth graze the sensitive skin just to hear him gasp before I kiss my way back up his body, hovering over him again.

"Tell me what you want," I demand, wanting to hear him say it again.

Blake is writhing beneath me, trying to push his hips up into mine, seeking friction. "You already know," he whines.

I grip his jaw, tilting his face so he has no choice but to look me in the eyes. "Tell me. Again."

Blake licks his lips, breathing uneven. "I want you to fuck me."

I groan at the words, my dick throbbing at the thought as I drag my cock against his and he moans again. "You sure?"

"Yes, I'm fucking sure. I've never wanted anything more in my entire life. *Please.* You know I'm not above begging. Is that what you want? I'll beg. Please, Liam, please fuck me. I—"

I kiss him hard, swallowing whatever else he was going to say. As hot as his desperation is, I can't hold back any longer. I reach for the lube and a condom in my bedside table, refusing to break apart from his mouth. Then I lift his hips off the bed and shove a pillow under his lower back, propping his ass up. I direct him to bend and hold his legs up to give me easier access to his hole. I slick my fingers before pressing one against his entrance, circling gently. His breath catches and he starts whimpering against the barely there sensation.

"Needy little thing," I tease as I stop circling him just long enough to squeeze the globe of his perfect ass, watching as he shivers, before pressing my finger back to his hole. "Let me take care of you, baby."

He nods frantically as I push in slowly with my lubed finger. I know I'm going to take my time with him despite his protests. The last thing I want to do is make Blake's first time anything less than perfect. The soft, warm, vise-like grip he has on my finger has my cock twitching in anticipation. I can only imagine how good his ass will feel squeezing my dick.

"Fuck, you're tight," I groan as I work to stretch him with my finger.

Blake moans, squirming, shifting his hips trying to take me even deeper. "Oh, fuck—"

"You like that?" I ask as I move my finger in and out slowly.

"Yes," he whimpers, pushing back against me.

I add more lube before bringing a second finger to his entrance, and he adjusts easily as I instruct him to bear down as I push inside of him. "So good for me," I murmur, leaning down to press a kiss above his collarbone as I work to stretch him out. "You're taking my fingers so well, B. Ready for more?"

"Yes," Blake breathes impatiently as he rocks his hips, fucking himself on my fingers. I love seeing how desperate he is, and I want him completely addicted to this feeling, so I give Blake what I know he needs. I crook my finger searching for that spot inside of him until his whole body jolts.

"There," he gasps with a cry. "Holy fuck, right there!"

I smirk, adding a third finger and working to stretch him even more before rubbing over his prostate again, watching as his blissed-out expression becomes even more dazed and he comes undone beneath me. "Think you can take my dick yet?"

Blake nods enthusiastically. "Yes. Yes, I want you so badly. Want your cock inside me."

I groan, lust pooling low in my gut as my own need spikes in response to how eager he is and how desperate he looks underneath me. I remove my fingers slowly and watch as his body shudders at the loss. Leaning down, I kiss him again, pouring everything I feel into the way our mouths move together. Hoping the way my tongue explores his mouth expresses what I don't have time to say with words, that each nip of his soft swollen lips reminds him just what he means to me. I want him to know how happy I am that we found each other, how much I've come to need him. I want him to feel cared for and appreciated because that's what he deserves, and I know this is a big moment for him, for us.

Eventually, I break the kiss and pull back just enough to look at him to make sure he's hearing me clearly. "If you don't like this, I'll stop. I promise. Just tell me."

"I want this," he reassures me, longing shining in his eyes. A part of me still can't believe that he's really so all in, but there's no hesitation or concern written in his features as he smiles up at me. "I need you, Liam."

I grab the condom, open the wrapper and roll it on before reaching for the bottle of lube again. I squirt more into my hand and cover my straining cock, stroking my shaft as he watches with wide eyes. I spread the excess on his already prepped hole before lining myself up at his entrance. "Relax for me, baby. Deep breaths."

He does exactly what I say, looking like my perfect fantasy as I push through his tight ring of muscle. As soon as I feel the head of my cock sink inside of him, he gasps. It's somehow even better than I imagined, and every instinct in me is screaming to slam inside, to bury myself deep in this man that I've fallen for, but I force myself to go slow.

I want this to feel good for him. I need it to be everything he's imagined and more.

Wrapping my hand around his cock, I stroke him to give him something else to focus on while he adjusts to the new sensation of me inside him. Whispering words of encouragement in his ear, I lean over him and admire how hot he looks with his legs butterflied for me. "You're so fucking pretty, baby. I can't believe I'm the first man to ever be inside you. You're doing so good for me. Taking me so well. That's it, B, breathe. You're incredible."

Each word seems to help him relax further and he melts against me as I slowly sink in deeper, inch by inch. He's so hot and tight, and I swear it's the best fucking thing I've ever felt.

I'm almost fully inside of him and he gasps. "Fuck, you're so big—oh my god—"

I still for a second, letting him adjust and peppering him with kisses on every inch of skin I can reach. "Breathe, you're doing so good," I remind him.

His breath shudders out as he tilts his hips up further, still holding his legs up behind his knees. "More," he begs. "Please, Liam."

There's no way I could say no to that. I sink in further and let out a grunt when my cock is completely buried inside of him. "You okay?" I rasp.

Blake nods. "Yeah, just—fuck. You're so deep. You feel so big. You're huge."

I smirk, pressing a kiss to his jaw. "Want me to move, B?"

"Yes," he gasps. "Please."

That's all I need to hear. I pull back enough so that just my tip is inside of him before I slowly push my hips forward again. I set an easy pace to let him get used to this new feeling. I want to devour him, want to fuck him so hard he can't think about anything else for days, but there will be more time for that. I also want his first time to be everything he didn't know he needed. I want him to feel me everywhere—want him to crave this connection. To crave me.

I drape my body over his, leaning down to grab a fistful of his hair, yanking his head back so I can kiss him, swallowing his moans as I fuck into him. The sounds he's making are driving me wild, inspiring even more possessive feelings inside of me. "You're mine," I growl against his lips as I thrust into him a bit harder. "You belong to me."

"Yours." His voice breaks on the word. "Fuck, I'm yours."

My hips pick up speed, I'm desperate to push him over the edge, for him to shatter beneath me in the best way, completely overwhelmed by the pleasure I'm introducing him to. I want him to know how much I'm his too. I adjust my angle again, and I know the exact moment I hit his prostate because Blake chokes on a moan, his whole body tensing as his arms wrap around me, fingers clawing down my back. "Oh, fuck—"

"Right there?"

"Yes," he cries. "Fuck, Liam, right there—don't stop, don't fucking stop."

I tighten my grip in his hair, yanking his head back even farther, loving the control he gives me as I kiss him. I swallow every desperate moan that spills from his lips as he completely unravels beneath me, and it's the hottest thing I've ever seen. Every sound he makes, every twitch of his muscles, every plea, only makes me want to claim him even more.

"You like being fucked like this, huh, straight boy?" I say against his lips, my thrusts continuing to pick up speed.

Blake whimpers as he looks up at me through his lashes. "Only you," he breathes. "Only want you, Liam."

The caveman part of me loves knowing I'm the only one who's ever been inside him. Loves knowing that I'm the only one he's completely handed control over to.

"You're so pretty like this, baby." I groan again, pressing my forehead against his.

Blake gasps at my words, his whole body shuddering beneath me. He truly is breathtaking with flushed cheeks and wild eyes. He lets out a whimper, and I know he's getting close, so I reach down to stroke his cock again.

"Come for me," I order, moving my fist in sync with my thrusts. "Come while I'm inside you."

Blake lets out a broken sob, his entire body clenching around me as he finally shatters, coming hard between us, coating his chest with his release.

The way he squeezes impossibly tighter around my dick has me following him over the edge, spilling inside the condom. I've never wanted to fuck someone bare before, but I wish there was nothing between us. I want to fill him with my release, mark him as mine from the inside and then watch my cum drip out of him. Just the thought of that has my cock twitching once more inside of him.

I drop my forehead to his again, still catching my breath before pressing a kiss to his temple. He's panting beneath me, body still trembling. I brush my fingers through his sweat-soaked blond hair, tracing down the side of his face, watching as his hazel eyes flutter back open. He's looking at me like I hung the damn moon, and I can only hope that means it was as good for him as it was for me.

"You're so pretty when you come," I whisper.

His face goes red and he buries it in my shoulder as he laughs. "Shut up."

I chuckle, tightening my hold on him as my hand smooths over his neck. "Nope. You're mine. I'll call you pretty as much as I want because you are, baby. You really are."

His breath hitches and I think he's going to roll away from me, but he just whispers into my skin, "Say it again."

I want to give Blake everything, so I do just that. I press my lips to his forehead, then his cheek, then finally back to his lips. "You're so fucking pretty, B," I rasp against his mouth.

He wraps his arms tighter around me like he can't stand even an inch of space between us, and as much as I love how he melts for me, I know I melt for him just the same.

The last thing I want is to leave him for even a second, but I want to make sure Blake feels taken care of, so I force myself to slip out of bed and head to the bathroom to grab a warm washcloth.

By the time I get back, I half expect him to be passed out from everything we just did. But instead, he's watching me with so much affection in his eyes that it knocks the air straight out of my lungs.

I sit beside him, gently wiping him down, taking my time because I like the way his body relaxes under my touch.

"You okay?" I ask, my voice rough.

"I'm perfect." Blake hums his confirmation. He's stretched out in my bed and it's my new favorite visual. I want to take a picture, make it my phone background, get a huge canvas printed and hang it on the wall so that I can always see him just like this.

But he's staying, I can have the real thing.

I toss the washcloth in the empty laundry basket in the corner of the room and climb under the sheets, pulling him close. His body immediately molds to mine, and I'll never get used to how right he feels against me. His leg hooks over my hip and his face buries into the crook of my neck. It gives me the perfect positioning to tighten my hold on him and trace lazy circles against his bare skin.

After a moment, he shifts slightly, just enough to tilt his head up so our eyes meet. "I had a really great day with you today," Blake sighs.

"Me too, baby" I murmur, pressing a kiss to his temple. "I'm so glad you got to meet my dad. He loved you just like I knew he would." I pause for just a moment before forcing the rest of my thoughts out. "I just wish you could have met my mom, too."

Blake tilts his head up to look at me. "Will you tell me about her?"

I swallow against the sudden tightness in my throat, a familiar ache that never fully fades. Every time I think about her, I feel an overwhelming mix of happiness and grief. "My mom was incredible. She cared so deeply, just like my dad. I know she would have loved you too. She and my dad did everything together, it was so obvious how in love they were. They really set the foundation for how I view relationships." I smile to myself at memories of them always laughing, smiling for no reason, working together as a team even to do the simplest things.

Blake is quiet for a moment as he moves his fingers to trail around my collarbone. Then, so soft I almost don't hear it, he says, "I wish I knew what that was like."

My chest tightens as I pull him even closer, like somehow holding him tighter could make up for everything he's missed. I wish I could rewrite his past, give him the kind of love he deserved from the very beginning—the kind that doesn't come with conditions. Not that his parents don't love him, I'm sure they do in their own way. But it's obvious from everything he's told me about them, and from how disappointed he sounded explaining that they didn't care to be in town to meet me, that their way was never quite enough for Blake. He craves affection, warmth, a love that doesn't make him wonder if he's asking for too much. It sounds like the only connection he's ever gotten that from is his dogs.

I want to give him all of it. I don't want him to ever question how I feel about him, exactly as he is.

"Keep going," he encourages. "What was your favorite thing about her?"

I take a breath, sifting through years of memories. How do you pick just one thing about someone you loved so much? But I do have something pretty amazing I haven't told him about yet.

"She was a planner, and she wasn't about to leave this earth without imparting every ounce of wisdom she possibly could on me. She left a detailed list for my dad of ideas for the farm, things to do with me that she'd wished she could do herself. She even bought me a present to open for all of my birthdays until I turned twenty-one, each accompanied by a card that was full of advice for me for that stage of my life."

My mind drifts to the bottle of whiskey she gave me for my birthday that year. I still have it, untouched except for the one drink I know she'd wanted to share with me. It felt too important to drink casually, so I've been saving it. I want to toast with it on my wedding night, when my future babies join our family, maybe when we accomplish something from her list on the farm. I want to save it for the big moments in life, the ones where I'd want to celebrate with her.

"My twenty-second birthday was probably the hardest, knowing there wouldn't be any more gifts or cards from her. My dad admitted that she wanted to buy me presents until I was one hundred, but she felt guilty with how much all her treatments were costing." I sigh at that and Blake notices. He squeezes me tighter, placing a kiss on my jaw, not rushing me, just letting me know he's here, so I keep going.

"I love revisiting her cards. I have all of them, and she's got some damn good advice. I just wish she could have told me herself instead of having to write it all down, but I'm so lucky to still have my dad and that I had a mom who cared so much to even think to do that in the first place." I think about all the ways my dad has been there for me over the years, how he never let me feel like I was missing out by only having one living parent.

"My dad has always been one of those men who's just a natural father," I tell him. "Like he was meant to raise children, always making it look easy. I'm not sure if they ever wanted more kids, but they always made me feel like I was their whole world. And she was it for him, you know? He's never dated, never even seemed interested. Their love was the once-in-a-life-time kind, and that's what I want."

That's what I want for us.

His fingers are still dancing around my skin as I let the weight of what I shared settle between us. He takes a moment to absorb what I'm saying and then speaks. "Do you think we could have that? That you could have that with me?" His voice is soft, but the insecurity in his tone is so far from his usual cocky demeanor, that I feel a flash of guilt that I've ever made him question my feelings or my commitment to him.

I turn to face Blake fully, wanting to look into his eyes, hoping he can see the honesty shining in mine as I cup his jaw in my hand. "Yeah, B. I do. I wouldn't have let us get this far in if I didn't."

He exhales sharply, like he's been holding his breath waiting for me to confirm it. He still looks hesitant though, gaze roaming my face, searching for something. His lips are parted, like there's something else he wants to say caught in his throat, something he's not sure if he's ready to voice. I recognize it because I feel it too—the weight of emotions that are bigger than either of us expected.

I'll take the leap for both of us. I don't want to give him any more reasons to doubt the way I feel about him.

"You don't have to say it back if you're not ready," I murmur, brushing my thumb over his cheek. "But I need you to know that I love you, Blake." I've been afraid to admit it, even to myself. But I think I've known for awhile now, and after today, finally seeing him in my world, there's no use in pretending I'm not completely in love with this man.

His breath stutters, and for a second, he just stares at me, eyes wide like he can't believe I actually said the words. Then, his face splits into the softest, happiest fucking smile I've ever seen.

"Say it again," he whispers.

I lean in, pressing our foreheads together, letting my lips brush over his as I repeat it, slower this time.

"I love you."

A shaky breath leaves his lips, and then, "I love you too," he says, voice raw with emotion. "Fuck, I love you so much."

The second the words are out, before I even get a chance to process how hearing them makes me feel, he's kissing me, pulling me impossibly close like he's afraid I might disappear.

But I'm not going anywhere.

I kiss him back with everything I have, sealing the words between us, pouring every ounce of love I have into him. He melts against me, and my racing heart begins to settle, the feeling of him so close providing me with a sense of peace unlike anything I've ever known.

This is it.

This is the love I've been waiting for.

2 7

BLAKE

Producer: Have you ever been in love before coming on this show?

Blake: Ha. Absolutely not.

*L*iam's alarm wakes me up, and I want to chuck his phone. The thing must be broken. It can't possibly be time to wake up already. I glance at the window and confirm that it's still dark out and exhale a sigh of relief as I shut my eyes and settle back into Liam's warm arms that are wrapped around me in his bed. *He must have set the wrong time.* We should have another hour or two before we actually have to get up.

But then his arm slides away from me and he places a soft kiss on the back of my neck. "Time to get up, sleepyhead."

He did not just say that.

I groan, rolling over to chase his warmth, and when I find he's already abandoned the bed, I pull the covers up tight over my shoulder and squeeze my eyes shut. I know he mentioned something about getting up early to do farm things, but surely this is a prank. Some "welcome to farmlife" hazing. He can't possibly expect me to get up when the sun isn't even out, *right?*

"Don't you want to go feed your babies, *daddy* Blake?" he teases, and that gets me to reluctantly open one eye, peering up at him skeptically.

"You're serious?" I mumble, making him laugh.

"I warned you that we'd have to get up early, but it's not even that early. It's just winter so it's still dark out at seven-fifteen. The cameras are probably already waiting for us outside."

Goddamn those fucking cameras.

I finally force myself into a sitting position, opening both eyes to look around, half assuming the cameras would be in here to catch his cruel joke for the show. Thankfully, though, it's just us in here. *Fuck, I think he's serious.* Then what he said catches up to me, and I realize that means it's time to go see my babies!

"Daddy's coming," I say as I throw off the blanket and jump out of bed. I know they can't hear me, but I don't *actually* know. Dogs have better hearing than people, maybe other animals do too. So, on the off-chance chickens have super hearing, I figure I should reassure them that I'll be there soon. It also makes Liam laugh, so today is already a great morning, despite the ungodly hour it is, *even if it is after seven.*

Liam also insists that I wear his clothes so my "fancy shit," as he lovingly called it, doesn't get dirty. I love that we're similar enough in size to do that sort of thing. I'm also *very* into the hungry look he's giving me while I'm wearing his old college T-shirt under one of his thick flannels that smells just like him.

Maybe he'll let me keep wearing his stuff after I've moved in. Even if he doesn't explicitly order me to. If it has him looking at me like that, I'll gladly wear his wardrobe every day. Yep, it's decided—I'll still steal his clothes anyway.

There's a slight sting in my ass as I move around, but I kind of love it. The sensation is a pleasant reminder of what happened between us last night. Liam fucking me was everything I had hoped it would be and more. The feeling of him filling me up from the inside was unlike anything I've experienced before, and I already want more. I know he's mentioned something about enjoying both topping or bottoming, and if he wants me to, I definitely won't say no to the chance to fuck him. But, if I'm being totally honest, I'd be content to have him top me for the rest of our lives.

Even better than the truly mind-blowing orgasms, *Liam told me he loves me.* No one has ever told me those words. I've never felt them for anyone either. I still can't believe how lucky I am to have met Liam the way that I did. I don't think I would have even thought to consider a relationship with a man if it wasn't for the show, and it's by far the best thing that's ever happened to me. I'm glad I wasn't able to identify gender, and instead, just went with what felt right.

Liam definitely feels right.

He even has an extra coat for me, so we head right for my babies, and as Liam predicted, the camera crew is outside waiting.

"With it being winter, there aren't quite as many daily chores to do this early in the season, but since my dad's been on his own here, I want to check over some things, and maybe start knocking stuff off the list he's got going for me," Liam explains as we cross the field to the coop. "Plus, we'll want to make sure the animals have enough feed and water. We'll come back a little later in the day to get their eggs."

"And hangout with them?" I check, because I fully intend to spend as much of my day with the chickens as I can to get to know each and every one. I want to help Liam with the other stuff too, but as much as I wish I could claim to know what I'm doing when it comes to fixing things up around the farm, or even doing the daily chores, I'm completely clueless.

I hope he's ready to teach me everything he knows. I don't

plan to stay as incompetent as I currently am for long. I've felt a connection to this farm, a sense of home that's been lacking in any of the other places I've lived since we first got here. I want to be a part of it, to make my own impact on this place that feels so alive with the history of Liam's family. I want to help him make it into the best possible version it can be, the one he mentioned his mom dreamed of. I wish that I could have met her, she sounds like such a wonderful person. The total opposite of the woman who birthed me.

"You'll have plenty of chicken-time today, I promise," Liam answers with an indulgent smile. He reaches down to interlock our fingers between us, and I swing our arms a little, trying to rein in my excitement over seeing them again. If he wasn't holding my hand, I likely would have jogged ahead by now, but I don't actually know how to open the coop for the day. Liam and his dad showed me how to lock everything up last night, but they'll probably have to show me again because I was too bummed about saying goodbye to all the chickens to really absorb everything.

"Good morning, my sweet babies," I sing off-key as Liam opens the coop and the chickens spring out to greet me.

Liam is laughing, saying something about them just looking for food, but I know they can sense how much I love them already, and that they want to spend time with me just as much as I do with them.

Liam walks me through everything that we have to do to get ready for the day, and I really do try to focus. But between all the adorable chickens surrounding him, and how hot he looks confidently moving around the space as he lifts heavy bags of feed like they weigh nothing, it's safe to say I'm distracted.

After Liam finishes everything with the chickens, he has to use his bossy tone that he usually reserves for bedroom activities to finally get me to agree to leave. The cameras, *which I kind of forgot about yet again,* have been filming us since we left his house this morning. They've been following us around the property as Liam seems to work through a mental checklist of the farm's equipment, making sure everything is working properly.

I have no clue what he's doing, but he sure looks hot doing it. How did I ever ignore how attractive men clearly are? We're in a barn, an "outbuilding" I think they called it, that looks like it's used for storage. He's shed his layers and his farm-earned muscles are flexing, demanding all my attention as he looks at the engine of something that wouldn't start.

Eventually his dad joins us, handing us each a cup of coffee. We thank him, and Liam quickly sets his down to resume inspecting what Wyatt informs me is a driveable lawn mower. I chug my mug, desperate for the caffeine to work its magic. I'll need to get Liam one of those coffee pots with a programmable timer if he's going to wake me up this early on a regular basis so I'll at least have hot coffee to look forward to at the ass crack of dawn.

Wyatt laughs, eyeing my now empty cup. "Want a refill?"

I glance at Liam, wondering if he'll mind us leaving him. But I actually did want to talk to his dad alone. "Liam, would you mind if your dad and I got some more coffee and enjoyed it with the chickens?" I call out, and he waves us off, promising to find us when he's done.

We detour to Wyatt's kitchen for a refill, and he grabs his own mug before we head back outside. "You really seem to like these birds, huh?" he says casually after I call out to them, announcing our arrival. "Have you been around hens in the past?"

"Never," I say with a huge grin. "But I love them already. I have a dog, Lucky, and she's been the most important thing in my life until recently. She's really sweet with smaller animals and kids and stuff so I think she'll fit in well here. I know she'll love all the extra space to run around and play. I try to give her as much of that in the city as possible, but it'll never compare to all this. I'm hoping when I move here we can get even more animals, maybe some cows and goats. I love the plans you guys have for the farm and bringing more people here. It's a really special place, and I'm excited to be a part of it all."

My answer must have been the right thing to say because Wyatt's smile grows and his eyes seem to shine. "That's all we ever wanted for him, ya know," he says, sounding like he's far away, maybe lost in memory. "Someone who could care about this place as much as he does. Or at least, because he does."

That seems like as good of an opening as any, so I stand a little taller and take a deep breath, gathering my courage as I turn to face him. "Wyatt, I know you haven't known me for long. Less than a day, I guess, but it's important to me that you know how much I really do want to build that future with your son. I'll admit that this wasn't what I was expecting when I signed up for the show, but Liam has helped me to realize that the life I had in the city wasn't much of a life at all. I'm in love with him, and I want to do this right, even if the cameras make everything a little strange," I say quietly as I glance at the crew member who followed us here.

He's giving me an encouraging smile as I ramble, and I feel like I'm getting a glimpse into Liam's childhood. I can't imagine having this type of parental support all my life, but I'm so glad that Liam did. I take another moment to center my thoughts before I continue, wanting to focus on getting the important part out before I get too distracted by the chickens running around our feet.

"Sir, I know how much Liam admires you, how much the marriage you and your wife shared has inspired him and what he wants for his own future. I know he's an independent person, and that this isn't some old-fashioned requirement I 'have to do,' " I say using air quotes. Wyatt gives me another encouraging smile, and I take a deep breath before continuing. "There's nowhere else I'd rather be, no one else that I would rather be with, and I think it would mean a lot to Liam if I got your blessing before I ask him to marry me," I blurt out, hoping I said it right.

Wyatt is positively beaming, though, so I think I got the point across okay. "That's real kind of you to ask, son."

I know he means that in the casual way older men sometimes refer to guys that are younger than them, but that doesn't stop my heart from skipping a beat at the term. "I think Liam's mom would have liked that," he goes on, unaware of how his word choice has affected me. "She would have liked you and your enthusiasm. You obviously make him happy. I haven't seen him look as calm and settled as he did last night in years, and the fact that he waited until this morning to start fixing things up around here shocked me."

He chuckles and places a firm hand on my shoulder, giving it a quick reassuring squeeze. "Of course you have my blessing to marry him. I'm looking forward to having you and Lucky join us here."

In this moment with Wyatt, I feel more love than I ever have from my own parents, and I can't help myself—I throw my arms around him in a tight hug, grateful that my second cup of coffee is nearly empty and that I don't splash him with it.

He must sense how much I need the embrace because he hugs me back firmly, not letting go until I do. After meeting him in person, I didn't have any doubts Wyatt would say no, but it's still so exciting to have checked that mental box off and that it went even better than I had hoped.

I'm one step closer to marrying Liam, and I can't wait.

"Did I miss something? Why are we hugging?" Liam asks as he enters the fenced-in chicken area.

I look over at him as he approaches, his bright smile and warm blue eyes focused on me, more love shining in them than I ever thought I would deserve. The animals swarm his personal space, probably looking for more food. In his backwards base-ball cap, worn T-shirt, and jeans, with a bit of a classic red flannel visible beneath his open coat, stubble lining his jaw, surrounded by the chickens, he looks like the perfect farmer. He looks like *mine* and everything I never knew I wanted, everything I want our future to be.

I don't really make the conscious decision, I just fall down to one knee, scrambling for the ring box in my pocket that I've been carrying around since I bought it with Chad. The chickens seem excited that I'm closer to their level, and more flock to my side, vying for my attention. As much as I would love to propose while holding a chicken, *because that would be fucking adorable,* I couldn't possibly single just one of my babies out for the honor like that.

"What are you doing?" Liam says, sounding amused. His eyes are wide, but there's a grin stretching across his face, so hopefully he won't be upset that I didn't make this moment more romantic or something. No, fuck that, just because I'm being spontaneous doesn't mean I can't make this romantic as hell.

He's close enough now that I can take his hand in mine as I look up at him through my lashes, and I'm reminded of the first time I dropped to my knees for this man. My cock starts to thicken at the memory, but I will myself to calm down and focus. "Liam, we both know when I signed up for the show, I never imagined I would be here today, in love with a man, making plans to move to a farm and leave my life in the city behind."

"And I don't even like sports," he teases, smile growing even wider.

"Exactly! You are not at all the person I would have pictured myself marrying," I say with a laugh. "But Liam, you are the only one I could ever see myself having a future with now. You've taught me so much about what it really means to love someone, to be loved by another person. I've never had that before. I know you don't give a shit about my family's money or what number I was in the draft picks. I love how kind you are, how hardworking and passionate you are about your life here and continuing your family's legacy. Earning your laughter is my new favorite thing in the world. You're the first person that I've ever dated that I've wanted to spend all my time with. Even if we're just sitting in the same room, I want to be near you—"

"And probably on top of me," he interrupts.

I aim a shrug his dad's way. "I like to share personal space. Don't worry, he loves it."

Wyatt is glancing between us with watery eyes, a huge smile on his face.

"To answer your question," I continue, still laughing a little, enjoying how perfectly casual this huge moment feels. I'm not nervous, just excited to finally show him the ring I picked out, and to claim him as mine in this new way. "I was hugging your dad because I asked for his blessing to propose to you, and I couldn't possibly wait another moment when he gave it. I'm glad you came to us here, because asking you to marry me in front of our babies feels way more romantic than if I'd found you in that shed by the lawn mower."

Liam bursts out laughing, and we all join in, even the camera guys are chuckling. "Well, are you going to officially ask then, or was that the whole speech?" he asks when we all calm down.

"Fuck, did I not do that yet?" We're grinning at each other like lovesick fools, and for once, I'm so glad there are cameras on us so I can remember this moment forever. I can't wait to go back and rewatch this with him for years to come. "Liam, *lover,*" I draw out dramatically, loving the eye roll I earn from him. "Will you make me the happiest man alive and agree to marry me?" I officially ask, opening the ring box to show him the black band I chose for him.

"Of course I'll marry you, baby," he says, then he cups both sides of my face in his rough palms and drags me up to meet him in a searing kiss. My entire body heats up at the feel of his stubble scraping across my cheeks as our mouths tangle and our bodies press together, like we're desperate to eliminate any space between us.

When I hitch my leg up around his hip, there's a deep throat clearing that reminds us both that we're not alone, and we reluctantly pull away at the same time.

"I got this for you while I was with Chad in the city," I explain as I take a small step back to put the ring on for him. "I also got a silicone one that I know you'll probably end up wearing more with all of the work you do around here."

Liam's smile grows soft at that, and I can tell he appreciates that I put in the extra effort. "Well, you beat me to proposing. I wanted to propose to you, but I was planning to use one of the rings the show offered since I figured they'd be nicer than what I could afford for you," he admits.

"I don't want to overstep," Wyatt cuts in, coming closer as he removes a chain from around his neck, and I see him pull a necklace with a ring around it out from his shirt. "I certainly didn't expect Blake to drop down on one knee in the middle of the chickens not even two minutes after our conversation." He chuckles, and I shrug.

"I didn't want to go another moment without Liam being my fiancé," I explain.

"Like I said, I think his mom would have appreciated your enthusiasm." He offers me a soft smile, holding out the necklace in his hand to Liam. When I look at his expression, it's clear that it means something to him, his eyes are wide in surprise, and he tentatively reaches out to take the chain from his father.

"I'd planned to offer you this in private before either of you proposed, but Liam, if you would like, I think it would have meant a lot to your mother if your partner got to wear the ring she had made for me."

It's a gold band with a small row of diamonds in the middle of it. Fuck, it's so cool. And the sentiment is making me so emotional. *Don't cry, don't cry.*

"She didn't want to be the only one with diamonds," Wyatt explains to me. "And she used the jewels from her own mother's ring to make mine. But I've always worn it around my neck, tucked into my shirt for the same reasons you probably got Liam the silicone band, so it's in pretty good shape. If you'd rather get something new, though, I won't be offended."

"Dad, if you're sure?" Liam checks, and I'm glad he doesn't feel the need to ask me. That is easily the coolest ring I've ever seen, and the backstory makes it so much better. I'll be fucking honored if Liam offers it to me.

"Of course, son," Wyatt says with a firm nod.

Liam holds the ring in his hand, turns to me, and drops down on one knee.

LIAM

Producer: You just got engaged! How does it feel now that it's official?

Liam: This feels like the start of what I've been waiting for my whole life. Blake leads with his heart and I love him for that. I'm ready for forever with him.

"I thought I'd have time to plan something big for this," I admit. "Something romantic. But I don't need any of that. Everything I want to say to you, everything I want for our future, it's already right here." I gesture around us, voice filled with emotion over how this proposal has played out with him taking the lead.

"I love you, Blake, and you deserve a proposal too. I love the way you fit right in on the farm, how you fit into my life like you were always meant to be here. I love the way you love me. I never knew it could be like this—this easy, this right."

Blake's eyes shine as he looks at me and I give his hand a little squeeze.

"So, I'm asking you to stay," I continue. "To keep building

this life with me. To keep being the best part of every day. To be my husband. To live here on this farm and build a future with me." I swallow hard, emotion thick in my throat. "Marry me, Blake. Be my forever."

Blake's already nodding before I even finish speaking, happiness shining in his eyes. "Yes, of course I'll marry you, babe. You know that, but thank you. I'm actually really glad that you proposed too. This is all so much better than anything I could have imagined a few weeks ago. I didn't expect this to feel so special."

I knew he'd say yes. *I mean, he literally just proposed to me,* but it still feels so surreal. I just needed him to have this moment, too. To feel just as wanted and chosen as he's made me feel.

I slide the ring onto his finger and it fits perfectly, like it was always meant to be his.

I smile to myself as I lean in, capturing his mouth with mine again. I keep it PG—well, mostly. There's definitely some tongue. But I'm painfully aware of the cameras still hovering around us, and the last thing I need is for one of them to clear their damn throats and once again ruin the moment with my fiancé.

My fiancé.

Damn, I like the sound of that.

We break apart and Blake has the biggest grin on his face as he says, "Well, I guess it's time to plan a wedding!"

The next twenty-four hours fly by on the farm, mostly consisting of Blake continuing to spend all his free time with the chickens. He tells them all about Lucky, and he's got some absolutely ridiculous ideas that I'm positive have all come from social media. He seriously suggests getting tiny pants for the chickens.

"You know they make them, right?" he says, like I'm shaking my head because I doubt him, not because it's a ridiculous suggestion.

I pinch the bridge of my nose and laugh despite myself as I ask, "Blake. Why do the chickens need pants?"

He gasps dramatically, like I'm the one suggesting a crazy idea. "You wouldn't understand, Liam. They deserve fashion and self-expression too."

Apparently, this is also the moment that I find out my dad is now on Blake's side because he laughs throughout the conversation and tells Blake he'd love to see it.

This is my life now.

But despite Blake's obsession with being the chickens' daddy, we're able to squeeze in everything we need to before heading back into the city. My dad gives both of us big hugs before we go and tells us he'll see us in two weeks for the wedding.

It still doesn't feel real.

Now, we're back at the fancy hotel the show is using as their headquarters in the city, and I think it'll end up being the wedding venue too. I'm sure the hotel will be thrilled for the exposure if the show ends up being popular. The producers have a lot of stuff planned for us to prepare for the big days, and as much as I would prefer to be back on the farm with Blake, I have to admit it's easy to get swept up in the excitement of the show, especially now that the hard part is over. I've already found my person. We're engaged. Now I can enjoy all the over-the-top wedding related stuff that I probably never would have experienced if I got married in my small town.

They make it seem like we have so much to do, but most of it is just picking from the preselected options they've had set up for us—venues within the hotel, catering, floral arrangements—all of which Blake has endless opinions on. I'm sure the audience will be entertained at how this man, who thought he was straight mere weeks ago, has now decided he needs "subtle rainbow decor wherever possible." I have no idea how that's going to turn out, but I'm happy to let him take the lead and give my opinions when he asks.

I'd really do anything to make this man happy.

Despite my excitement, I can't deny that a part of me is still waiting for something to go wrong. It's not Blake, I'm sure that I want to marry him, but I can't get rid of this gnawing anxiety in my gut that something isn't right. Maybe it's just being in such a fancy setting where I feel so out of place when I'd always assumed I would get married on the farm. Or that we're doing all this planning away from my dad. I don't need a ballroom or whatever they're pushing on us, but I remind myself the farm isn't an option. I'm already thinking about how we can do some-thing special there by ourselves that would be just for us when the big production is all said and done.

I'm grateful for the show bringing us together, so if that means we end up with a bougie rainbow wedding in the city, and if it makes Blake happy, then I'm happy to do it. At the end of the day, I'll be marrying the man of my dreams and that's what really matters.

Today, the show is going to film us making calls to friends and family, finalizing the guest list, and getting our tuxes. I'm probably most excited about that because we actually get to do something outside of the hotel. It feels like they just keep drag-ging us from vendor to vendor in the same building, and I'm over it.

I'm really glad they aren't forcing all the men still left on the show to shop together. I really don't care to pretend about most of their tuxes. However, the producers did like the idea of us inviting some of the other contestants to our appointment as a part of our friends and family list if we wanted to.

I shoot Jace a text. I feel like we really bonded in a way that I haven't been able to when attempting to maintain friendships as an adult. After meeting so many of Blake's friends during his hometown visit, I was reminded of the fact that most of my interactions with people in my day-to-day life are related to the farm in one way or another. As much as he's looking for that sense of family that he's missing, I've realized that maybe I should have been investing more time into my friendships. Some of my friends have confirmed they can make it to the wedding, but none of them are in town yet. It'll be nice to feel like I have friends at the appointment that are there for me too.

LIAM:

You free to tux shop?

JACE:

You never told me how the proposal went, just that you were engaged, give me the details!

LIAM:

Well, technically we both proposed, but he beat me to it. Surrounded by chickens. It was kind of perfect.

JACE:

That's sort of adorable.

LIAM:

It was, I can't wait to catch you up more in person.

JACE:

I can't believe we get to be hot grooms together!

LIAM:

Do I need to do anything special to qualify as a "hot groom"?

JACE:

I'm bringing Kieran to give you all of his opinions, he's the only one in this relationship who should be giving fashion advice. I'm sure he'll love hyping up whatever chaotic options Blake picks out too.

LIAM:

As you should. I love how unserious he can be. Blake can wear whatever he wants. It's his day too.

JACE:

See, this is why you two work.

LIAM:

Damn right. See you soon.

Blake is vibrating with excitement before we even step into the store. "This is going to be so fun," he declares, practically bouncing on his heels as he loops his arm through mine.

I can't help but lean in and press my lips against his forehead.

We step into the boutique the show booked for us, a swanky, upscale place that looks way too nice for me to be setting foot in, and an associate greets us with a perfectly polished smile. "Grooms! Welcome. I'm Sam and I'll be helping you today. Can I get you any champagne, water, coffee?"

Knowing what Blake wants before he even opens his mouth, I say, "We'll take a coffee and a water, thank you. We should also have a few more joining us." I don't think much of ordering for him, but he's got a satisfied smirk aimed my way, so I don't think he minds.

"Great! I'll be right back. Take a seat and get comfortable while we wait or feel free to start looking around."

Blake wastes no time dragging me toward a rack of tuxedos, eyes already zeroing in on a deep emerald velvet jacket. "Okay, but look at this one." He yanks it off the rack and presses it against his chest.

I huff out a laugh. I knew he was excited to go shopping in an expensive place, but I can tell he's feeling extra ridiculous today.

"You'd look hot, but it also kinda screams 'rich asshole at a Christmas party.' "

Blake smirks at me. "I *am* the rich asshole at a Christmas party! Wait until we have to go to some of my parents' events. It'll turn you into a rich asshole too. Those people are insufferable."

I laugh again, shaking my head just as the door swings open.

Jace and Kieran stroll in, hand in hand, and I smile at them as they make their way over. Before they even get to us, Chad and Ash follow. It feels great to still have people here supporting us. Kieran immediately claps his hands in front of his chest once when he's in front of us. "Show me the options!"

Blake shows off the emerald velvet jacket. "This color probably isn't right, but I'm loving the idea of doing something more fun than a black tux."

It seems everyone's fine with skipping the pleasantries and diving right into wedding talk.

Kieran steps closer, inspecting it with a critical eye. "Love that for you, and I agree this color isn't really in season. Let's find something that's still a statement, but in the right way."

"What's the vibe you're going for on your wedding day?" Jace questions, using words I understand far more than whatever Kieran was talking about.

"I'm still deciding," Blake admits. "I definitely don't want to be boring. I kind of want to do something that'll piss my mom off since my parents doubted I'd be walking down the aisle in the first place. Obviously, I also want to like it too because I know I'll enjoy the pictures and videos for the rest of our lives. And I don't want to embarrass Liam if I go too bold." He turns to face me with a sheepish grin, but he should know better than that by now.

"This is *your* wedding day, you know that, right?" My tone might be a little harsher than I intended as I arch my brow at him, but I also want to drive home my point, so I think it works.

"Wear whatever you fucking want, B. I just want you to be happy."

Blake's face lights up and he gives me a slight nod before focusing his attention back on the blue jacket that's now in his hand.

Jace turns to look at me next. "What are you planning to wear?"

"I'll probably go with a black suit."

Blake gasps like I've somehow offended him. "Nooo, Liam, babe, hear me out. Do you really want me to get up there in something cool and sexy and unique, and then have you look like you didn't even give a shit to pick something out. What about charcoal? Or"—he tugs me toward another rack—"navy. Sexy but still classic, plus it'll look so cool with your eyes. Black is so boring."

Kieran nods. "I love what you could do with different shades in a blue color palette."

Sam returns with our drinks, setting them down on the counter. "I also pulled some options based on your fittings questionnaire. Feel free to take a look."

Blake immediately reaches for a navy tux with black satin lapels. "Ooooh, Liam, this." He holds it up to me, tilting his head. "Yep. Hot as hell. We're trying this one."

I take a sip of my water before taking the tux from Blake's hand, kissing him softly on the mouth, and heading into the dressing room.

"Wait!" Blake practically yells in the nearly silent store. "Take these too," he says, shoving a couple more options in my arms.

Shaking my head, I can't stop from smiling as I do exactly as he says.

"Hurry up. I need to see just how sexy you are in a tux. I'm worried that I'll try to strip you out of it when we're supposed to be saying our vows."

"You do know we're in public, right?" Ash says, and I can only imagine the look on Blake's face right now. I can hear the other guys out there laughing, and I kind of love how Blake has no chill in front of our friends.

I try on the first one Blake was so excited about, the navy tux. Sam was kind enough to assemble the entire outfit, so I pull on the white shirt first before the rest of the ensemble. I shake my head, smirking to myself as I pull the jacket on and adjust the lapels. I have to admit, Blake has good taste, and Sam got the fit just right for everything. The tux fits like a dream.

I step out of the dressing room, and immediately, the group goes silent. They're all sitting in chairs, waiting for me, and Blake freezes mid-sip of his coffee. His eyes rake over me so shamelessly, and I love that I've done the impossible and rendered him speechless.

"Okay, yeah," he finally says, voice slightly hoarse. "You're definitely wearing that. Holy shit, babe. You look *hot*." He's got the biggest smile plastered on right now, but his eyes are dark, like he's picturing exactly what he wants to do to me. My chest aches with how much I love him and how lucky I feel that we made it here together.

Chad lets out a low whistle. "Damn, dude. If he wasn't already obsessed with you before, you just solidified it. I've never seen him this smitten."

Blake finally blinks, shaking himself out of whatever fantasy he's just played through in his head. "Turn. Let me see the whole thing."

I humor him, doing a slow turn, and before I even complete the full circle, Blake is out of his chair, putting his hands on me like he physically can't help himself.

"You're so sexy," he says again in a breathy tone, and I can't help but smile. "I mean, you always are, of course. But this is a whole new level." Then he leans in close and whispers, "I definitely want you to fuck me in that tux after our wedding."

I chuckle, sliding a hand around his waist and pulling him closer. "Glad you approve, and I think we can make that happen."

I brush a quick kiss against his lips before heading back into the dressing room to change. If picking a tux gets him this worked up, I can't wait to see what he does when I'm actually standing at the altar.

I'm barely back in the dressing room when I hear Blake enthusiastically asking Sam about his options.

Sam chuckles, assuring him that they already set aside options for him as well. "I pulled a few styles based on what you mentioned too. Do you have a preference?"

I hear Blake hum and it sounds like he's tearing through the rack. "I mean, obviously, I want to look hot as hell. But also, like, husband material. Like, *wow, that guy definitely landed the man of his dreams and is about to say 'I do' in the most stylish way possible.* You know?"

"Oh, totally," Ash deadpans. "That was very clear. You just made Sam's job so easy."

"You're supposed to be on my side, Ash."

"Just grab something and get in the dressing room. You're turning into such a groomzilla," Chad teases.

I walk out just in time to see Blake carrying three options into another dressing room. The first two are good, he looks as handsome as ever, but when he steps out in the third option—a lighter-blue tux with black lapels, my heart slams against my ribs.

He looks unreal.

Blake is silently standing in front of the mirror, staring at his own reflection like he's never seen himself before. I slowly walk over to him and wrap my arms around him.

"Oh," he says softly, smoothing his hands down the jacket. "What do you think?" he asks as he turns to face me.

Kieran lets out a low whistle. "Yeah, that's the one."

Chad nods. "This is it, dude. No question."

But I barely register what they're saying because I'm too busy drinking him in as he awaits my reaction. Although, I'm sure my face completely gave me away.

"This *is* it," I echo their words. Then I lower my tone so that only he can hear me. "You in this, walking toward me? It's perfect, baby."

Blake lets out a deep exhale, like he was holding his breath. "Yeah?"

I nod, stepping forward holding his jaw to guide his gaze to meet mine. "You look incredible. How do you feel in it, though? That's what's important."

"Happy, confident. Like I'm doing this for me and not because it's what my parents want."

Maybe I've been underestimating how much pressure Blake's parents have put on him. I'm glad he seems to be moving past it, though. Smiling, I lean down and kiss him slowly. Once again, trying to hold back from deepening it because we're in public and we have an audience—and the cameras.

Someone clears their fucking throat though. *Of fucking course.*

I swear, I never want to hear another person clear their throat in their entire lives.

Then I hear Ash say, "Love this moment for you two, but if you keep making out in front of me, I'm going to have to bill you for emotional distress. I can only handle so much jealousy and longing in one day."

Blake laughs against my mouth before pulling back. "You just wish you had someone this hot to kiss."

"Yeah, I do. That's exactly what I want." Then I swear I hear him mumble, "It feels so good to say that out loud," to himself. Then he quickly spins to the camera person with wide eyes. "I didn't sign anything today, you can't put any of that in the show." They assure him that they're not about to out someone on a queer show, and Ash settles again.

I turn to give him a knowing smile. "You'll find it, Ash. I know you will." Then I grab Blake's hand. "Now, come on, fiancé. Let's go check out before you start insisting on an outfit change for the reception."

"I mean… it wouldn't be the worst idea…"

"Blake."

"Fine, fine." He squeezes my hand, smiling. "Let's go."

29

BLAKE

Producer: What are you looking forward to most about being married?

Blake: As grateful as I am for the show bringing us together, I'm excited to spend time with Liam *without* all the cameras around.

Today is my fucking wedding day! *I actually did it*. My thirtieth birthday isn't for another month, and I'm about to walk down the aisle with my person. I can't believe how lucky I am that I not only followed my parents' stupid ultimatum and won't lose access to my trust fund, but that I actually found the person I want to spend the rest of my life with in the process.

As much as I hate to admit it—because I still think the whole threat of cutting me off if I didn't settle down was stupid—it was also undeniably the best thing that's ever happened to me. There's no way I would have signed up for the show without the possibility of being cut-off hanging over my head, and I also don't know that I would have ever thought to give dating another man a chance in the real world. And it brought me to Liam, who is everything I need.

Even my attitude about my family's money has changed since I met Liam. Before, I was terrified of what my life would look like if I lost it. I had no sense of direction, no purpose other than making Lucky happy and having a good time, and that life-style wasn't cheap. Now, though, I'm grateful to have that money because of how I want to use it to help Liam and his dad achieve their dreams for the farm. *It really has become my dream too.* But, even if I wasn't rich, I know we'd still be happy. I think I finally understand what my dad said to me almost two years ago about really finding his purpose when he met my mom. Not that Liam himself is my purpose. As much as I want to spend my days making him happy, I still feel like my own person, but the life we're going to build together feels so much more meaningful than anything I was doing before meeting him.

The ultimatum hasn't been my focus for a while now, but I can't ignore the fact that now that I'll fulfill my parents' require-ment, Liam and I will be financially set. Obviously, I still want the money. We'll use it to put *Moore to Love Farms* on the map and turn it into the coolest destination farm in New York. Fami-lies are going to want to come from all over to visit, and we're going to give them the best farm experience possible. I'm so excited to go back with Lucky this time. Only a couple more days to wrap this show up and get Lucky, and I'll be officially moving in. I can't wait.

I'm sure I'll tell Liam about my parents' threat eventually, but every time I've considered bringing it up, I've talked myself out of it. I don't want him to question my motivation for being with him. He was already so concerned about being the first man I've been with, I don't want him to think I'm only marrying him for the money. He said he wanted to be chosen and I'm choosing him fully. I want to marry him regardless of their deadline or threats, so I don't even think the ultimatum really matters anymore. No use giving him something to stress about when we're so close to our happily ever after.

The last two weeks of wedding planning have flown by, but I'm more than ready for this show to be over. We've done countless interviews this week with Andy talking to us individually, as couples, and even other pairings and groups that the producers deemed would make good television.

They wanted one with me, Liam, Rachel, and her fiancé, which I absolutely did not want to do, but before I could even complain or try to get us out of it, Liam firmly declined. It was really sexy watching him stand up for us like that—I could barely wait until we were alone to strip down and present myself to him. Bottoming is definitely my favorite, I'm kind of obsessed with it. Not just because the feeling of him inside of me—stretching me out, filling me up— is so fucking amazing, but I also think I've become a bit of a pillow prince with how much Liam spoils me in bed. I've never had such a high libido before, and it's not that I'm not an enthusiastic participant in everything we do together, because I am. It's just so fucking hot when he takes control, bosses me around, or manhandles me so that we both get exactly what we need. I never thought I'd love submitting to him like I do, but I'm *really* into it. And then when it's over, and we're both wrung out and satisfied, I love how he takes care of me, cleaning us up and holding me until we fall asleep, or until we're forced to get out of bed to do something for the show.

The rest of our time this week has been spent coordinating the actual wedding details so we had a say in making it our own, even if all the couples are getting married at the same venue of the hotel. There are a few different event spaces within the hotel, but only three couples can actually get married on each day. I know Liam is happy that Kieran and Jace are tomorrow, though, so that we can be at each other's big days.

I finally got ahold of my parents a few days ago to confirm that they'll be here, my mother sounding shocked but reluctantly pleased that I was actually getting married. She did say she "hoped the producers know what they're doing and that my wedding won't be cheap and tacky," but at least my dad congratulated me. My brother and sister are also able to make it with their families. Not that we're close, but it'll still be nice to have them here, I suppose.

We still have a couple of hours before the ceremony, but the show has us separated in different suites to get ready and hang out with our friends and family. I'm not about to spill on my hot as fuck suit before the ceremony, so we won't change for a while. For now, we've got hockey on and we're enjoying some snacks. I wish Liam could be here too, but I'm trying not to focus on that too much. Today is the last day the producers can tell us how to handle our relationship and the last day they'll be following us around endlessly. We'll have the rest of our lives to spend together; I can wait a few more hours. Even if I really don't want to.

"Knock-knock. I'm assuming none of you are prepared enough to already be dressing, so you're all decent," my mother's voice cuts through the room like a knife, tearing apart whatever good vibes we'd been soaking in. Why did I want her here again?

I turn to see that both of my parents have entered the suite and my mom smiles at the camera. My father is dressed in a traditional black tuxedo and he looks great, very polished and sophisticated. My mother at his side has obviously spared no expense on her own appearance. Her hair is freshly dyed and in an elaborate style on the top of her head. The amount of makeup she's wearing could probably be classified as a mask, and I can't tell if the lack of expression on her face as she glances between my friends and where our suits are hung up is because she's unimpressed by our fashion choices, or if it's more indicative of recent botox injections.

And then I register her dress, reacting aloud before I can filter myself. "Mother, what the fuck are you wearing?"

"Pardon your language, Blake! I'm sure your future wife doesn't want to hear that vulgarity."

Wife? *Shit, did I not mention I'm marrying a man?* I tried to call them so many times to confirm if they would be here. By the time they actually answered, I think I was so focused on if they were coming, I must not have actually told them anything about Liam. *And of course, they didn't ask.*

I don't think they'll actually care, though. They have progressive friends, some of my mom's charity's biggest donors are members of the LGBTQIA+ community. Sure, they've made some ignorant comments about same sex couples in the past, but even those memories seem distant. I can't remember anything like that in the last few years.

No use easing them into the idea now. "Well, it's a good thing I'm marrying a man then, because he doesn't care if I swear. And lucky for you, because I'm pretty sure most women would hate you if you showed up wearing *that* to their wedding, especially the first time you meet them," I say, gesturing to her dress, but she's tilting her head to the side like she's confused. "Mother, you look like you're wearing a wedding dress!"

She glances down at the light silver, form-fitted, sparkly gown she has on as though she can't remember what she's wearing. "Darling, this is obviously not a wedding dress," she dismisses with a wave of her hand and an eye roll. "And I think I misunderstood the joke, your wife swears like a man?"

"No, I think you heard exactly what I said. I wasn't trying to hide it from you guys or anything. I thought I'd already told you about Liam, but it's been hard to reach you recently while you were traveling."

"Since when are you gay?"

"I'm bi, actually," I correct, and I see her shoulders visibly deflate.

"Oh, thank god. Then you can just marry a woman. If you need more time, we can talk about it. We never meant to pressure you into settling down so much that you resorted to marrying one of your friends to get the money."

My friends have been exchanging uncomfortable glances since my parents walked in here. Chad knows about the ultimatum, but he's the only person I ever told about it.

"Why don't we go see if they'll give us any whiskey to have in here," Chad says, clearly seeing this conversation is going to go poorly. He excuses himself from the room and my other friends awkwardly follow.

"Mother, it isn't like that." I huff out a breath, frustrated that I have to have this conversation at all. "Being bi doesn't mean that I'm going to just pick someone else because you think that gender would be easier for you to support. You wanted me to settle down and get married, to find someone to share my life with. I've done exactly what you hoped I would do. I'm in love, getting married *today*. It shouldn't matter what that person's gender is, you should just care if I'm happy." Exactly like Liam's dad did.

The comparison between our parents is jarring, a stark reminder of what I don't have, but have always wanted from my own. I turn to my father to see how he's taking the news. He doesn't look angry or upset, I didn't think he would, but he does look a little surprised still, wide eyes avoiding my gaze as they fix on my mother.

"You know what, I thought that it was important for you both to be here today, but for the life of me, I can't remember why. I'm getting married to someone I really love, who loves me back just as much. If you can be happy for us, then I'll see you at the reception. If you can't, then I guess you won't care that I'm leaving the city. I'd like to spend this time with my friends now if you could leave us alone," I say, walking to the door to hold it open for them.

My mother looks horrified by my demand, but it's like she can't get anything out, moving her mouth without sound. They both slowly exit the room, and my dad turns around as my mother is huffing down the hall. "I'm sorry, I'll talk to her. She's just surprised. I think we both are."

I don't say anything more as I turn around and head back into the room, letting the door slam shut. My friends return shortly after and they don't have any liquor with them, which is probably for the best. I don't need any today, I want to be totally clear-headed so that I can remember every happy moment of marrying Liam.

He'll be my husband today. It's easy to be happy when I think about that, so I push all thoughts of my parents out of my mind and focus on my man. In a few short hours, we'll be done with this show and can finally be together without worrying about cameras or other people interfering with our relationship.

I can't wait.

LIAM

Producer: It's your wedding day. What's going through your mind right now?

Liam: I think I'm still trying to process that this is real and it's happening. A few months ago, I didn't ever think I'd be on a show like this, and I definitely didn't think I'd be getting married to a man I fell for without seeing his face. But here we are. I just want to get to the part where he's mine and I'm his.

Today is surreal. I haven't seen some of my college friends in years, and to have them drop everything to come stand by my side on such short notice makes me realize that even though I might not see them as often as I'd like, I'm really lucky to have them. Between them, John, Jace, and my dad, it's obvious just how strong my support system really is.

I have a tendency to forget that with how much the farm consumes my time, but seeing them all here today, dressed up, joking around, it's a nice reminder that some friends stick around no matter how much time has passed or how shitty I am at keeping in touch with them.

I've also been thinking about my mom a lot today. I know she'd be happy for me and Blake, and that she would love his excited, outgoing, happy-go-lucky personality. I can totally picture her telling me that she's glad I found someone who's so carefree when I'm always so stressed out about the farm.

Part of me still can't believe we're getting married today. Maybe after the ceremony it will feel more real, or maybe I'm just really emotional today with all my people here, and so many thoughts of my mom, but I can't deny there's still that part of me that doesn't fully believe this whole thing happened like it did. *Like who let* me *of all people be on a reality show?* I'm just a random farmer, and this all feels very glamorous compared to my normal life. Looking back to the beginning of this show when Blake didn't even make my top ten is even crazier to think about, but I'm so glad I told myself to keep an open mind.

Blake is everything I needed. He's the best thing that's ever happened to me, and I can't wait until all this fanfare is over so that we can get back to a more casual reality.

A soft knock on the door draws my attention to my dad walking in, and the camera man turns to face him.

"How're you feeling today, son?"

I let out a breath and smile. "Good, I think. It doesn't feel real, though. I can't believe I found him only a few weeks ago, and in such a short time, we've made it here."

My dad reaches a hand out and places it on my arm. "Your mom wouldn't have thought it was crazy at all. She always said true love found you at the perfect moment, when you were both ready to receive it."

"She would have loved him, wouldn't she?"

"Absolutely," my dad agrees with the biggest smile on his face. Then he turns to my friends. "You guys mind giving us a minute?"

They all nod their agreement and head out the door.

He turns back to me once he sees we're alone, then he

reaches inside his suit pocket and pulls out an envelope. "She wrote you one last letter. Wanted me to give it to you on your wedding day."

I see the handwriting on the envelope and my throat is immediately tight as I fight back tears. I never thought I'd see another letter after my twenty-first birthday. I cherish every single one that my mom left for me, and knowing that she's with me in this unexpected way today makes everything even more surreal. My fingers shake as I reach out to take it from my dad, and I immediately pull him into a hug.

"Thank you," I whisper.

"She wanted to make sure she could still be here with you, no matter what."

I nod my head into his shoulder, not wanting to let go.

"I love you."

"Love you too, son. I'll give you a minute," he says when we break apart.

He claps me on the shoulder before walking out of the room, leaving me with the letter. I hold onto it for just a moment, tracing my name on the front where she's written,

For Liam's Wedding Day!

I steady myself, needing to take a deep breath because I know this will make me even more emotional than I already am. I'm just about to rip the adhesive on the back when I hear another knock at the door.

"Come in," I call out, tucking the letter safely into my pocket, already feeling raw. I don't want to be distracted when I read it.

The door swings open, and for a moment, I think it's one of the other contestants. In walks a woman who looks like she's attending her own wedding in a sparkly white dress. Her blonde hair is perfectly styled and her makeup is flawless. But her hazel eyes that match Blake's give her away, and I realize who she is before she even speaks.

"Hello, you must be Liam," she says in greeting. "I'm Blake's mother."

"Hi, Mrs. Barclay," I say, walking over to her.

Blake's told me enough about his parents for me to know that she's not the type to offer much warmth or affection, so I extend my hand instead of going for a hug, wanting to make a good first impression. She takes my hand briefly and offers me what I can only describe as a condescending smile filled with pity. She directs her attention to the camera person still in the room and asks them to give us a minute. They politely excuse themselves, but I don't think Blake's mother is aware of the other cameras that have been set up to blend in throughout the room without needing anyone to operate them, and I'm not going to say anything.

That small ball of anxiety that's been churning in my gut all morning suddenly grows in size as her expression immediately gives me a bad feeling about why she's really here.

Then, with a smile I can tell she's perfectly crafted, she says, "Listen, Liam. I'm sure you're a nice young man and all, considering you were somehow able to convince my son he wants to marry you, but let me be clear about something."

Fuuuuck. I don't like where this is going.

"Blake is easily influenced," she continues. "He has no real direction in his life, so he just follows whatever path is laid out for him at any given time. We tried to push football when he was younger to give him a sense of purpose. It was clear he'd never have the brains for anything more difficult or productive, but he couldn't even manage that. It's sad, really." She sighs, like she's actually pities her own son and isn't sounding like a horrible parent right now. "That's why we gave him the marriage ultimatum. We thought it would push him to finally take his relationships seriously, like his siblings have. Then he'd have no choice but to make something of himself with a good wife by his side."

I'm sorry, did she just say… marriage ultimatum?

"Um, what ultimatum?" I choke out the word, sure I must have heard her wrong. Blake would have told me if anything like she was suggesting was true. *Right?*

She purses her lips. "Of course he didn't tell you."

I don't say anything. *Can't* say anything. Just wait for her to continue as I feel like my entire world is tilting off its axis.

"We told him he needed to be married by his thirtieth birthday, which as I'm sure you're aware, is next month. Or we'd cut him off."

My stomach plummets, that anxiety I was trying to ignore earlier seems so mild compared to the absolute panic level of dread and adrenaline now coursing through my veins. I need to calm down, but despite the deep breaths I'm attempting, I can't help but feel a sense of deja vu, like I'm back in that college dorm, walking in on my boyfriend hooking up with someone else. Like the happy future I've built up is just in my head and the harsh reality is crashing down around me to reveal I'm just being used by someone yet again.

There's no way he's marrying me for money, though, right?

He told me he loves me. He proposed to me first. He said he wanted to move to the farm and help my dad and me make it as great as we know it can be.

None of this is making any sense.

His mom is either unaware or unconcerned with the mental spiral she has set off inside me, continuing like this is a casual chat and not possibly the worst moment of my life. "Now, he's here, pulling this 'I'm bisexual' nonsense when he's only ever dated women. I know he was unhappy about the ultimatum, but I never thought he'd go this far just to spite us. We told him we'd give him more time so he could find a wife." She sighs like this is so inconvenient for her to have to explain to me. "It's impressive, really, I didn't think he had this level of commitment in him. But he's proved his point. It can end now."

My heart is racing at what feels like a very dangerous rate, and I'm distantly concerned that I might be about to throw up on this woman's very expensive-looking dress. I don't want to believe he'd use me, but why would she make this up? I know I need to call Blake, I need to hear his side of the story, but what if it's all true? I'm desperate for him to have some logical explanation for this, but what if there isn't one?

God, why wouldn't he just fucking tell me?

Is it because she's telling me the truth? Has this whole thing been about money to him, am I just a pawn in this family's schemes?

I don't want to believe that.

But then I remember his vague comments about his parents being sick of him not holding down a real job, about him only having to start thinking about money recently. Of how quickly he jumped from calling himself straight to wanting to be with me. My stomach clenches as a message he sent me way back in the beginning, before we'd even met, is suddenly clear as day in my mind. We were talking about what we'd do with the prize money if we finished the show, and he'd said he would "just be happy to leave the show married" and that his "new spouse can decide what they want to do with it." Is that because he knew keeping his parents' money would be worth more than the prize money anyway? Because at the end of the day, the only thing he cared about was getting married?

"I'll make this easy for you to understand," his mother continues in a smooth, practiced voice that I now absolutely hate. "If you marry Blake today, we *will* cut him off. He needs a wife who can give him children, not some *buddy* to hang out with and continue the same aimless life he's been leading for years. And as you know, Blake has no skills, nor work experience. He has no drive."

A part of me wants to defend him, say that isn't true, but I don't know what to think anymore, so I'm still stunned into silence as she goes on.

"I'm sorry that you got caught up in all this. But if Blake lying to you about his motives isn't enough to make you want to end things, if he's somehow truly convinced you to care for him, then I'd like to be perfectly clear that you two staying together will only hurt you both. He doesn't really love you, the only thing he's ever cared about in his life is his dog. Whatever he's said to you has been about keeping his money. He'll change his tune when he suddenly has nothing, and if you go through with this, that's exactly what he'll have. Nothing. His life as he knows it is over, understand? You'll be stuck in a marriage with someone who doesn't actually want to be with you."

She looks at me expectantly, like she's waiting for me to respond.

I stand there frozen, her words spinning in a loop in my head as the room begins to feel like it's shrinking. I want Blake, I want him so badly. I *love* him. I want to marry him. But was any of it real? And even if it was, can I cost him everything?

Even if everything about him lying to me isn't real, there's no way I can support him the way he's used to. The farm barely scrapes by as it is. There's no *wealth,* and I've seen the way Blake lives. Even when we've talked about the farm, and he seemed excited, it was about wanting to upgrade things. What if we can't afford to do that? Could he handle the kind of lifestyle that having almost no money leads to?

She clears her throat, giving me a pointed look.

"Does Blake know you're here? Know that you're saying this to me?" I manage to choke out.

Her expression doesn't change and I know there's no way she's going to give me an answer. She doesn't care about me or my feelings, she just wants me gone. I still don't know what to believe about Blake, but I truly can't comprehend the type of mother who would sacrifice her own son's chance at happiness just for her own ego. *And why? Because I'm a man?*

I have a long list of insults I would like to use to label this woman. But I can't even focus on that as my thoughts keep going back to Blake.

What if this wasn't real?

What if everything I thought we were building was just... a convenient way for him to keep his wealth?

What if he chose me because he had no other option?

Was he going to marry someone, *anyone* from the show, no matter what?

Has his real search for happiness been about the money all along?

The weight of all my past insecurities comes rushing back in full force. The feeling of not being enough. Of being someone's second choice, of being the backup plan.

Now, of being the mark to manipulate in the name of money. Clearly this conversation is over, so I walk past her, needing to find Blake. *I need him to tell me this isn't true.* That there was no ultimatum that led to him deciding to be with a man for the first time instead of just ending it when we met.

When I make it to his room at the end of the hall, I push the door open and he instantly smiles when he sees me. *That fucking smile.* He's already in his tux, and he looks like my biggest fantasy.

But I can't let him distract me, I need to ask. Need to know.

"Hey, babe, what are you—"

I don't let him finish. I can't get sucked in by his disarming smile and cheery tone. I need to ignore his charm. I need to get this out. "Did your parents give you an ultimatum? That you had to get married by thirty or they'd cut you off?"

He stills.

Completely freezes.

And I have my answer.

I *need* him to deny it. To immediately say, "no, of course not," but the way he's looking at me, completely shocked, guilt shining in his eyes, he might as well have ripped my heart out and stomped on it.

"Liam, just—just let me explain—"

"Did they?" I bite out.

Blake exhales like he's trying to delay the inevitable. "Well, technically, but—"

I can't do this. If he says anything else, I can't hear it above the static in my head, the swarm of emotions of shock and anger and hurt that flood my system. I can't believe I was about to marry someone who only agreed in the first place because it's what he thought would be the easiest way to get money.

"I can't do this," I barely manage to say above a whisper. Blake's eyes widen in panic, but I don't let him speak. "I can't, Blake. I can't do this right now. This is a huge bomb to drop on me on our wedding day."

The cameras are pointed at us, and I need to get away from them. I can't take the scrutiny for a second longer. I already feel like an idiot, I won't let them draw this out and make it even more embarrassing.

Blake moves forward to reach out to me, but I step back. "Please, don't," I plead. "I just… I need to go."

"Go where?" His voice sounds panicked too. But is he upset that I'm leaving? Or does he think he'll lose his money if I do? Little does he know the new twist his mom just threw in there— that if I do marry him, he'll lose it all anyway.

Was he just never going to tell me? What was his plan in all of this? Marry me, get the money, pretend to be happy on my family's farm just long enough to serve me divorce papers and cash out? Stay until he could run back to his fancy condo in the city where he could laugh about it with his friends? *"Remember that one time I married a guy to prove to my parents that they shouldn't cut me off? Ha-ha, so fucking funny."*

Blake looks so upset, and I want to believe it's at the idea of losing me, but this has all been too much to process at once, and I know that there's no way I'll be able to calm down enough to rationally make any major life decisions anytime soon. *Like getting married.* I need to get away from all of this right now and get some fucking air.

I shake my head. "I don't know. I just know that I can't marry you today. I can't say yes to someone who doesn't choose me for me with no ulterior motive." I wipe the tears from my eyes, knowing that I'm about to leave here unmarried today. "I just wish you told me."

Before he can say anything else, I walk out of his room. Then I practically run out of the hotel and into the street. I need to get away from those fucking cameras, I need space to breathe before I figure out what the fuck I'm supposed to do now.

BLAKE

Cameraperson: Fuck. I did *not* see that coming.

Producer: Shut up and keep filming.

"*I just know that I can't marry you today. I can't say yes to someone who doesn't choose me for me with no ulterior motive.*" Liam's words echo in my head like a broken record, but no matter how many times I replay what just happened, I can't believe it's real.

I was so happy only a few minutes ago, so excited to marry him and start our lives together. I look down at the blue tux I just finished putting on. I'm supposed to marry him wearing this. We picked coordinating outfits. We looked hot as fuck standing next to each other at the boutique. Trying them on for our friends was fun, silly, and such a great memory.

How could he think I don't want him?

How could he walk away that easily?

I'm standing in the middle of the suite, still staring at the door Liam just walked out of. He made it abundantly clear he doesn't want me to follow him, and even though I really want to,

I don't think I can move at all. I'm internally screaming at myself to chase after him, and yell, and beg, and do whatever I can to force him to listen until he understands that whatever he thinks about me right now, about our relationship and how I feel about him, isn't true.

But my body isn't responding. I'm frozen in place.

Is this shock? Could this be a nightmare I'm about to wake up from and realize none of it is real?

But then an arm is wrapping around my shoulders, guiding me to the couch closest to me. Someone is talking softly near my ear, encouraging me to sit down I think, but I'm not really comprehending their words. I fall more than sit on the couch, still numbly staring at the door. Every part of me is wishing and hoping and praying to anyone who will listen that Liam will open it again and be ready to talk to me.

But it doesn't open.

He doesn't come back.

Is it really over? Was I really so close to having everything I didn't know I wanted—someone to love, who loved me, a home, a supportive family, the animals—only to have it fall apart at the last possible moment?

I feel like I'm back at training camp, being told by the coaches that I wasn't good enough for a spot on the team. That they expected more from me, but I just wasn't cut out for the NFL.

I thought that would be the worst thing that ever happened to me, that the memory would forever haunt me as the worst day of my life.

But it doesn't even come close to right now.

This is so, so much worse.

I thought I loved football more than anything, that getting to play professionally was the only thing that could make me happy.

I was so unbelievably wrong.

The excitement I felt getting drafted, the promise of playing in the NFL, that can't even begin to compare to how I've felt the last few weeks planning my life with Liam. Every day that I've spent with him has been filled with so much joy and laughter. There have been quiet moments of peace that I've never experienced before. I'm not worried about entertaining him or making sure he's having a good time like I sometimes am with my friends. I've never felt like I needed to prove my worth to him like I do with my family.

I felt like I had finally found my purpose in life, planning for everything we could do to improve his farm. Like the life we were building was the one I was always meant to live. The few days that we spent there were more rewarding to me than any of the years I've spent in the city.

And now it's just… gone?

Even if he's furious with me for not telling him about my parent's ultimatum, how can he really believe I don't love him? That our connection is fake or forced?

"Do you want to talk about it?" Chad asks, and I guess I've been sitting here for long enough that my friends' voices are cutting through my racing thoughts. They're all sitting around me, like the world's worst huddle, probably so they can have a clear view of how I handle my life falling apart. I glance around at the pitying expressions they're offering, unsure what the fuck I'm supposed to say to them. There's still a camera pointed at me, but honestly nothing they get now can make this any worse, so the audience might as well see how heartbroken I am.

"Did you really only agree to marry him for money?" Ash sounds nearly as disappointed in me as I am with myself.

"No," I insist, because by the time I proposed, the money was the last thing on my mind. We got engaged because we're in love, no matter my motivation at the beginning of the show. I'm confident in that.

But then I deflate back onto the couch, deciding to give my

friends the truth, if only so they might be able to help me work out what to do next. "But, it was the main reason I signed up for the show, and it also played a factor into why I was so willing to date a man when I had always thought I was straight. Well, that and the connection we formed."

"And you never told him?" Chad checks. More than anyone, he understands the journey I've been on because of the ultimatum. He was the only person I ever confided in about it, and hopefully over the last couple of weeks as we've all gotten to interact, he's seen how Liam has become so much more important to me than the money ever was.

"Obviously I should have told him," I concede. "But honestly, it stopped being about the money for me a long time ago. I'd give it all up right now if it meant Liam and I could still get married. Wealth has never made me as happy as he does. The only reason I've recently thought about it at all is because I want to use that money to help Liam expand his farm."

Ash looks more sympathetic now as he squeezes my arm in support. "Maybe it isn't over. That was a lot for him to find out on his wedding day. He probably feels a bit blindsided, and like he isn't in a good spot to be able to say 'yes' to you today. He could be more open to hearing your side of things once he's cooled down and is away from all *this*," he says, gesturing around to the cameras. Liam has never loved being filmed, and has tried to keep most of our important conversations away from the cameras, so that tracks.

Fuck, I hope he's right.

"How did he find out, anyway?" Chad asks, and I snap my head in his direction.

"That's a great question. You're the only person I've ever told about it, and since it obviously wasn't you…" I trail off, thinking for a moment, but I know there's only one other person to blame.

"My own parents must have sabotaged the wedding they

were so desperate for me to have." I've never thought I had the world's best parents by any stretch of the imagination, but this whole experience has really shown me just how horrible they really are. I'm so pissed off and hurt and fucking sad. I'm angry for Liam, too, because he didn't deserve what I'm sure was the wrath of my mother, and I'm so fucking angry at myself for not telling him.

Fuck, fuck, fuck!

It never felt like a good time. Between the rocky start with thinking he was a woman, then Rachel, and then how good things were. Our timeline just moved so fast, and I didn't want to ruin what we had by planting doubt in his mind. I *want* him, and I never wanted him to question my motivation for being with him. But by not telling him, I realize I just exacerbated that doubt and all his insecurities.

My anger seems to be enough for my legs to start working again. I push up from the couch and storm out of the room on a mission to find the assholes who gave me their DNA. The people who are supposed to love me unconditionally, but have only ever cared about how *I* affected *their* image.

The cameraperson follows me out of the room, and I can hear him mumbling into a phone about finding my parents, and someone responds that they're in the hotel bar, so that's where we go. They're sitting at a raised table with my siblings and their spouses not far from the bar, an almost empty martini glass in my mother's hand, and a more full scotch in front of my father.

My mother notices me, or more likely the camera, first, and my father turns to see what has her suddenly sitting up straighter and putting down her drink. "Blake, what are you doing here? Shouldn't you be getting ready?" my dad asks, sounding surprised. He's never been one to lie, he isn't very good at it, so his reaction seems genuine enough for me to direct my fury at my mother, *just as I suspected.*

"You evil bitch," I spit out at her.

Her eyes widen, and her mouth opens, but that must be the only range of emotion her plastic face is capable of expressing.

My father's face, though, is very clearly displaying his surprise at my insult. "Blake! You don't speak to your mother that way. What is going on with you?"

"Why don't you ask your wife?" I sneer, directing all my attention at the woman I desperately wish I wasn't related to. "Why don't you ask her why my fiancé just told me he couldn't marry me before leaving the hotel?"

"Darling, what happened? I thought we talked about supporting them?" he asks, sounding alarmed as he turns to stare at my mother.

She glances at the camera before having the audacity to lie right to my face. "Liam left? I'm not sure why you think I would have anything to do with that. Are you alright?"

I'm not a violent person, I can't remember ever wishing anyone else physical harm. But right now, I can't stop myself from fantasizing about all the horrible accidents that could result in my mother's untimely demise. Not like I have anything left to lose today. But as much as I truly hate my mother right now, I know it wouldn't actually help anything. And Liam would probably be disappointed if I did anything to hurt anyone.

Plus the fucking camera is right in my face.

Fuck, I'm so sick of these fucking cameras! Can't a man have a public breakdown without being recorded?

I take a deep breath and attempt to remain calm as I call her out on her bullshit. "Liam asked me if my parents had given me an ultimatum to get married by thirty or be cut off, and obviously the only people who know about your threat are the two of you. So tell me, Mother, why did you feel the need to interfere in my relationship *hours* before I was set to get married?"

As soon as the words are out of my mouth, I know the answer. "Is it because he's a man? Are we really adding 'homophobic' to the long list of reasons you're a shitty human? I bet all the queer people who donate to your charity will just love to see how you sabotaged your own son's same-sex marriage."

"Debra, is that where you disappeared off to?" my father scolds, sounding appalled by my accusation. Maybe one of my parents will prove they give a shit about me after all.

"Don't be ridiculous," my mother hisses, eyes bouncing between us and the camera, no doubt calculating how she can redeem her reputation. "You were the one who was clearly lying to the poor boy. He didn't deserve to have you trick him into a relationship." Her tone is dripping with false concern now, and it makes me feel physically sick to think that Liam might actually believe that's what happened between us.

"I didn't trick him into anything!" I nearly shout. "I'm in love with him. I told you that! And the last few weeks have been the first time in my life that I've ever been truly happy."

My mother rolls her eyes, and I know whatever final, desperate part of me that was holding out hope that I could one day have a good relationship with this woman, is officially gone.

My siblings are gaping at us, gazes pinging between my mother and me. My father must have seen her roll her eyes too, because he gasps at the motion before turning to me. "Blake, the only reason I agreed to this ridiculous ultimatum in the first place was because I could see how unhappy you were. I know I'm too focused on my job, and I've never been good at making time for you, but I really did hope it would be the push you needed to find something you're passionate about. Love can be a powerful motivator."

His admission completely surprises me. My father has always been the easier parent for me to get along with, but after my football career ended, it was like we didn't have anything left to talk about. I thought that meant he no longer cared.

Now he's making it sound like he's always wanted me to be happy?

Could he really have been that shitty at showing it all these years? Or did we both let my mother's actions overshadow his own?

"I was never planning to actually cut you off. You're my son, I just wanted you to have some direction in your life, and I thought this would be the motivation you needed."

"Seriously?" I definitely do shout it this time.

"Well, yeah." My father shrugs, and I ignore the huff of complaint from my mother, too shocked by this new information.

Before I'd signed up for the show, I'd been consumed by their ultimatum for so long. Trying to find someone to marry was all I cared about until I met Liam, and I shifted my focus to learning more about him and planning our future on his farm. It's unbelievable to think after all this time, it was just an empty threat.

At the same time, I know I never would have met Liam without it, so in a fucked-up way, I'm glad they did it. No matter how devastated I am right now to not be marrying him today, I wouldn't trade the time I've spent with him for anything.

Wait a fucking second.

His words echo in my head again. *"I just know that I can't marry you today. I can't say yes to someone who doesn't choose me for me without an ulterior motive."*

Liam said that he couldn't marry me *today*. Not that he never wanted to see me again.

He said he couldn't say yes to someone who doesn't choose him, *but I do*. I would choose Liam over the money in a heartbeat. I would choose him over anyone and anything.

And I intend to do just that.

If Liam needs me to prove to him that I'll choose him every day for the rest of our lives, I will. Even if we never actually get married. Even if I never touch another cent of my parents' money to show him how much more he means to me than it ever did.

I look down at my finger and twist the ring he gave me, the

one his mother made for his father. He wouldn't have given it to me if he didn't love me, if he didn't want to build a life with me.

I promised him my future, and I intend to keep that promise.

If he needs some space to cool down, I'll give it to him.

But I'm not giving up on us.

I promised to help them on their farm, and I have a feeling I know someone who might be slightly more willing to hear my side of things when I explain how much I love his son and just want him to be happy.

He might even let me stay with him until Liam is ready to talk.

Liam deserves to be happy, and I'm selfish enough to think I could be his happily ever after. Until he explicitly tells me to get out of his life, I'm not going anywhere.

LIAM

Losing my mom at ten years old felt like the world cracked in half. At the time, it felt like my dad and I were stranded on the wrong side of life without her. It was a slow, excruciating kind of pain, one that built and built as she grew weaker and weaker until it finally swallowed her whole. And then, just like that, she was gone.

We knew it was coming, but knowing didn't make it hurt any less. Nothing prepared us for that kind of loss. The grief, the absence, the helplessness of it all—knowing that nothing we did could have changed the outcome, that no amount of love or bargaining could have bought us more time.

But at least I understood it. Understood losing her to something no one could fight forever. Even if I fucking hated cancer with every fiber of my being, I could wrap my head around what was happening. I had time to process it.

None of it was her fault. She fought. She held on as long as she could, for me, for my dad. And ultimately, it wasn't her choice to leave. Losing her was like a slow-burning fire we all saw coming but were powerless to stop.

Losing Blake was like a sudden, violent explosion—unexpected and over before I could make sense of the wreckage.

Because while I'm positive my mom would have never left if she had a choice, Blake did. He made a choice.

And it wasn't me.

Well, he wouldn't have chosen me if he wasn't in a blind dating situation with an ultimatum to push him to date me. A man.

Losing someone to lies and deception, to the reality that I was never the first choice from the start? That I was just a means to an end, or a loophole? This is a different kind of pain. One that feels like it's clawing its way through my chest, hollowing me out from the inside.

I was *so sure* about us. So sure he was my future, that he was it for me. I let myself believe that what we had was real. That I'd found my person. I like him so much. I *love* him, and I thought I made it clear. He said the same words back to me, even if I said them first. But the second his mother's words sank in, and I had to question what I really meant to him, it felt like the ground was ripped out from under me.

Now, I'm waking up alone in my bed. Again. When I thought I would be waking up next to my husband. We should be wrapped up together while he asks for five more minutes. But he isn't here. It's just me and my broken heart that won't allow me to focus on anything other than how much I miss what I thought we had.

Even though Blake was only here for three days, I'd built an entire life in my head of our future. Working together to expand the farm with the money we made from the show. Hanging out with the chickens and building them what would probably have been a chicken castle more so than a coop, knowing Blake. Drinking coffee together on the front porch, cooking together in the kitchen, and falling asleep together in our bed.

But, obviously, he's not here. It's the third day of waking up without hearing a word from him.

He's going to be asleep for hours still, on his fancy mattress, in his expensive condo, with all his money. He'll probably find a wife soon, just like his mother wants, and he'll forget all about his bi experiment with me.

I go through the motions of my morning routine, but my mind always drifts back to thoughts of Blake. I've been throwing myself into work, trying to bury the pain and heartbreak, but it's no use. I've made a list of things to fix that don't actually need fixing, cleaned things that weren't dirty, and completed chores twice just to stay busy. But even working from sunup to sundown hasn't allowed my thoughts to stray from him.

Nothing helps, and nothing makes it stop.

The hardest part of my days is feeding the damn chickens.

The spot we got engaged, where *he* proposed to *me*. Was it just so he'd have a guaranteed yes and get his money?

My mind spins as I enter the gate to their yard, stuck on that proposal that felt so sincere, and the way he'd refer to himself as their daddy. I haven't had the heart to tell the chickens yet that it's just me again. The thought alone makes my throat tighten when I imagine speaking the words out loud. I know they don't care, but his supposed love for them was infectious, and has me feeling like they really were his children, even after such a short time. I clutch the feed bucket a little tighter as I scatter the grain. They, of course, don't know that anything has changed. They still run up to me, excited to eat and be let out for the day. Blake probably isn't even someone they remember.

But in such a short time, he's taken over every inch of this farm for me.

This whole place reminds me of him, and before I can stop it, my vision blurs and tears start falling. I can't believe I have any left in me after the last three days, but lo and behold, here they are. I try to swipe them away, but they won't stop. This has happened every time I've come over here. It's inevitable, the pain is so fucking deep, so raw, that I can't hold myself together even during normal tasks.

I really thought he loved me. I believed that he chose me because he wanted to be with me. He was *that* good at lying. I couldn't even see the deception.

Every time I try to reason with myself that it *must have* become real for him at some point—that he couldn't fake the emotion he put into our relationship, the intimacy we shared— his mother's harsh words come back to me in full force.

"He has no real direction in his life, so he just follows whatever path is laid out for him at any given time."

I dab my eyes with my shirt and realize just how much I've been crying. I guess I should head back to the house to eat something and change. I think I need a minute.

I'm so mad at myself about it too. I'd tried so hard to keep my guard up this time, until I was absolutely sure. But he made me believe he wanted this as badly as I did. I finally let myself think that I could have the kind of love my parents had. *I even told him that.* I confided in him. But this whole time, it had been an act, a way for him to make sure I said yes so that he could get his money.

Am I just a complete fool to believe that any of what we had was real? *I must be.*

Thoughts of my past relationship keep rushing back to the forefront of my mind—the man who strung me along, let me believe we were building something together, all while keeping another relationship in the background. Those feelings that I thought I'd gotten over, of how small and stupid I felt when I found out. How used he'd made me feel when I'd realized I was just an *option* when once again, I had thought I was his future.

This feels so much worse, though. Blake was supposed to be my forever—when I was just a payday to him.

My heart hurts, a constant stabbing pain in my chest that's

impossible to ignore as I drop onto the couch and continue to cry. I'm exhausted by my own grief after days of enduring this. My whole body aches at this point.

And because everything seems to be harder than it needs to be right now, there's a knock at the door right after I settle on the couch. I don't even try to hide my groan, my dad has been trying to give me space, but it must finally be time for him to come check on me. He keeps telling me he can handle the farm chores, but if I sit here for too long, wallowing in my sorrow with nothing to give me a sense of purpose, I don't know if I'll ever go back outside. I'm scared I'll lose myself completely in the despair I'm feeling.

I force myself to stand, grumbling the entire time I shuffle to the door, I really don't want to have to pretend I'm better than I am in front of my dad. It's bad enough that Blake deceived me, but he'd won my dad over too. I hate that he believed in us as much as I did, and that he's now forced to have a front row seat to my heartbreak after seeing how happy I thought Blake and I were.

I open the door, trying to muster up the strength to fake a smile, but it's not my dad.

It's Blake.

What the hell is he doing here?

"Hey," he says softly, gently, like he's approaching a wounded animal and doesn't want to be attacked.

I wipe my tears from my cheeks and try to pull myself together, though I know he's already seen what state I'm in. *Whatever, I'm in this emotional state because he broke my heart.* I shouldn't have to pretend like I'm okay when I'm not. He can see just how much he broke me with his lies. The thing I told him I hate more than anything.

"What are you doing here?" I finally manage to ask, wishing I sounded angrier.

"I had to see you, L."

I shake my head because I can't do this right now. I'm so raw already, I can't hear that he's sorry, but he did what he had to do for his parents and their money.

"Blake, I can't—"

"No," he interrupts. "Just, please, Liam. I need to get this out. Please let me explain before you decide you're done with me."

I remain silent, staring at him blankly. He's the one who did this, I didn't *decide* anything. But he looks determined, and I don't think getting rid of him will be as easy as shutting the door in his face. So, I resign myself to a few more minutes of torture in his company, to stare at the man I wanted to spend my life with.

I'd rather hear whatever excuse he's come up with now, rip the Band-Aid off. Maybe it'll give me some closure, rather than sitting here wallowing in my confusion over what really happened, letting the questions tear me apart.

"I was an idiot," he starts. "A coward. I should have told you about the ultimatum the second we got serious. I should have told you, and I'm *so* sorry. I don't know why I didn't. I mean, I think a part of me was scared that if I told you, that you'd see me the way my mom does—a spoiled failure who couldn't amount to anything on my own."

He lets out a huff of air, and I open my mouth to argue, but he holds up a hand.

"I know that's not how you see me, Liam. I do. But when you left, it felt like she was right. And I'm so sorry you were blindsided, that you felt betrayed. I never wanted to hurt you, and I hate that just because you're a man, she deemed you not good enough for me. I had no idea she was such a homophobic bitch. I regret not telling you. I know it'll be the biggest regret of my life."

I can tell he's angry, but if we're doing this, I know I need to ask the questions I've been stewing over the last few days. I need to know exactly what happened. "Did you know?"

His brows furrow, clearly confused by my question. "Know what?"

"That she was going to say that to me? Threaten to cut you off anyway if I married you?"

His expression hardens, and I see realization dawn in his eyes.

"No." He huffs. "Absolutely not. I had no idea she even said that until right now. I had no clue she was going to speak to you at all." He stands up a little straighter. "Is that why you left, babe? Because she threatened to cut me off if we went through with it?"

No, you lied to me. You never really wanted me, you just wanted your money. I'm trying to remind myself of the real problem here. Sure, what his mom did was shitty, but he's the one who hid the ultimatum from me in the first place. If he ever truly wanted our relationship to last, he would have been honest with me about it. We talked about money, and he had plenty of opportunities to come clean after we'd gotten serious. I told him how much honesty mattered to me. He knew and he still chose not to tell me.

It's hard to focus on that, though, when his handsome features are filled with what looks like genuine longing, like he wants this conversation to actually resolve things between us and not just ease his guilty conscience.

I'm… confused.

I can't help but feel a little ashamed, either. I probably should have stayed to talk things through more, even if I knew we couldn't get married that day. I wasn't going to be in a place to walk down the aisle, the news was too shocking, and I just needed to get away from the cameras. But should I have told him what his mom said?

I nod, numbly, before finding my voice again. "It was part of it." He's looking at me with so much hope, but I can't forget the rest of why I left. "But the main problem was you lying, Blake. You made me feel like a pawn in your scheme to keep your family's money. How was I supposed to feel, when I told you honesty was so important to me, and you never told me about this huge thing? I assumed you only dated me, a man, because of the money. How can I trust what was real and what was you manipulating me to agree to marry you so that you could fulfill the ultimatum requirement?"

"It stopped being about the money a long time ago, Liam," he assures me. "I swear to you, I don't care about any of that. My dad admitted that he wasn't going to cut me off after I confronted them." He swallows hard and grabs my hands, looking me in the eyes. "But I *will* give it up. Every penny. If you need me to do that to prove that you're what's important to me, I'll give it all up."

His voice cracks, and I know what that offer would mean for him. Losing his wealth would change his entire way of life. *Is he serious?* What could he possibly have to gain from promising me that?

Other than another chance to be with me... could he really mean it? Was what we had real after all?

"Please, L. I will do anything to prove to you that you're what really matters to me. I choose you, Liam. I promise I will *always* choose you—over money, over anyone else. I just want *you*. Everything we shared was real, and I'm so sorry that I didn't do enough to make you believe that, that what she said was enough to plant doubt in your mind."

His voice is breaking more and more with each plea. Part of me wants to reach out and pull him into my arms to comfort him, but I don't move.

"I don't care what it takes," he continues. "I'll donate it. I'll put it in a fund for the farm. Anything. You tell me what you want me to do, and I'll do it. The only thing I need is you. Just you."

I exhale slowly. I want what he's saying to be real so badly. I want to be able to believe him and forget all about the last few days.

But it isn't that simple, and there's something I still need to understand.

"Why did you come on the show, Blake?"

He swallows and steadies himself. "The money," he admits. "I won't pretend like it wasn't my reason for signing up. Chad was the only one who knew about the ultimatum. He mentioned the show when he saw how much I was struggling with dating. At the time, I figured, why not? I'd get married to some girl that was only looking for a husband anyway, and we'd have the money and be happy enough. But then I met you, and I knew that kind of aimless future would never really be enough. I met you and everything changed because *you're it* for me, Liam. No one else."

He looks sheepish as he steadies himself to say the next part, and the guilty look on his face has my gut sinking.

"I need to say this because I'm promising complete honesty, but please know I love you exactly the way you are, Liam." He swallows and lets out a deep breath, obviously nervous to say whatever he's about to.

I hate this. I want to believe that this whole breakup has been a misunderstanding, but I need to hear everything before I let myself hope.

"When I found out I matched with you, a man, I thought about leaving. I really did. And while the money definitely crossed my mind, the louder thought was how excited I was about the relationship I'd been building with you, Liam. I wasn't ready for it to end. I thought to myself, *how different could it really be?* You were still the same person I wanted to stay up all night talking to, the person I'd really grown to care about, and I knew I wanted to stay for *you*."

The tears that haven't stopped for long since I left the city threaten to fall again, but I have to get through this. "And?" I push.

"And it turned out to be the best thing that ever happened to me. The money became totally and completely irrelevant, because *I love you,* Liam, and I want to spend the rest of my life with you. I don't care about your gender, I care about who you are, how kind and strong and independent you are. I care more about seeing your smile and earning your laughs than I ever did about my life in the city. I love everything about you." He swipes a hand through his hair then looks me right in my eyes, begging me to believe him. "I still want this, if you'll have me. I'm sorry things got so fucked up, but I will prove to you every day for the rest of our lives how serious I am about you."

I squeeze my eyes shut. I can't look at his desperate expression while I process this. I'm still hurting, but it suddenly feels a little easier to breathe.

Ten minutes ago, I was trying to forget all about him. Can we really move on that easily? Can I trust him again after one conversation? This is about more than a simple miscommunication, trust goes so much deeper than that, and I think this whole thing has highlighted some of my own insecurities and unhealthy trauma responses. If we jump back into a serious relationship like nothing bad had happened, I don't think that would be setting ourselves up for a very healthy relationship. Taking a deep breath, I try to keep my voice steady as I make a decision. "I believe you, I just… I need more time."

Blake nods immediately. "I know. I didn't expect you to forgive me right away. That's why I'm staying with your dad."

"You're what?" I ask, convinced I misheard.

He looks away, suddenly nervous about his admission. "I know you, Liam. I knew I would need to earn your trust back, and I don't think I can do that from the city. Plus, I didn't want to be away from the farm any longer than I had to be. So, I've been talking to your dad and he agreed to let me stay with him."

"You're serious?"

"Dead serious," he says, eyes locked on mine. "I want to prove to you that I still want the future we were planning. Even if we never get married, I don't care. I want to get back what we had. As long as I get to be with you. That's the only thing in the world I truly care about."

My mind is all over the place, I didn't expect any of this. "Blake—"

"I love you," he interrupts. "I love *you*, and I don't care how long it takes. You're worth waiting for, and I'll be here whenever you're ready. I'll prove it to you every day just how much I love you."

I do believe him, but trust isn't something that instantly returns after an apology—even one this big and sincere. He seems to understand that, though, I can't believe he's already coordinated staying with my dad. I wonder how much groveling he had to do there.

"Wait, is Lucky here too?"

"Yeah, your dad instantly bonded with her. They're probably still cuddled up on his couch. I've done a lot of research on how to introduce dogs to chickens, and it needs to be a slow process, so he promised to keep her inside."

Well, that's fucking adorable. As impressed as I am by his gesture, and as much as I know my heart is already opening itself up to him again, I also know that I need to give myself the time he's offering. I need to do this, both for me, and to give us any real chance. My emotions have really been through the wringer these last few days, and I know I'm still holding on to some hurt and hesitation over what happened. I need to be sure I can truly and completely forgive him, or it might end up causing problems for us down the line.

"I don't know how long it will take," I admit. "This has brought up a lot of shit from my past I thought I'd already dealt with. I went to therapy and everything, but I guess it was deeper than I realized."

Blake nods and reaches out a hand to take mine in his. It's not a tight grip, more so a gesture to let me know he's here to listen and support me. "If you want to talk, I want to listen."

I hesitate, but remind myself he deserves to know. He just bared his soul to me, and if we're going to make this work, I can offer him the same in return. Clearing my throat, I give his hand a little squeeze and offer a small smile. "I was with this guy in college who made me think I was his future. It was nothing like *this*"—I gesture between us—"not even close. But for being that young, it felt real. Turns out, I was naive to think that, because he was still long-distance dating his high school girlfriend the entire time. I walked in on them having sex and was shocked to find out I was the other guy."

Blake lets out a groan and his face turns red as his grip on my hand tightens a little. "Are you fucking kidding me?" he practically growls.

"I wish I was." I shake my head. "I felt like the biggest idiot. Like I should have *known* that I was just an experiment to him while he was living another life, the one he actually wanted to be living. He ended up marrying her, and I was left with a lot of healing to do around being someone's second choice and experiment. It's part of why honesty is so important to me because that situation was so shocking. He also really liked football and sports. I spent a lot of time trying to be enough for him, and it turns out no matter what I did, it never would've mattered."

As much as I don't want to hurt Blake, I need to get the next part out. He said total honesty, and I need to show him that same level of respect. "That's how I felt when your mom told me about the ultimatum, Blake, and even more so when you couldn't deny that you'd hidden it from me. Like I was a convenient experiment to you while you earned the money you were really after. It felt like walking in on them all over again. It seemed like once you married me, you'd secure your wealth and could move on with your straight-guy life, forgetting all about me."

"No. Never, Liam. My straight-guy life is so over. I want my future to be you and only you." He steps forward, cradling my face in his hands, forcing me to meet his hazel eyes that are welling up with tears. "You're it for me, babe. There is no moving on. You're not convenient, you never were. You're my person. The *only* person I want to spend my life with. My mom is a selfish asshole who cares way more about her image than she ever has about her own children, and I'm sorry I didn't protect you from her hate. I'm so sorry she made you doubt yourself, and us, and I promise, you never have to see her again."

I simply nod.

"Thank you for telling me," he says as he pulls our foreheads together.

"I'm sorry, Blake. I'm sorry for not having more of a conversation before leaving. I just needed to get out of there, and hearing that it was true hurt so much. I still need time, though," I remind him, pulling back even though there's a part of me that never wants to let go. "I need to make sure we're in a good place before we can move forward so there's no tension or resentment that comes up in the future, but know I still care about you, and I still love you."

"I know," he assures. "And I'll give you as much time as you need. But I'm not going anywhere. Unless you *explicitly* tell me to leave. I'm not trying to force myself on you if you really want to be done. I promise to respect you if you tell me to go. I'm just trying to show you how much you mean to me, and to continue to choose you. If I ever earn the right to wear this again, I'll be honored."

He takes my hand, carefully placing my father's ring, the ring I gave him, in my palm before gently closing my fist around it. Then he leaves a soft kiss on my forehead before turning to walk out the door.

I'm still kind of in shock over what just happened, over how much might have changed in that one conversation.

I want to be with him, desperately. But I also know I need to work on my own issues before I can fully forgive him, and before we can have any shot at a future where a part of me doesn't still resent him and everything that happened.

But it looks like we have time to do that now, so let's see how this goes.

33

BLAKE

I've learned *a lot* about farming from Wyatt and Liam over the last few weeks. Lucky has settled in even better than I had hoped, and she loves playing with her new chicken friends. She might not officially be a livestock guardian breed—I learned that's a thing—but she's definitely assumed the role of one, and I know she's much happier here than she was in a high-rise.

The little preview I had during our hometown visit was definitely not enough time for me to appreciate everything that goes on here. No two days are the same. Sure, we still need to wake up with the sun every morning, and there are chores like feeding my babies that have to happen each day, but I'm constantly amazed by everything Liam manages to juggle.

Some piece of equipment or structure seems to break down or need repairs every other day around here, and Liam just knows how to fix them all. He doesn't call someone for help, or even look up how to do it online. If something needs his attention, he addresses the problem and quickly has it fixed and working again.

And that level of competency is really fucking hot.

Liam started talking to a therapist pretty soon after I got here. It's so cool that you can do that over a video call. I had no idea. He told me that he wanted to work on himself a bit more before he was ready to be in a relationship again. It sounded like a great idea to me—I can use all of the help I can get—so I asked for the details and have been talking to a different therapist in the same practice as well.

My therapist and I have been talking a lot about my parents, and they obviously know all about my situation with Liam. They've been giving me tools for healthy communication and other things that I never saw modeled growing up. While we haven't progressed our relationship yet beyond friendship, I'm hoping I'll be able to be a better partner to Liam, because he deserves nothing but the best.

I have to constantly remind myself that even though I'm madly in love with him, Liam still needs more time. He's been honest from the start—he wants to make sure he's not carrying old wounds into something that could actually last. We've talked a lot about trust and communication, and how hard it is to believe you're chosen when your past made you feel like a placeholder. He's working on unlearning the story that love always comes at someone else's expense or that he's just someone's experiment. I know it's not about me—he needs to believe he's enough. But I also know I want to be the one he fully lets in when he's ready.

I can't touch him like I want to, and I shouldn't be telling him how good his worn jeans make his ass look, *but damn.* Every time he repairs something, I want to drop to my knees and show him just how impressed I am by all the hard work he puts in around here.

But we're not there yet. Hopefully, we will be soon, and we'll have years and years together for him to teach me everything he knows. I'm hoping we'll just look back at this time as a short hurdle we overcame in our life together by both working on ourselves while still choosing to stand by each other. But for now, I'm appreciating him from a polite distance.

The flirting, though, I'm not as good with filtering. I can't even help it; sometimes the words just slip out of my mouth before I can stop them. I've lost track of the amount of times I've accidentally called him "L," or "babe," but I'm always quick to apologize.

Luckily, Liam hasn't seemed to mind too much. The first few times it happened, he froze, clearly unsure how to respond. But as the days have gone on, I think he understands now that I'm not trying to push him, and that it's just a knee-jerk reaction I'm struggling to control. When he was over at Wyatt's place last night, cooking dinner, explaining to me the best way to prepare the soup he was making, I'd accidentally said "thanks, babe," as he handed me the spoon to try some and he just shook his head, laughing while obviously fighting a smile.

I'm trying not to get my hopes up that it means I'm winning him over again. I meant what I said about giving him time. But I also really wish that time involved some cuddling. *Friends can totally cuddle, right?*

It's May now, and we've already been busy planting some of the early crops. The last frost seems to have passed, so Liam and Wyatt have been talking about planting the rest of the summer vegetables shortly. We've also been talking a lot about the farm plans, and I'm so grateful they've included me in their conversations. It took some convincing, but Liam agreed to let me fund the upgrades we've been making. The barn that we've been renovating to house the future animals is almost ready, and I can't wait to get more. We've been putting in a lot of time designing the layout for their land to optimize every space for this new venture, while also keeping the option open to add more later on if it ends up being popular. We're only about three hours northwest of the city, so we think plenty of people will make the trip here if we have enough for them to do, not to mention all the people who live closer than that.

The show has also been doing a lot of advertising in the last few weeks to prepare for its release, and we're hoping that if it ends up being popular, we can use that attention to attract more visitors. Both Liam and I have already seen an increase in followers on our social media just from the promos that have been running, so hopefully people will like us on the show enough to want to come see the farm.

I'm nervous to finally watch the premiere tonight. In a lot of ways, I feel like a totally different person than I was when we began filming, and I don't know that I want to see the reminder of how I used to be.

Liam agreed to watch it with me and even invited me over to his place. I can't help but feel like we're on a date. He's popping some popcorn for us now while I pull up the first episode, and I love how domestic this is. I can almost pretend like we're still together and this is just a normal night for us as a couple in our home. Pretend that I won't have to walk across the field to his dad's house in a few hours.

I'm dreading having him see how confident I was that he was a woman, but at least that part isn't a secret. I'm hoping we can laugh off how big of an idiot I was, and that maybe when we get to the later episodes, he can watch me fall in love with him all over again, and it'll help him to forgive me.

"This is going to be so strange to watch," Liam says as he sits on the other end of the couch, placing the popcorn bowl between us.

"Yeah, are you ready to watch me make a fool out of myself for the entire world to see?" I joke.

"Don't be so dramatic." He rolls his eyes, smirking at me before adding, "It's a national show, so only people in America will get to see you embarrass yourself."

I burst out laughing, loving that he's comfortable enough to tease me again. "Alright, here goes nothing." I hit play on the first episode and Andy's dazzling smile fills the screen as he gives a short rundown of the show's premise and structure. Before I know it, they're playing the interviews from that first day to introduce all the contestants, and we're touring our rainbow apartments.

The episodes are an hour long, and they've released the first four tonight. I really hope Liam is up for watching them all, because I know I'll be too focused on what's out there already to get any sleep without seeing it for myself.

"I can't believe how confident I was that I was straight," I comment when they show my interview about what I'm looking for in my ideal partner.

"Yeah, you swallowed my cock pretty quickly, straight boy," Liam responds conversationally. He obviously wasn't trying to flirt or taunt me with that remark—I know his growly tone for those sorts of comments well, and that certainly wasn't it. His eyes are wide as he looks at me, though. "Sorry, I wasn't trying—"

"It's fine, Liam. I know you weren't," I assure him, reaching over to give his knee a friendly squeeze.

Liam's intro is so sweet and wholesome, far more grounded and thoughtful than mine. I wish that I could go back in time and give that man the happy ending on the show he deserved, but I'm not giving up, and I really do think we'll get there. I mean, I'm still here after all. He hasn't kicked me out yet. Maybe we'll be closer to it for the reunion episode they're planning to shoot after the entire show has aired in a few weeks.

The rest of the episode establishes the cast and shows the first round of speed dating. "Did I really only talk about football? How did I ever land another date with you?" I'm joking around, but Liam has a guilty expression when I glance at him. "What's wrong? Why do you look as guilty as I did when I had to tell you I let the chickens into the main house?"

"I don't know if I should tell you or if watching it will be better…" he trails off and I look back at the screen, considering what he could possibly look so worried about.

"Eh, I'll wait and watch it," I decide, figuring he can always add details that were edited out if he needs to, but I'm too eager to see it to stop for him to warn me about something I'll end up watching soon anyway.

They only show a few more clips from those first blind dates. Apparently, our date was entertaining and bad enough for them to actually include, but obviously a lot of those were cut in the editing stage of the show. Then they show us all learning about the ranking system, where we choose who we want to continue to see in the next round.

And Liam.

Doesn't.

Pick me.

I'm not on his list, *at all.*

Ten spots and my name doesn't fill *one.*

I can't help it, I burst out in uncontrollable laughter. After watching our first date back, it's no wonder he didn't want to keep talking to me. Obviously, he'll reconsider and add me back onto his list after I put him at the top of mine, but the fact that I was so confident about him from the get-go, and he didn't even have me on there at all, is so fucking funny to me.

There were so many things that could have gone differently, and we wouldn't have ended up here. One or both of us not going on the show. If Liam had refused to reconsider me. If I had put him lower on my list so he didn't even have that option. One of us could have had a different conversation with another contestant and ended up chasing a different connection.

But none of that happened, and here we are, watching our love story unfold. Even if we aren't at our happily ever after yet, I truly believe that's still where we're headed, and I love all the little things that went right along the way.

"You're not pissed I didn't rank you?" Liam hesitantly asks.

I try to calm down, looking his way to give him my full attention as I answer. "Definitely not, it's fucking hilarious. After that disaster of a first date, no one could blame you. I was so confident that we were having a great two-sided conversation, and you were clearly not enjoying yourself. I'm sorry that I was so focused on myself then. Hopefully you agree that I've changed quite a bit since we started filming." I know I'm fishing for his praise, but I can't help it.

"Yeah, Blake, I can definitely agree to that," he says with a soft smile that makes my heart race, then his expression grows more serious. "I'm sorry I never told you about that."

I shake my head gently. "I appreciate you saying that, but honestly? Don't worry about it. Just another weird little piece of the puzzle that makes up our story, right?"

"Right," he confirms, that softer smile back in place.

I pry my gaze away from his handsome features to focus back on the show. I'm gripping the arm of the chair to stop myself from climbing into his lap as I remind myself over and over again that I'm giving him time and space. I need to be good for him, and right now, that means respecting boundaries.

But, fuck, if it isn't the hardest thing I've ever done.

LIAM

I didn't realize how emotional it would be to sit here with Blake and watch our love story play out from the beginning.

With everything else we've had going on, I kind of forgot about not picking him in that first ranking. I realize I could've told him on the show, but the reason I didn't wasn't because I was hiding something, per say, it was because I was trying to protect his feelings.

I didn't want him to feel… like… a backup option.

Oh.

Fuck.

Kind of like how Blake didn't tell me about the ultimatum.

I know he explained himself already and made it crystal clear he wasn't trying to deceive me or lie to me; he was trying to protect me because the money didn't matter. My therapist and I have talked about it extensively.

Still, I felt so blindsided at the time that it was hard not to question his sincerity. If I hadn't been carrying the weight of that past relationship trauma, I probably wouldn't have reacted so strongly.

I know Blake, though, and regardless of the fact that he kept the ultimatum from me, he isn't a manipulative person. He didn't mention it because he didn't want me questioning his motivation for being with me. Because he actually does love me. Just like I love him, even if I didn't tell him I didn't initially choose him.

I'd been so wrapped up in my own pain, so tangled in my past, that I couldn't see it for what it really was. Just as my initial ranking of him made no difference once I got to know him, the ultimatum didn't matter when he got to know me.

I never thought watching our experience back on the TV would stir up so many emotions, but it definitely is. Not only everything between us, but seeing Blake connect with Rachel through the beginning rounds is more painful than I anticipated.

I glance over at him, and he's completely unaware of the revelations I'm having as he watches the show. I do feel like I'm in a much better headspace personally than I was when he first showed up here. My therapist has been helping me to give less power to my own self-doubts and anxieties. I've been feeling more and more ready to start working on things with Blake again, but I've been afraid to make that final leap. Maybe I am finally ready to close this gap between us.

Sitting on the couch with a whole cushion of space between us feels wrong. All I want to do is reach for him—pull him against me, press my lips to his temple, to his lips, hold him in a way that tells him just how much I've missed him. Because this distance feels wrong. I want him curled against me, his head on my chest while I run my fingers through his thick blond hair.

This must be so hard for Blake, too. He always wanted to be touching and as close as possible. He likes knowing he's wanted, and I love giving him that through physical connection.

But I don't move yet. I need to make sure I'm ready for this, because once I go back, everything changes.

Instead, I watch the show and our past selves on the screen— the two idiots who didn't know they were about to fall in love.

Blake isn't the same person who walked into this experiment thinking he was straight and only caring about money. The man sitting next to me has grown so much. He's fought for me and continues to prove himself every day. Just like he said he would.

And I do trust him.

I want him back.

Yup, I'm ready.

I clear my throat and shift slightly closer to him on the couch. "Hey," I say.

"What's up?" he says casually, obviously unsure of where I'm going with this.

I inhale deeply. I know this is what I want. "I think I'm ready."

"For what?" he asks, still confused.

I shift, moving the bowl of popcorn to the coffee table before turning my body toward him as I reach out to take his hand in mine. "To move forward with us, if you're ready too. I miss you, even though you haven't gone anywhere. We've been separated for too long, and I do trust you, Blake, and I'm sorry if it felt like I didn't. Watching this back has made me realize just how far we've come, and I don't want to keep moving backward. Thank you for being so patient with me while I've been working on myself."

His mouth drops open slightly, and I watch as his face shifts from disbelief to absolute fucking joy. Then he's lunging at me, wrapping his arms around my shoulders, knocking me back into the cushions, and I let out a laugh as I wrap my arms around him too.

"Fuck, I've missed you," he says before peppering kisses all over my face. "You have no idea!"

"I have *some* idea," I tease, squeezing him a little tighter. "I missed you like crazy too. Even if I saw you daily, it wasn't the same."

He pulls back just enough to look at me, and the joy on his

face is so pure I can't help but smash my mouth to his. His lips feel like coming home and he sighs into me, tongue teasing at the seam before I open up for him. Before long, he's rutting against my leg and letting out a moan before pulling back.

"So, can we"—he wiggles his eyebrows suggestively, licking his lips as he grips my thighs—"you know. Make up properly? I've missed your dick so much."

I smirk, tilting my head. "Oh, you think you get to go right back to bottoming again?"

"Wait. What?" Blake acts like I just broke him.

"You think you just get to waltz back in, bat those pretty eyes, and I'll bend you over like nothing happened?"

"Well, I mean… yeah, kinda," he whines. "So, we *don't* get to have sex? I thought you said you wanted to be together again."

Oh, Blake. So naive.

"That sounds like a punishment for me, too. And I definitely don't want that."

He has the most confused look on his face, like he's never once thought about topping me. I guess that just goes to show how needy he is for me. *Fuck.* It's almost enough for me to give in. *Almost.*

I trail my fingers up his side, teasing him with light touches. "We can do that if it's what you really want, I never want to pressure you into anything. Or, if it interests you, we can keep playing into the apology angle for one more night. You can prove to me just how much you trust me. Let me tie you to my bed so I can use you like my own personal sex toy."

Blake's jaw drops and his face goes bright red.

"Yes, that one, definitely that option." Then, before I can really process his answer, he's scrambling off me and yanking me toward the bedroom—the show completely forgotten. Okay, looks like he's very, *very* on board with the idea.

By the time we make it to my room, his chest is rising and

falling rapidly, and his hazel eyes are wide with anticipation. He licks his lips, looking me up and down, clearly as eager and excited as I am for what I have planned.

"You want to be tied up, baby? Used by me?" It seems like he does, but I want to really make sure he's okay with this.

His eyes flutter closed for a second like he's lost in the fantasy of what I'm suggesting. "Yeah. Yeah, I really do."

He looks almost overwhelmed by how much he wants this, and I know he's ready to give up control. If Blake wants to be owned by me, then that's exactly what I'll give him.

My smirk deepens, my fingers trace down the column of his throat, and I pull him to me. I press my tongue into his mouth for just a few seconds before pushing him back.

"Then get naked and get on the bed," I command.

He whimpers, and I can visibly see his body relaxing, see how much he's already loving handing over control. He rips off his clothes until he's beautifully naked—cock already hard and straining toward his abs as he jumps onto the bed.

I shake my head as I watch him, taking my time. "Eager little thing, aren't you, B?"

A blush creeps over his skin again, but he just nods.

I take my time walking over to my dresser to grab a tie from the second drawer. I almost never wear these things, so might as well be resourceful. With the silk fabric in my hand, I walk back to Blake and his breath hitches as he watches with anticipation.

"You trust me?" I double check as I straddle his hips.

"Yes," he breathes without hesitation.

I lean in, mouth brushing against his ear, and he squirms as my fully clothed body drapes over his naked one. "Then be a good boy and give me your hands."

He shudders beneath me and obeys immediately. He lifts his wrists toward me and completely surrenders. Fuck, my own cock is fighting against the confines of my jeans, and part of me wants to rush through this, to finally feel him inside of me as quickly as

I can. But I fight off that impatience. I want to take my time and enjoy this. I know how amazing it will be if we draw this out a little, if I really tease him.

I take one of his wrists, wrapping the silk around it, tying it to the headboard, and making sure it's snug but not uncomfortable. He pulls at the tie, testing it, but it holds firm. "I'll just start with the one wrist so you can tap my thigh if you need me to stop. I have other plans for your mouth."

I move off the bed while he lays there, muscles flexed, veins bulging, and the head of his dick flushed red as I strip out of my clothes. His cock twitches as I move toward him, but I ignore it despite knowing how desperate he is for friction.

Instead, I move up his body, straddling his chest. He parts his lips immediately, jaw falling open for me, knowing exactly what I want. I grip his jaw, tilting his face up. "I'm gonna fuck your face," I tell him, brushing my thumb over his lower lip.

He nods frantically, tongue darting out to wet his lips. I drag the head of my cock against them, smearing my precum. His tongue flicks out again, tasting me, and he moans. His eyes flutter shut like he's savoring it, and fuck, if that isn't the sexiest thing I've ever seen.

"Open," I instruct, voice practically a growl with how turned on I am.

He obeys instantly, yet again, and I press forward, groaning as his mouth wraps around me. Warm, and wet, and perfect. I push deeper, feeling his throat relax until it contracts around me when I hit the back of it. I grip his beautiful blond hair and start to move, shallow thrusts at first to test his limits and let him adjust. But soon he's moaning around me, and I lose any restraint I thought I had, thrusting deeper and faster, still making sure to pull back so he can breathe, but fucking into his mouth the way I know he wants me to.

His eyes flick up to mine, glassy and faraway, and I groan

again at how blissed out he looks. "You love this, don't you?" I rasp.

He nods the best he can with his lips stretching around my cock, spit dripping down the corners of his mouth. He's perfect, absolutely fucking perfect. Then suddenly, he's tapping my thigh, and I immediately pull back.

"What is it?" I pant. "Fuck, did I hurt you?"

"Just need more, shift a little higher." He smirks, and I do as requested. Before I know it, he's dragging his tongue down my cock, over my balls, and lower—until he's *right there.* I'm so grateful we both showered the day off before getting cozy tonight to watch the show.

I shudder, my entire body going boneless the second I feel the first flick of his tongue against my hole.

"Jesus fuck—"

His free hand is gripping the wrist that's still bound above his head, like he wishes they were both tied up, but I want him to be able to communicate if he needs to. Not using his hands only makes him work harder, and he presses his face closer, licking slow and deliberate, before circling the tight ring of muscle with the tip of his tongue.

"Oh, fuck." My head drops forward, my hands moving to grip the headboard as I rock my hips, grinding against his mouth, letting him eat my ass the way he clearly wants to. His moans vibrate against my hole, and I can't help the way my hips move of their own accord. I have to brace myself against the headboard to keep myself upright as I come apart on his tongue. It's been so long since I've been on the receiving end of this, I'd almost forgotten just how amazing it feels. He's opening me up in a way that has my cock absolutely aching for release.

"God, Blake," I gasp. "You're gonna make me come just like this."

He moans in response, his tongue pushing in deeper, and I

can't take it anymore. I need his cock. I force myself away from his tongue, quickly tying up his other wrist before reaching for the lube and a condom in the nightstand. I slick my fingers up before turning to straddle him facing the other direction. I want him to be able to watch, but not touch, as I replace the loss of his tongue with two fingers of my own. I work myself open quickly, eager to lower myself down onto his cock and give it the attention he's craving.

I look over my shoulder, wanting to enjoy the image of how he's tied up and completely at my mercy. *Fuck,* I love it. Love seeing him squirm, love the little whimpers that escape as his hips thrust up into nothing, seeking any sort of relief.

"You're so desperate, baby," I tease, working a third finger inside myself. His eyes are pleading, his body trembling with the effort to not touch. I smirk, teasing my fingers in and out of my hole, avoiding my prostate so that I can take my time. He's a moaning, pleading mess as I torture him. "You want me to ride you, don't you?"

"Please," he begs. "Please, Liam, I need to be inside you."

I chuckle, pulling my fingers from my hole, making a show of how wet and stretched I already am for him. His cock is leaking where it twitches against his stomach, and I can tell he's barely holding on.

"Patience, B," I soothe, reaching for the condom as I turn back around to face him. I tear it open with my teeth, shifting to roll it down over his straining erection and he jerks his hips up instinctively, but I pin him down with a firm hand on his stom-ach. "Toys don't rush things. You take what I give you," I remind him, slicking him up with lube, stroking just enough to drive him even more crazy.

"Fuck, babe—" His voice is needy, and his head slams back against the pillow, hands still bound above him.

And then, finally—*finally*—I position myself over him, lining up his cock against my entrance, and sink down.

BLAKE

*F*uuuuuuck.

Holy goddamn. Mother of fucking titballs.

There's a distant part of my brain that wonders if my internal swearing even makes any sense, but that thought is forgotten as Liam lowers himself further onto my cock. His ass is squeezing my dick so fucking tightly, I'm worried I'm going to come already and ruin this before I have a chance to enjoy it. But his teasing—or torture—really got me closer to the edge than I'd care to admit.

I'm in heaven right now, though, there is no other way to describe what I'm feeling. The pleasure is so intense I'm struggling to focus on anything at all. Like if Liam wasn't on top of me right now, I might just float away. His body is so warm, his hole slicked from the sexy way he prepped himself for me. Wait, *not for me,* for himself, *to use me* for his pleasure. My dick twitches inside of him at that thought, of being his toy, and as much as I fucking love bottoming, this is also mind-blowing.

My cock might be in Liam's ass right now, but there is no denying that he is still the one fucking me as he slowly raises and lowers his hips, his hands holding me down, his fingers digging into my pecs. Part of me wants to thrust up into him, force a faster pace, but there's a bigger part of me that wants to finally give in to this sensation of him owning me, to stop trying to focus on the details and just *let go.*

I'm distantly aware of his hand shifting higher up my body—his weight no longer pushing down onto me—caressing up my chest before tracing my collarbone and settling just below my neck. My eyes must have closed at some point, because I have to force them open to meet Liam's dark possessive gaze.

"Fuck, straight boy, you're being such a good toy for me."

A whimper escapes my mouth, and I wouldn't be surprised to find out I'm glowing with how happy his praise makes me feel. But toys don't talk, so I don't respond as I stare up at him adoringly.

"Do you like that, feeling like something I own?"

I nod quickly and he shifts his hand higher, wrapping his long fingers around my neck without actually putting any pressure there. My chest is rising and falling rapidly now as I hold his gaze, completely consumed by this moment between us.

"More," I plead in a high-pitched, needy tone that I don't recognize.

"Want me to squeeze?" he checks, the hungry look in his eye making it clear he likes the idea.

"Please, yes. I want that, to feel like I'm completely and totally yours."

We might not have made it down the aisle, but right now with Liam staring at me like I'm a gift, like I'm more than he could have ever asked for as he continues to ride my cock, this moment feels divine, like the beginning of something sacred. The relationship between us is stronger than it ever was before as we embrace this dynamic that brings us both so much pleasure. I'm still not completely convinced this is real, that Liam is really giving me another chance. This all seems way too good to be true. If it is some sort of dream, then I don't want to wake up.

"Just a second, you need a hand free again," he mutters, stretching to pull the tie loose from my wrists. "Keep one hand above your head," he commands. "Put the other tight around my wrist and let go if you need me to stop, *for any reason.*"

I quickly nod, eager to have his hand return to its position on my throat, something in me settling when he does. He's stopped the motion of his hips now, and I'm desperate to have him move again.

"Any reason, Blake, I mean it. If you even loosen your grip, I'm stopping. I never want to hurt you."

I smile up at him, sure my expression is a little dopey but I can't help it. I grip his wrist tightly, wanting to assure him how eager I am for this. He slowly increases the pressure of his hold on my throat. I can still breathe, but my head starts to feel fuzzy as his grip must restrict the blood flow. Now I really do feel like I'm floating, looking into his eyes as he raises and lowers his hips again, more quickly now.

He loosens his hold, no longer applying any pressure to my neck, and I feel an overwhelming rush of euphoria as the blood returns. He moves one hand to work his own straining erection. He's really picked up the pace of his efforts riding my cock, and the combination of that pleasure and this new high, that his hand around my throat has left me with, has my orgasm violently crashing into me. My dick jerks inside of him as it fills the condom, shooting more of my release with each wave after wave of what must be the longest and most intense orgasm of my life.

I'm glad I'm already on my back because I completely check out, unable to think or move as my release finally comes to an end. Liam lets out a deep moan as thick ropes of his cum cover my chest and neck, making me feel owned by him in another way.

He slowly raises himself off me, wincing slightly at the loss of me inside of him. Then he removes the condom from my softening cock, ties it off and moves to the bathroom to get rid of it. I close my eyes, still feeling a little dazed as he unties me and must get himself cleaned up. I feel like I should be helping him with that, but no matter how good my intentions are, I still can't find the strength to move.

Liam returns with a warm washcloth to clean me up as well, murmuring soft praises about how good I was for him, and how happy I make him, as I fight the urge to fall asleep. I want to stay awake, to talk about what this means for us, how happy I am that he's giving me another chance, to find out what his expectations are now that we're together again.

But as he crawls into the bed next to me, resting his head on my shoulder and pulling the blankets up to cover us both, I lose the battle, giving in to the dreamland that's calling to me.

LIAM

*W*aking up this morning is everything.

For the first time since that awful day in the city, I wake up with Blake in my arms. It's so much better than the empty bed. When I open my eyes, I'm met with his warm hazel ones staring back at me. *Oh, how times have changed.* That first morning on the farm, I never would have pictured this man waking up before me. Yet here he is, waiting for *me* to get up, tucked against my chest, fingers drawing patterns against my skin.

I tighten my hold around his waist, pulling him even closer, pressing a kiss to his forehead. "You waiting for me, baby?" I rasp, voice thick with sleep.

Blake grins and presses a kiss to my jaw. "Yes."

I can see a flicker of hesitation, and I know there's still so much we need to discuss. I'd planned on talking last night, but Blake passed out, which I completely understood with how intense our sex ended up being.

"Whatcha thinking about?" I ask, running my hand up and down his bare back. I wait, letting him take his time to collect his thoughts.

"Are we still engaged?"

The question makes my stomach flip. It's not that I haven't asked myself the same question repeatedly as I considered us getting back together, but hearing him ask doesn't make it any clearer. "I don't know," I admit honestly.

Blake bites his lip, considering my words. "I mean, we were supposed to be married by now," he says quietly. "And I still want to be."

My heart beats a little faster because *I do too.* I never stopped wanting him, or us. But I also don't want to rush it.

I cup his jaw and run my thumb over his cheek. "Blake, I love you. You know that, right?"

He nods. "Okay," he says quietly.

"And I *do* want to marry you, but I also don't want to rush it. I don't want us to feel like we have to prove anything to anyone. I want our relationship to be *ours.* Not something we do because of the show, or for money, or because it's what someone else expects of us. I don't want to do anything because we feel like we have to for the reunion. I just want us to have time to be together the way that we want to."

Blake exhales slowly, like he's been holding his breath this entire time. "Yeah, I want that too."

"So let's not worry about the fiancé label for now. We can officially get engaged again when it feels right for us. It doesn't change the way I feel about you, or the fact that I want our future to be spent together. I just want it to be for us, okay?"

Blake smiles, leaning down to nudge his nose against mine. "Okay. But, for the record, you're definitely still my future husband, so can I call you that?"

I chuckle, tugging him against me and press a kiss to his lips. "Of course. And you're *mine.*"

We stay like that for a while—wrapped up in each other. It feels like we're finally back on the right track, like we're exactly where we're supposed to be. Since his dramatic move to the farm, I haven't doubted that Blake was my future. I just needed to be in the right headspace to *choose* it again. And now, we can.

After a few minutes, I finally nudge him. "You ready to get up and go feed the chickens?"

"The chickens! Yes. Daddy's coming!" he yells dramatically, even though they definitely can't hear him.

I roll my eyes and laugh, savoring the reminder that my life with him will never be boring. I get dressed quickly and follow him out the door.

As we walk over toward the coop, I turn to him. "So, what's on our to-do list now that you're officially moving in?"

He stops in his tracks like this is shocking news to him. "I am?"

"Yeah, baby. We'll get your stuff today from Dad's and move you in, although I don't know if he'll let Lucky come too with how attached he is." I thought living together was a clear next step, but I guess not. Especially not with the way he launches himself at me, wrapping his arms around my neck and kissing me with excited passion.

When he finally pulls back, his entire face gets serious. "Liam. Future husband. I meant what I said to you when I first showed up at the farm. I want to put my money into *our* life. Into the farm. I know I've put a little bit in already, and before you get weird about it, just accept that this is *my* dream too."

I sigh, it's been a bit of struggle to accept his money, even in the small amounts we've used already, but I do know he really wants to do this. He's proved it. It's time for me to prove that I trust him too and let him get what he wants. "What are your grand plans?" I check, trying to sound as excited as he is, despite knowing that I'll probably have a headache after hearing the answer.

He perks up immediately, realizing that I'm not going to argue with him about the money. "Okay, so first, goats!"

"Goats?"

"Yes, we *need* goats. I've already picked out names, babe. I've done some research and you have to have *at least* two so I think we should start with four."

I had a feeling this conversation would immediately go to more animals. "Blake—"

"No, no, just hear me out," he pleads. "Goats are good for farms. They eat weeds. They're cute! And we can get those little pajamas for them!"

"What is with you trying to dress up the farm animals, B?"

"Fine, *overalls*. We'll get them overalls."

I groan but I know it's useless, he's already committed to this and named them. "What else?"

"Alpacas."

I actually laugh at that. He says it so seriously though, like he's put a lot of thought into this. "You're out of your mind."

"I am not!" he exclaims. "They're profitable, Liam! We could sell the wool. Make blankets. Plus, they're fluffy and adorable and I love them."

I cross my arms and level him with a look. "Uh huh, and how much research have you done on all these animals?"

"I'll have you know, a lot. It's my entire TikTok algorithm. They're all I see. I know so much now."

"Oh, Jesus." I laugh to myself.

"Trust me, I have so many ideas, and the animals will be great for bringing families to the farm! Petting zoos are the best. I'm officially taking over the expansion plans."

I tug him in, whispering against his lips, "I love you, Blake. So much."

He smiles against my lips and presses a kiss to my mouth. "I love *you*, Liam."

And at this moment, I know we're going to be okay because we have each other. As ridiculous as his ideas might sound, I love that he's making plans for *us*. That this isn't just my farm anymore, it isn't just my dream, my future. It's ours.

EPILOGUE ONE

BLAKE

A Few Weeks Later, May

The final episodes of the show released last week for streaming, and it feels like all of America has seen our love story unfold. I might be biased, but I think our relationship and all the drama that occurred during filming is the reason that the show became so popular.

Sure, when it came out that Jace and Kieran had grown up together and that they hated each other's guts, there was obviously some interest from the viewers as well, but I still think we had a more captivating story than them.

Everyone who made it through enough of the show to at least meet their partner in person is back tonight for the live filming of the reunion episode. Andy is seated in the middle of the stage that's been set up in front of an audience that seems way too big for the soundstage. The audience is packed. Apparently a lot of people wanted to be here for this.

Jace and Kieran are seated together on a love seat, along with the rest of the couples who are still together to the left of Andy.

Those who didn't say "I do" are all seated in single chairs to the right of Andy.

The show put Liam and I in our own armchairs and explained that it would be more dramatic to start out this way. Then when it's time, they'll swap our chairs with a love seat after it's announced we're still together.

We're moments away from starting as the crew gets everyone in the audience to quiet down by holding up signs with instructions. Someone counts down the final moments before we must be live, and Andy's booming voice rings out across the studio.

"Good evening, fellow romance lovers and reality TV show watchers. We have a very special episode planned for you all tonight! We have brought back the cast of the inaugural season of *Love Without Labels* to bring you the latest updates and gossip over how life has been since the show stopped filming!"

He pauses to smile and make eye contact with a few of the couples seated on the stage before turning back to face the audience. "Are they still together? How is life away from the cameras? And the real reason I think most of us were so eager to tune in tonight—what really happened between Liam and Blake?"

I can feel my cheeks heating at the mention of my name, but I try to cover up any nerves with a big smile of my own. *I have no reason to be nervous. Liam and I are better than ever.* We've spent the time since the show aired working together to really improve the structures around the farm and prepare to open our pumpkin patch, and I successfully convinced Liam to fill the largest barn on the property with animals for a petting zoo.

The baby highland cows we purchased should be ready to leave their mom any day now, and I can't wait to see my newest children again. The goats have been amazing, even if they are a bit destructive, and Lucky has loved spending time with her new siblings, even if she does prefer to spend most of her time with Liam's dad. And Liam and I have been looking into the best place we can get alpacas. I feel like we're building a great future for ourselves, and I really hope that we can attract other people to come see how special the farm is.

It's crazy to me just how much the farm feels like home in such a short time. It feels far more like a home than the city ever did, and I've made Chad come experience the farm life twice so far. I think he finally sees the appeal. Liam's childhood best friend, John, just ended up moving back home kind of unexpectedly, and it's been great to spend time with him too.

Andy has a script of questions to run through, starting with some of the contestants who got less screen time, before moving to Jace and Kieran. Obviously, I'd heard what happened between them on the show when they first met the person behind the anonymous profile, especially since Jace and Liam became close during the process. But the producers and editors weren't sure exactly what had gone down between them in the past, so their shift from anonymous dating and picking each other, to hate, to being in love was a little jarring.

They weren't nearly as good at monologuing to the cameras as Liam and I were.

Andy tries to get more out of them about why they were so opposed to each other initially, but they both give very vague answers, not revealing much, which I can respect. Even Andy's bubbly optimism starts to flatten when they give their fourth or fifth nonanswer and it becomes clear that they're not going to turn this into some tell-all that I'm sure the audience and producers alike were hoping for.

After what feels like forever, Andy finally turns dramatically in his seat to face Liam and I, crossing his legs and folding his hands in his lap like he's settling in, ready to catch up with old friends. "Hello, boys!"

"Hi, Andy," I respond conspiratorially.

"Well, I think that we all know you two are the ones

everyone was willing to sacrifice their first-born for while trying to secure tickets to tonight's taping."

"There does seem to be a lot of people here," Liam responds casually as he looks out at the audience, playing into the teasing approach the producers wanted us to take. Sure, we could go the Jace and Kieran route and refuse to give them anything, but Liam and I have talked extensively about the benefits our popularity could bring the farm, so we're willing to play along.

Plus, it's kind of fun.

"Blake, I think we have to start with you, did you *really* think you were straight when you applied for the show? A lot of people online have speculated that you wouldn't have signed up at all if you weren't at least open to the idea of being with a man."

"Those people might be smarter than I am," I joke. I've seen all of the backlash online, so this isn't news to me. There were a lot of people, especially when only the first few episodes were released that *hated* me. I was called every word for insensitive, biased, ignorant, sexist—you name it and someone was labeling me that way.

Luckily, after the first few episodes, I seemed to win people over with my willingness to adapt once I met Liam and loved him for him, regardless of his gender. Supporters for my "embraced bi-awakening" rose up to defend me, loudly praising our relationship for setting an example of people realizing their sexuality later in life. They particularly loved the way I came out to my friends at the hockey game and told them they could get out if they had a problem with me or Liam.

Then when news of the ultimatum came out, the fandom was split again. Some people still believed me saying that there's no way I faked my feelings for Liam even if money was involved. But a lot of people assumed the worst like Liam initially did, so it will be interesting to see how tonight goes.

There was another group who said I was an actor, planted by

the show to boost ratings, and that there was no way someone could go from identifying as straight, to so publicly dating a man as quickly as I did, and the drama of the money only seemed to add fuel to their claims that everything was scripted.

I like to tell Liam that if there had been cameras in our room and those people could have seen the first time he fucked my face, then they would believe me, but he just shakes his head and laughs whenever I suggest it.

Universally though, my mother is hated by all. According to my father, she was livid when she found out there had been cameras in the room when she talked to Liam. That episode led to my parents separating, so I haven't gotten many updates on her since then, which is perfectly fine with me.

"Well, Andy, can I be honest with you?" I ask sincerely, like there aren't hundreds of people staring at us right now and cameras shooting from five different angles.

"Of course, Blake, we're all friends here."

"Absolutely," I respond, just as cheesy, really getting into it now. "Well, the truth is, yes, I did believe I was straight. Maybe on some level, I was cool with the possibility of being with a man, but I wasn't lying when I labeled myself that way. It's what I believed to be true at the time. But the real motivator for me signing up for the show was the ultimatum my parents gave me. They threatened to cut me off, so I needed to be married, and I wasn't particular about who I would be tying myself to. I just wanted to keep living my expensive life in the city the same way I always had."

"We'll come back to the ultimatum in a moment, but can you tell us a little more about when things changed for you? I think we all saw how heartbroken you were when Liam told you he couldn't go through with the wedding."

"Well, I think before I even met Liam, I was excited about the possibility of actually liking the person I could marry, which might sound like a basic requirement for a spouse, but when I tell you I went into this show with minimal expectations about my partner, that's the truth."

Andy laughs at my response, and I try my best to avoid looking over at Liam. I know I won't be able to hold back the way I feel about him from my expression, and we want to keep people interested as I continue.

"When we met, obviously I had the moment of shock, realizing how stupid I'd been with my assumptions, but there was still that part of me that was really excited to see where things could go with the person I'd been talking to. I had to reevaluate some assumptions I'd made about myself as well, and at the end of the day, I'm actually really glad that I had the ultimatum as that initial excuse to keep seeing him."

"So the ultimatum—I think everyone knows about it by now —luckily our dedicated camera crew caught the confrontation with your parents, as well as your mother's conversation with Liam. Did you watch that part?" He pauses for me to nod before continuing. "Well, your dad made it seem like you were never really at risk of losing your money. Have there been any problems there?"

"No, I still have access to everything. I just have a much better purpose for spending it now," I assure him with a huge grin, still avoiding looking at Liam.

"And do you still talk to your parents? You had some choice words to say about your mother."

"My dad and I are working on a more honest and open style of communication. My mother and I haven't spoken since what should have been my wedding day," I answer honestly.

Andy nods solemnly. "Well, I'm happy to hear things seem to be improving with your father." Then he sits up a bit straighter to dramatically look back and forth between Liam and I before pointing a finger at each of us and crossing to the other.

"Okay, okay, I think the real question we've all been dying to ask, is what the hell happened after Liam left? Have you two spoken before today? Was the truth about the ultimatum really enough to tear you apart forever?" Obviously Andy already knows we're back together, but his voice cracks at his final question, really selling how emotionally invested he seems to be in our relationship.

"We've talked before today," I say with a smirk.

"Aaaaaand?" Andy prompts desperately.

"And apparently I wasn't clear enough when I tried to end things with Blake," Liam says lightly, one corner of his mouth turned up as he holds in a laugh. "He showed up on my farm a few days later with his dog and all his packed bags, ready to move in with my dad. He said that I never actually broke things off with him, that I just told him I couldn't marry him that day. I said something about needing to be with someone who chose me. So, he was choosing me and the life we had planned, and he promised to give me the time and space I needed to trust him again before we officially got back together."

"Well... did it work?"

Liam finally shifts his gaze to meet mine, both of us smiling as we finally get to tell the crowd we're together. "It did," is all Liam has to say for the audience to erupt. People are cheering and clapping, someone shouts out that Liam shouldn't have forgiven me, and someone else yells that they'll marry me instead. It's chaos for a few minutes while the show's staff tries to calm the audience down.

They must cut to commercial, because a two-person couch is brought out and exchanged for Liam's and my seats so that we can sit together at last. We weave our fingers together, placing them on Liam's thigh, and eventually Andy is able to continue. "People certainly have strong opinions about you two. Has that made it difficult to navigate resuming your relationship?"

I nod at Liam to answer. "To be honest, we've been able to get to a point where we don't care what anyone outside of our relationship has to say about it. We're grateful for all the support that we've seen online and on all our social media. We're actually planning to open the farm up as a family destination this fall, so we're hoping that our new followers will help to spread the word, and maybe some will even come meet us to support the farm and all the new animals Blake has insisted on adopting," he teases.

"That sounds fantastic, I know I'll visit!"

"Thanks, Andy."

"Alright, final question. Now that we've confirmed you two are together again, can you tell us what that actually means? Are you two still planning to get married? Are you no longer engaged but dating? What did that conversation look like?"

"Oh, Liam is absolutely still my future husband," I assure them, and Liam smiles indulgently at me.

"I agree. But we've also decided that rushing into a marriage didn't make sense for us. We've had parents and producers telling us why we need to get married for so long, that we lost sight of why we'd want to be married in the first place. We're in love, and I'm confident that Blake is my person, the one epic love I had always hoped to find." Liam squeezes my hand as he brings it up to his mouth, leaving a kiss on the knuckle.

"We want to wait until getting married feels like something we're doing only for us," I add to clarify. "We're committed to each other, which is all I need." Liam leans in for a quick kiss, and the audience "awwws" along with Andy.

We might not have had the picture-book ending that the show planned for us, but I think what we have now is so much better.

EPILOGUE TWO

LIAM

October

I never thought I'd be waking up to the sound of a goat screaming outside my window, but that's my life now.

I groan, shoving my face into the pillow. Jolene, our chaotic little gremlin of a goat must be somewhere she's not supposed to be. *Again.* "Jolene" is what I get for letting Blake name the animals. He gave them all pop star inspired names and hypes them up by following them around with a camera all day. Even though they are literal farm animals, they act like they're the ones in charge here.

Beside me, Blake is *dead asleep*, with Lucky rolled on her back right next to Blake despite the fact that Jolene is begging for attention. I don't know how he does it, but I decide to let him sleep, pressing a quick kiss to his forehead before climbing out of bed.

Today is the first morning of our Fall Festival, there's no use in me staying in bed, I'm far too excited to go back to sleep.

Mom would be too.

This was always something she dreamed of—bringing more

319

of the community to our farm and making it a place people want to come rather than just a spot to pick up produce and leave. She wanted it to be a core memory for families, and I'm excited we're finally able to make it happen.

Fall has always been my favorite in upstate New York, but now that Blake is here and we're finally making this happen, it's even better. We have a field full of pumpkins, games set up, a corn maze, a petting zoo that the animals are probably going to like more than the humans because Blake's trained them to love attention, and even a live local band.

I grab a cup of coffee and step outside into the quiet, crisp October air. The farm looks like something out of a Hallmark movie, and honestly, that was kind of the point. There are pumpkins piled high in wooden crates for people who don't want to go into the field, hay bales stacked up near the entrance, and a parking area we set up waiting to be filled.

The peace of taking in the view only lasts about thirty seconds before I see the chaos. The goats have already gotten out of their pen, Jolene standing on top of the shed. *How does she even get up there?*

"Don't do it," I warn, and she doesn't listen. *Of course she jumps.* She's fine, and I roll my eyes at the crazy animal. I sigh and walk over to the chickens who I know are eager to get out of their coop. I throw out some feed for them and collect their eggs.

Next, I move to the cows, filling their trough with fresh water and checking to make sure they still have enough hay, and they do. They're far less excited than the chickens or goats to see me, but they're so damn cute. I know they're going to be a huge hit today at the petting zoo.

The goats on the other hand, *they better behave.* Blake has given them so much attention that they expect snacks every time they see a human, which I guess is good for a petting zoo, but it gets pretty annoying when it's just us here. I bring them alfalfa hay and check their water while they jump all over everything that isn't nailed down. The goats are a handful, but I do love them.

Then there's the alpacas, they just watch me with the most judgmental stares. It's quite rude, but I ignore their attitude and make sure they have food and water too.

By the time I make it back to the house, Blake is at the kitchen table, scrolling through his phone.

"They love me," he says dramatically, holding it up.

By *they*, I know he means the internet and his followers. Somehow, Blake has turned into a viral sensation. He started by posting silly farm updates, recording himself talking to the chickens like they were his coworkers or dressing up the goats, but people loved it. They still do.

He posts new videos almost every day and he's been hyping up the Fall Festival for weeks now.

"I think today is going to be a hit," I say, grabbing his coffee from his hand and taking a sip before handing it back.

"Obviously." He grins. "The people are so excited for our opening and they all want updates."

The farm was already growing in popularity from the show, but since Blake started making videos, we've been busier than ever. Our summer produce membership was completely sold out and we actually had to turn people away. We did build a roadside shop, though, and any extra produce we had, we were able to sell there. It turned out to be successful, and Blake absolutely loved being the one to run the store. Between the shop, the video content, and the animals, he really is living his best life, and it makes me so damn happy to see that this really *is* his dream too.

"Speaking of updates," he continues, pulling out his phone and flipping the camera to selfie mode. "We're live, babe!"

I stare at him in mild horror as he zooms in on my face. I should be used to this by now, but his antics are always amusing in different ways.

"Say hi to the people, future husband."

I just blink at the camera, then deadpan, "Help me."

He laughs, pointing the camera back at himself. "Guys, don't listen to him. I treat him so well. Anyway, today is day one of our big Fall Festival and we finally finished setting everything up last night. Who's ready for a tour?" he asks the camera like they'll respond.

He grabs my arm before I can protest and drags me with him as he narrates what we're walking past to the phone. "We've got the pumpkin patch over here." He points. "The corn maze is behind me. Who wants to take bets on how many kids get lost? I'm kidding! I'm kidding! It's pretty tiny so it's not hard this year. And last, our star attraction…"

He flips the camera to the goats. "My babies!" he yells happily.

As over-the-top as Blake is—about well, everything, especially the farm—it's part of why I love him so much. It's also why I know this festival will be such a hit.

TODAY WAS TRULY BETTER than I could have ever imagined.

Blake really helped Dad and me make Mom's dream a reality. I glance over at my dad where he's petting Lucky and feel a deep sense of pride in my chest that he got to experience this. That we did it.

"You look happy," he says, and I nod.

"It's just surreal, this was always something Mom wanted."

His answering smile is warm. "She'd be proud of you, son. She'd love this."

I smile to myself as my throat gets thick with emotion. My eyes land on Blake, who's still with the goats. He seems like he's checking in with each of them to make sure they had as much fun as he hoped they would today.

My dad nudges me. "You ready?"

I let out a slow breath and nod. "Yeah, I am."

I walk toward Blake, my heart pounding in my chest. He's still busy paying attention to the goats so I grab his hand and tug him toward me.

"Hey, babe. Oh my god, today was awesome! Wait, what are you—"

I don't answer, I just drop to one knee, holding the ring in my hand that he gave back to me all those months ago, and his mouth falls open.

"Blake," I start. "You are the best damn thing that has ever happened to me. You showed up in my life, to the farm, and you've made everything infinitely better. Better than I ever could've imagined. Your happiness is infectious, and I love that life with you is never boring."

Tears well in his eyes and I let out a deep breath.

"I told you I don't want to rush anything," I continue. "And I still don't, but you know I've already chosen you. Now and forever, I choose you. I love you, and I don't want to wait another second to make you my fiancé again. Marry me, Blake."

He nods frantically and throws himself in my arms. "Yes. Fuck yes, babe!"

I pull him to me and whisper in his ear. "I love you so much, today was perfect."

"I love you too. I can't wait for every day with you. They're all perfect."

I grab his hand, sliding my dad's ring back on, and then pull him with me toward the house, knowing there's one more thing I want to do to cement this amazing day. We turn to my dad who says his congratulations and waves us off. When we get to the house, I go right to the liquor cabinet and pull out the bottle of whiskey.

"Mom left me this for my twenty-first birthday," I explain. "I've been saving it. I thought we'd toast with it on our wedding day, but today feels just as special. You helped her dream come true, and mine and dad's. This is something we've been dreaming about forever, but you made it happen. I can't wait to spend the rest of our lives together."

Blake nods, reaching out for my hand, squeezing it gently. I pour us both a glass, then pull a small envelope from the cabinet drawer.

Blake's breath catches. "Is that—"

I nod. "The letter she wrote me. For my wedding day."

His fingers tighten around mine.

"I couldn't read it that day," I admit, my voice cracking. "Not after everything."

Blake nods in understanding.

"But I want to read it tonight. With just you. No cameras, no waiting for whenever we actually say 'I do.' Today feels just as special, way more than whatever ceremony the show would have planned."

I let out a slow breath, unfolding the letter with trembling hands. Her familiar handwriting stares back at me, and I blink rapidly, forcing back the tears already threatening to fall.

I take a deep breath, then begin to read.

My sweet boy,

If you're reading this, it means you've found the kind of love your dad and I always dreamed you'd have. A love that makes you smile every day, that makes life bigger, richer, and fuller. The kind of love that makes you better.

Your dad and I had that. And my greatest wish for you is that you do too.

Love is a choice, Liam. Every single day, you will choose each other. And if you've chosen this person, then I already love them too.

Dance, laugh, celebrate, and hold each other close

through it all. And know that I am celebrating with
you. I'm so proud of you.
I love you, always.
Mom

I exhale shakily, wiping at my face as Blake squeezes my hand so tight, it almost hurts. He doesn't say anything though, just lets me feel every emotion her letter has inspired.

After a few moments, I take a deep breath and lift my glass.

"To Mom," I say.

Blake lifts his glass to meet mine. "To Mom."

The whiskey burns as it goes down, but when Blake leans in to press a soft, comforting kiss to my lips, I swear I can feel her here with us, smiling.

And I know with absolute certainty—he's the love I've always dreamed of finding.

THE END

What's Next?

Looking for more from us?

WANT to read about Jace and Kieran AKA JR and KD???

Keep reading for the prologue of The Reality of Wanting My Bully book two in the Love Without Labels series! This book will also take place during this first season, but don't worry the timeline and vibes are very different than this one. This is unedited and subject to change.

The Reality of Wanting My Bully *contemporary MM romance*

. . .

AND THEN???

LIAM AND BLAKE'S bachelor party of course! The Reality of Ever After *LWL novella* see what happens during the bachelor party in Vegas

WANTING My Husband *LWL spin-off not on the reality show, woke-up married MM romance*

SEASON *Two of Love Without Labels*
The Reality of Wanting Them *contemporary MMM blind dating reality show romance expected early 2027*

PREORDER our next books so that you don't miss what's new!
Cove Lake College
One More Dare *contemporary MM college romance expected August 2026*

STANDALONE
Not Another Dark Romance *contemporary MM dark romcom expected September 2026*

AFTERWORD

We did it! We wrote a book together!

Honestly it was super fun and you'll definitely be seeing more cowritten projects from us because having a friend to go through all of this with makes it so much better.

SPEAKING OF MORE... Want to read about Jace and Kieran AKA JR and KD???

PREORDER LINK

Keep reading for the prologue of The Reality of Wanting My Bully book two in the Love Without Labels series! This book will also take place during this first season, but don't worry the timeline and vibes are very different than this one. This is unedited and subject to change.

THE REALITY OF WANTING MY BULLY (DECEMBER 4TH 2025)

PROLOGUE

Jace
Present Day
January 2025

I'm about to meet my future spouse.

At least, I hope I am.

Somehow, KD agreed to move in with me despite the fact that we've never met in person, and I don't know if I've ever been this excited about anything before. I have no idea what they look or sound like, how old they are, or even their gender, but none of that matters to me. I know who they are as a person.

We've been dating on *Love Without Labels* for the last week, which might not seem like a lot of time, but somehow the connection I feel with K seems more meaningful than any other connection I've had in the past.

I'll be the first to admit I was skeptical about the whole process when I signed up for a "label-free dating show," but I needed a change. Something—anything really—to distract me from the pattern of failed relationships I've fallen into. I know it's my own damn fault that no one can ever live up to the version of *him* I've built up in my head over the years, but I can't help making the comparisons.

For as long as I can remember, Kieran Delaney has been the ideal person to me, and I don't know how to quit my obsession; I don't know how to stop measuring everyone I date against him. I watch every video, like every post, know about every public appearance, product launch, and endorsement deal. Sometimes it feels like I still know him—even if I use a fan account he wouldn't recognize—while he probably wishes we'd never met in the first place. It's been over a decade since I've seen him in person, and Kieran has probably forgotten all about me. *I need to try to forget about him, too.*

When my last girlfriend dumped me, claiming "I cared more about some stranger on the internet than her," I knew I needed a dramatic change. I tried to delete all of my social media apps and quit cold turkey, but that only lasted a few hours. I've never had the best self-control, and after I'd updated myself on everything "Sparkles" that I'd missed, I was doomscrolling when I saw the ad for *Love Without Labels*.

Something, maybe fate, maybe because I was overtired and should have been sleeping hours before, made me want to know more. I followed the link to the application and saw contestants would be isolated during the process, cut off from the rest of the world—and more importantly, their phones—to focus on dating other participants on the show.

It seemed perfect. They would literally force me to give up social media, and I could potentially meet someone without being distracted by whatever Kieran was doing that day. Even if it seemed unlikely that I would actually get chosen for the show at all—let alone match with anyone I could spend the rest of my life with—I knew I had to try.

Maybe it isn't fair for me to have signed up for the show when a part of my heart will always belong to him. It's not like anything could ever happen between us anyway, especially given how I treated him and how things ended between us.

Now here I am, pulling my suitcase behind me as I follow one of the show's producers, Jay, as he escorts me to the new apartment I'll be sharing with KD. This whole process has been kind of surreal, and there's a part of me that hasn't quite accepted that I'm actually a contestant on a reality show at all. But I'm embracing this once-in-a-lifetime experience, and I'm so excited to meet the one person here who's captured my interest.

I follow Jay into the elevator, leaving the anonymous part of the show behind, ready to jump into this next chapter. I'm taking deep, measured breaths, trying to calm my racing heart as I wonder—for probably the last time—who it is I've been bonding with over the countless messages and hours talking through the show's distorted voice technology.

What if it's him? the annoying voice in my head asks for the millionth time.

I'm not proud of the fact that all I could think about during my first date with KD was that they share the same initials as Kieran. But I'm not a complete idiot, I know there are probably tens of thousands of people in New York whose first and last names also start with K and D.

This KD is by far the coolest person I've talked to in years. We clicked right away, and despite the short amount of time we've been dating, I do feel like we have a real shot at a future together. Talking with K has been so easy; they're really fucking funny, kind, and there hasn't been a single moment of awkward silence or tension between us like I experienced in some of the other dates early on.

I'm so relieved and excited they also like me enough to have agreed to move in with me and enter the next phase of the show together. If the next week of sharing an apartment goes well, we might even be engaged soon. I feel like I might actually be ready to build a life with someone without constantly wondering about what might've been if things didn't end the way they did back then. *K could be it for me.*

Jay motions for me to get off the elevator first. "Apartment 13 on your left. KD should already be in there."

Kind of an ominous number to include on a dating show, but thirteen was also my jersey number in high school, so what might seem like an unlucky sign to most feels like confirmation that I'm exactly where I should be. I run my fingers through my unruly hair like that might somehow tame the mess of curls.

I push open the door, eager to meet the person who I could spend the rest of my life with… and my heart shatters.

It's like I can feel it being ripped apart in my chest, splitting right down the middle as I'm torn in two. Half of me is elated, overwhelmed by the person standing in front of me, because I was right. We are perfect for each other, and no one else could ever compare.

But the other half of me, the more logical, rational part, is shattering in a way I know I'll never recover from. It doesn't matter what happens after this; no one will ever be able to help me fit all the broken pieces of who I was before this moment back together.

Because it wasn't just a silly crush that turned into an embarrassing obsession—there really might have been a chance for something real between us. This moment proves it.

But I fucked that possibility up years ago.

THE REALITY of Wanting My Bully *contemporary MM romance*

ALSO BY

Lexi Amber

Chicago Awakenings

Accidentally Joining His Cult *contemporary MM romance*

Accidentally Falling For My Best Friend *contemporary MM romance*

Accidentally Falling for Her- The Girls *contemporary FF romance companion novella*

Accidentally Living With The Captain *contemporary MM romance February 2026*

Bec Benson

Straight To You *contemporary MM romantic suspense*

All In December *contemporary MM holiday romance*

Co-authored

Love Without Labels

The Reality of Wanting Him *contemporary MM romance*

The Reality of Wanting My Bully *contemporary MM romance*

The Reality of Ever After *LWL novella expected March 2026* The bachelor party in Vegas

Wanting My Husband *LWL spin-off expected mid 2026* not on the reality show

ABOUT LEXI

Lexi is an American author who is obsessed with queer happily ever afters. Most of her time is spent with her two kids, but if they're asleep then she is either reading, writing, or watching hockey.

Professionally trained as a nurse, Lexi decided to start writing when she became a stay at home mom and the characters in her head haven't stopped talking since.

Lexi also loves Diet Coke, traveling, and Halloween. Her house is probably obnoxiously decorated for whatever holiday is next because she thinks that little things that make people smile are important.

To read unreleased chapters early, and be the first to see art/covers/behind the scenes join my Patreon! patreon.com/Lexi Amber

Signed copies of solo work and lots of fun merch at Lexi amber.com

ABOUT BEC

Bec Benson is based in the Northeast, lives for the first sip of hot coffee in the morning, genuinely believes emo music can make you happy, and is obsessed with mgk.

More about Bec and upcoming work at Becbenson.com

ACKNOWLEDGMENTS

Thank you so much to everyone who helped make this book possible!

Both covers were created by the very talented Rebecca at Story Styling Cover Designs and the amazing cover image was done by Wandar Aguiar. Copy edits were done by Raven at Raven Quill Editing, Proofreading was done by Lindsey Middlemiss.

Chapter images and character art drawn by Kierofoxen—thank you so much for all of the art you've already done for us, we can't wait to get more!

Sensitivity feedback was done by Jonathan Samuels—your unhinged comments were everything and we can't thank you enough for the feedback and entertainment!

The biggest shout out and thank you to our beta readers! Bryoni, Ashley, Debbie, Jenny, Charley, Em, Ronan and Alyssa —Thank you for all of your feedback! The first version that you saw ended up being a very different one than this. We'll always have Blake 1.0 LOL.

Our amazing PA Brittany aka Campfire Edits has also been such a lifesaver! I'm so glad that we all met when we did and and that this community has brought us all together.

Extra from just Lexi- I'd also like to thank my very supportive husband who believed in this dream before I did, and who's encouraged me every step of the way. I definitely couldn't have done any of this without you.

Thanks to my parents who've been very supportive, even if I hope they never actually read any of my books.

And to my kids, thanks for napping, going to bed on time, and letting mommy work, even after I quit my nursing job to stay home with you guys. I'll love you forever and always no matter what.